CW00585275

The Cleaner

www.penguin.co.uk

The Cleaner

MARY WATSON

bantam

TRANSWORLD PUBLISHERS
Penguin Random House, One Embassy Gardens,
8 Viaduct Gardens, London SW11 7BW
www.penguin.co.uk

Transworld is part of the Penguin Random House group of companies
whose addresses can be found at global.penguinrandomhouse.com

First published in Great Britain in 2025 by Bantam
an imprint of Transworld Publishers

A CIP catalogue record for this book
is available from the British Library.

ISBNs
9780857506030 (cased)
9780857506047 (tpb)

Text design by Couper Street Type Co.
Typeset in 12/15pt Minion by Jouve (UK), Milton Keynes
Printed and bound in Great Britain by Clays Ltd, Elcograf S.p.A.

The authorized representative in the EEA is Penguin Random House Ireland,
Morrison Chambers, 32 Nassau Street, Dublin D02 YH68.

Penguin Random House is committed to a sustainable future
for our business, our readers and our planet. This book is made
from Forest Stewardship Council® certified paper.

For my father, C.C.V. Watson (1943–2020)

Prologue

Midsummer

Houses know. They watch, taking in every small thing. They see when you're lonely or loved-up or lying. They know all your untold hiding places. And when you're heartbroken, or afraid, they might watch a little closer. Houses are witnesses. They carry the secrets of those who think they're safe inside.

A house will tell you those secrets. If you're patient enough to listen.

Tonight, Woodland House learned a new secret.

The summer kitchen is empty. There's no one in the courtyard through the wide open bifold doors. Beyond, in the apple orchard, the sounds of laughter have stopped. At the large metal sink, she runs water over her hands. It isn't the first time she's washed blood from them.

She scrubs her nails, even though there are no traces of blood left. With shaking fingers, she pulls at the buttons of the blouse she's wearing but her hands are wet and unsteady. She tears it over her head, a button flying across the flagstones, and thrusts the stained fabric under the stream of water. Watching the tainted water swirl down the drain, she pushes the images from her mind: the unmoving body. The reddened knife on the floor.

From the room next door come the sounds of others. A man's low, keening cry. A woman's anguished voice. She takes the bar of soap from the sink and begins to scrub again.

Chapter One

FOUR WEEKS EARLIER

I steered my bike into the narrow, winding road, past high stone walls and iron gates, where large houses hunkered in landscaped gardens. Tall trees peered over the walls, time-worn sentries keeping guard. To the left, a stone plaque declared *The Woodlands* in gold lettering.

When I reached the bend in the road, I checked my watch. Twelve minutes after nine. It was a dangerous corner, the turn sharp. Hedgerows leaned in, making the lane even closer. There were fewer houses here, and it felt secluded. Cut off from the rest of the world.

The distant rumble of a lawnmower, a faint fiddle endeavouring, the thick blinds on upstairs windows as parents tricked their children into falling asleep. The summer night sun brighter than I could ever have imagined.

Everyone safe inside their houses.

And out here, only me.

I took the bend, stopping when I saw the large pothole, the tarmac crumbled into the deep crevice. I sized it up, willing my heart to slow.

At the end of the lane was a sign marked 'Private!' It didn't stop people from climbing the gate and entering the bluebell woods, though. I was there only yesterday, my feet planted in the carpet of blue-purple flowers on green.

Their little noddy heads on my bare ankles, while butter-flies rose and landed. From around me came a low hum of bees.

I checked my watch again. Nine thirteen.

Then, behind me, I heard a low roar. A car accelerating as it turned out of the T-junction, heading this way.

I waited, gripping the bike handles, and counted down from forty. At fifteen, the car was nearer, on the far side of the sharp bend. I pushed down on the pedals.

Nine, eight. Holding tight, I picked up my pace, making sure to aim for the rut in the road just ahead. *Push harder, go faster.*

Seven, six, five. There was so much room for error here. My hands were slick with sweat, and I grasped the bars even tighter.

Four, three, two—The car took the bend. Squeezing my eyes shut, every muscle in my body tensed, I hit the pothole.

The wheel jammed into the crumbling tarmac, and the judder spread from my hands through my bones. Letting out a yelp, I fell forward, jabbing my hip on the handlebars. All I knew was gravity, the pull of the rough ground, the blur of the wildflowers on the side of the road. I bounced off my knee and landed hard. For a moment, I was jolted out of my skin, out of my body.

Sharp pain tore through me. I clutched my knee, cursing under my breath. It hurt so much more than I'd thought it would: everything felt bruised and raw. The world seemed to tip to the side.

The Jeep screeched to a stop. Doors flew open, and two men in soccer gear rushed out. I looked down to find that my old grey cotton joggers were ripped at the knee and blood was trickling from the broken skin there. There was a pile of fresh dog shit where I sat cradling my knee, and the stench of it turned my stomach. I gulped deep breaths to steady the wildness inside.

'Are you all right?' The younger man – the driver – called as he glanced at me, then the bumper. He was lean and athletic, with dark blond hair and striking features. He moved nearer until he was towering over me. 'What happened?'

'Did the Jeep hit you?' The older man crouched beside me as I dropped my backpack from my shoulders. He flicked a practised eye over me. He didn't look like a man who was easily fooled, so I made sure to twist my face with pain. It wasn't hard. 'Where does it hurt?'

The smell of dog shit rose from the ground, and with it my discomfort. These men and their easy confidence, their after-sport glow.

'The Jeep didn't touch you.' The driver sounded uncertain, though. 'Was it the pothole?'

'It came so fast.' I gestured to the sharp bend. 'The car.'

The two men glanced at each other, and a dart of satisfaction shot through me. They knew they had been going too fast. It was a blind corner, and habit was a dangerous thing. They were used to the road being quiet after their weekly soccer game. Strangers didn't often venture this way. I was a deviation, a break in the norm.

'I'm Lincoln – Linc,' the driver said. 'And this is Paul.'

'You took an awful tumble,' Paul said with cheerful sympathy. 'Let's get you back on your feet. Sure, you're still in one piece.'

He straightened up, reaching out a hand, but I ignored it.

'It hurts,' I pushed. 'Maybe we call the police?'

The men looked at each other, worry shadowing their eyes, and Paul dropped his hand, saying, 'How about we see if anything is broken first?'

'I live right there.' Linc pointed to a house hidden behind

trees. But I knew that already. 'And Paul here is a doctor. Please, come inside and we'll patch you up.'

If only it were that simple.

'Bring her in, and I'll move the Jeep and the bike,' Paul said. He was a bear-like man, tall with a body that straddled the line between muscular and overweight. His cheeks were slightly jowly, and his thinning hair was a little longer than you'd expect. Despite the concern clouding his expression, he seemed like a man who smiled a lot.

Linc nodded at the bike. 'Your wheel is damaged.'

I let out a gasp of real dismay when I saw the skewed front wheel. I couldn't afford to get it fixed.

Linc held out a hand and this time, I took it. I tried a step, but my ankle buckled and my hip screamed; my head spun and I thought I might fall again. At my halted intake of breath, Linc looked at me and said, 'May I?'

Then he lifted me into his arms and stepped towards the gate. It was unexpected and intimate, and I felt my cheeks grow hot. Tentatively, I wound my arm around his neck, but I couldn't look at his face, suddenly too close to mine. I barely dared to breathe. Instead, I turned away, looking at a black cast-metal sign that said *Woodland House* in silver Celtic lettering.

Linc walked up the garden path, carrying me in his arms as if I were a bride. The delicate perfume of the flowers in the summer night, the steady feeling of his chest and arms as he held me. The reassuring rhythm of his breathing. I wondered if he, like Nico, enjoyed playing the saviour.

The house loomed above us, old-fashioned in style with large bay windows and an imposing door frame. It was unlike anything I was used to back home. But the smell of sweat on Linc's soccer jersey was strangely comforting. Familiar, somehow. Like Nico, long ago, when he coached the under-twelves down at the civic centre. The thought of Nico in the sunshine on the threadbare pitch made me smile, and for a brief, welcome moment, I forgot. But too quickly, it all came rushing back and my smile fell.

The front door opened, and I turned my head to see a woman waiting at the threshold. She watched us approach.

'That's Amber, my wife.' Linc glanced down at me as he carried me between the rose bushes. I met his gaze, took in his hazel eyes and golden-brown hair, and it felt like I was on a wild carnival ride. Being here, in The Woodlands, so far away from home, carried in the arms of a stranger. Everything was finally starting.

But as he studied me, Linc's brow creased. Something was bothering him. Maybe I seemed familiar. As if he knew me from somewhere – but how was that possible? A foreign girl picked off the side of the road. Feeling a flash of alarm, I averted my eyes, fixing them on the woman instead.

Centred in the white door frame, she was like a Polaroid image come to life. Amber.

Her face was carefully blank, her arms folded. She was blonde and slim, dwarfed by an enormous red-and-cream kimono, a barefoot queen in her robes. Beneath, she wore black leggings and a tank. For some reason, I drew closer to Linc's chest.

'A little accident at the bend,' Linc called out as he walked me up the steps.

'We're going to fix her up,' Paul said cheerfully, climbing out of the Jeep, which he'd parked in the drive. 'Amber, can you bring the antiseptic cream? Gauze?'

Still holding me firmly, Linc stepped over the threshold on to geometric tiles. Wide-eyed, I took in the stained-glass front door we'd passed, the staircase with the iron railing, the chandelier. I noticed everything, committing it to memory.

On the left was a living room with velvet and leather and magazines. On my right, a room with floor-to-ceiling shelves of books. Two large, lean dogs watched from the living room. One of them let out a low growl. Mama Bear always said that dogs had a nose for trouble, that they could smell robbers and ghosts. These dogs eyed me carefully, as though they knew.

'That's Edward and Bella.' Linc nodded to the dogs. I raised an eyebrow. Linc laughed, and I felt a rumbling in his chest, 'Not my choice. I prefer books written before the twenty-first century. Amber is a terrible romantic.'

We moved to the large kitchen, which had clearly been modernized recently. Linc carried me past the kitchen island and the long blonde-wood dining table to the glass walls, where couches and armchairs were arranged. I could imagine Amber curled up, tea in hand, the sun streaming into the room.

'What's your name?' he asked, placing me gently on the brown leather couch.

'Esmie.' My knee throbbed with pain. Short for Esmerelda Theodora Lorenzo. Loves music, cats, volleyball. Excellent cook. Daughter of Beatrice Lorenzo, known as Mama Bear by those who love her. And sister of Nico.

In this unfamiliar place, it was easy to forget who I was, so I made myself repeat those words like a mantra, as though they could keep me grounded.

'Can I?' Linc waited for me to nod before he rolled up my joggers, carefully skimming my bloodied knee. He examined it a moment, then raised troubled eyes to mine. 'I'm sorry.'

'You didn't hit me,' I conceded reluctantly.

'I spooked you.'

It's not your fault, I wanted to say. But I didn't. Because it would be easier to get what I needed if he felt guilty. If he thought he owed me.

'Let me take a look at that.' Paul sounded jolly as he came into the kitchen holding my backpack. He placed it beside me and pulled up a footstool. I thought then that he must be a good doctor – that his calm, confident manner must work well to settle jittery patients.

Would it work on a patient who was jittery because she was lying?

'Esmie?' I realized I'd missed a question from Linc, who'd crossed to the other side of the kitchen.

'Sorry, what did you say?'

'Can I get you something to drink?' Linc opened a cupboard. 'Tea, or something stronger?'

'Something stronger.'

'Whiskey OK?'

I nodded, and Paul examined my ankle. 'Does it hurt anywhere else?'

'My hip.' My lips were dry. Despite my discomfort, I couldn't help looking around the room. The flooring and fittings were smart, but the place was messy. Pots and pans spilled from the sink. There was a half-drunk glass of wine and a book on the table. The floor hadn't seen a mop in days. Outside, through the glass doors, many, many apple trees disappeared into the distance. My eyes ate it all, greedy.

Linc set a glass of amber liquid on the table beside me. Neat, with no ice. I eyed the drink, wishing he'd asked how I took it. I'd never drunk whiskey without Coke.

Paul pulled on surgical gloves and wiped some grit out of the graze on my knee. His touch felt strange outside a clinical white room.

'You're from abroad?' Paul asked, as he cleaned my wound with his blue-gloved bear paws.

'I am.'

'Where from?'

I made a show of wincing. 'Ouch.'

'Sorry. You long in Ireland?'

'I came last week.'

'You're here for the language classes? To improve your English?'

'I am here to learn, yes.' Though perhaps not in the way he understood.

'There're plenty young folk like you about town. From Brazil, Mexico, all over. Must be a right blast. So, what's the verdict, then? Do you like it here?'

'Sure.' Then, without meaning to, I added, 'I like the Irish music.'

'Ah yes, the music. Do you play?'

'Banjo. And guitar.' It had been a while. I'd lost the urge when Nico came home nearly six months ago. When things had changed so much, and for reasons I couldn't fully understand.

'Where did you say you were from again? Brazil?'

To avoid answering, I took a drink of whiskey, but with nothing to dilute it, the burn that came with the large gulp had me sputtering.

Paul chuckled. 'Takes a bit of practice.' He stood up. 'The ankle isn't sprained but if it hurts, put it on ice.'

I nodded, but I was distracted. On the far side of the island, Linc and his wife were having words. With her arms straight down beside her, her body was a rigid line. She hissed, 'Always too fast.'

'You're good to go.' Paul peeled off the blue gloves, his mind already elsewhere. I felt a burst of alarm. Not yet. Not before I'd done what I came to do.

I reached into my backpack and pulled out a few cropped,

photocopied sheets, 'I was bringing these. Before the accident.'

I spoke carefully, as if I were unaccustomed to the words. When I landed in this strange new land a week ago, I'd realized that when most people looked at me – brown-skinned, accented, quiet – they simply saw 'foreign'. They assumed things – that I liked spicy food for example, though that one happened to be true. That my mother tongue wasn't English. Also, true – but that didn't mean it didn't come easily. Not that they needed to know – I'd get what I came here for more quickly if they didn't think I could understand them.

'I came for work.' I handed two flyers to Paul, who passed one on to Linc.

'You're a cleaner?' Linc asked.

I nodded again. Paul read the flyer. I looked down at my hands, feeling self-conscious as he said the words aloud: '*Hardworking. Committed. Reliable. Accepting new clients now. Call Esmie.*' There was a stock image of a sparkling feather duster – I so obviously wasn't a graphic designer.

'Well, how's this for timing?' Paul laughed.

'Serendipitous,' Linc agreed.

Serenfuckingdipitous, Linc.

'You're in luck, Esmie.' Linc smiled at me as though I'd won the lottery. 'Just this week, our cleaner told us she'll be away for two months. Family illness. Amber's been in a flap, saying how hard it is to find someone to fill in, especially since we're out of town and these narrow country roads can be a little off-putting.'

'But you obviously don't mind a bit of a cycle,' Paul added.

'Laura looked after a group of us,' Linc continued. 'Three houses, all here in The Woodlands.'

Amber watched from behind the kitchen island. She

pushed back her hair to reveal long drop earrings with a yellow-brown topaz stone that matched her eyes. She'd said nothing to me yet.

'I can work three houses.' I tried not to sound too eager. 'I like cycling.'

'That's great.' Linc beamed. 'Isn't it, Amber?'

'It's getting late,' Amber said, clearly reluctant to commit now. 'We should talk in the morning.'

'Just give it a go, Amber,' Linc coaxed. 'If it doesn't work out, then . . .'

He shrugged. How easy that shrug was, how privileged. *If it doesn't work out, then no harm done.* Not for him, anyway.

'We only need a cover for two months.' Amber turned those topaz eyes on me. 'You don't look much more than eighteen. How much experience do you have?'

I held her gaze. 'I am twenty-five. I'm only in Ireland for two months.'

Still Amber hesitated. 'Let me get back to you tomorrow.'

I twisted the edge of the flyer in my hand, trying to quell the panic sparking in my chest. 'Please, my bike. It is broken.' I sounded wheedling and pathetic. 'I have to pay to fix it. I promise, I am a good worker.'

Amber chewed her bottom lip. Resentment flashed in her eyes. I'd made her feel guilty, and she didn't like it one bit.

'I have reference,' I added.

'Amber, come on.' Linc waved an impatient hand. 'She has references.'

Amber stared at Linc. Paul stabbed a single, large finger at his phone as he composed a message. Linc slung an arm around Amber's waist, resting his hand on her hip. The silence in the kitchen grew.

'Fine.' Amber relented. 'Come Monday at ten. I'll talk to the others.'

'I'll be here.' I restrained myself from letting out a loud exhale.

Amber gave me a tight smile and picked up her wine from the table. She walked out of the room, her kimono fluttering behind her.

'I'll run you home,' Linc said, reaching out a hand. 'Can you put weight on your ankle? And don't worry about your bike. I'll see to it.'

I took his hand and he helped me up. I tested my ankle, felt the dull throb in my hip, my knee, and nodded.

As I limped from the kitchen, I ran an eye over the food-spilled surfaces, the red spatters on the backsplash. The caked mud near the door, the dog hairs layering the floor. Then, in the passage, the dust gathering on the intricate geometric pattern on the tiles, the smudges on the stained-glass front door.

I had my work cut out for me. But it would be worth it.

In the front seat of the Jeep, I studied Linc as he clipped in his seatbelt. In his mid-thirties, he was attractive. Sporty. He turned and smiled, catching me staring.

'You all right?'

I felt a faint blush colour my cheeks, and nodded. I was now. Just not in the way he meant.

We backed out of the drive, and Linc took the bend slower this time. Chastened, as if he'd learned a lesson.

The dark was creeping in, finally, casting the rolling fields, the low, jagged stone walls in blue light. The trees were in full leaf, and tiny winged insects dived down to the windscreen. Vibrant scents of earth and grass and flowers wafted in through the open window. I watched as the Irish countryside passed by, so different from home, and elation swelled inside me. I had to press my lips together to keep from smiling.

I'd done what I'd set out to do.

I would be coming back.

Linc drove through town, following my directions, and stopped at the house where I was staying, not far from the centre. Without traffic, the drive was only ten minutes, but it was a different world from The Woodlands. He idled outside the run-down three-bedroom bungalow, where two cars and a van were packed into the small drive.

'I'll let you know about your bike.'

I thanked him, got out of the car, and walked up the short path. I felt his eyes on me all the while. Shutting the door, the smell of damp long settled into the walls still hit me; I didn't think I would ever get used to it.

I leaned against the door as I let out a breath. Only then did I allow myself to feel relief. I'd done it.

After a moment, I checked my phone, my heart sinking as I saw a missed call. Mama Bear. Finally. I'd been texting and texting, but I hadn't heard from her for several days.

Everything OK? I sent off a quick text, fear squeezing my heart. **Nico?**

The response came immediately: **No change.**

Nico is a fighter. My thumbs flew across the screen. **He'll get through this.** But I didn't know if I believed my own words. How do you fight when you're not even conscious?

Nico was in a coma. In a terrifying white room with beeping machines that meant uncertainty and peril. He was out of reach, and we couldn't know if he would come back to us. With each passing day, it became more unlikely.

And while he slept, I had to keep running.

I walked to my room, the pain in my heart making my palms ache, thinking about Nico and how much we loved him.

Nico, who'd been lost to us long before the terrible night he was rushed to hospital.

There are many ways to kill a man. A stab to the heart, a gun to the temple, a head held under water. A fistful of pills, a garrotte, a rope.

Then there's the way that makes a man witness his own death. Where day after day, month after month, he watches himself diminish. Whatever had happened in The Woodlands, it had destroyed Nico, slowly and surely. The cruellest murder kills from within.

I sank to my bed, thinking of Nico when he returned to us. The uncertain months that followed. And then, that cool May night when I was forced to run. Now, eleven days later, he was still in a hospital bed, unable to wake. Like Snow White, in her coffin of glass. Except this was no fairy tale. No one was going to save Nico with a kiss.

But I could get the witch who poisoned him.

HOME

The girls didn't remember when they'd first met. It must have been in the time before memory, because neither could think of a life without the other. It seemed to Esmerelda that Simone had always lived with her dad in the run-down house next door. There was never a Friday evening when Simone didn't come to theirs, clutching a shopping bag that held her pyjamas and underwear.

Esmerelda never asked why Simone stayed every weekend. She understood with that same intuitive knowing why Simone's dad got that lazy look in his eyes, that strange, sharp smell on his breath, why his tongue turned even meaner. They never spoke about how every weekend the house next door filled with unfamiliar men who arrived with bottles tucked under their jackets, the women with their tiny shorts and high heels. The music and laughter that pierced through their dreams. Esmerelda understood, before she had the language for it, that Simone's dad was not a good man; and Mama Bear had taught her that good was everything.

Mama Bear was like a mother to Simone. She wasn't given to idleness or fun, but she made all three children feel loved and cared for. She gave the best hugs – deep, tight, squashy hugs where the children were enfolded in

17

her soft breasts – which was why Nico had named her Mama Bear.

Mama Bear worked as a cleaner and had little patience for mess of any kind. She brought much-needed order to Simone's world with her sharp-edged view of life. There was good and bad, right and wrong, proper and improper, seemly and unseemly. She taught this clear moral terrain to both girls. She taught them, kindly but firmly, that actions had consequences.

They learned this the hard way the day of the fire.

It had taken the two girls twenty minutes to pile the wood and stuff it with rolled-up newspaper in their small cement-and-dust backyard. Simone lit the match, meeting her best friend's eyes; dark brown, just like her own.

'Make a wish,' Esmerelda told Simone, then shut her eyes. When she opened them, Simone was staring at her, the match lit.

'Did you wish?' Esmerelda asked.

Simone nodded, then dropped the match. Standing on the brown grass, the girls watched, hand in hand, as the flame caught.

They'd meant to make a small fire. They'd wanted to see the flame take hold. They'd wanted to whisper all their wishes, then watch the pile burn down to nothing.

But the flames grew higher.

'Esmie! Simone!' Mama Bear had yelled from the window, her voice thin with fear. 'What the hell are you doing?'

They hadn't expected the fire to grow so quickly. They hadn't realized how the wind and dry grass would cause it to spread. They were just two young girls who'd played with matches. The wood pile collapsed, sparks flying, and Esmerelda turned to see the terror and fascination play on Simone's features. The fire began to eat the old fruit crates stacked at the side of the fence, greedy flames searching for more.

'Ma,' screamed Esmerelda, jumping back as a spark landed on her T-shirt. 'Ma, help.'

Then, suddenly, Nico was there. 'The hose,' he said. 'Esmerelda, catch.'

There'd been a hosepipe ban that summer, and it was wound up like a snake. Nico threw the pipe towards the girls, but it was tangled. Simone darted forward to untwist it while Nico set upon the stiff tap, struggling to turn it.

Mama Bear stomped outside, her bad back making her gait heavy. Tossing water from a bucket, she doused some of the flames. Then water spurted from the hose – first one reluctant burst, then another, before a steady stream came out, spraying Simone's face and soaking their shoes.

When the fire was out, Mama Bear lined up the three children in the kitchen. Only Nico could meet her eye. She was shaking, with rage or fear or both, and they had never before seen that look on her face. And then, only one time after.

'Who did this?' she said, her voice ominously low.

Simone pressed her lips together. Esmerelda looked into the distance.

'I will ask just once more.' Mama Bear's voice went even lower.

'It was her.' Esmerelda couldn't help the words. 'Simone lit the match.'

Simone turned to her best friend, her betrayer, her eyes narrowed.

'I didn't,' Simone burst out. 'It was your idea.'

Mama Bear rarely raised her voice. But she'd been taught that discipline, which was a kind of love, required pain. Since Simone's dad didn't care enough to give her a belt,

Mama Bear wouldn't hesitate to show how much she loved this girl who wasn't her daughter. Her mouth set, she opened the kitchen drawer.

'I did it,' Nico said quickly. 'It was my idea. I lit the match. I started the fire.'

Mama Bear stared at him a long time. 'Are you sure?' she asked eventually. 'Actions have consequences, you know that.' She took the leather strap from the drawer.

Nico paused, then gave one quick nod. 'I started the fire.' This time he lied more firmly.

Mama Bear released a slow breath. 'If that's how you want it.' She examined the two girls solemnly. Simone studied the laces on her shoes. Esmerelda was riveted by the wood whorls in the kitchen table. Then Mama Bear said to the girls, 'Leave.'

Nico bowed his head, ready to accept a punishment that wasn't his. Before they left the kitchen, he glanced up at the girls, giving them a smile that was as quick as it was dazzling. They watched him, feeling warm and afraid and loved.

'Come.' Simone grabbed Esmerelda's hand, the brief betrayal forgotten, and they ran to the window. They peered inside where Nico leaned on the table, his hands gripping the edge. Mama Bear's mouth was tight; she took no pleasure in this. She raised the man's belt, a remnant from long-ago days that neither Nico nor Esmerelda could remember. Nico dipped his head as the hard leather hit his bare thighs. Esmerelda's hands went to her mouth. Simone breathed in sharply. Mama Bear raised the belt again.

Nico looked up at the two girls. His eyes shone with unshed tears.

He smiled.

Simone had never really paid attention to Nico before; he was simply the older brother she ignored. The older brother

Esmerelda adored. But as he held the table, taking *her* consequences, she began to suspect that he was more than she first thought.

Esmerelda didn't take her eyes off Nico, watching as he flinched. She knew that he'd meant to spare her, but how could he, when every hit caused her heart to squeeze with a pain worse than ten belts on her legs.

Chapter Two

Monday

The bell pealed through Woodland House as I waited outside at nine fifty-five on Monday morning, thinking about actions and consequences. It felt almost cosmic: this single most important lesson that had been drilled into us from childhood was the reason I was there. It was why I now peered through the stained-glass door, seeing a woman take shape on the other side.

Because, consequences.

Amber opened the door, giving me a quick smile, saying she had to take a call now but I'd find everything I'd need in the utility room. She gestured in the direction of the kitchen and said, 'Go on through,' before disappearing into the study.

Alone in the entrance hall, I imagined Nico here for the first time, raising an eyebrow at how grand it was. I imagined him looking up at the huge chandelier, amusement playing at his lips. I imagined him placing a hand at the side of his mouth, whispering, *Someone's overcompensating.*

But Nico wasn't here.

Walking down the passage, I thought about how he'd pumped his fist and roared when he heard he'd been awarded that fucking scholarship. He'd be studying in Ireland, with some of the best in his field.

The tense ride to the airport the day he left. His tight hug near the departure gates as he grabbed each one of us in turn. I'd held back my tears, catching my breath at how much it hurt. In contrast, light shone in his eyes: he was living the dream.

'It will be worth it, I promise,' he'd said softly.

'Look after yourself,' I'd half laughed, half sobbed while I smacked his arm. Then he'd turned to leave.

Three years without Nico.

How would we live without him, this golden man? Four years older, Nico had always taken charge. He was everything: helper to the older people in our road, soccer coach, youth counsellor who lit up a room every time he entered it. He was a good son and a good brother. He was my best friend.

We'd watched him walk away, each of us holding him in sight until he turned the corner. At the very last moment, he glanced back and grinned, melting the hearts of the three women who loved him. The older woman, her shoulders stooped from years of hard labour. The younger two – his sister and his fiancée, our hearts full, as he blew a last kiss.

And then he'd come here.

Today, memory felt like a weapon.

Outside the kitchen door, I paused. I pressed the heels of my palms beneath my eyes, making sure that no tears spilled.

Get it together, I scolded myself. I counted to five, but the memories persisted. I made myself think of music, of quick, light fingers on banjo strings. The bell-like chuckling that always made me feel all right. A little calmer, I pushed open the door.

Linc was at the kitchen table. He was typing, hands flying across his laptop keyboard. He reached for the mug beside him, not taking his eyes from the screen.

It was like I wasn't even there.

I found a bucket and cloths in the utility room, grabbed some cleaning potions with unfamiliar names.

Holding the bucket, I said, 'Linc?' I had to ask him about my bike – I'd walked over this morning and I really needed it back. I tried his name again, but Linc was absorbed in his screen. Nico hated it when I interrupted his work, so I gave up, resolving to try later. I went upstairs, peering inside each room, and taking mental snapshots of their lives.

Houses tell you about the people who live in them, and Linc and Amber's bedroom had a lot to say about her. A mirrored closet took up an entire wall, the clothes shoved inside and falling from the shelves. The fine silk dresses carelessly dropped to the floor. Amber was lazy.

Long blonde hairs clogged the shower drain. Toothpaste spit flecked the mirror. Discarded make-up pads littered her dressing table. Amber was messy as hell.

Beside her bed was a tall stack of romance novels where large-muscled men held pretty women in pretty dresses. Amber believed in happily ever after.

A spread of make-up. Bottles and vials and serums and creams, many of them promising the same thing. Amber had more money than sense.

Prescribed antidepressants labelled *Do not drink alcohol* on the bedside table next to a glass stained with the dregs of red wine. Amber had a complete lack of regard for consequences. More than that, she probably craved the consequences because they brought adventure to her life of privilege and plenty.

Why did Amber need antidepressants? Had something triggered a depressive episode? Was Nico that something?

I poured out the bucket of dirty water and examined Amber's now gleaming en suite bathroom. Then I went to the top of the stairs, where I'd placed the dustpan and brush.

Voices came from the study below, and I stilled. Amber was talking, her words fast and annoyed.

I peered down. Through the iron railing, the study door was open. And inside, I glimpsed Linc's muscular calves, dusted with golden-brown hair as he crossed the room. If I went down only a few steps, I'd hear more. I hesitated, my feet at the very edge of the top step. *Unseen*, I reminded myself. *Invisible.* I took a deep breath to steady myself.

Picking up the hand-brush, I moved slowly. Down two steps, then another. On my knees, I positioned the brush on the top step and listened.

'This can't go on indefinitely,' Linc railed. 'It's been months, Amber. Months.' One of the dogs sleeping in the hall cocked an ear.

I swept the top step, digging the brush into the corners.

'Ceanna's not herself, Linc. She's . . . troubled.' Exasperation crept into Amber's voice. 'You know how my dad's death affected her. She's back in that same dark place, and no one can reach her there.'

Out of reach. Like Nico. My knees ached on the hard step.

'What's Ceanna's plan?' Linc pushed on. 'To keep Eden's papers shut in the safe for ever? To smother her genius in a locked box?'

'Probably.' Amber sounded gentler now. 'Would that be so bad?'

I brushed harder, sweeping the bristles down the skirting, along the banister. The wooden hand-brush bashed into the iron rail, a loud clang echoing.

The silence was laden. I waited with bated breath, shoulders up to my ears. I could not get caught eavesdropping on my first day. It would ruin everything.

'Amber.' Linc's voice was taut. 'You know what they mean to me.'

I sank to the step, leaning against the wall as my shoulders released. The dog watched me with soulful, accusing eyes.

'Yes,' Amber replied. 'Everything.'

I couldn't tell if she was resigned or bitter.

'You have to reason with her,' Linc said. 'Tell Ceanna we'll find an expert, one who understands antiques. One who'll cause minimal damage.'

'What about the safe trap? Dad was so oddly paranoid those last weeks. He could well have armed it.' Linc swore softly as Amber continued, 'But what does that matter – you know Ceanna will never risk the damage. Not to an antique that's been in Dad's family for God knows how long.'

'Ceanna needs to stop clinging so tight to the dead.' Linc's voice rose, all remnants of calm lost. I could almost hear Amber flinch in the following silence. 'Sorry, I shouldn't have said that.' A drawer slammed shut, making me jump.

I inched down another step and resumed brushing. Fine dust flew into the air, catching in my throat as I tried to understand how Amber was caught between her husband and her sister. Was this a warped mirror image of my own situation, our own cursed triangle?

'It's killing me, Amber,' Linc went on. 'I could be the

world authority here, the top of my field. Everything I ever dreamed of, so close. I need to get into that safe.'

There was another pause, and Linc pushed on, softer now. 'Your dad's death broke something in all of us. We need to find a way to heal. That's what Malachy would have wanted. Just as he wanted me to have Eden's papers.'

As I bent over the step, breathing in their dust, I could picture them in the study. The tall windows and high ceilings. She with her beach waves and silk kimono, glowering at her husband, not forgiving his harsh words.

Nico had once told me that in every couple there was the lover and the beloved. The one who wooed, and the other who was elevated by their affections. It didn't take a genius to figure that Amber was the beloved here. Propped on the pedestal of Linc's adoration.

Which meant that every argument between them was predetermined: he would always cave first.

'Amber,' Linc said, his voice now cajoling. 'I said I'm sorry.'

Leaning down towards the study door, I saw his legs again, now moving closer to Amber. Silk falling on her smooth calves. I looked away, fixing on the dirt on the banister; these hadn't been cleaned properly for some time.

'I suppose you've asked the ghouls to come on Wednesday evening?' Amber still sounded peeved.

'We talked about this,' Linc sighed. 'Come on, babe, let's not fight.'

'They're boring, Linc.'

'Other people aren't there to entertain you.' His voice was clipped now, as though the shadow of a different argument hung on to his words. 'They're not ghouls, they're my research assistants, and I like them.'

'Fiona's boring. And you're boring when you're with her.'

There was a rustle and a bump, the click of a latch, and

when Linc spoke again, his voice was muted. 'Can we do this later? The cleaner's here.'

'The new Laura is upstairs. She can't hear us.' Amber dismissed me easily. I had no illusions that I mattered to her, yet still I felt a disgruntled churning inside. *The new Laura.* Did she even remember my name?

'She seems nice.'

'Nice,' Amber repeated disparagingly. I could almost see her shudder, her pretty face twisted with distaste. 'Yes, I think she is nice.'

'Amber . . .' Linc made her name sound both placatory and like a warning.

The floorboard creaked beneath Amber's light step. The dog stood up, eagerly watching the door, and I resumed my brushing with vigour. There was a layer of grime on my hands, my skin gritty from their dust and dirt.

'Does the new Laura seem, I don't know . . . familiar?' Amber was a little nearer now, right at the door. My brushing hand stalled. Heart drumming, I listened for Linc's reply.

'Familiar?' Linc sounded distracted.

'Yeah, like I've seen her somewhere before.'

I held my breath.

'Don't see how that's possible. She'd barely been in the country a week when we plucked her out of the ditch. Must have one of those faces.'

'I suppose you're right.' Amber paused. 'Where's she from?'

'What's that? I'm right? Now those're words I don't often hear.' Linc sounded playful.

'Must be a rare star alignment. Where's the new Laura from?'

'Brazil? Or was it Mexico?' Linc was walking now. 'That's what Paul said.'

I rolled my eyes at Paul's remarkable ability to decide the facts from unanswered questions.

Moving down another step, I pushed my earphones into my ears as Linc emerged from the study. A leather satchel in one hand, he lifted a set of keys from the hook beside the front door with the other.

I watched Linc from the corner of my eye, thinking how he worked at the same university where Nico had studied while he was here. Linc was arts faculty, while Nico had been a science PhD student. Through word of mouth, Nico had learned about the room-for-rent at Ceanna's, heard she was looking for a responsible graduate student lodger. He'd moved in soon after he arrived, immediately liking the quiet, green neighbourhood. In those early days, he'd told us all about the neighbours he'd met: Ceanna and Amber, the mismatched sisters. Their dad, Malachy, a silver-tongued old rogue. Linc, who was married to Amber, and Paul, the next-door neighbour, both of whom loved sport as much as Nico did. And Paul's wife, Isabelle, who was reserved and kept to herself. In time, the stories stopped, like a veil had closed over Nico's life in The Woodlands.

The dog – Bella, possibly – danced around Linc, its nails clacking on the tiles. He rubbed Bella's head, then Amber tugged on his T-shirt and pulled him in for a kiss. I turned my back to them.

'Be good,' Linc said, and I heard the door shut as he left for work wearing shorts and a faded T-shirt. Nico had been so careful with his grooming, always neatly dressed in shirts and jeans, aware of how his background made him different, how he always had to compensate. The utter privilege of Linc going into work in shorts almost made me laugh. Linc, I'd bet, never worried about being taken seriously.

I felt Amber's eyes on me, watching me on the stairs. I continued down, brushing with brisk efficiency.

But inside, I was taking stock of the conversation that I'd heard, noting the tensions that had been revealed. Filing away everything I'd learned.

Chapter Three

Monday

Amber hadn't moved from the bottom of the staircase. 'You don't have to do that.' She sounded irritated. I ignored her, brushing the dirt that had caked on the outside of the banister. The old Laura clearly wasn't very thorough. 'You don't have to do that.' This time the words were louder, almost laced with anger.

I straightened up and turned to watch her warily. I pulled the earphones from my ears, even though I wasn't listening to anything. I just wanted Amber to think I couldn't have been listening to her and Linc.

'We do have a vacuum cleaner, you know.' Her hands were on her hips now. 'It's quicker. Easier.' And under her breath: 'It's not the damn eighteenth century.'

'I prefer . . .' I held up the brush and trailed off.

Mama Bear preferred the brush, too. I had a sudden image of her vigorously sweeping the backyard. There was a large jacaranda tree nearby, and the ground was often carpeted with the fallen purple blooms. It had vexed Mama Bear during the flowering season, which had endlessly amused us.

I dropped my hand holding the brush, feeling a sharp ache in my chest.

Amber regarded me for a moment, then said, 'Come.'

She stalked down the passage towards the kitchen. I followed, scurrying down the stairs. Her kimono swirled as she stepped through the kitchen doors, then into the bright utility room. Cleaning products lined the shelves, and I'd never thought a washing machine or tumble dryer could be beautiful, but somehow Amber's sleek, gleaming machines were. I counted three vacuum cleaners – robot, cordless and plug-in – and a steam mop that looked like it had never been used.

Amber lifted the cordless vacuum from where it hung on the wall. 'Use this.' It was a command.

I held back a moment, taking time to study her again. Those remarkable yellow-brown eyes that matched her topaz pendant earrings.

Then I realized that Amber was also studying me. Not bothering to hide it, her eyes examined mine; my wide nose, my cheeks that must have been pink from cleaning, my dark hair tied in a short ponytail.

'You're pretty,' Amber said, and I frowned at the unexpected judgement. Just as when she'd called me nice earlier, it felt like an insult.

'Amber?' A voice called from inside the kitchen.

Amber was still watching me, her outstretched arm gripping the vacuum. 'Be careful.'

I stared at her, hackles rising. Amber was right; I did need to be careful. But where did Amber see danger? My shoulders braced, as if for attack. Was Amber warning or threatening me?

She reached her arm closer to me, impatient. 'It's expensive.' Then she muttered, 'God knows there's enough broken around here.'

She was talking about the vacuum, I realized with some relief.

Smiling politely to mask the hardness inside me, I took it from her.

'Amber.' The voice came again, louder now.

'Coming,' Amber called. She returned my smile with a tight one of her own. 'Always take the easier path. Now, come meet Isabelle. Paul's wife.'

I followed Amber into the kitchen. Standing behind the counter was another woman. This one was the opposite of Amber. Just looking at her, I could tell this was a quiet woman who didn't like drawing attention to herself. She was composed, with black shoulder-length hair and dark eyes lined with shadows. She looked to be in her forties, older than Amber by at least ten years. The slight sag of her cheeks lent a sadness to her face.

'You must be Esmie,' she said. 'I'm Isabelle Blake. You met Paul, my husband.'

The garden door opened, and we all turned to look at the woman stepping inside the kitchen. She was very like Amber, though her figure was fuller, her face pale and haunted. This was a more serious version of Amber, without the tiger eyes. It had to be the sister, the one Amber and Linc had been arguing about only minutes ago.

'Cee, hello.' Amber's greeting sounded strained. She pushed her hair behind her ears, unable to meet her sister's eye. 'I didn't know you were coming over.'

'How could you?' the woman said mock-graciously. 'You didn't bother to answer my phone calls.'

Ceanna's catty remark, Amber's barely concealed eye-roll – the obvious tension between the two women was just like being at home.

Amber recovered herself quickly. 'It's good you're here. You can meet Esmie. She's filling in for Laura for the next two months.'

The woman turned to me, and the blood red of her

lipstick stood out on her pale face. 'I'm Amber's sister, Ceanna. I live down the boreen.'

'We're so relieved Linc and Paul found you,' Isabelle said. Found me. Like some lost thing.

'Hello.' My throat felt tight. The unfamiliarity of my surroundings, the daunting luxury, made me sound timid, which I wasn't – but no harm to have these women think I was. Let them not know they'd let a snake inside until it was too late.

'Paul said you're from Brazil?'

'Mexico,' Amber corrected helpfully.

Now would be the time to settle the misunderstanding. But I didn't.

In her hands, Isabelle held a typed sheet. 'We're going to keep ticking over with Laura's schedule – two four-hour days here with Amber.' Her eyes and skin suggested mixed racial heritage, some South Asian perhaps, and she spoke with the same lilting accent I'd heard around the city. I was curious how she fitted in; if she hovered at all at the edges as I did. I didn't think so. Not when she spoke so confidently and carried herself with an assured elegance. We might share a similar skin tone, eyes and hair texture, but I guessed that was about it.

'Two days here?'

Amber raised her eyebrows at me defiantly. 'The house gets messy. The dogs, you know.' She picked a hair from her sleeve and let it float to the floor, her eyes locked on mine.

'And two four-hour sessions at mine – I run a tight ship.' Isabelle dipped her head and checked me over. Her lips pursed ever so slightly, as though she were assessing if I was up to the challenge, but found me wanting. 'Then one three-hour afternoon at Ceanna's.' She pointed to the days marked on the schedule.

36

'And the cottage.' Amber held Ceanna's eye as she said this, and Ceanna scowled. I looked between the sisters, hungry to know why Amber seemed so frosty, why Ceanna was mute with fury.

'The cottage?' I asked, trying to follow the unspoken conversation. In the pocket of my leggings, my phone buzzed with an incoming message.

'My dad's cottage,' Amber said airily. 'Three Oaks. Friday afternoons OK?'

'We're not selling the cottage, Amber,' Ceanna snapped.

'We still have to sort and clean it,' Amber hit back.

'I can do Friday afternoons,' I interjected, before the sisters really got into it. I allowed myself an inward smirk at Amber's 'we', when there was zero chance she was getting those delicate hands, with their perfectly rose-pink nails, dirty.

'Good.' Amber clasped her hands together. 'We need it scrubbed down and everything boxed. We've sorted most of his personal items, but Three Oaks has been in Dad's family for eighty years so there's a lot to do.'

My phone buzzed again; a second message.

'He's dead,' Ceanna added abruptly. The words clearly caused her pain, and she used them like a blunt instrument. 'Six months ago. To the day.'

My mind raced, searching my memory for Nico's mentions of Malachy Kelly. Because six months ago, give or take a few days, Nico had lost his scholarship and was forced to return home. But I couldn't recall much: Nico had liked the old man, found him hilarious. He visited when he could.

'That's Dad, there.' Ceanna pointed to a photo on the fridge.

I moved closer, examining the picture of a younger Amber beside a tall man with a craggy face and thick eyebrows. He seemed distinguished and imposing, and charged with vitality. On Amber's other side was Linc, in university robes and a ridiculous hat.

'At Linc's graduation.'

Graduation. The word was a knife.

Nico would never graduate. Not after what had happened here.

Before he came here, Nico used to talk about that damned degree as if it were a magical elixir. With this degree, he'd told us, he'd dance into his dream job as a neuroscientist. With this degree, we wouldn't need to live in that tiny four-roomed house any more. With this degree, he'd take care of Mama Bear so she could retire after decades of hard, physical labour. With this degree, he'd say, my girls will wear gold.

He'd say those words as if they were a mantra, a prayer. A vow. *With this degree.*

Then everything changed. When he came back six months ago, it was unexpected, with a year of his time abroad unfinished. He didn't dance into his dream job; he couldn't, not with his studies abandoned. The four-roomed house was still home. Mama Bear still cleaned. None of us wore gold.

When Nico walked away from us the day he left, when he turned for that last glance, we didn't know that this was an ending. That Nico as we knew him would never come back to us.

The three women were giving me odd looks, and I realized I hadn't yet responded. 'I'm sorry,' I murmured, trying to keep my voice bland and uninterested. 'It was sudden?'

'He'd been sick.' Amber sounded unnaturally bright. As though this was so painful she had to pretend it wasn't. 'Heart problems.'

Nothing to do with Nico then. I filed the information away, relieved.

A third message vibrated in my pocket. Was it Mama Bear? News of Nico? Nausea rose at the back of my throat.

'Right, glad that's all sorted,' Isabelle said, looking down at something, and I took the moment to check my phone.

Three alerts from a messaging app. When I left home, I'd deleted all my social media accounts, all apps with private messaging. Or I thought I had.

Glancing up to make sure the women were still talking to each other, I quickly opened the app. There were three unread messages, all from a user I didn't recognize:

Where are you?

Where ARE you?

Where the fuck are you?

It felt like a hand was covering my nose and mouth, and I couldn't get air. I read the words again. I knew who'd sent them.

Relax. I forced myself to take a deep breath. *She doesn't know where you are.*

'Esmie?' Ceanna was looking at me curiously. 'You look like you've seen a ghost. You OK?'

'Fine.' I tried to smile, but it felt like a grimace.

Isabelle handed me the schedule, a neat table of the week with times colour coded. Beneath was the hourly rate and Amber's, Ceanna's and Isabelle's phone numbers. Linc and Paul might have found me, but managing me had quickly become the women's job.

'Now, if you could just provide the contact details for your references?' Isabelle said.

My heartbeat picked up again. 'I only have one?'

I didn't like how Isabelle was looking at me. Were her dark eyes suspicious? Or was she just cautious by nature? She struck me as uptight, unyielding.

Amber was entirely uninterested in references, preferring instead to examine her split ends. Ceanna was on the other side of the kitchen, getting a drink of water. She caught my eye and smiled with her blood-red lips.

'If that's all you have, then I suppose it will have to do.' Isabelle continued to study me, and I felt like a butterfly on a board beneath her gaze. Dropping my eyes, I examined the schedule again.

When I looked up, all three women were watching me. Amber, Isabelle, Ceanna. Names I'd heard so many times in those early months when Nico first arrived. Dinner parties at Amber's, renting a room at Ceanna's, walking through the bluebell woods with Isabelle.

The sound of birdsong from outside. The distant cries of children playing. But inside the kitchen, for a moment, the silence was all I could hear.

I looked at Amber, who wore her entitlement as easily as she wore her silk kimono. I looked at Ceanna, whose smile was as sincere as if it had been painted on her face. I looked at Isabelle, at her cool self-containment and wary eyes.

All of them respectable suburban women. Living in this leafy area with its large houses. Each of them careful to keep a face on.

But I knew without any doubt: one of these women had been fucking the lodger.

In this kitchen was the woman who had destroyed Nico. And I was here to return the favour.

Chapter Four

Tuesday

Revenge was one of those words that meant something different, depending on how you looked at it. Revenge could be small and petty, a sign of moral weakness. Or it could be majestic, biblical: a grand retribution, an eye for an eye, a tooth for a tooth.

Two years and nine months ago, Nico had left home with his head full of dreams. Now, he was in a coma. And in between was The Woodlands.

A wrong had been done, and it was up to me to make it right.

This morning, I strolled through the bluebell woods, taking in boundless shades of green, from the rich mossy stones to the lighter hues on the higher branches. The cries of birds, the rustling foliage, a red squirrel darting across the beaten path. I'd never known a place could feel like this, heaving and aware. I was due at Isabelle's soon, but now, embraced by trees, I wanted to think about what had happened, and what was to come.

On the flight over, I'd considered appealing Nico's dismissal through the proper channels – approaching the university, for example – but I didn't need a psychic to tell me how the proper channels would play out for someone like me. The scrutiny at airport Immigration, the newspaper headlines about arson attacks on buildings earmarked for refugees, the far-right agitation about immigrants, all confirmed my suspicions about what little clout I might have here. Everyone I'd encountered had been friendly and kind, but I didn't rate my chances with a proper channel.

I'd known it all along: revenge was the poor woman's justice. The last resort for the powerless.

When Nico returned, he told us they'd pulled his scholarship and not a word more. He refused to talk about how he'd lost it, but the reason seemed obvious: it was hard to hide his new fondness for whiskey and pills in such a small, close house. We'd put his silence down to shame. A deep, unspeakable shame that he'd failed himself, and worse, that he believed he'd let us all down.

It never made sense, though. Nico was driven. Nico had immeasurable self-control. He hadn't been swayed by the temptations of our neighbourhood, where drink and drugs and guns could easily be found.

Five and a half months after he returned, he finally let it slip: he'd fallen in love. That was the missing puzzle piece.

Love.

He admitted to a secret romance with a woman, one from The Woodlands, despite being engaged to be married. And this – not the drinking or the benzos – was the reason he'd lost his funding.

The truth came out by accident one awful night when he uttered those words in a heated moment: *I loved her. She betrayed me. Because of her lies, I have nothing left. That's why they pulled my funding and kicked me out.*

He'd fallen in love, and it had been a gut punch to learn. And then the woman he loved had sabotaged him. We didn't know the hows and whys, I could only surmise that at the end, when things soured, she'd told lies about him cheating or stealing. It was bad enough that his funding was withdrawn and Nico was told to return home.

I leaned against a tree, thinking about our little house tucked into a valley of vineyards, our sunshine home. It had been filled with music and laughter. The smell of fried dough and sugar. Once it was our haven, but after Nico returned it felt heavy and hopeless.

Then, one unforgettable night, it became a place of terror.

The last time I'd seen Nico, his eyes had been rolled back in his head. I'd cradled him to me, my tears mingling with blood.

My world came to an end that day. We were, all four of us, irreparably broken.

Nico's life hung in the balance, and I had been forced to run.

I pushed away from the tree; it was time to get to work. I ambled through the woods, watching the sun wink in and out of sight, confident in my plan. My path to justice would be subtle, cards played close to the chest.

I loved her.

I would find out who Nico's lover was.

She betrayed me.

I would find out what mattered most to her.

Because of her lies, I have nothing left.

And I would take it away.

Stepping out of the woods into the sunshine, I noticed a silver Toyota sedan parked a little way down. Isabelle was talking to the person in the driver's seat. She appeared annoyed, huffing as she folded her arms.

Hearing my footsteps, Isabelle turned to me with an unconvincing smile. She was nervous, I realized, with a jolt of interest. I raised my phone to my ear as if taking a call, and Isabelle continued her urgent, hushed conversation.

'That's right,' I murmured to no one, as I approached Isabelle and the Toyota. I ran a careful eye over the car, noticing that it was new and well kept. Sidling nearer, I tried to see the driver, but Isabelle shifted, deliberately blocking my view. Their conversation fell silent as I passed.

'Hello, Isabelle.' My cheerful greeting was jarring in the sudden quiet.

Isabelle nodded, turning her back to me. Tension lined her shoulders, making me certain that she was hiding something. A dark sort of excitement sparked deep in my belly. That of a predator on the prowl.

I glanced back, but in the bright sunlight, I couldn't make out the driver. Isabelle waited until I was metres away before she spoke again. I could just about make out, 'Fine, tonight. Not here. You can't come here again.'

The driver responded too quietly for me to hear.

'Begley's, ten o'clock.' A pause, then Isabelle exploded: 'Yes, I know it's a shithole. What do you expect? A five-star hotel?'

I glanced back, and Isabelle's face was as hot as a blistering January afternoon back home. She glanced at the windows of the neighbouring houses, clearly hoping that her outburst hadn't been witnessed. She wasn't the kind of woman who enjoyed airing her dirty laundry.

Turning my back to her, I allowed myself a triumphant smile. They were planning to meet later, and I knew when and where. I would go, too. I would see what she was hiding. Fired up, I gathered pace, making for the gate.

A high wall surrounded Isabelle's house. Beside the tall gate was a stone plaque declaring in a simple, elegant script: *No. Three, The Woodlands.* I hid my scoff as I pushed open the gate. This house told you straight away that someone important lived here – someone too important to use a damn numeral.

Nico would have found it ridiculous, and suddenly I ached to know what he thought. I wanted to travel back in time, watch him take in his new neighbourhood when he arrived here nearly three years ago.

The house loomed above me. My feet crunched lightly as I walked up the neatly kept white pebble path towards the front door. How many times had Nico walked down this path? Did his heart skip? Did he anticipate time with his lover?

'You're early,' Isabelle said from behind me.

I turned to watch her walk down the path, tall and stately. The agitation I'd seen on the street had passed so completely it was almost like I'd imagined it. She was put together, neatly buttoned into her linen shirt-dress. I tried to imagine Nico with her, making her laugh. I couldn't see it.

'This way,' Isabelle said, going inside. I followed her through the passage, observing the polished wood, the expensive-looking vases. She stayed three steps ahead as we wound through the kitchen and into a large, neat utility room.

I halted abruptly when I saw that everything – the drawers, the shelves, plastic containers, even the different laundry soaps – bore small, printed labels. I took in the typed words marking *Isabelle* on the pink detergent for delicates, or *Liadh Sport* and *Ava Swimming* on plastic tubs of shin guards and swim goggles.

The woman was clearly a domestic tyrant. My lips twitching, I wondered what Nico would have made of this.

This one, I imagined him whispering, *has a stick up the ass.*

I bit my bottom lip to keep it from quirking up. Isabelle looked at me curiously.

'As you can see, the house is big, but it's well kept. We need you to make sure it stays that way.'

'Very well kept,' I agreed, reading more labels on the plastic tubs – *Tapes, Scissors, Soaps, Clothes Pegs* – and this time I couldn't hide the smile. The woman labelled her pegs. 'Wow.'

'We like our home to be immaculate.' Her reply sounded rote, as if she was using someone else's words. 'Flawless.'

I stared at Isabelle a moment, picturing her alone in this room with a label-maker, and it didn't seem funny any more. A brief, unwelcome wave of pity stirred in me. Then I realized she expected a response.

'Of course,' I murmured. 'Your home is beautiful.'

Her expression remained blank, and for a second I thought she might say something, but she simply nodded. She gestured to the cleaning caddy on the countertop. 'I've put everything you'll need today in there. I'll update it each time. You'll also find a list of jobs I want done.'

She examined me, not ashamed to run her eyes over my face, my cheap leggings and thin white T-shirt. I could see her drawing conclusions: poor, practical, neat. Her gaze was unexpectedly incisive, and with a flash of panic, I worried she could see more. Maybe the hurt, maybe the fear. Maybe the lies.

I slid out of her eyeline and reached for the cleaning caddy. 'Where do I start?'

Of the three, this was the woman I needed to watch out for.

But it seemed Isabelle wasn't quite ready to let me go. 'Tell me about yourself, Esmie. I can't quite place your accent. Where did you say you were from again?'

Blood pulsed in my ears. The fewer lies I told the better, but I was going to have to lie about this. There could be no connection between me and Nico.

But really, how many times did they have to ask that same damn question? What difference did it make to them where I was from? It wasn't like they actually cared. I was a minor inconvenience, an outsider who entered their most private spaces. It was easier to keep me at arm's length. Safer. I made them feel vulnerable, so in every other way they avoided looking too long at me. So why keep asking that wretched question?

'I come from a small town,' I stalled. I spoke in the quiet, demure voice I'd adopted here. Soft and uncertain, so that I sounded ill at ease with the words I used. 'Nobody knows it . . .'

Isabelle's phone rang, and she glanced at the number. Irritation clouded her features, and she stepped back. I concealed my relief by checking inside the cleaning caddy.

'Excuse me,' she said. 'I have to go out. If I'm not back when you leave, just pull the back door shut.' Seeing my raised eyebrow, she added, 'It's safe here. Safe as houses.'

But that wasn't true now, was it, Isabelle? It hadn't been safe for Nico . . .

She frowned at me. 'You should get started, there's a lot to do.' Then, raising the phone to her ear, she left.

Isabelle and Paul's bedroom was massive. I was certain our entire little house could fit inside. It was elegant with Persian rugs, white wainscoting, and grey wallpaper with the palest silver thread. There were seats set into each of the three large windows. On one side of the room was an enormous bed, and on the other a chaise longue covered in a patterned silk. Through one door was an unnecessarily large en suite bathroom. I stepped through another door, into a bright, spacious dressing room with mirrors and shelves and rows of hanging clothes.

I ran a hand along Isabelle's dresses. Somewhere there had to be a photograph, a memento, a letter. I had evidence that Nico had written at least one to his mystery woman, and I was fairly certain there were more.

I knew there was a chance that his lover, whoever she was, had burned his letters or thrown them away. But with a passion this grand, one that had utterly derailed Nico's life, traces had to remain. Fading track marks that signalled an addiction. A secret tucked into the back of a wardrobe. I would find it. I would find her.

'What are you doing?' The voice came from the dressing-room door, and my heart leapt. I had no brush, no cloth, nothing to show I was cleaning. *Careless*, I berated myself.

I turned to see a young woman with bronze skin and brown hair. She wore a school uniform, but she had to be in her late teens. Isabelle had told me she had two girls. The older daughter, Ava, was away at university, and I had to clean her room once a week. The younger daughter, Liadh, was preparing to take her end of school national exams and I was not to get under her feet. My hand flew to my chest and I said in that quiet little voice I was coming to despise, 'You scared me.'

'Did I?' She smiled, but it wasn't friendly.

'I was just, uh, looking for dust.' I shifted uncomfortably, gesturing to the shelf above the clothes rails. I was certain she could hear my heart, it felt so loud.

'Oh, you're the new cleaner,' the girl said, her expression clearing. 'I'm Liadh. Listen, I know my mam is really particular, but you don't have to clean my room. I don't like people in my space.'

'I'm Esmie,' I said. 'Of course. If you like.'

But Liadh had already lost interest in me and my talk of dust.

She perched on the stool at the dressing table and picked

up a make-up brush, then turned to face the mirror, the light from the window turning her hair gold. With a careful stroke she ran the brush across her cheekbone, then sucked in her cheeks, admiring her reflection.

With a quiet exhale, I reached for the caddy and went to the dressing-room door.

I hadn't found anything, but I wasn't discouraged. I was only getting started.

Chapter Five

Leaving Isabelle's room, I went to the small sitting room at the opposite side of the upstairs passage.

It was simply furnished, with a writing desk, a wooden chest and two worn armchairs. The entrance was in line with the open double doors to the master bedroom where I'd left Liadh putting on make-up in the walk-in closet. I stared at the desk, biting my lip. Did I have time to nose around before she came out?

Then I looked up and, above the desk, I saw a shelf holding bronze figurines. The shock of them was a punch to the gut.

They were strange, ugly statues, made from bronze with a blue-green patina, each the length of my hand and forearm combined. A girl with sea for hair, her thighs more fish-tail than legs. A man with an aviator hat and goggles that had merged into his eyes. I drew closer. Not because I liked them.

Because I'd seen one before.

Nico had one just like this. He'd brought it back with him when he'd returned in disgrace. I'd hated it immediately. Hated how it reminded him of his failure.

His was a thin blue-bronze woman in a heavy coat that hinted of a straitjacket. The Doctor's Wife, it had been

called. I remembered the feel of it in my hand; the smooth-
ness of her jacket, the bumpy texture of her face.

I remembered it flecked with blood.

My heart in my throat, I reached for the sculpture of
the man wearing a doctor's jacket, the folds of the fabric
appearing to bind his arms from behind. It was like Nico's
sculpture; they were clearly a pair. On the base was a
small label: The Doctor.

Why did Nico have the matching partner to Isabelle's
statue? Had he stolen it? Or was it a gift from a lover?

With shaking hands, I put down the sculpture. Eyes darting, I inspected the room for potential letter-sized hiding
places. I hurried to the wooden chest, rummaging through
a pile of folded blankets. Straightening up, I scanned the
room, zeroing in on the desk drawer.

It was locked. I pushed back the hair that had fallen out
of my collapsed ponytail. The key had to be here. I searched
the desk, combing through a box of thank-you cards, lifting up the carriage clock. Urgency rose within me as I
checked the door again and pulled the desk from the wall.
Nothing.

Where was that key? I pressed my fingers to my cheeks,
forcing myself to slow down. I gazed around the room and,
slung over the chair, I saw Isabelle's Mulberry cross-body
bag. With an eye on the door, I opened it.

Isabelle's bag was, unsurprisingly, pristine. No crumpled
tissues or fluff-covered mints. Just a purse, a glasses case –
and a set of keys. With a victorious fist-pump, I danced
back to the desk.

My eyes snagged on the doctor statue again, leaving an
acrid taste in my mouth.

Choosing the smallest key, I slid it into the lock. Every
Pandora hesitated in front of her box, and before the
key turned, I stalled, fighting an inexplicable urge to leave.

Go far away and never return. But my need for answers, for retribution, was greater than my instinct for self-preservation. I would avenge Nico, no matter the cost.

The key turned easily, revealing a large cash box and several folders bearing warranties and receipts. Beneath the folders was a slim notebook. The blue cross-grain leather cover was familiar. I picked it up, suddenly breathless, stroking the cover. Didn't Nico have a book like this? I was sure I'd seen something like it on his bed when he'd video-called with Mama Bear. I'd noticed it because it looked expensive, the kind of luxury Nico would love but couldn't afford. Eager, afraid, I opened the book, finding no name, no identifying details.

On the third page there was neat cursive writing, like Nico's. Drawing in a sharp breath – *could it be this easy?* – I lifted the book. Then, with a plummeting in my chest, I realized my mistake. The writing wasn't Nico's – it was less slanted, with more loops. This wasn't Nico's book. I shut my eyes momentarily, cursing under my breath.

Then I brought the book nearer, forcing myself to rally. Just because it wasn't Nico's, didn't mean there wasn't anything to learn. Leaning against the desk, I read the first lines.

1.

Sometimes the woman wondered if she were some alien thing, inhabiting this body. A tiny, microscopic creature, a parasite who had taken over the host and couldn't find a way out.

How could she be real when she barely recognized the woman in the mirror? She felt trapped, inside this life. Inside this body.

She was locked in a tower, in the middle of the ocean. And there was no one to let her out.

The words felt like a raw, bleeding wound. I felt nasty, as though I had just walked in on a deeply private act and stayed to watch.

Would that stop me from reading on? No. Because for Nico, I would trample through the privacy of these three women in my search for clues. Nothing was sacred.

2.

Last night, she sliced the kitchen knife through her hand.

It happened quickly, the blade slipping from the hard avocado seed and sinking into the inside of her palm. Through skin, through flesh. The pain was immediate. Sharp and deep. The woman stared at the red spilling on to green, then on the marble cutting board below.

She'd frozen, watching the blood, until her younger daughter noticed with a cry. The older daughter insisted they go to A&E. The woman let them lead her to the car, watching the bloodstain grow on the pink-and-white towel.

The daughters fussed as they stalled in traffic, while the woman tried to reassure them that she was fine.

Oh Mam, you'd have a bullet in the brain and you'd still insist that everything is fine.

The woman couldn't explain it. Yes, her hand hurt. The knife had gone almost through. Her body trembled as if the temperature had suddenly dropped. She had to clamp her jaw to keep her teeth from chattering.

But at the same time, she couldn't explain how she felt strangely awake. A creature kept in ice, now coming into thaw. Her brain was electrified, jolted out of a stupor. Everything felt more intense; the bright lights and noise of the emergency department, the large blue eyes of the triage nurse. She couldn't hold on to what they said to her – words fell and floated, impossible to piece together.

The woman couldn't explain how that wound was an awakening, the cold touch of something unfamiliar. How in the strangeness of the hour, she was given this sudden, awful clarity.

She'd been sleepwalking through her life.

In that restless emergency room with a kitchen towel wrapped around her bloody hand, she was more alive than she'd been in years.

It was fragile, this awareness. Already it was receding, lost in the relentless tide of laundry, and chicken on Wednesdays, and Mam where's my shin guards?

She could not continue with this life.

She had to make sure she didn't forget.

She would not lose herself again.

The rest of the page was blank. My face folded into a frown. What the hell was this?

It felt like a novel that Isabelle was writing, but it also felt real. As though Isabelle was writing about herself; I could see Isabelle in the woman she'd conjured on the page. But what was truth, and what was the fantasy of a bored, pampered housewife?

From the hall came the sound of the bedroom door opening, and I was wrenched back to the real world. I shoved the notebook beneath the folders. Before I shut the drawer, I spotted a silver latch key behind the cash box. A duplicate drawer key?

Pocketing it, I returned Isabelle's keys to her bag. I grabbed the polish, retrieved the bronze doctor from the desk, and hastily arranged everything as I'd found it. An actor ready for her scene.

Later, when I was ready to leave, I met Isabelle on the stairs with a red sports bag slung over her shoulder. Intrigued, I studied her with a surreptitious, sidelong glance. There was a tinge of pink in her cheeks, and her eyes sparkled. She did not look like a woman sleepwalking through life.

I peered back at the shelf with bronze sculptures, thinking of the solitary wife who'd sat on Nico's bedside table.

If the words I'd read were true, then maybe Isabelle's awakening after the avocado accident had made her ripe for an affair with a hot young foreign man.

Maybe her solution was to inject the stupefying ordinariness of her suburban existence with a little transgression. And maybe, looking at the flush on her cheeks now, after she broke him, Isabelle replaced him with a new Nico. Like Amber finding her new Laura.

Maybe she was meeting her new Nico tonight, at Begley's.

'You're finished?' she asked as we passed on the stairs.

'Yes.'

'Then I'll see you Thursday.'

I looked down, searching her palm for a scar.

But her hands were closed, clenched into fists, as if to be here at all was to be fighting.

Chapter Six

Tuesday

Isabelle was right: Begley's was a shithole.

The bar was half empty. The floor was sticky beneath my shoes, the lighting dim yet oddly glaring in places.

It was ten minutes before ten and I sat at a table in the corner, waiting for Isabelle to arrive, still unable to think of anything but that doctor sculpture.

I studied the room, watching a young couple argue quietly, a group of students gathered around a wobbly table. A stag group bunched at the pool table, downing shots. A man laughed as he placed his arm around a blow-up doll in a red dress. At a window table, a solitary woman checked her phone impatiently. She was perfectly made up, her face a masterclass in contouring and smoky eye. In another corner, an older woman swayed to the music. A lone man danced with energy. The stag crowd let out a cheer, and I rolled my eyes to see one of them getting handsy with the doll.

'Justin's getting lucky tonight,' the stag men crowed, as Justin held one hand over the doll's mouth, the other slipping between its legs. I turned away in distaste.

Checking the time, I went to the bar and placed my order. Nico had talked about how much he'd loved Guinness, how he wanted me to try it when I visited. With a lump in my throat, I ordered a pint.

I caught my reflection in the cloudy bar mirror: the serious, sad eyes; the simmering fury that was now etched into faint downturned lines at the corners of my mouth. My hair was down, and I'd put on make-up for the first time since I'd arrived. Removed from context, and without my usual uniform of leggings and a T-shirt, I hoped Isabelle wouldn't recognize me. I would need to be careful.

I was watching the door when a hand grabbed my wrist. I whirled around to find Justin leering down at me, his face red with drink. With rising anger, I strained against his grip, but he was stronger. 'Aren't you a cute little thing.' He swung me around, then dropped me on the groom's lap.

'A present from your best man.'

The groom caught me awkwardly, his hand uncertain at the small of my back. He seemed as surprised as I was and made no attempt to hold me as I leapt off his lap. As I staggered away from him, my whole body trembled with fury and fear.

I glared at the men, loathing them with every inch of my being. It was obvious they'd flown in for the weekend, which meant they were scarier drunks. More untethered. Removed from their civilized selves.

When Justin lunged for me again, I was ready. With righteous satisfaction, I landed my elbow in his gut. He stumbled back, and I pulled my Leatherman knife from my jacket pocket. I grew up on streets rougher than these, and I'd learned always to be prepared for trouble.

Holding Justin's eye, with a vicious smirk I stabbed the blow-up doll, the plastic deflating against my hand. It sunk to the table, the slinky red dress tangling with the collapsing plastic.

'What was that for?' Justin's mouth was an angry gash.

'Oh my god, she murdered the sex doll,' a student called drunkenly. 'She's a murderer. Murderer!' He stood, pointed a finger at me, laughing. People were staring at me, and I ducked my head, cursing the attention.

'Donal, don't be an arsehole.' Another student put a hand on his arm, bringing down the pointing finger. She looked at me apologetically. She pushed back her black fringe, then guided Donal to his chair saying, 'Let's get you some water.'

I watched the woman with the fringe settle drunk Donal, and the familiarity of it was both comforting and rage-inducing. I'd been the woman with the fringe so many times, smoothing back Nico's hair when he was sick after one of his drinking binges. Suddenly, I ached to feel his thick curls. I'd give anything to be with him right now.

The bartender approached me, an accusatory look in his eyes. I quickly slipped the knife into my pocket before he had a real reason to throw me out.

Then I saw Isabelle at the door, and I stiffened. I felt the bartender's eyes on me as I whirled in the opposite direction, with the alacrity of the guilty.

She wasn't alone.

I'd only seen them for a second, but I'd immediately recognized Ceanna beside Isabelle. She seemed to look right at me.

I bent my neck so that my hair fell over my face, hiding my features. My ears were ringing, a loud, shrill hum, and I prayed they hadn't noticed me.

The bartender frowned, then nodded to my drink. 'Why don't you go on back to your seat?' He was watching me suspiciously, and I felt a burst of resentment. I wasn't the trouble here.

Taking the Guinness from the counter, I returned to my seat. I searched out Isabelle. She'd taken a table at the half-wall, neatly placing her bag on it. Ceanna, wearing a huge brown trench coat like an old-fashioned spy, pulled out a chair and sat down. She played with her earlobe, staring absently into the room, and I knew she hadn't copped that the woman she'd seen at the bar was her cleaner.

I'd been so sure that Isabelle was here to meet a lover. That I'd discovered a secret. The argument outside the silver Toyota had seemed so much like a lovers' spat, with them arranging to meet here, away from the prying eyes of the neighbours. So why bring a neighbour along? And who had she come to meet? Disappointment settled like lead in my stomach.

I took a sip from my glass, pleasantly surprised by the dark, creamy taste. Across the room, Isabelle tracked a subtle eye over the crowd. She took in the arguing couple, the woman with the smoky eye, the students. She stopped at a table near the stag party. I bent my head over my phone, and her gaze passed right over me. Tucking her blazer around a chair, Isabelle strode to the bar.

At the table, alone in her trench coat, Ceanna was a picture of misery.

I thought back to what Nico had told us about Ceanna. The last few years had been hard on her. She'd lost her husband and infant daughter in a car accident three years ago, about five months before Nico first arrived. Bereft, she'd sold their home in Dublin and moved back to The Woodlands to be near her father. They'd been very close.

And then, six months ago, she'd lost her dad, too.

Isabelle placed two glasses of wine on the table. There was an ease between the two women, and it made me wonder how close they were. Whether they talked about their most intimate fears. Whether they knew each other's secrets.

My glass was half empty when Isabelle stood up and made for the back exit. After a beat, I followed. She went down a flight of stairs into a dimly lit passage, following the sign for the toilets. Keeping back, I started down the stairs, listening for her heels on the tiled floor. They halted suddenly, and I pressed against the wall, holding my breath.

An endless moment passed as I waited, hoping she wasn't retracing her steps. Then the beat of Isabelle's heels resumed, moving further away, and I let out a slow breath. Cautiously, I carried on down the stairs.

At the bottom of the stairs, turning a corner, I stepped aside to avoid bumping into the woman with the smoky eye. She was striking to look at, exquisitely groomed, and smelled of rose perfume.

'Sorry,' I said automatically, as something fell from her hand. Reaching down, I saw a small brown paper bag. Before my hand could close around it, the woman grabbed it.

'I've got it,' she said, tucking it into her handbag. I studied her for a moment. She was achingly thin, the bones of her hips and chest reminiscent of a nineties model.

The woman walked away, and I pushed open the door to an eight-stalled toilet with faux-wood surfaces and low yellow lighting. Isabelle faced away from the door, now wearing reading glasses and intent on her phone. Keeping my head down, I slipped into the first stall, leaving the door open a crack.

From the stall, I watched her take off her glasses and pack them away. Then she pulled out a stash of twenties. Glancing up at the main door, she counted them quickly before tucking the money back into her bag.

Pulling back to the graffitied toilet wall, I took a deep, steadying breath. I'd seen nothing untoward, just Isabelle reading something on her phone and counting through a bundle of notes. But I felt sure that something significant had just happened. I could tell from the way she zipped her handbag, her eyes darting to the door. The wariness in her shoulders. The set of her lips as she counted money beneath the flickering yellow light.

Something was off; I felt it in my bones. But what?

Isabelle pressed her hands to her eyes and I quickly slipped out of the stall, hastening to the door. When I looked back, I saw her palms still pushed to her face, as if they could stop her head from hurting. She seemed small and bothered in the dingy toilets. Just the previous day, I'd thought her too confident and elegant for us to have much in common. Suddenly I wasn't so sure.

I hurried out into the passage, certain that I hadn't been seen. On my way up the stairs, I walked past the student with the fringe. She smiled at me as we crossed, as if we were old friends. Maybe we were. That's all I had these days. Brief encounters in the back passages of dingy bars. Everything else was broken.

When I returned to the bar, the best man reached out his arms to me saying, 'There she is.' His words were slurred. 'I was told I had to say sorry for manhandling you.' Justin arranged his features in an exaggerated sad face. 'Sorry.' He dragged out the word like a child forced to apologize, and slapped his wrist for good measure.

'Let me make it up to you,' he said. 'I'll buy you a drink. Join us.'

I would have to be out of my mind to sit down with a group of drunk men. Then I noticed the expensive watch on his wrist, the branded clothes he wore.

'I'll play you.' I nodded to the pool table. I'd dropped the soft, hesitant voice and I felt a wave of warm relief, like I could be myself again. 'But let me warn you, I'll take your money.'

Justin laughed as if I'd said the funniest thing. But he had no idea. I wasn't as good as Nico, but I'd spent enough time in pool halls with him and I could carry a game. Besides, Justin and his friends were so far down the road of inebriation that my level of skill was likely irrelevant.

I lined up a shot, sinking two balls. When I missed the next, I stepped back and glanced around. Isabelle was alone at her table now, nursing a fresh glass of wine. She checked her watch, and I sensed she was impatient. Ready to leave. Had the mystery silver Toyota driver stood her up? I searched the bar for Ceanna.

'Your go,' Justin said, stepping too close.

I moved away, and that's when I saw her. My eyes widened in surprise. Ceanna was dancing by herself on the other side of the room. She was nothing like the woman I'd met in the kitchen.

She'd taken off her jacket to reveal a short red dress. She danced, rolling her hips, reaching out her arms above her. She drew the attention of both men and women, who tracked her red dress into the darker part of the room. She watched them back, a knowing look in her eyes.

I played my round, sinking two more balls before I missed. All the while, I was aware of Ceanna immersed in the music, following the beat with languid, sinuous movements. Her eyes were shut now, and she closed her fingers around the hem of her dress, raising it higher as she shook her hips.

At his turn, Justin walked around the pool table. When he took position, I moved closer and whispered, 'She looks like she's having a good time.' His wallet bulged out of his back pocket. Justin glanced up, his shot going wild.

'You distracted me,' he said. He seemed more sober now. I had to be careful.

'Have another go,' I said generously. Justin went again,

but he was too aware of Ceanna, our game no longer interesting to him. He was still staring at her when I slipped the
wallet back into his jeans pocket.

I did warn him that I'd take his money.

'I'm out,' I said, placing the cue on the side of the table
and stepping back. Justin barely noticed me.

I made my way to the door, leaving the crowd of drunk
men behind. They seemed wilted now. Sweaty and red-eyed
and not exactly having fun. The groom stared morosely
into his beer. The smoky-eyed woman had left. I couldn't
see the student with black hair and the fringe.

Ceanna danced on, uninhibited. She knew she was
watched, and she didn't care. Courted it, even.

Was this who Nico had fallen in love with? She was
clearly very sensuous, comfortable with her sexuality.

Was this all it had taken for Nico to ruin everything? A
woman in a red dress, and a cheap bar. A dull disappointment stabbed at my heart. I was suddenly tired. I wanted to
either drink too much or sleep.

I left the stuffy bar and walked for twenty minutes, going by
the bay and watching the moon over the water.

At the house where I rented a bed, there were men in
the living room playing cards and drinking spirits. The
small space was hazed with smoke, not quite masking the
smell of damp.

'Esmie, come and play,' the men called.

I smiled, shaking my head. 'Not tonight.'

'A woman got in touch, asking for a reference.' Marko's
deep voice rumbled across the room. His Eastern European
accent was thicker with the drink. 'I told her, that Esmie –
she's a bad, bad girl.' He let out a shoulder-shaking wheezy
chuckle at his own joke. 'Drinks a man under the table,
then takes his money cheating at cards.'

'Thank you,' I said with a grin, knowing he was joking. He'd have told Isabelle exactly what she needed to hear. I'd offered him payment but he'd declined, preferring to do it for the mischief.

Passing the kitchen, I heard talking and laughing from inside, but I was too tired even to say hello. After using the bathroom, doing my best to ignore the mildew around the window, I shut myself in the room I shared with Fabiana. Her shift started at five in the morning, and she was usually asleep by nine.

I took the stolen money from my back pocket and counted six hundred and thirty euros, an insane amount to carry while wasted. My conscience pricked; I wasn't a thief, really. But I remembered how Justin had grabbed at me, as if I were little more than a blow-up doll. Then I didn't feel so bad any more.

Guilt was a luxury I couldn't afford while I was here. On the outside, I was spending the summer in a pretty Irish university town. One with quaint shops where flowerpots hung above cobblestone roads. But on the inside, this was a war zone and I had to do everything I could to survive.

I put the money in an envelope. With a Sharpie, I wrote LAURA and taped it to the top of my bedside cabinet drawer. I paused when I saw the worn, folded page peeking out beneath my T-shirts. I hesitated, then pulled it out, holding it to my chest while I got into bed.

It was a page from a letter. There was no salutation or sig-nature, but I knew Nico's handwriting well. Settling into my pillow, I read again the words I'd read a hundred times.

Please, please, please talk to me. Why won't you answer my messages? Have you really forgotten me? Or do you fool yourself into believing you are alive without me?

*You said it yourself: you are nothing without
me. You said it when we stole out in the middle of
the night. When we ran together down the road to
the bluebell woods, your lips on mine, your hands
wandering, and you begged so prettily. Have you
forgotten our tree, the one we marked? The tree
where I, bound and yours, made you feel?*

*I lost everything because you did not speak the
truth when it mattered. But I would give it all,
gladly, to be together again. You are in deep
beneath my skin, and I cannot settle without you.*

*My love, my viper, I forgive you and every lie
that fell from those beautiful lips. If you'll have
me, I will find a way back to The Woodlands.
Back to you.*

Call, and I will come.

I'd found the letter hidden inside the lining of Nico's suitcase, along with a roll of cash tied with an elastic band. One
thousand euros. I found it the night I needed it most, an
unexpected answer to a prayer I'd never thought I'd say.

Nico had been rushed to hospital, Mama Bear whispering urgently to him while she held him in the back seat. A
devastating Pietà.

I packed a bag, left my home and spent four nights hiding
in a warehouse, desperate for news about Nico as I waited
for my flight to Ireland. A flight that had been booked
months before, when I'd dreamed of visiting him here.

When Nico came home, his scholarship lost, we'd thought
the ticket wasted. That night, it became my passage to
safety.

I'd read the letter on the thin mattress in the cold warehouse. Afterwards, I wanted to tear it into tiny shreds. But
I made myself keep it. A memento of that night when Nico's

head split open, the night Mama Bear had warned me to run.

This letter was proof that Nico had loved one of the women from The Woodlands. It was proof that her lies had cost him everything.

I missed our tiny four-roomed house. Our home. I missed Nico.

I missed myself.

Chapter Seven

Wednesday

Ceanna's house was down a blink-and-you'll-miss-it narrow gravel lane. It was older, a seventies bungalow with no upstairs and a small, unkept garden. Linc still hadn't returned my damaged bike, and my cheeks were stinging from the wind after the long walk. I'd asked Amber about it before I left there two days ago, but she'd given me impatient eyes and said, 'How should I know?'

Stepping over the yellow-flowered weeds on the stone path, I consulted my mental notes. Ceanna was thirty-nine; eight years older than Amber. After the terrible accident that killed her family, Ceanna had moved back to this area because she wanted to be near her father. She sublet two of the three bedrooms in her house to graduate students. Nico was her first lodger, and it had been clear he'd been happy with the arrangement, finding Ceanna friendly. Easy.

Exactly how easy and friendly, I planned to find out.

I hesitated at the front door. Nico would have seen this door with its chipped green paint every day. The potted plants, overrun with tall, wild grass. Something twisted inside me. This had been his home. The place where he slept and studied. This was where he'd been in those long months he felt lost to us. I reached out a tentative fist, dread and anticipation tangling in my chest, and knocked.

'Nasty chill in that wind.' I whirled around to see Ceanna behind me, carrying a basket of plants. When she'd danced seductively in her red dress, there had been a wildness about her, a recklessness that was as frightening as it was alluring. Now, in the cold light of day, she seemed a different woman. Today I saw the grief etched into her face, that strange, sad light in her eyes, and the downturn to her mouth.

Was Nico a rebound affair for Ceanna? A mistake made in grief?

Would it change my plans at all, if so?

She stepped in ahead of me, and I breathed in a scent of soap. Not the pretty florals with tea overtones that Amber favoured, but a masculine scent that reminded me of Nico. A common supermarket teen-boy soap that pressed at the open wound in my heart.

'Come to the kitchen; it catches the afternoon sun.'

The walls of the dark, narrow passage were crowded with photographs. Ceanna went ahead, a pagan nun in a shapeless white linen dress with a huge cardigan and bare feet. A narrow white linen scarf wrapped around her chin-length hair like a huge headband. She seemed like a different person than the woman dancing at the bar, that bold persona discarded along with the slinky red dress.

Ceanna put down her basket and flicked the kettle on. 'So, this is the house. It's not big, but' – her mouth turned down apologetically – 'it is awful messy.'

'It's fine,' I soothed. But she was right. It was awfully messy. The kitchen table was cluttered with magazines and papers. There were heaps of books and jackets on the chairs. I suspected things didn't have a place in this house. That they were put down and that's where they stayed.

Jars of herbal remedies, minerals and supplements jostled on the counter. There was a tub of powder called

Moondust, and I had to restrain myself from rolling my eyes. Of course this version of Ceanna – the basket-of-flowers-and-linen-scarf Ceanna – took something called Moondust.

'I take it every night.' Ceanna saw me looking at the container. 'It keeps me balanced. Settled.'

'What is it?'

'A mix of herbs and minerals. All perfectly natural.' She gave me a brittle smile. 'Three years ago, I was in a dark place. I took a heap of prescribed medication to get me through that time. Then I started a new med, and it turned out I'm one of the few who gets an extremely bad reaction. I found myself parked on the side of the road at four in the morning, thirty kilometres from home. I had no recollection of how I'd got there.' Her eyes were lit with sorrow. 'Only a little while before, I'd lost my husband and my daughter because of a drunk driver, so I couldn't believe I'd endangered other people by sleep-driving. I weaned myself off everything. Started finding natural remedies, finding peace through meditation and yoga. Moondust is one of the herbal cures that helped me turn my life around. You should try it.'

My ice-cold heart melted just a little.

Ceanna looked away, and the pink in her cheeks suggested she was embarrassed at how much she'd revealed.

'Where do I start?' I edged towards the door. There was a lot to do. I'd be hard pressed to finish it all in three hours, never mind have time to nose around.

'Sit for a moment.' Ceanna placed two mugs on the table.

I did so reluctantly, watching Ceanna pull small yellow flowers from one of the plant cuttings in the basket. She rinsed them, then dropped a handful in her mug, which she then topped up with boiled water.

'St John's wort,' she said in response to my unspoken question. 'It came up early this year.'

I had to think a moment before I remembered: a natural antidepressant. I thought back to the awe I felt when I first visited this neighbourhood, imagining that just living in such beauty and affluence must make life easier. But it hadn't taken long to begin to see the cracks in the facade.

'I'd like us to be friends, Esmie.' She pushed a mug with still-steeping black tea towards me.

'Sure.' I shifted in my seat, unable to meet her eye. It was a different version of Isabelle's list: polish the sculptures, clean the fridge, be my friend. I wondered if she was genuinely interested in me, or if this was all about her. Maybe it made her feel good about herself, her act of goodwill for the day, talking to the poor foreign girl. Or maybe Ceanna was sad and lonely and needed someone to listen.

I could do that for her. Until I knew the truth.

Ceanna's grief was a thick cloak around her. Losing three of her most precious people in only a few years must have been traumatizing. A burst of sympathy swelled. 'I'm sorry. About your family. And now your father.'

'Thank you. I miss them every day.' She raised the cup to her lips and blew on it. 'Dad was a good man. He was very protective of us. He was the only one who could rein Amber in.'

She took a sip from the mug and her mouth pulled down. I realized it wasn't the tea that caused the strange expression on her face, but talking about Amber. A touch of dissatisfaction, a hint of longing.

'Rein Amber in?' I asked. 'I don't understand?'

Ceanna stared at the flowers floating in her tea, then looked up, pasting a smile on her face. 'Do you have siblings?'

The mug grew heavy in my hand. Tucking a loose strand of hair behind my ear, I tried to think what to say. I didn't know how to answer – if I should answer. I put the mug on the table, unable to drink the hot, bitter tea. I paused until it was almost too long, then had an idea. 'I have a brother.'

It was smart, I realized, to talk indirectly about Nico. I couldn't give myself away, but I could fish. I was here to dissect, to pin them beneath my gaze as they let me into their homes, and then pull everything to pieces until I understood. Referencing a brother would help me do that.

I could talk about how he was a studious young man, and did she know anyone like that?

'Is your brother older or younger than you?'

'Older,' I said. 'Three years older.'

Suddenly, now that I started talking about Nico, I didn't want to stop.

'He's very clever. Loves sports.' The words came out in a rush, as if from a clogged pipe that had been cleared. It had been so long since I'd spoken about him, the Nico he was before. 'Very handsome.' I laughed, but it sounded a bit like a sob. 'He has a girlfriend. Six years.'

'There'll be a wedding soon then.'

'My brother . . . he isn't well.'

'He's sick?' Ceanna tilted her head, sympathy on her face. But her eyes shone, and I felt a sudden flash of apprehension, an uncomfortable inkling that she was somehow buoyed by my sadness.

'He's . . . he's sleeping.' Said like that, it sounded peaceful.

'A coma?' she asked, and I nodded. 'Oh, Esmie. I'm sorry. And his girlfriend . . . she left him because of that?'

My head jerked up. 'No. She loves him.' It came out too rough, and Ceanna raised an eyebrow. I fought to bring my voice back under control. 'It is difficult.' And I was so far away. I felt a constant anxiety about home, about what was happening there. How I was being edged out.

'You get on with her?'

I sighed. 'We were friends first. Since we were children. She was next door.' My hands closed around each other in my lap. 'Her father, he wasn't a good man. So she stayed in our house every weekend.' I realized my words were coming out too fluently, so I made myself slow down and injected uncertainty into my voice. 'Her father died, and then she lived with us.' Sharing Nico's room, his small bed. 'We're family.' Weeds, twisting together. 'Sisters. Like you and Amber.'

'This woman your brother loves, what's her name?'

The name was at the tip of my tongue. It wanted to be said. To be spoken out loud: *Simone. He loves Simone.*

I shook my head. I couldn't say it. I didn't know what Nico had said to Ceanna. I wasn't worried about them connecting my Esmie to Nico's Esmerelda – he'd always preferred the long form, even when we were children. But Simone was only ever Simone.

Beautiful Simone, I could almost hear Nico saying. *Perfect Simone.*

Vicious Simone.

Fear balled in my gut. It felt that even saying the word out loud, Simone, would be dangerous. To say the name was to summon the presence. There was no room for Simone here.

'Your brother, then, do you want to tell me his name?' She was looking at me with a hungry kindness. Perhaps Ceanna herself sensed this poisonous sorrow I carried and it stirred hers, made her settle in her own sadness.

'Lucas,' I lied with a smile. So many lies.

Pushing the abandoned tea further back on the table, I tried to avoid that dissecting eye, felt pinned by the intensity of her gaze. I made to stand, but she put a hand on my arm and the scent of Nico caught me unawares, making my head spin. Did that soap remind Ceanna of Nico too? Was that why she used it? She was a very attractive woman – Nico couldn't have missed that. Her beauty was a light that shone from within, carried in her grief-stricken eyes.

'Not yet.' The words weren't barked, but it was unmistakably an order.

Bitterness curdling, I sat back in the chair. So much for being friends. From the clutter of books and newspapers, Ceanna extracted a lighter and held it to two pillar candles at the centre of the table.

'For healing.'

She stared at the candles and suddenly I couldn't stand it, this new-age mumbo jumbo when the disaster was so very real to me.

'Where?' I stood up too fast and clutched the chair to steady myself. 'Where do I clean first?'

I felt a sudden wave of resentment. The congealed remains of a smoothie in the blender. Something white and sticky splotched on the floor. Then I thought of Nico and the times I'd cleaned up his vomit. I straightened my shoulders. I would do this. I would do this and more.

'I have a new lodger moving in this evening.' Ceanna rose from her chair. 'The empty room – the one just after the bathroom – hasn't been let since last November, so it needs a deep clean.'

Since Nico.

The room had been empty since Nico. Something dark and vicious streaked through me, almost tripping me up. Maybe the residents of The Woodlands weren't as unaffected by Nico as I'd thought. Good.

'Why so long?' I fought to speak lightly as I followed her to the utility area.

'The last lodger left and—' She exhaled. 'Well, there'd

been difficulties.' She gestured to the small alcove off the kitchen. 'Right, everything you need is in there. Clean cloths on the second shelf, vacuum, mop. It's all there.'

'What do you mean, difficulties?'

Ceanna pressed her lips together. 'Sometimes you think you know someone and it turns out you were wrong.'

Wrong about what? There was an untold story in her eyes.

'My one-thirty will be here soon.' Seeing my confusion, Ceanna explained. 'I made the garage into a little wellness centre. Massage. Acupuncture.' Moving to the outside door, she added, 'I'll be busy until five. Shut the door behind you when you leave.'

'Did something happen? With your lodger?' The question came rushing out before I could stop it, and I braced myself for suspicion and discovery.

'There was some . . . upheaval.' She picked up her phone and checked some app I didn't recognize.

'Upheaval?' I frowned. 'I'm sorry, I don't understand the word?'

'Problems. He caused problems.' Ceanna's tone was clipped. 'He left. It's over.' Her words were final: she was not going to say any more. Slipping her phone into her pocket, she was clearly upset. Ceanna stepped out of the door and then she was gone. I could have screamed with frustration – the answers were so close, but so far away.

My phone buzzed, and that customary dread grabbed my chest. No one messaged me any more, unless it was trouble.

You know I'm going to find you.

A chill ran through me. She was devious and manipulative, and I knew her too well. She could sneak through Mama Bear's phone to get my new number. Trace every step I'd taken to find out where I was.

And then this place would become dangerous too.

I'd call home tonight, I resolved, struggling to shake the unease that had come over me.

Tucking my phone into my tight hip pocket, I looked around the kitchen. This was where Nico had made his morning coffee for more than two years. I tried to imagine him at the fridge. Or standing at the microwave, waiting for his dinner to heat up. But I couldn't feel him there. I pressed the heels of my hands to my eyes and took a long, deep breath. Then I collected what I needed from the alcove. It was time to get to work.

I passed a bedroom and a bathroom; then, at the next door, I reached for the handle. Bracing myself, I stepped inside his room.

And there he was. It hit me immediately, the feel and even the smell of him. I had to stop, steady myself against the door frame, because it was as if Nico was there. The walls were painted a deep indigo colour. His favourite.

The room was just big enough for a desk and a single bed in the corner. The window looked out to an ivy-covered wall. I could hear him in the silence, the way he filled it when we were alone together. Comfortable and complete, we didn't need to talk because we were connected by something that ran deeper than words.

I could picture him sleeping on that bed. At the desk, working deep into the night. He'd always put in the hours, starting early in the morning and still going late at night. Nico never watched TV. If he read fiction, it took him months to complete. Sport and science, that's what he liked most.

I stood in his room, the wall holding me up, and I could feel him there. Not the man who hid pills in his desecrated textbooks, but the Nico before. The one who thrummed with life. Whose vigour was infectious.

I went to the desk, ran my fingers over the wood whorls.

77

I felt the cushioned desk chair – too soft, Nico wouldn't have liked it – then leaned my head out of the window, looking at ivy creeping over the stone. My throat thick, I sat on the bed, then curled up in a ball on the bare mattress, my head on his pillow. I wanted to sit a moment, with the ghost of him.

I burned to speak to him. To tell him that I was in his other room, on his other bed, in the place where he'd last truly lived. That I liked this shade of indigo more than the one back home. I wanted to ask if he remembered the delicate scent that came from the trees and moss and ivy outside the window here. I wanted to ask him if Ceanna had danced for him while wearing a tiny red dress. If he'd placed his hands on her hips, if he'd kissed her neck.

I realized then that I was crying, huge tears tracking silently down my face. I curled up on his bed and wept into the bare mattress. Because I missed him. I wanted to be with him so badly. But nothing would ever be the same again.

HOME

Simone hesitated at the door to Nico's bedroom. She smoothed her hair and fixed her dress. She said a quick prayer to the god of lost girls. Then, she stepped inside.

Nico was at the desk, wearing a deep blue-indigo T-shirt that matched the walls. Out of the window was the pale brown dirt road, the patchy grass and distant green-grey mountain.

His smile lit up the room, pulling her like a magnet.

Lately, she felt an odd twisting in her gut when he was near. A desperate urge for him to see her, draw closer to her. It was madness – he was Nico. And she was just Simone, the girl next door. A girl whose own father didn't care about her.

Sometimes she feared that she was a little parasite who'd attached herself to this family, drawing from their warmth. Not enough to stop, though.

She thought about Nico all the time. He was the last thing on her mind before she fell asleep, the first when she woke up. She felt like a string-pull doll that only came to life when he was around.

She reached into her pocket and pulled out a chocolate bar. 'Do you want this?'

Nico leaned back in the chair, resting his feet on the desk. He nodded, folding his arms across his chest.

She didn't move to him. Instead, Simone wagged the chocolate bar in her hand, looking him in the eye. 'Well then, come and get it.' Her heart was thundering in her chest.

He smiled slowly, unfolding himself from the chair. Simone hid the bar behind her back and teased, 'Nuh-uh, what's the magic word?'

When younger, they'd wrestled and played, his touch as familiar as Esmerelda's. Now, it felt all the more thrilling that it had become strange.

'Please?' Nico lunged for the bar but Simone shifted out of the way, laughing.

Simone shook her head. She held the bar above her head, taunting him. As Nico reached her again, she put it behind her back.

He lunged, grabbing her in a full body tackle, and together they fell on the bed. Giggling, she squirmed, but Nico pinned her down. 'Is it "Simone is the best"?'

She shook her head, laughing.

'What about "All hail Queen Simone"?' Pushing her into the mattress, Nico tried to prise the bar from her fingers, but she held firm. He held her tighter, and she couldn't get up.

'Nope. Close, though.' She suddenly, unexpectedly, nipped his arm. Hard. She tasted his skin; sweat and soap and him. It made her want more.

Surprise loosened his grip, and Simone wriggled out from under him. She moved to get off the bed, but he grabbed her and tossed her down again.

This time, as they wrestled, him hovering over her, she saw something new in his eyes. A hunger that she'd never seen there before. Emboldened, she slipped the chocolate bar down the bodice of her dress and raised an eyebrow.

Nico looked at it, the intensity in his eyes growing. They were both still, frozen in place, and her body was on fire.

'It has to be "Simone is hot."' He raised his hand and touched it to her chest. Simone waited, holding her breath.

His fingers brushed the embroidered edging. Then they dipped beneath the cotton bodice of her dress and he swallowed. He trailed his fingers down, reaching for the plastic wrapper and brushing her skin. 'Or' – Nico's voice was hoarse – 'Simone is beautiful.'

Their eyes met. He pressed his body down on hers as his fingers gripped the wrapper. His eyes dropped to her mouth and his head dipped.

'Hey Nico, we need to—'

They heard the words from outside the room and they both sat up quickly, adjusting themselves. Simone leaned against the wall while Nico went back to the desk.

'—decide what we're getting Mama B for Christmas. Oh Simone, I didn't realize you were here.'

'Hello, Esmie,' Simone said, wishing with all her being that her friend hadn't come. They'd been so close. He wanted her, she'd felt it.

'Esmerelda!' Nico sang her name, giving her an affectionate smile. 'You're right, we're running out of time.'

Esmerelda flopped beside her on the bed, entirely oblivious to what she'd interrupted. 'What do you want for Christmas, Nico?'

'Maybe chocolate,' Nico said, watching Simone. 'More of these.' He lifted the mushed chocolate bar he'd extracted from her dress, peeled the wrapper and took a large, greedy bite.

'That's too boring,' Esmerelda complained. 'What about you, Simone?'

'I'm fine. Don't really need anything.' Simone hated

Christmas. It was always disappointing. Her dad was rarely sober during the holidays, and she bore the brunt of it.

'Seriously, you must want something?' Esmerelda said with a laugh. 'What do you most want in the whole world?'

'Honestly?'

'Honestly.'

'You guys.' The words came out quickly, and she could feel her cheeks burning at the raw truth. 'You made me part of your family. I couldn't ask for more.' She tried to hold back the words, but they poured out. 'Sometimes I feel like I – that there's something wrong with me. Like I'm too difficult, hard to love. But when I'm with you, I'm OK. I think I would die without you three.'

Simone looked down, embarrassed at her outburst. She'd been so close to kissing Nico, and she'd blown it all with her word vomit. How could he want her after that?

Then she felt arms squeezing her tight. Esmerelda held her and said fiercely, 'I love you, Simone. You're the sister I never had.'

Over Esmerelda's tight hug, Simone finally looked at Nico, hardly daring to see how he'd responded to her brutal honesty.

But Nico was watching her with a strange new light in his eyes. He looked at Simone as if he could see *her*, beyond the surface to the murky depths below.

And he liked what he saw.

Chapter Eight

Wednesday

I woke with a start on the bare mattress in Nico's old room, alarmed and disorientated, to the vibrations of an incoming call. Reaching for my phone, I saw that I'd been asleep for half an hour. Cursing, I got up off the bed and answered.

'Esmie, thank God.' Amber's voice was loud. 'There's an emergency. We're having friends over tonight, and on a fucking whim Linc asked this new professor in his department to join us, and now he tells me she's badly allergic to dogs, and I can't sort everything out all by myself.' Her words were laced with anger. 'You have to come.'

'I can't,' I said, working to keep the sleep out of my voice. 'I'm working.'

'I'll pay you time and a half.'

'I'm at Ceanna's. I can't leave.' I looked around guiltily. I'd barely started.

'Ceanna's only paying three hours. Come as soon as you're done.'

'I started late.' *Well, fell asleep.* 'I won't finish before five.'

She exhaled with unrestrained irritation. 'Five, then.'

I hesitated. I was still feeling raw, undone. The back of my neck was itching, as though I'd developed hives. I wanted to go back to my narrow bed in my small shared room and hide under the covers.

'Please, Esmie. I'll pay you double.' And then she sounded softer, more desperate. 'There's so much to do, and I need help. You'll be done before eight.'

'OK.' I shut my eyes briefly. I would push on. I might learn something. Besides, I needed the money.

Then, pulling myself upright, I started cleaning. I worked hard, tugging the bed from its corner, lifting the rug. I cleaned vigorously, as if brushing and scrubbing could dislodge whatever of Nico was entrapped here.

When I was finished there, I went to the desk and pushed it away from the wall.

Soft as a wing, something glided to the floor.

I had no right to be angry about the mess, I told myself again and again. I fixed my eyes on the stain on the suede armchair as I cleaned it. I refused to look at the room. 'The afternoon room', as Amber called it, without any irony or awareness of affectation.

'Some friends came round last night,' Amber had said without expression, before turning to walk out.

When I'd left two days ago, I'd been proud of my work. The house had been gleaming. The afternoon room had been fit for a magazine spread. Today it was trashed, like the aftermath of a party thrown by teenagers when their parents were away. Cigarette butts on the floor. Forgotten beer bottles hidden behind the leather bench and cake trampled into the wooden floor. Underwear stuffed down the side of the armchair. Through the glass doors, in a sheltered nook, a used condom lay discarded in a corner.

There were no dog hairs – not in here, anyway. Seething, I realized that Amber had lied. She had just called me in because she couldn't face her own mess.

I attacked the stain with renewed vigour. It wasn't only

84

Amber summoning me that had angered me. I was angry about the way Ceanna had talked about Nico. I was angry with Nico.

But mainly I was angry because of the photograph I'd found, the one that had been wedged between the desk and the wall. Had Nico left it there deliberately? Or had it slipped back there, unseen?

The picture was in my backpack, folded over and over so I wouldn't have to look at it again. On the back, in Nico's handwriting, were two unsettling lines.

She begged so prettily but
He tore off her clothes and jewels

The photo had been taken in the woods. Nico naked, aroused and tied to a tree. Nausea rose within me just thinking about it.

'Are you trying to clean up a crime scene, Esmie?' I jumped at the boom of Linc's voice from behind me. I looked up to see him in the doorway, observing me with a bemused smile. He was in a smart dark grey suit, and with his thick dark blond hair and hazel eyes, he looked dashing. I felt self-conscious in my boring black leggings, the plain tank top.

When I'd sat with Ceanna, the idea of being her friend had been awkward but within the realm of possibility. I could clean her toilets and, despite the unevenness, we could light candles and be friends.

But with Amber and Linc, the divide felt insurmountable. It wasn't just the yawning chasm between the glamorous couple and the hired help. That was there, sure, but it wasn't the main thing. What separated us was the gap between the haves and the have-nots, but not in a material sense. Stuff didn't matter to me. I didn't need a house like this, or the obviously expensive clothes that Amber wore. My needs were simpler. When Nico was with us, I had. And when Nico wasn't with us, I lost the sun around which my world had orbited. Then I didn't have.

Whatever it was that filled people up, that made them complete and alive – mine had been emptied that night when Nico was hurt.

'Let me guess.' Linc sighed. 'It was a lot worse when you got started.'

He was right. I'd cleaned most of it, and although the smell of booze and cigarettes lingered, the mess had been reduced to a rubbish bag, a box of bottles, and stains on the rug and chair.

'Amber said she'd had friends over.' I got to my feet, feeling suddenly shy.

He arched an eyebrow. 'Looks like they had fun.'

'You weren't here?'

'No, just back from Cork.' He checked his watch. 'With less than two hours to spare before our guests arrive.' He was relaxed, jovial, but there was something hard in his eyes. 'Amber shouldn't have asked you to clean this.'

'It's OK.' I said that a lot these days, I realized. I seldom meant it. 'You are not worried?'

'Should I be?' His smile reached his eyes, crinkling the skin at the sides.

'It's just . . .' I dropped a hand. 'Amber is stressed.' Her exact words had been, *God, I have such a fucking hangover. This dinner is the last thing I need.* She'd held her fingers to her temples, her skin even paler than usual, and dark smudges beneath her eyes.

'Ah,' he said. 'Suppose I'd better get stuck in.' He made to leave, then paused. 'Thank you, Esmie.'

When he smiled, his eyes were on mine and it felt like the winter sun on my face.

'It's OK.' I meant it marginally more this time.

'Well, I owe you. Amber is not happy with me right now.'

A moment later, I remembered that I needed to talk to him and ran to the door. 'Linc!' But he had disappeared. Damn, I'd have to ask about my bike later.

When I'd finished cleaning up Amber's little party, I vacuumed and dusted downstairs, removing all traces of the dogs. It turned out there really was a professor who was violently allergic and Amber had walked the dogs to Ceanna's house while I'd attacked the afternoon room. I headed out with the cordless vacuum, between the leafy trees, down the gravel path to the summer kitchen, which had been set up for the dinner.

The thick walls of an old stone shed had been repurposed to make a rustic garden kitchen with a brick oven where something delicious was already cooking. The bifold doors were completely open, and the kitchen extended outdoors where the dinner table stood. The nearby trees were strung with fairy lights. All around the table were shrubs planted in large old milk cans and giant clay pots. Beyond, the grass and apple orchard. It felt peaceful here. Like I could rest for a moment, and be safe.

But then I examined the chair cushions and found them all covered in dog hairs. I sighed, then got to work.

Amber appeared and, humming, she began setting the table with vintage crockery, wildflowers and simple silver candlesticks. Everything pretty, she disappeared again. By the time I'd removed the last dog hair, my stomach was growling. The smell of whatever was slow-cooking in the brick oven had me ravenous.

I went back into the house and found Amber in the kitchen, intricately icing small cakes.

'That looks really good.'

She glanced up at me and gave a small smile. 'Thanks. No more dog hairs?'

'I was careful.'

'I'm sure you were.' This time, the smile reached her eyes. 'You really saved me this evening, Esmie. Last night . . .' She paused as though lost for words. 'I didn't mean for things to get so out of control. And then I woke at two this afternoon and I panicked.'

I smiled sweetly, all the while thinking, *What would Amber most hate to lose? What would hurt her the most, if she no longer had it?*

Linc came into the kitchen, now wearing dark jeans and a smart shirt. He smelled good and again, I found my eyes turning to him. Wanting to look at him.

'Hey, Esmie.' He smiled. He knew, of course. That I liked looking at him. That I was a little wide-eyed, a little awestruck. I wondered if he enjoyed this admiration from his students.

'Linc,' I said, before I missed my chance again. 'I need my bike. Can I take it back with me now?'

He winced. 'I meant to fix it for you. I'm so sorry.' Then suddenly he seemed to realize that I didn't just teleport to work. 'How have you been getting in this week?'

'Walking.'

'Esmie.' The dismay was so thick, I wasn't sure if it was genuine or if he was laying it on. 'You should have said something.'

A stab of irritation. How did he think I'd been getting in after he'd damaged my bike? But he didn't think. For him, and everyone else here, I ceased to exist the minute I left. I was a non-player character in their beautiful world.

But that was my secret power. That was what gave me access to their private spaces. That was how I would get justice for Nico.

'It's OK.' Again, those stupid words.

'No. Listen, I'll drive you home and I will fix the bike tomorrow. I promise.'

'You don't have time now,' Amber protested with a scowl. 'Neither of us do. Get one of the ghouls to do it.'

'They're not my servants, Amber,' Linc snapped at her. She lifted the tray of cakes and I saw her eyes were tight.

He considered for a moment. 'Why don't you work here this evening? You can help out in the kitchen, keep on top of things? I'll drive you home after.'

I glanced at Amber, uncertain, in time to see her give him a sharp look.

'It's the ideal solution,' Linc said, ignoring her and sorting through a pile of books on the kitchen table. 'This way we don't have to face the clear-up and a mountain of dishes at midnight or in the morning. Esmie, you won't be run off your feet, I promise. Most of the time you can sit here and read a book or watch TV.'

Or, I thought, *take advantage of the uninterrupted time to continue my search.* I nodded.

'This won't be double pay.' Amber sounded sour.

'That's OK.'

The doorbell rang. Amber took off her apron and stepped out from behind the kitchen island. 'I'll get it.'

'That's probably Fiona,' Linc said. 'I asked her to come early.'

'I can't stand Fiona,' Amber grumbled. 'The way she sucks up to you.'

'Be nice,' Linc called, as Amber went to the door.

He picked up a book from the kitchen table, and turned it over to glance at the back. The front cover faced me. It was pale blue with a black-and-white photograph of a woman's face.

'*The Heart in the Wood.*' I read the title. '*Entrapment in the Work of Eden Hale.* Who is Eden Hale?'

'She was an important poet, philosopher and artist in the sixties and seventies. I did my PhD on her,' he said, flipping the book over, and I had a sudden image of Linc writing tiny words all over the body of a woman. Feeling an unexpected tingle, a muted stirring of a sleeping hunger, I shifted uncomfortably.

He tapped the book. 'This was written by our allergic guest. The new professor in my department. She's *supposed* to be the world authority on Eden.'

'Supposed to be?' I said, bolder than I'd intended.

But it didn't matter – the smile he gave me was dazzling. 'I am, of course. No one knows Eden Hale better than me.' His words were certain. Possessive. 'I just wish the selection committee for the Poetry Chair could have seen that.'

My eyes widened with confusion, an invitation for him to keep going.

'I applied for her job a while ago. I was sure that with my publishing record, my books, the grants I've secured, my teaching awards, the conferences I've organized, my unmatched knowledge of Eden Hale, I would get the promotion. Instead, they hired someone from the outside.' It was clear from the tightness in his voice, the fire in his eyes, that despite the intervening months, this was a fresh wound. 'I'd spent a year preparing. I did *everything*, and—' He broke off abruptly, seeming to realize he wasn't being charming any more. He hitched the handsome smile back on to his face.

'She wrote in the sixties and seventies?' I asked, keen to steer the conversation to safer ground.

From the front door, Amber's voice carried to us. 'Well, Fiona, tell him to hurry the fuck up.'

'That's right. She published her first poem at sixteen and died when she was only twenty-nine years old.' Same age as Nico. The echo made me shiver. Linc held the book beside my face. 'You don't have to meet someone to know them.'

His words sounded heavy. As though he meant something else by them, and I was suddenly afraid. But Linc couldn't know who I was – could he?

He put a hand on my shoulder and turned me to the ornately framed mirror. The single piece of grandiose opulence in the otherwise modern room. He stood behind me, one hand on my shoulder, the other holding the book next to my face. I was so surprised by his touch, I just stood there. The heat from his fingers, those long, elegant fingers, on thin cotton, on my skin, and that stirring only grew. His grip seemed to tighten as he met my eyes in the mirror. I didn't look away.

'There's something about you that reminds me of her.'

And in my chest, a warm melting sensation.

His wife's heels sounded down the passage. I reminded myself to keep my armour up, not be swayed by Linc's obvious attractiveness and pretty words. As Amber pushed the door open, Linc dropped his hand and stepped away from me, too quickly to be smooth, still holding the book in his hand.

'Your fucking students, Linc.' Thankfully, Amber didn't seem to notice the strange new note in the room.

As he moved away from me, the image of Eden Hale was still imprinted in my mind. Her hair was piled up on her head, and an overlong fringe hung in her eyes. Her face was narrow and her nose big for her otherwise delicate features. Large, soulful eyes. She was, at the same time, seemingly above the pleasures of this world and also the girl who hooked up with boys in the back of the car.

'What have you done with my students, Amb?' Linc said jovially, pouring red wine into a glass.

'They went looking for a cake. Fucking ghouls.'

'A cake?' Linc sounded bewildered.

The sound of voices and footsteps came down the passage. The high laughter of a young woman.

'We're here,' she sang as she stepped into the kitchen, holding a plate with a home-baked chocolate cake. This evening she wore dark berry lipstick, but I knew her immediately. She was the woman with the fringe from Begley's. The drunk student tamer.

Before I even had time to worry about the coincidence, she glanced at me, showing no recognition. There was no conspiratorial smile this time. We were not old friends. My black leggings and grey tank top were camouflage, blending me into the kitchen walls. Disappointment settled into me, that I was right there and still she couldn't see me. I'd felt a kinship with her last night at Begley's, watching her handle the drunk student. But tonight, she was just like everyone else.

'Fiona, come in. Did you bake that pretty cake? Is there nothing you can't do?' Linc was smooth and confident, and Fiona blushed as she put the cake on the island, where it looked a little flat beside Amber's artfully iced fairy cakes.

'Sorry, we forgot it in the car.'

'It looks delicious. Thank you.' Amber gave Fiona a dazzling smile, as though she hadn't been bitching about her minutes ago, and kissed both of Fiona's pink cheeks.

'We stopped for these.' A man around my age came into the kitchen, carrying a bunch of freshly picked wildflowers. He wore a leather jacket, a white T-shirt and jeans. His skin was a warm brown, the colour of cinnamon bark, and his smile was cheerful, his eyes sparkling. He looked strong. Cool. He reminded me of Nico before.

He gave the flowers to Amber saying, 'Thought you'd prefer them wild.'

'I do.' Amber smiled at him. 'It's Caden, right?' She placed her small hands on his big shoulders, kissing him as she had Fiona. 'I think we met only once before.'

'Twice.' Caden smiled.

'Cade joined us from the States two months ago.' Linc poured two glasses of wine as he spoke, so he didn't see how Amber was watching Caden take off his jacket.

Her eye caught mine, and she raised her eyebrows slightly and laughed. 'Esmie, would you give me a hand in the summer kitchen? The others will be arriving any minute now.'

Perhaps Caden reminded Amber of Nico, too.

Chapter Nine

Wednesday

The guests arrived over the next fifteen minutes. Isabelle came into the kitchen, wearing heels and a dark cloud wrapped around her like furs. She'd been bright-eyed when I'd said goodbye the previous day, but now she was subdued. Her loud red-and-black printed skirt and blouse seemed to mute her further.

Paul, a step behind, was large and exuberant. He put his bear paws on Amber's shoulders as she kissed him on the cheek; then he finger-gunned me in greeting before cornering Fiona.

'You're one of Linc's PhDs, you say?' he boomed. It was as though he had to fill Isabelle's silence, to balance her quiet simmering with his loud bubbling. 'What's your name?'

I watched Isabelle watch Paul talk at Fiona. Her expression was inscrutable. She was staring at them so intently, I'd normally have said she must be jealous of her husband's attention to the younger woman. But it didn't feel like jealousy. Her steady gaze felt more like . . . curiosity.

Then Amber appeared at her side. 'Isabelle, I don't think you've met Fiona?'

'I haven't,' Isabelle confirmed, still watching.

'She's Linc's right-hand woman. I don't know how he'd cope without her.' And gliding around the kitchen, saying all the right things, Amber gathered her guests through the arch into the afternoon room. The chandelier glowed, thousands of crystals illuminating the now spotless room. The bell rang again and again. From the passage came voices, the undulating song of greeting as more and more people arrived.

Ceanna entered wearing the same white linen dress and headscarf as earlier. My conviction grew that this was a costume, that Ceanna was assuming a homespun, lady-who-drinks-picked-herbs persona. Separate to her woman-who-dances-in-dingy-bars-in-a-red-dress persona. Ceanna was a chameleon, then – different things to different people at different times. And amidst her changing camouflage, it was impossible to know her true colours. A mystery, and one that Nico might have enjoyed uncovering.

Beside her was a thin bearded man I guessed was Arvind, her lodger and maths post-doc. A tidy man, whose bedroom was sparse and smelled of lemongrass. Through the narrow arch, I watched them laugh and talk easily.

Linc's voice was like the main singer in a chorus, all the other voices fitting around his. I collected a mug from the kitchen table and peered around. From this vantage point I could see the people in the room, their bright colours and shining jewellery. The floral notes of perfume, the softly played Dizzy Gillespie. Nico used to love jazz; he'd listen to it while he worked through the night. And then he left, and when he came back he hated music.

I washed the dishes from Amber's baking and cleaned the mess she'd made, stealing occasional glances into the afternoon room.

Amber came into the kitchen. 'Will you help me carry these outside?'

I went with her to the summer kitchen, carrying a tray of glasses. She chatted easily, pointing to where they hid a spare key, in case they weren't home when I arrived. Amber seemed more relaxed with me now, after I'd bailed her out.

It was still bright, but Amber turned on the fairy lights and lit candles. Behind us, the guests came down the garden path, following the ever-charming Linc. Isabelle trailed a little behind everyone. She was talking to Fiona, their heads bent to each other.

When everyone was seated, bottles of wine on the table, Linc triumphantly carried the heavy cast-iron pots from the brick oven. I slunk away.

After washing the wine glasses, I slipped my thin hoodie over my head. Now that I wasn't cleaning so vigorously, I could feel that the evening had cooled. I made my way to the shared study beside the front door. I hadn't had a chance to look through it yet because Amber had spent most of Monday at her desk.

The far side of the large room, framed by windows in both walls, was Amber's. Her desk was a blonde wood with a huge bunch of peonies in an antique-looking vase. Near the door, Linc's desk was made of darker wood with a leather inlay that I ran my fingers over, then picked up a stapled printout.

TO BE UNMADE
Eden Hale

Entrapment, for most people, is inevitable. The details of
routine, of the familiar, all serve to imprison us. We are
the sum of our experiences. But unlike the sculpture whose
shape is deliberately fashioned, we are not made with

vision or foresight. We are accidentally and haphazardly made. We do not know, as we take shape, what we are becoming. *The very shape of ourselves is another cage.*

The words stirred something inside me that made my heart pound. The idea that I was caged inside myself made my clothes feel suddenly suffocating: my leggings squeezed my calves; my hoodie choked my throat.

Hearing footsteps in the passage, I darted to Linc's shelves. I was holding a copy of *Grimms' Fairy Tales* when he appeared at the door and stopped short at the sight of me, his eyebrows raised in surprise.

'I'm looking for a book.' I waved the fairy tales at him in explanation. 'That's OK?'

'Of course.' He arched an eyebrow at the book in my hand. 'But Esmie, I'm sure we could be more adventurous than that.'

He smiled, his voice light, and my breathing stuttered. Was Linc flirting with me?

'The dinner is good?'

'Got to be honest here.' He was looking through the bookshelf but shot me a mischievous glance. 'Our new professor, the one I'm trying to impress, is deathly dull.'

'Impress?' I said. 'Or outshine?'

His smile froze and his brow furrowed. 'Your English is better than I thought.'

My cheeks burned as I looked back at the shelf. That was way too careless. I was letting my guard down with Linc, and that was too risky.

'Here it is.' He pulled out a small paperback and handed it to me. 'This contains some of Eden's most popular essays and poems. Do you like poetry?'

I took the book from him. *The Heart in the Wood and Other Writing.*

'It wasn't my favourite at school,' I confessed, opening to the first page.

'Esmie!' Linc said my name in mock horror, eyes sliding to mine. Definitely flirting with me. 'We're going to have to fix that.'

Flustered, I studied the page, but my mind was leaping around and I took nothing in. I peered up, and Linc was looking at me with the strangest expression on his face. I couldn't tell what he was thinking, but it was the first genuine warmth I'd felt from someone else in too long. In the lamplit room, I felt myself embracing it, my lips quirking up despite myself.

'There she is,' Linc said, returning my smile. His words were playful, but his tone wasn't. I couldn't look away.

Then, reality washed over me like a bucket of cold water, and I made myself look at the page again. Nico. I was there for Nico.

'Which is your favourite?' I flipped through the book, and the pages fell to where the place had been marked with a red ribbon.

Linc moved closer until he was standing beside me, looking at the book over my shoulder. 'Eden Hale never married, took many lovers – both men and women, often at the same time. She was happy alone, practically living in the woods. She smoked too much and drank whiskey for lunch. She was bold, but ethereal. The neighbours thought her a witch.' He touched a finger to the page, his hand inches from mine. 'That one. That's my favourite.'

I skimmed the poem. 'The Heart in the Wood'. It was all angst and trees. Not my kind of thing at all. Until a line caught my eye:

She begged so prettily but
He tore off her clothes and jewels

'What's this about?' I said, looking up at him, trying my hardest to hide the shake in my voice at seeing those same awful words that Nico had written on the photo. There was something else too – they'd shadowed something else, something just out of reach . . .

'This poem is based on a folk tale called "The Sweetheart in the Wood". You know the story of Bluebeard? It's similar.'

Then I remembered: Nico had written those same words, *begged so prettily*, in the unsent letter to his lover too. But why?

'Bluebeard? The man with dead wives? Locked in a room?' I asked, suddenly too hot.

'Yes, but in this version, a beautiful young woman is courted by the sweetheart. He tells her to come to his grand old house. And she does, diligently trailing peas deeper and deeper into the woods where she finds the house. The bride goes inside, where she's warned by a bird to be careful.'

'What is in the house?' I felt a sense of foreboding; then I felt silly. *It's just a story.*

'She walks through the rooms, going deeper and deeper into the house.' Linc's voice was rhythmic and husky, and I thought, *I could listen to him all night.* 'The bride enters a room and finds . . .' He paused, drawing out the moment until it was almost comically long. 'Buckets of blood.'

'And of course, she runs away?' I was half joking, but I looked up at Linc, too aware of his shoulders, his arms, his chest. The smell of him, a heat beneath the aftershave and red wine.

And I felt it was me who'd ventured into a dangerous house. Like I should leave, before it was too late. Like I should never have come in the first place.

'You clearly haven't read the story.' He grinned, shifting

closer to me, his leg brushing mine. I swallowed, not moving away.

'What is in the next room?'

'Bodies,' Linc said, his eyes playful. I wondered if he felt it too, this strange something that agitated between us as he told this story. 'The bird began shouting that the sweetheart had returned, warning the bride to hide.'

I grimaced. 'This is not good.'

'She hid under the bed, and the sweetheart entered . . . with another woman.'

'The bride saw him with another woman?' I said, thinking I'd read all the wrong fairy tales in my childhood. This sounded – what was the word Linc had used? Adventurous. Dark. And, I hated to admit, alluring.

Or maybe it was Linc I was finding alluring. My thoughts were mixed up. I should have stepped away, but I couldn't. My legs refused to move.

Hunger, I told myself. The dull ache in my stomach reminded me that I hadn't eaten since before Ceanna's. That must be why I was so confused. So affected – by the story and by the man beside me.

'The bride watched him with his next *victim.*' Linc pointed to that disturbing line, where my finger had rested. 'She begged, prettily, but it didn't help. He tore off her clothes and cut off her finger, which rolled under the bed.'

'How does it end?' I needed him to stop. For whatever was budding between us to stop.

'In the traditional story, the sweetheart and his house were burned to ashes.'

'No "they all lived happily ever after"?'

'Fairy tales are dark and gruesome,' Linc said. There was fire in his eyes, and I could imagine him in front of a class. Everyone listening with rapt attention. It was impossible not to look at him, to be drawn to him. 'Eden Hale changes the ending. She has the heroine embrace the sweetheart's darkness. She marries the villain—'

'Villain?' I interrupted, as if I didn't know.

'Sorry. It means a very bad man.'

Or woman, I thought, but didn't say.

'In Eden's version,' Linc continued, 'they fall in love and live together in the house in the woods, luring unsuspecting men and women who stray there.'

'The bride also becomes a villain?' Unsurprisingly, the idea appealed to me. Was I not doing the same?

'She embraced her inner darkness.' Linc paused, his eyes holding mine, and I knew those words meant something to him. Something important. And he wanted me to understand.

'Her inner darkness?' I pushed a strand of hair behind my ear, and Linc's eyes tracked the movement.

'A lot of Eden Hale's work is about what she called "unbecoming": unmaking ourselves and accepting the darkness within. She believed that we are all trapped, basically. In many different ways, and that fairy tales could guide us out of our cages.'

'Like the bride who is now a villain?'

'The woman who becomes unmade,' Linc corrected.

Linc spoke on, about unbecoming and wildness, and I could see his passion for his work run through his body. The way he stood, ready and electrified, as if these dusty old books had lit a flame deep inside. One that burned so bright, it warmed even me.

I wanted to stay here listening to Linc talk, even if half of it made no sense. I wanted to be warm, if only for a few minutes.

'Would you like that?' Linc said in a low voice. 'To be released from everything that holds you down?'

The longing was a weight in my chest.

Down the hall, a door closed loudly. I stepped away, finally set free from whatever spell had held me rooted. A fog seemed to lift from my brain, making me aware of where I was. Who I was with.

I'd forgotten myself.

And that was a risk I couldn't take.

Chapter Ten

Wednesday

L inc stepped away from me.
'I should probably get back. I left a plate in the kitchen for you.' He inched to the door. 'Keep the book. I have several copies.'

I wasn't here to get drawn into the strange ideas of a dead woman. I turned the book in my hand, Linc still watching. This was what he'd chosen to dedicate his life's work to? I was baffled.

Drinking whiskey and rewriting fairy tales was one thing. Believing that they were some kind of spiritual evolution was unhinged. Clearly living in the woods had detached Eden Hale – and Linc – from real life.

I looked again at the bookshelf, hoping Linc would leave so I could continue snooping. But he waited, watching me take in the books as if he had all the time in the world, and I gritted my teeth in irritation.

'Go on.' Linc smiled faintly as he waited at the door. 'Get your dinner.'

He stepped aside so I could leave first.

Flirting with Linc, I'd learned nothing about Nico or his lover. I'd wasted this chance to nose through the study and couldn't risk getting caught in there again this evening.

In the passage, Ceanna was emerging from the bathroom.

She gave Linc a look, and the disdain in her eyes spoke volumes. Intrigued, I glanced back and saw Linc's jaw harden. Their dislike was mutual, then, and I was eager to know more. Perhaps my conversation with Linc hadn't been a complete waste of time, after all.

I went through the kitchen and picked up the dinner Linc had left there for me. My empty stomach ached, and I liked Linc a little more for remembering. Walking to the utility room, I eyed the plate hungrily, not bothering to flick on the light.

I examined the buttons and dials on the microwave, thinking about the way Linc's eyes had shone when he spoke about Eden Hale and her weird little poems.

Why had Nico copied those awful lines on the photo I'd found? The image they evoked made me shudder. I didn't have to be a poetry expert to feel that something was off with Nico quoting lines about tearing off clothes and jewels while the victim begged. And written on the back of *that* picture, which had clearly been taken in a moment of intimacy with his secret lover. I felt queasy again. Those were details I did not want to dwell on.

Then movement outside, through the glass door, caught my eye. Caden was leaning against the garage wall where he lit a cigarette, cupping it with both hands. Amber went towards him – an assured, sultry walk. Deliberate. She took the cigarette from him and put it to her lips.

A slow sort of agitation building inside me, I observed the pair as they talked, her body angling towards his. She inched closer, a slow creep to close the gap between their bodies. She lifted the cigarette to his lips, holding it as he took a long drag. It did not look like they'd only met twice before.

She leaned in to him, and I was both appalled and fascinated. I wanted her to kiss him, and that shook me. Maybe I wanted proof that Amber was as malignant as I suspected. That she was entitled and demanding. That she would cheat on her husband – because that would put her in the frame for Nico. But this strange voice inside, the one that whispered, *do it do it do it*, was motivated by something different.

Then I realized: it was because my world had upended. In the aftermath of Nico's fall from grace, a part of me took perverse delight in watching the destructive behaviour of other people. Misery loves company, and I'd never felt it more acutely than standing there in the darkened utility, holding a plate of cold food.

I put the plate in the microwave and set it for three minutes. Outside, Amber and Caden had drawn even closer. Her face was tipped up to his. He threaded a hand through her hair and pulled her to him as the microwave hummed. From the dark utility room I watched Amber reach up and, without restraint, kiss her husband's assistant.

The microwave pinged. I lifted the cover and the food sizzled with heat, the smell of it making me salivate. Then, a movement in the shadow drew my attention, and I looked across from the garage towards the cobblestone path. And there she was, beneath a tree – brown hair, the white linen dress – watching the kissing couple. Ceanna.

The shadows enhanced the lines of her face. In her white dress, she seemed like an angel. Beautiful, a calm exterior at odds with the turmoil beneath.

She seemed like someone Nico could love.

She didn't walk away, nor did she intervene. Instead, she stood in the shadows and observed.

But she did not see me watching her.

Later, when all the guests had left, I carried the dishes from the summer kitchen back to the house. The evening was warm, the night sky an indigo blue. I was unused to unending days where the sun didn't seem to fully set. It felt unreal to me, this never dark sky, an impossible thing. Against reason, it stirred hope.

I was loading plates into the dishwasher when Linc came in from seeing off the guests.

'It was a good night?'

'It was.' He rolled up his sleeves and began washing the glasses. 'You get on OK?'

'Sort of.' I'd searched the drawers in the living room, found nothing. 'Is Amber in bed?'

'She's walking home with Ceanna.'

'Amber and Ceanna are close?'

He snorted. 'Depends on the day.'

'They must miss their dad.' Amber said he'd been sick, but it still snagged on my brain that he died around the same time that Nico left. Had Malachy's death made Amber or Ceanna do something to lash out at Nico? Was there a connection?

'It's only been six months.' Linc stacked a glass on the drying rack. 'We all thought he'd live for ever.'

Was there a touch of bitterness in Linc's voice? I looked up at him, but it was sadness I saw on his face.

'It was hard for Amber and Ceanna. Malachy was confused, paranoid, saying irrational things like someone was trying to hurt him, poisoning his food.' Linc shook his head. 'I thought it would solidify their attachment to each other, but instead it widened the rift between them. It took Ceanna back to a dark place.' His voice and gaze seemed faraway, back in that difficult time. 'Malachy's death was drawn out and traumatic, and I wish it had been quicker.'

Linc's unburdening was sudden, out of the blue. His words were too complicated – too fast if he were really speaking to me, someone who wasn't supposed to be fluent in English. They all did it. Maybe they didn't want to appear condescending by simplifying their speech. Or maybe that was the benefit of talking to me: that I wasn't meant to fully understand. Maybe I was little more than a sounding board to them. What did it matter anyway? I wasn't there to make friends.

'I'm sorry,' Linc winced. 'I don't know why all of that came out. I find it really easy to talk to you.'

Sounding board, then. Or confessor. But I could use that. Let him think I was some sweet, soft girl who listened quietly, unjudging. That I was just the cleaner. And maybe then, he'd tell me the hidden stories. The secrets kept by these four walls. We both reached for the towel at the same time, our fingers brushing.

'I like hearing you.' I gave him my best attempt at a shy smile. 'You must be a very good teacher.'

Linc ran a hand over the back of his head and cleared his throat.

'That's Malachy?' I pointed to the graduation picture that Ceanna had shown me the first day.

'Yes. And there's one from when he was much younger.' Linc nodded at a framed photo on the shelf. It was of a burly young man with an arm slung around a petite, brown-skinned woman. 'With Eden Hale.'

I shut the dishwasher.

'Amber's father knew your poet?'

'Malachy was her stepbrother.'

I raised my eyebrows. 'That's lucky.'

'I met Amber because I was interviewing Malachy. Eden Hale wrote a story based on "The Sweetheart in the Wood", which was never published. She refers to it in her essays, but there's no record of it anywhere. I wanted to ask Malachy about this missing story.' He gave me a sheepish look. 'I was horribly nervous. And Malachy was difficult. He didn't answer any of my questions, grilling me instead about the poems. Trying to catch me out. It was awful.'

His eyes were sparkling as he recounted this story, one he presumably told a lot.

'I was about to give up when the most beautiful woman I'd ever seen breezed into the cafe, dropped a kiss on his cheek, then gave me a filthy look and said, "Who the fuck are you?"' Linc laughed. 'It was love at first sight. And over the years, Malachy and I grew close.'

Close enough for Malachy to will him Eden's papers. Which were in Ceanna's safe. It was all starting to make sense, the tension between the two of them.

We finished the dishes, and Linc grabbed his car keys. We set off down the unlit road. He talked easily; about his students, about poetry, about Eden Hale, the dinner.

'Amber cooked?' I asked, and he nodded. 'She's really good.'

'Amber's good at everything she does.' He kept his eyes on the road ahead. 'She's always welcoming, especially to my work friends.' Did I imagine the shadow over his words? 'She makes these dinners into something fun.' Then he added as an afterthought, 'Amber's good at fun.'

Well, it certainly seemed that way.

I let out an inadvertent yawn, and Linc looked rueful. 'Do you have an early start?'

'Not too bad,' I said, resisting the urge to yawn again. 'I'm cleaning Isabelle's house.'

'Definitely can't be late for that,' Linc said with a broad smile, and I couldn't help returning it.

'Her house is tidy.' She really only needed me one day a week. 'Not . . .' I bit my lip. Not like Ceanna's I was about to say.

'Not what?'

'Not too much work.' But I was distracted, thinking about Ceanna's house. That picture I'd found behind the desk in Nico's old room, now tightly folded and stashed in my backpack. I wasn't sure what about this naked, horny picture troubled me the most. Was it how tightly Nico had been tied, or was it that he was in the woods, getting his kink on? Or was it that dark look in his eyes?

And then it occurred to me. His hands. They'd been tied together not with rope or a belt, but with a piece of fabric. I tried to remember. It was a scarf, I was sure of it. Excitement sparked in my stomach.

Linc pulled up outside the house. Cars and vans were packed in the driveway.

'You live with friends?' He nodded to the brightly lit house.

'It's a house share.' Room share, really, but he didn't need to know that. 'Most of us are just passing through.' I had my hand on the door, impatient to get inside. I needed to look at that picture again.

'It was nice, chatting with you this evening.' That deep dimpled smile again.

I couldn't make him out. Linc was a natural flirt, that was obvious. But again, I felt targeted. As though maybe he enjoyed the unevenness between us. Maybe he got a kick out of flirting with the woman who cleaned up after him.

He took out his wallet and counted through a wad of notes. 'This is for tonight.' I could tell just from a glance that it was more than he owed me. I couldn't help feeling that he was buying more than my time, my labour. But what? I took the full amount regardless.

Inside, I went straight to the bathroom. I pulled the picture from my bag. Smoothed it out. Made myself look.

Binding Nico's wrists was a green scarf with a tiny white

flower pattern. Silk, probably. Zooming in to the tied hands, I took a picture with my phone, then folded the photograph into small squares again.

I would find this scarf. And when I found it, I would know which woman had lied about Nico.

Chapter Eleven

Thursday

The next morning, I pushed open the front gate to Amber's house, relieved that it was the last time I'd walk the six kilometres to The Woodlands. Linc had texted earlier, saying to meet him in the garage to get my bike. At last.

I headed around the side of the house into the back. Through the glass walls, I could see Linc and Amber in the kitchen. I couldn't hear what they were saying, but it was obvious from the rigid lines of Linc's body that they were arguing again. Linc snapped shut his laptop and walked away, Amber following after him. I inched closer, taking it all in.

He shot something over his shoulder and walked into the utility, leaving Amber alone in the kitchen. She stood there, abject, for ten seconds, then she flipped her hair and belted her jacket. She grabbed her laptop bag and strode towards the front door.

I turned quickly, making a show of admiring the wild-flowers that grew along the high stone wall. They were alien to me, the bright whites and pinks and yellows on verdant green, so unlike the sun-faded summer foliage back home. The rows and rows of vineyards and brown earth that defined the landscape of our town. Suddenly, I needed to know the names of these plants, if they had any meaning.

Facing the flowers, I slid my eyes to the door, aware of Linc stepping outside. I ran my hand over silky petals, hoping he hadn't seen me through the kitchen windows.

'Good morning, Esmie.' Linc moved towards me, doing a decent approximation of cheerful, only narrowly missed. 'Have you been waiting long?'

'Just got here,' I said breezily.

Linc pressed the fob to open the rolling garage door. 'Shall we go in?'

Some of the burnish had faded since last night. Linc was more subdued this morning, a few frames off from the charming professor. The garage door rolled open to reveal a shiny pale green bike leaning against a ride-on mower. I couldn't see mine anywhere.

'Your bike isn't worth fixing. It will cost more to repair than you'd get for it. This is Amber's but she never uses it, so it's yours.'

'I can't take this,' I protested. 'It's too expensive.' Besides, how dare he dismiss my bike so easily? Not worth fixing. I felt tired, suddenly. We stood less than a metre from each other and yet we were worlds apart.

'I damaged your bike,' Linc said. 'I insist on replacing it. I'm just sorry it took me this long.'

'I'll bring it back,' I conceded. 'In August. When I leave.'

'So soon?'

'This isn't home.' I had the sudden urge to tell him more, but clamped my lips shut.

He checked his watch and said, 'I have to see a student shortly. Can you shut the gate behind you? Amber's off to Dublin for client meetings.'

Pushing the bike out of the garage, I gestured to the flowers and blurted, 'What are these? Their names?'

'Red clover, cow parsley.' He pointed to each. 'And there, buttercups and foxglove. You'll find plenty of these in an Irish summer.'

I'd look them up later, I resolved. The lush growth, the unfamiliar plants, even the birdsong sounded different, and the strangeness of the landscape made me feel out of place. Maybe I'd feel more anchored if I knew the names of things here. 'I like them.'

Something shifted in Linc's face. He held my gaze and said, 'There's a lot to like.' Then he nodded and walked so briskly down the path it felt like he was fleeing.

Alone in their back garden, I checked my watch. I was impatient to begin my search for the green scarf, and I had some time before I started at Isabelle's.

Ever cautious, I waited a few moments to make sure Linc didn't return. I listened carefully, hearing only the empty lane, interrupted by the occasional bark of a distant dog. It was brutally quiet out here in The Woodlands. The kind of silence that grew heavier and heavier until it felt oppressive.

I checked the time again. A few fat drops of rain fell. After a minute, I retrieved the key from beneath a potted plant. Just as Amber had said. Strange how easily she trusted me, a complete stranger, because of my role in her life. Because I was just the cleaner.

I unlocked the kitchen door and eased inside just as a heavy shower began. I made straight for the stairs, unable to wait another moment to start my search.

Near the foot of the stairs, I stopped at the hall closet and went through the jackets, hats and scarves. Out of the corner of my eye, I caught a glimpse of Amber's swirling screensaver in the study and I felt a similar swirling in my gut. What if I could get into her computer? Check her emails for messages from Nico? Her calendar, to see if she'd scheduled anything with him? It was too good an opportunity to resist.

Keeping an eye on the door, I woke her computer. The wallpaper was a photo of her and Linc in a field of yellow flowers. With their arms around each other, they smiled at the camera. Only then did I see that the computer was password protected. I grimaced – of course it was.

I stared at the desk, thinking of the time I went with Mama Bear to a client's house. I'd wandered into his study, a serious room dominated by dark, heavy furniture. I'd crawled beneath the desk, because I found small, enclosed spaces comforting. Safe. Tucked to the side was a small drawer, one you wouldn't see if you didn't know it was there. I'd opened it and found photographs that I definitely shouldn't have been looking at.

That was the first time I understood the divide between what people let you see and what they didn't.

But here, now, it gave me an idea, and I began a systematic examination of the desk.

Then, hearing a sound from somewhere in the house, I froze.

I waited, holding my breath, half expecting Linc to appear; perhaps he'd forgotten something. Then it sounded again – just the alert of the tumble dryer. I sank into Amber's chair, my legs boneless. After a moment, I resumed my check. Running my hand beneath the top, I felt the shape of something. I pressed and pushed, and a narrow drawer slid open.

I leaned forward, excitement rushing through me. I picked up a birthday card dated to the previous year, and signed *Love, Dad*.

Malachy's last card, I thought with a pang.

My fingers felt thick as I scrabbled through mementos of Amber's life. I pushed aside a hospital bracelet with *Dana*

Kelly written in faded lettering. Her mother's name, I was certain. There was a creased photo of Amber kissing a dark-haired young man. On the back was scribbled, *Amber and Steve.* I flicked through more mementos from old boyfriends, then picked up a small card saying, *I'm sorry. I shouldn't have said those things about Linc – Cee.* Funeral sheets, a wedding invitation, a photo of Ceanna with a baby. A whole life in a narrow drawer.

Looking through her keepsakes, I would have to be made of stone not to feel some sympathy for Amber. But if she were responsible for Nico losing his scholarship, his slow downward spiral, I would break her slowly. I would hurt her, destroy her, hair by hair, bone by bone.

At the back of the drawer were letters. They were tied together with a thin velvet ribbon. The top envelope was blank, no name or address. There was a loud drumming in my ears as I reached for them, pulling the ribbon loose.

A hard knock at the front door made me jump a foot high. The doorbell rang once, twice.

I grabbed the letters. The knock sounded again.

I shut the drawer and made for the wall, ready to press myself against it until the caller left. But I was halfway across the room when a face appeared at the window. I raised my hands to my mouth, letting out a cry. He knocked on the glass.

'Come on, Esmie, open up.' Caden sounded irritable. 'It's wet out here.'

I looked around the room for a place to leave the letters. Caden was watching, so I made for the door, stuffing them beneath my T-shirt. Smoothing my hair as if that could calm the wild thumping of my heart, I reluctantly opened the door. He stepped in, out of the rain. He moved towards me, forcing me to stumble back into the study.

'Where's Amber?' he said. He looked around the room as though he was seeing it for the first time. He stared at Linc's desk, at the stack of papers there, then at Amber's. He turned back to me, leaning forward, nostrils flaring slightly. 'I need to see her.'

'She's not here,' I said, making a snap decision to play it cool. Caden wouldn't know my schedule. He wouldn't know I wasn't supposed to be here today.

'Do you know when she'll be back?'

'She's out for the day.' I stood stock-still, feeling the press of the papers beneath my thin T-shirt. I swallowed. If Caden looked down, if he paid attention, he'd see the shape of them there. He inched closer, as if he could smell my agitation.

'Excuse me.' I stepped past him. But as I moved, I felt a hand close around my wrist.

'I saw you last night, going into the dark utility room.' His eyes were boring into mine. I fought the urge to look away. 'Did you see me?'

I looked down at where his hand gripped my wrist. He held it almost tight enough to hurt. Then I looked up at him, not hiding the amusement in my eyes.

'I saw nothing.' I wrenched my hand away. 'Amber's not here. You should go.'

I started for the passage. *Give it a minute*, I told myself. Then Caden would be gone. No one would know I'd been here. I didn't dare go upstairs to look for the green scarf now, no matter how much my curiosity burned.

I'd taken only one step when an envelope slipped down beneath my T-shirt. It fell to the rug, and I gasped an inadvertent 'no'. I reached for it, but Caden was quicker.

'What's this?' he said, grabbing the envelope.

'That's mine.' I swiped the air, but he held it out of my reach. He was looking at me with a gleam in his eyes, and this time it was like he'd snared me in his gaze. Like he could see more than I was willing to show.

'Is it?'

'Yes,' I said, reaching for it again, and this time he let me take it.

'Yours? A university headed envelope?'

I glanced down and saw with dismay that he was right. The front left corner of the envelope was stamped with the university crest.

'I took it, OK? To send something home.' I replied to Caden. 'It's one envelope. Linc won't miss it.'

Caden searched my face, as though he knew I was lying.

'I have to work now,' I said, suddenly hot with anger at him. This was not his business. What was he doing here anyway?

He held up his hands as if in surrender, but I could feel his hard eyes on my back as I walked out of the study. I glanced down at the envelope, seeing the rough edge where it had been torn open, and felt a burst of panic. If Caden had noticed that tear, he'd know I'd lied. I pressed the envelope to my stomach, holding the other letters close, as I opened the front door and stood aside, signalling that he should leave.

Caden inclined his head as he made for the door.

When he'd finally gone, I leaned against the wall and shut my eyes. I realized with a thud of dread that I'd made a huge mistake. My one trump card had been my invisibility – and I had made myself visible to Caden. I pressed the heel of my hand to my temple, willing myself to calm down. After a moment, I pulled the letters from beneath my T-shirt.

There were six in total, each in a worn blank envelope. I opened the first one, and saw at once that the writing wasn't Nico's. My greedy eyes scanned through the effusive declaration of love and desire, then checked the date and signature. I dropped the letter, staring at the stained-glass door, trying to gather myself, disappointment warring with relief.

They were from Linc, all from the beginning of their relationship. Not from Nico. There'd been not one thing from Nico in that drawer where Amber kept her mementos.

If they'd been lovers, there would have been something, I was sure of it. I'd found a treasure for every person she'd cared for, and Nico wasn't one of them.

Pushing away from the wall, I thought about the old letters from her husband, stashed away as if they were talismans of some long-lost grand love.

Then I remembered Amber sidling up to Caden last night. Maybe that's exactly what they were.

Chapter Twelve

Thursday

The letters replaced, I slipped out through the kitchen door and hid the key beneath the potted plant. The air was sharp, almost electric, after the shower. The scent of wet earth and flowers, the dense green of trees in full leaf, made everything feel charged and alive. Nico would have revelled in this, but today it made me wary. The world around me seemed too awake, watchful, when I was trying my best not to be seen.

I crossed the damp stone and the sun peered out from patchy cloud. A little further, in the orchard, the tiniest impressions of apples were beginning to form. Drawn to them, the tip of my finger traced the still unshaped fruitlets on the branches. It was funny, I thought, how it all went on regardless – the ever-moving circle of death and birth. Despite every bad thing, growth would push through. Whether we liked it or not.

I checked the road before slipping out of the front gate. It was deathly silent, as usual. Sometimes, it felt like this cluster of three households, all on this quiet side of the bend, was a world unto itself. Only hedged-in fields overrun with tall grass and wildflowers, and old, old trees. The road itself swallowed by the bluebell woods.

Walking over to number three, I felt I was making some progress. The absence of a single memento for Nico pushed Amber down the leaderboard of likely lovers, and so I switched my thoughts to Isabelle. I couldn't see it. She was too self-contained, too uptight to be tied to a tree in the bluebell woods while Nico tore off her clothes and made her *feel*. I couldn't see her letting go like that.

Unless that was the allure of Nico: the uptight housewife with her label-maker melting in the arms of her exotic foreign lover. I let out a bitter snort as I reached the outside gate to number three. It was locked today, and I pressed the bell. A buzzer sounded as the gate released.

In the utility room, Isabelle had left a typed list of very specific things to do: wipe the skirting, clean the grouting, dust the books, and wash the shelves in the study. I exhaled loudly. What next? Clean the oven with a toothbrush? Pick the lentils from the ashes?

I just wanted to get upstairs and search her wardrobe for the green floral scarf.

In the passage, I almost bumped into Isabelle. She lifted her sports bag and said, 'Esmie, I won't be back until this evening. I baked fresh scones – help yourself.'

She gestured to the kitchen, and that's when I saw something that nearly made me gasp: a scar right in the centre of Isabelle's palm. A cut, long healed. An interruption in the clear, smooth skin. One that might have been caused by an avocado slipping, and a knife sinking into flesh.

A cut that made the words in Isabelle's secret notebook less like fiction, more like real life.

If it were true that a woman's destiny could be read by the lines of her hand, this indicated a violent detour. An inexorable change from what was meant to be.

I looked up to where Isabelle's eyes followed mine, seeing them fall upon her palm. I wondered exactly what she'd done to make sure she didn't lose herself again. What price she had paid.

After collecting the caddy, I headed upstairs. I went to Isabelle's room first, searching her large wardrobe for the green scarf. I hunted everywhere – the shelves, inside hatboxes, beneath the neat piles of clothes, under coat collars. Nothing. I clenched my fists and let out a quiet, strangled scream. And that's when my phone buzzed with an incoming message.

Esmie?? Haven't you taken enough from me??

I shut my eyes and cursed under my breath, when really I wanted to open my chest and roar. What exactly had Mama Bear told her? If she'd said anything—

A wave of vertigo washed over me. My phone buzzed with another message.

I really fucken hate you.

As if I didn't know.

Leaving the bedroom, I paused just outside the door. Everything felt red raw. Loud screaming music pumped from inside Liadh's room, an echo of the turmoil inside me.

She was gunning for me, I thought as I continued down the passage. I could feel the crosshairs searching for me.

I had to move quicker. Before there was no longer anything holding her back from coming to find me.

In the upstairs sitting room, I unlocked the bottom drawer of the writing desk with the latch key I'd had copied. I returned the borrowed key and took out the notebook. The story resumed after a blank page.

3.

The best stories, she always thought, were stories about girls. Lost girls, damaged girls, foolish girls. And this one was no different.

Girls in danger.

Not many people would have thought that the woman was in danger.

If Isabelle was telling her own story in these pages – and I was increasingly certain that she was – calling herself 'the woman' was unsettling. It was as if Isabelle had become detached from herself, like she really was some sort of parasite inside an indifferent host. It made me feel odd, mildly panicked.

The woman hadn't known, in the beginning, that Danger dressed itself in ordinary clothes. The woman didn't know, as she wandered the streets of the university town where she lived, that Danger had good manners and a nice smile. The woman didn't realize, until it was too late, that the worst kind of danger disguised itself as safety. That it made you think you'd found a haven, a safe place, until one day you realized the walls pressed in, making it hard to breathe.

The woman, before she met Danger, didn't realize how subtle punishment could be. She didn't realize that the most she had to lose was herself. Until it was too late.

By the time the woman learned the shape and smell of Danger, there was only a thin thread of herself remaining. She learned too late that the soft mattress she slept on kept her asleep long after she got out of bed. That the silky sheets were slowly poisoning her – not real poison; the Danger was never that obvious.

No, her Danger was infinitely more sophisticated. This Danger manipulated you, made you question yourself, all the while pretending to look after you. Put you in a room so beautiful you wouldn't know it was a prison.

This Danger made you so small, the smallest you could possibly be, and said: there, that's when you're beautiful.

Be beautiful for me.

The woman tried escaping, of course she did.

The punishments were subtle . . . except when they weren't.

Isabelle's bedroom door slammed, and I threw the notebook back into the drawer as though scalded by it, catching my hand as I banged the drawer shut. My heart hammered as Paul, freshly showered, appeared at the sitting-room door.

He must have been in the bathroom while I searched her wardrobe. A bolt of terror went through me at the thought of him catching me there. That was way too close.

'Esmie, there you are,' he announced, his cheerful voice at odds with the hardness in his eyes. He looked at his watch and said, 'Come talk to me while I make coffee.'

He turned to walk down the stairs and, after a moment's hesitation, I followed.

In the kitchen, I asked, 'You don't work today?'

'Catching a flight later,' he said, pushing a button on the coffee machine.

I stood awkwardly while the coffee machine gurgled. When it filled, Paul added milk then held the cup out in front of me. I didn't want it, but it didn't feel like I had a choice. So I took it, wondering why he'd called me down. What could he possibly have to say to me?

Paul continued to pin me with his moody gaze, and I realized that something was on his mind. That there was something he wanted to say, but didn't know how to say it.

I felt a sudden urge to laugh. I was just the cleaner – no one minded their words or actions around me. They argued with each other; they tossed their underwear to the floor beside the hamper, unembarrassed. They left their hand-bags open and out.

So why was Paul – loud, confident Paul, who never quite aimed all his pee into the toilet – suddenly hesitant?

'Is everything OK?' I said eventually. I felt exposed by his steely medical eye.

'Yes, of course.' He sounded irritated, not bothering with his customary jovial tone. 'But I wanted to ask, does Isa-belle seem, well . . . a little distracted?'

'Distracted? I don't understand.' I felt an inappropriate bubble of nervous laughter rising. This was absurd – him consulting me like I knew his wife better than he did.

'Is she bothered? Preoccupied? Absent-minded?' Paul sounded frustrated, and it made the urge to laugh stronger.

I held his gaze, stubbornly refusing to understand.

'Is she worried or busy?' he tried again.

'She is busy, of course,' I conceded. 'Worried?' I shrugged one shoulder. 'I don't know.'

'Hmmm.' He nodded again, drinking deeply from his cup. 'I suppose you wouldn't.' He placed down the cup and said, 'I work long hours, and sometimes I worry about my wife. She's not one to complain, but lately she seems not herself. Distant.'

His words were spoken quietly, as if we were intimate friends, and it made my skin crawl. I glanced at the door, longing to escape.

Paul considered me. Then: 'I'm glad you're here, Esmie.' He didn't look glad. He looked almost menacing. I sensed a heaviness in him that made my palms sweat. 'It's good to have someone watch out for Isabelle.' He spoke slower and louder now, as if I were stupid, or didn't understand Eng-lish at all. 'Keep an eye on her. She's alone here during the day, and I worry.'

'Liadh's here.'

He waved a hand, dismissing my words and his daughter. He reached into his pocket and drew something out. A butter-soft leather wallet. 'I want to help my wife, and I think you can help me.' He extracted a fifty-euro note.

I pressed back again, the worktop now digging into me. 'I don't understand what you . . .' I faltered, but Paul didn't. He pushed the crisp note towards me.

'I can't take that.' My voice shook slightly.

'Of course you can,' he said, injecting the jolly notes back into his voice, and I noticed for the first time how close-set his eyes were. 'You're a good worker. Consider it a bonus.' He didn't move. 'The house has never been this clean. A-plus job, Esmie.'

I wanted to wallop him for his patronizing tone. Paul shook his outstretched hand with a hint of impatience. Reluctantly, I took the fifty from him.

'Have a think about what might be distracting Isabelle. Maybe she gets visitors during the day. Maybe somebody calls. We'll touch base again soon.' He looked at his watch and downed the dregs of his coffee, moving away from me. 'Is that the time already?'

Heat rose in my cheeks, and I took a tiny sip of the horrible, bitter coffee while Paul talked on, unhindered by my short, non-committal responses. My mind was reeling. Had Paul, under the guise of concern for his wife, just roped me in to be his snitch for hire?

'You not going to drink that?' Paul gestured to my still-full cup.

'Too strong.' I was thinking about the argument that Isabelle had with the mystery driver of the silver Toyota. I couldn't, wouldn't, say anything about that. 'I drink it and I'll never sleep again.'

Paul gave a practised chuckle and said, 'I'll remember that for our next chat.'

I didn't want there to be a next chat. 'I don't like coffee,' I said, plotting my escape from the kitchen.

'I need one strong cup in the morning,' Paul said conspiratorially as he stood up. 'Then a second around eleven, and I'm good for the day. There was this fella, Ceanna's lodger, who was completely addicted. He was on a scholarship, so he had to study a lot.' My heart began to race: Nico. He was talking about Nico. Paul shook his head, remembering. 'Even I couldn't drink the stuff he made.' He came closer to me.

I knew Nico's coffee well. Undrinkable.

'Ceanna's lodger? Arvind?' I avoided looking at Paul and tried to keep the tremor from my voice. I couldn't let him see how much this mattered to me.

'No, he's no longer here.' Paul took the cup from me. 'He left months ago. Glad to see the back of him.'

'Oh?' I picked up the kitchen cloth with shaking hands. 'Why's that?'

He poured my unfinished coffee into his cup. 'I don't like waste.'

I waited, impatient, for Paul to answer my question. Why would he be glad that Nico had left?

'Turned out he was an aggressive fella. Maybe it was all that coffee.' This time, Paul's chuckle was more of a harsh bark.

'Aggressive?' I cleaned the spilled coffee grounds on the counter with more vigour than was necessary.

Paul was studying me again, and I felt a dart of worry that I had shown too much interest.

'Some men have a troubling idea of masculinity.'

Anger stirred deep within me. I knew I should stop pursuing this. Paul was already looking at me too intently.

But he was wrong. Whatever had happened, he was wrong. Nico had his faults, but he was not aggressive. The idea of Nico as toxically masculine was laughable. I planted my feet on the expensive kitchen flooring and wanted so badly to speak up and defend the good, though flawed, man we loved so much. But I couldn't.

'What do you mean?' I tried to sound disinterested, but I failed. By that point, though, I barely cared about keeping up the facade.

'I don't know if it's because they hang out online and get fed these garbage ideas about manhood, or if it's the unrealistic images they see on porn. Call me old-fashioned, but what's wrong with being a gentleman? Men should protect and look after their women.'

'What did he do?' That pulsing in my ears.

'Dad.' Liadh pulled a face as she came into the room, and in that moment I could have throttled her. 'It's not the nineteen-hundreds any more. And please' – she shuddered delicately – 'do not talk about porn.'

She went over to the fridge, and only after taking out a yoghurt did she glance at me. 'Is it Thursday already?'

HOME

Esmerelda hadn't realized that she was engaged in combat until the night of the Miss Mardi Gras.

For as long as Esmerelda could remember, they'd gone to the local funfair, optimistically named Mardi Gras, which was held in the park opposite the community centre every year. Some of her earliest memories were of eating candy floss with Simone, and gripping each other's hands while being thrown around on stomach-churning rides. Towards the end of the evening, they would watch the beauty pageant, sighing at the pretty young women on the stage. Both Esmerelda and Simone loved the glamour of it – the sequinned dresses, the sash announcing the queen and her princess, the crown.

Both Esmerelda and Simone also loved competition.

This year, Esmerelda had entered the pageant. She was wearing a burgundy satin dress that the seamstress down the road had made especially for her. She'd never felt more beautiful.

'Esmerelda, look at you,' Nico had laughed, when she stepped outside the community centre where the other women had been changing. 'You're definitely going to win.'

Esmerelda hit his shoulder, smiling. 'You have to say that. You're my brother.'

But they'd been drifting apart. They'd once been closer than twins, but now it felt like Nico's path was moving away from hers, and it made Esmerelda anxious. This was right and normal, Mama had gently warned her. Nico had to make his own way, especially now that he had Simone, and she had to find hers. They weren't children any more. Esmerelda couldn't live in his shadow for ever.

Esmerelda hated that Nico and Simone were together. That they'd forged their own closeness, one that threatened to eclipse her bond with her brother. It had already driven a wedge between the two women, who were no longer as tight as they had once been.

That night, Nico tucked his arm into Esmerelda's, and together they walked through the park to the stage where the pageant would be held. It was perhaps a foolish dream to win a beauty competition, but it was her dream nonetheless and had been since she was a young child. She wanted the red-and-gold crown, and now, with Nico shining his bright light on her, Esmerelda felt like it could be hers.

Then he was checking the time, and she knew he was thinking about Simone. They had maintained an uneasy balance since Nico and Simone started seeing each other a few years ago. Esmerelda was sure it wouldn't last. It was a relationship born out of circumstance. Nico was with Simone because she was convenient, nearby. And because he felt sorry for her. Nico was protective of Simone because of her dad, and his instinct to save her had only strengthened after her dad died.

Just thinking about that night made Esmerelda angry. Simone was a liar, and she would never be good enough for Nico. He was a smart man. He would see the truth of her.

Then they were at the stage. Nico put his hands on her

shoulders and said, 'Good luck. Not that you need it. This is going to be a night to remember.'

Esmerelda beamed up at him, but before she could respond, she could feel Nico's attention wasn't on her any more. It had been snatched by something behind her. Someone. His eyes were lit up and a soft, dazed expression worked over his features.

'Wow.'

Esmerelda turned. Behind her, walking towards them, was Simone. She was wearing a pale blue scrap of a dress. Her face was made up and her hair styled into long, soft waves.

'What are . . .' Esmerelda trailed off. She didn't need to finish the sentence. She knew exactly what Simone was doing.

'You entered the pageant?' Nico slipped an arm around her.

'A last-minute decision.' Simone lifted one delicate shoulder. 'Come, Esmie, let's get on stage.'

The pageant passed in a blur. Esmerelda was hardly present for it. She'd been so excited at the thought of her childhood dream coming true, only to be upstaged by Simone at the last minute. She was livid. A burning anger roiled in her gut as she watched Simone strut across the stage, then smile as she stopped to talk to the interviewer.

Suddenly, she hated Simone. She was going to pay her back for this. The conviction only grew stronger when the red-and-gold crown was placed on Simone's head. They were calling her, Esmerelda realized. She was the princess – the runner-up. They shoved a bouquet of roses into her hands, and made her stand beside Simone and smile. When she looked at the photos later, all she saw was second best.

Then Nico was on the stage, the big wheel slowly turning

in the distance behind him. He dropped to a knee in front of Simone.

Esmerelda brought her hands up to her mouth, terrified.

'Yes,' Simone screamed. 'Yes, yes, yes.' And she was leaping into his arms, one hand holding on to her crown as she wrapped her legs around him and everyone cheered them on.

Nico was right. It was a night to remember.

Chapter Thirteen

Friday

Years ago, when I'd asked Mama Bear if she minded cleaning other people's houses every day, she hadn't answered straight away. She'd cut her apple into quarters, bit and carefully chewed. When she eventually spoke, all she said was that she used the time to think. That scrubbing and wiping and brushing allowed her buried thoughts to emerge, scum to the surface.

This morning, scrubbing last night's pots in Amber's kitchen, I was thinking, as usual, about Nico. About that night at the fair – blue painted fingernails, cheap satin sashes over slinky dresses, the sparkling crystal ring, the big wheel turning in the distance – and wild rage swept through my body.

'Esmie,' Amber said from behind me, her voice unusually strident.

I ignored her, my heart thumping in my chest. Had Caden told her I was here the previous day?

She spoke louder. 'Esmie.'

I turned to her, slowly pulling off the sudsy gloves. I tugged out one earphone, then the other. 'Yes?'

'Have you seen my emerald ring?' Amber's face was etched with concern. 'I was sure I left it in the pottery bowl in my bathroom, but it's not there.'

I frowned at her. 'I didn't go in your bathroom. Not today.'

Which she knew. When I arrived at Woodland House forty minutes earlier, I'd gone straight up to search Amber's wardrobe for the green scarf. But she'd been in bed, just lying there, staring out of the window. I'd apologized for disturbing her, in that quiet little voice I now loathed.

'The ring has a large oval stone and is set in diamonds.' Amber's hands twisted together. 'I always leave it in the bathroom pottery bowl when I take it off.'

'When did you see it the last time?' My calm voice belied my own panic. I knew exactly where fingers would point if her ring was missing.

'Yesterday evening.'

'I'll find it,' I assured her.

'Linc gave it to me. I can't lose it. Will you go up and look for it now?' Amber's eyes were wide and pleading. Her clear distress was intriguing.

'Of course.' I dried my hands on the kitchen towel. 'Is anything else gone? Maybe it was a thief?'

'No,' Amber said. 'Just the ring. Linc bought it in Paris. He hadn't planned on proposing. When he saw it in an antique shop, he just knew. The ring was so stupidly expensive, he had to ask his grandfather for a loan.' A light came into her eyes at the memory of his proposal. 'It had to be that ring, and no other. The moment he saw it, he saw our future.'

The look on her face, the softness, the fear, told me the ring was priceless to Amber, and not just because Linc had gone into debt for it. For the first time, she seemed vulnerable, and it tugged at me.

She really loved him, I realized. So much that Linc might be the breach in Amber's armour. And even though she'd moved down my leaderboard, I filed away this knowledge.

Suddenly Amber braced her hands on the counter, her

arms rigid as she leaned forward. Her breathing was coming fast and shallow. Cautiously, as if I were approaching a feral animal, I moved to her. 'Amber? You OK?'

She squeezed her eyes shut, shaking her head, and moved her hand towards me. I took it, feeling her arm against mine as she gripped my hand tightly. In the minute that followed, her breathing steadied, through deliberate, slow exhales.

'Do you think it's an omen?' Her words were pinched.

'An omen?' For once, I didn't have to feign my lack of comprehension. 'What do you mean?'

'The ring, disappearing. Is it an omen? A sign that something bad will happen?'

I let her squish my hand, astonished that she would think something so wild. 'No, Amber, no. No omen, no sign.'

'When he bought the ring, it was a sign that he loved me. Putting it on my finger meant we'd be together always. So why not a sign now that it has suddenly, inexplicably disappeared? I had it yesterday evening before yoga, and now this morning, it's gone.' She pulled her hand from mine and stood straight. A ragged breath tore through her body. It was the first time I'd seen her like this, afraid and with all her shields down. It was unnerving. I stepped back to give her privacy, quietly murmuring that I'd look upstairs.

'Esmie,' she called as I reached the door, my body stiff in anticipation of what she might say.

'Yes?'

'Thank you,' she said simply, and the smile in her eyes appeared true.

I went upstairs, feeling like I'd dodged a bullet. It seemed that was how I always felt these days, a sense of danger closely averted. And that glimpse of Amber, the softer Amber beneath the haughty facade, had left me shaken.

I shut Amber's bedroom door, scanning the room for

where I might find an emerald ring – and a green scarf. I didn't think it would be there, but I had to make sure. I opened drawers, tossing aside the half-squeezed ointment tubes. I ignored the vibrators, the handcuffs and toys, and noted the condoms tucked beneath the lining. For use with Linc – or someone else?

I went through her underwear drawer, moving each piece with cold, clinical method. I didn't pause at the lacy lingerie, each expensive piece designed to bring a man to his knees. That Amber valued her desirability above comfort didn't surprise me at all. I opened drawer after drawer, finding only evidence of her vanity.

I'd searched the room from top to bottom, confirming my instinct that the scarf wasn't there. And there had been nothing of Nico in her drawer of treasures, either. Maybe I could cross Amber off my list entirely?

The chime of the doorbell was loud and sudden, and I let out a muffled yelp. I'd been lost in my thoughts; I needed to pick up the pace. Moving silently, I looked out of the window and saw Caden on the front step, smoking a cigarette.

I cursed under my breath. From below, Amber's bare feet padded to the door. Leaving the bedroom, I stole to the top of the stairs, clammy with panic.

'Caden,' she said, sounding entirely back to normal as she opened the door. 'Linc isn't here.'

He took a drag of his cigarette and tossed it into the flower bed. 'Not here to see Linc.'

'Oh?'

'I'm here to see you.'

My heart was in my throat. Should I go down, and stop him before he said anything about yesterday? But what could I say? If Amber knew that I'd let myself in uninvited, and now her ring was missing, she would think I'd taken it, no matter that the times didn't match up. Of course she would; rich people always blame the cleaner. I'd lose my job. I would never find out who'd betrayed Nico. I would never get revenge. I gripped the iron railing of the staircase. As long as Caden said nothing about me being there yesterday, then Amber couldn't suspect me.

'What can I get you? Coffee?' Amber said, walking down the passage. They were almost immediately below me, and I stepped back. Caden grabbed Amber's waist, stopping her.

'I don't want coffee.'

Caden stood behind Amber, one hand gripping her waist. The other snaked into her hair. Her eyes flickered shut.

'What *do* you want?' She sounded breathless.

His hand moved from the ends of her hair to the base of her skull. Gripping her hair in his fist, he pulled her to him and she let out a little cry.

Her face twisted. Caden was hurting her. I moved out of my hiding place to the top of the stairs without thinking. Fists clenched, I was about to shout out, when I saw her arms wind tightly around his neck. His fist stayed in her hair, and with his free hand, he wrenched her shorts down to her knees.

I was frozen on the top step. Amber was kissing him, large sloppy hungry kisses which he broke only to pull off her loose tank. He was clumsily tugging her bra off her shoulders, she fumbling with his jeans button by the time I slowly took a step back, earlobes burning.

I turned away as they hit the wall with a thump. I walked into the guest room, where clean laundry spilled out of the basket, and tried to ignore the rustling of clothes, the small animal grunts. They confirmed what I suspected about Amber's hedonism. That Amber cared only about this moment, about immediate gratification. Maybe this was why she was freaking out about omens: because she was cheating on her husband.

As I folded the laundry, I heard a muffled whisper – 'Shh, the cleaner's upstairs' – followed by a giggle. But women who didn't care about consequences didn't really care if the cleaner heard.

'Again?' Caden said, but then they stopped talking. I let out a relieved breath that Amber was too distracted to ask what he meant.

My ears were hot as I folded a blouse, a green T-shirt, a thick fluffy towel that made me ache at its luxuriousness. Downstairs, they continued, not caring about how much noise they made. I worked systematically, while inside I burned with resentment that I could be so completely dis-regarded. It made me ache for home, for Nico. For deep, squeezy hugs from Mama Bear.

After the noises finally stopped, after the door clicked shut what felt like hours later, I crept downstairs. Amber was in the study, working at her computer. Caden had left.

She glanced up at me, her cheeks tinged with pink, her eyes shining with her secret. With the naughty thing she'd done, right there in the passage, right beneath my nose. Then I understood. Amber wanted to be caught.

Because she was drawn to disaster. She wanted to walk that line, knowing there was a danger I might have heard. It made it more fun. Amber wanted to teeter on the edge. Until one day she would fall right off.

I had a sudden, violent urge to push her over it.

'Esmie?' I realized Amber was staring at me.

'Yes?' I looked up at her. Of all of them, she was the easiest to hate. But did I think she was Nico's mystery woman? He'd been deeply addicted, passionately in love. Amber didn't seem capable of matching that. Amber was fickle and shallow. She was incapable of loving the way Nico required. And I couldn't see how Nico could fall for someone this small.

'Did you find my ring?'

'Sorry.' I shook my head. 'I didn't.'

But I wasn't sorry. Amber didn't deserve to wear Linc's ring.

Chapter Fourteen

Friday

Malachy's cottage was on the other side of the woods. I had to go through the trees, leaving the path at the heap of rocks (known in Ireland as a cairn, Amber told me). Keep north for five brisk minutes, until I reached the stone wall. Hop over, then I'd be practically in the back garden of Three Oaks.

'Red gate,' Amber had said. 'There aren't many houses down that way.' She handed me a set of keys.

Between the trees, I felt low, frustrated by the elusive scarf. I'd searched through both Amber's and Isabelle's bedrooms thoroughly. I'd have to wait until next week before I could go through Ceanna's.

In the meantime, I would hone my revenge plan. It was three-pronged and simple: find Nico's lover, learn what she cared about most, and take that away from her. While I had stalled slightly on the first part, I was gaining on the second. Cleaning their houses, I was quietly learning about all three. I was finding out what mattered. What they cared about most.

Looking around the trees, I wondered which was the one that Nico had been tied to. *Our tree*, he'd said in the letter, *the one we marked.*

A thought hit me with a mix of excitement and dread:

what if he'd marked this tree with their initials? Nico had carved NL + SW inside a heart on the jacaranda tree near our house. It was the kind of gesture Nico found romantic, so I was certain my hunch was right. If I found their tree, then I would know who she was. Then I wouldn't need to hunt for the damned scarf.

I took out the folded picture again, ignoring the dark lust in Nico's eyes. The tree had a straight trunk, some mossy stones in the background. I looked around me and groaned. Finding a specific tree in a forest was like finding a needle in a haystack.

I made my way through the woods until I came to the jagged wall and climbed through a gap in the ivy-covered stones. Down the lane, past hedged-in fields, I found the red gate.

I took a last look around, again admiring the otherworldly lushness. Patchy clouds hung low, making the greens even more vivid. Above, the skies were an explosion of silvers and greys, blues and purples; it was moody and intricate, letting out golden light before shifting again. The hedgerows were thick and full, narrowing the lane to a path. I ticked off the flowers in my head, pleased with myself – foxglove, cow parsley, red clover. I'd learned a few more too: centaury, elderflower and red valerian. The day was luminous, its beauty almost painful. So different from home.

I wished I could have come here under different circumstances.

In the small back garden of Three Oaks, a rickety wooden swing hung from one of three thick-trunked trees. The walls of the cottage were whitewashed, and the slate roof was speckled with moss.

The cottage was old, and I could only guess the secrets it knew after decades of silent witness. I shivered.

Entering the small kitchen, I halted at the sight of a tall figure standing there. I pressed a hand to my chest, my breathing heavy. 'You nearly gave me a heart attack.'

'Sorry,' Linc said sheepishly. 'Didn't realize you'd be here.'

I gave a shaky laugh, moved to the table. 'Amber wants me to do a deep clean. Start boxing things.'

'Ah,' Linc said. 'Ceanna can't be happy about that.'

But it looked like Linc wasn't happy about it himself. I dropped my bag under the small Formica table and took in the room. A jar of teabags perched on the counter, and the fridge looked ancient. Between the toaster and the kettle was a tray with yellowed boxes of medication. Out of habit, I studied them: warfarin, beta blockers, digoxin, diazepam. Old Malachy had quite the collection.

'Cup of tea?' Linc retrieved two mugs from a faded cupboard.

They were all so polite, obsessively offering me hot drinks before I went off to remove their pubes from the shower.

'No, thanks.' I couldn't understand why Linc was in his dead father-in-law's kitchen making tea, instead of at work. 'Why are you here?' It came out too blunt.

'When Malachy was alive,' Linc said, seeming not to take exception to my tone, 'I'd visit every Friday after work. Do a few jobs, admin, or fix his endless technical problems.' He shook his head and smiled. 'Malachy was a sharp man, but terrible with technology.' He raised an arm in the direction of the sitting room. 'But mostly I came to visit.'

His smile was sad, and it was clear that he'd had a close relationship with his father-in-law.

'You still come here on Fridays, even though he's gone,' I murmured.

'Yes.' He exhaled as the kettle breathed beside him. 'Now that it's summer and I have no teaching, I find myself gravitating here whenever I can.'

'It's just standing here, empty.' I thought of the small, crowded slum with its mouldy walls where I shared a room with Fabiana. Eight of us stuffed into three bedrooms, while Amber and Linc had a huge house and a cottage between them. *Strange old world*, as Mama Bear, master of the understatement, used to say when she was particularly pissed off.

'Now *that* is a source of contention.' Linc leaned against the counter. 'See, Malachy left the cottage to both Amber and Ceanna. But they can't agree on what to do with it. It makes them furious that they can't persuade each other. Amber wants to sell, or at least rent it out.'

'And Ceanna?'

'Ceanna wants to keep it as a shrine. She's too bereft to move in, she can barely visit, but she doesn't want anyone else living here either. And while the sisters argue' – his hand swept out, gesturing in the direction of the sitting room – 'I work on my monograph, my in-depth study of Eden Hale.'

'What do you think will happen?'

'Amber tends to get what she wants.'

'And what do you want?' Impetuous, the words slipped out.

Linc didn't answer immediately. I waited, sensing that my silence would draw him out. It seemed to me that Linc liked that I was quiet.

'For things to stay as they are.' Linc busied himself filling his mug with water, and I couldn't read his face. 'Eden Hale lived at Three Oaks. She and Malachy grew up here. When he married, Malachy bought Woodland House. But he always preferred it here.' Linc lifted his mug. 'I do too.'

There was a light in his eyes that I'd never seen back at Woodland House. It pulled me in, making it impossible to look away. It seemed he couldn't either. He watched me, holding me in that burning light. His hand tightened around his mug. Then a loud chime sounded somewhere inside, and it felt like I could move again.

Clearing his throat, Linc excused himself. I hunted for cleaning materials, then went through the kitchen door to the older part of the house. Through the open door to the left, I could hear the clatter of fingers moving quickly over a keyboard. The clear, determined thoughts of a man who knew his own mind. Just like Nico, before.

I used to sit on the beanbag chair beneath the window while Nico typed at his small bedroom desk. I felt a pang of longing so fierce it made my chest ache.

Later, when I was ready to leave, I went to find Linc.

'Linc.' The door was open a crack and I pushed it further. 'I'm leaving now, unless you . . .'

I trailed off as I looked at the room, my mouth falling open.

Books were shelved along one wall of the room, but the other three were covered with drawings and writing. Words were bordered with vines and flowers, some faded with time. A large red peony dominated one section, magnolias on another. A string of inked hearts weaved around short poems. Silver birds on cherry blossoms were painted on to a cabinet. Symbols and solitary eyes watched from the wall. Some words twisted, others spiralled, but most bunched together in paragraphs or couplets, the writing spiked and urgent. A few lines stood by themselves. The words slithered off the walls to the floor.

It was the most beautiful vandalism.

I moved closer to read the writing on the walls.

I am unmade. A snake losing its skin.

'Did Eden Hale do this?' I touched my fingers to the image of a snake. I glanced down to the wooden floor and saw words and vines twisting beneath my feet. Through the window, the stone wall was covered with ivy, and it felt like I'd stepped into one of her fairy-tale poems.

'She did.' Linc's voice was deeper now, and I could see how it affected him, being in this room. His laptop was on her desk, surrounded by her books, and I understood why he worked on his monograph here. Why he wanted things to stay as they were.

I caught snippets of Eden Hale's moods – *I chase what cannot be caught, and it frustrates me* – as I followed her words across the wall.

> *Monogamy is*
>
> > v
> >
> > e
> >
> > r
> >
> > y
> >
> > long.

It felt so intimate. But how could it be when it was laid out on the walls for everyone to see?

This room stirred something in me, a hunger. A reminder that I was more than just the cleaner. It made me feel achingly human. It made me feel restless.

Linc stood up and I noticed a single bed, covered with opulent red-and-gold fabric, behind the desk.

I walked along the wall, reading and touching. He opened a cupboard built into the wall beside the shelves. Inside was a heavy, antique-looking safe. It was studded with brass and, though I searched, I could see no dial or keyhole.

He took a wooden box from the shelf above the safe. He placed it on the desk and lifted a letter opener to the lock.

'Linc,' I said, alarmed. 'What are you doing?' It looked like he was breaking into the box. It felt illicit, wrong.

'This is our secret, Esmie.' The glint in his eyes was unmistakably flirtatious. This time, in this room, it hit me hard. His eyes felt as though they were feasting on me, and I didn't want it to stop.

His face seemed almost wolfish, and there was an urgency as he beckoned me nearer. 'Come, don't be afraid.'

He was drawing me in, and I sensed danger. But beneath the urge to step back, there was a pull. And for once, it wasn't about Nico. There was little in the cottage that would help me help him. This was all for me, wrong and selfish, and it gave me a thrill. My skin pricked, and suddenly breathless, I moved nearer.

'What's life without a little risk?' Linc worked the letter opener in the lock.

The lid sprung open and he moved to the bench, gesturing for me to sit beside him.

'What's that?' I asked, taking another tentative step. If we were caught, or if anything went missing, I would for sure lose my job. Linc, in contrast, seemed to be relishing the moment. But then, it was easy for Linc to break the rules; it always was, for men like him.

'Come here, Esmie.' His voice was lower, enthralling. He placed a hand on the teal velvet beside him.

I took cautious steps forward, drawn by the way he spoke to me, the way he looked at me. With everything that had happened to Nico, I hadn't felt like this, at the centre of things, in so long. I'd been scurrying at the edges, and now, someone was looking at me. Like I mattered.

Linc smiled at me, and I felt the power of his charm. He'd turned it up high; deep dimples and shining eyes. His gaze seemed to linger. Didn't it? Or did some secret part of me just want him to look at me, want it to be true?

Instead of sitting on the bench, I slunk to the floor, too aware that I'd been cleaning all day. My leggings were sticking to my thighs, my T-shirt tight and clammy. I worried I smelled of sweat and bathroom mould.

Linc placed the box on the bench. He reached inside and pulled out a stack of folded paper, tied by green ribbon.

Excitement rippled deep in my belly. Linc caught my eye, as though he knew that it was spreading from him to me. A pleasure that came from sharing something illicit. Perhaps Linc and I were not that different.

'These are Eden's business letters.'

A flash of disappointment shot through me as I watched his long fingers trace the thick paper.

We were in a room where the walls watched. I could feel the heat from his leg even though we weren't touching. Something hot and alive budded between us in the afternoon light, yet he was showing me the business letters of a dead poet?

'And her finished poems,' Linc continued, 'with some publicity photographs.'

I turned so I could see him better. The light in his eyes was the same as the preachers on the street who shook their finger and yelled about fire and brimstone. A zealot's light.

'Have you read them?'

'Obsessively.' The thickness of his voice told me this was no exaggeration.

'OK. Wow.' I broke his gaze, unnerved by the intensity of his passion.

'I know, isn't it amazing? Sometimes when I hold these in my hands, it's like she's here with me.'

This time, I must have let my scepticism show because he studied my face and, misreading, he laughed. 'Don't worry, Esmie, these documents are all mine. I was teasing you. Malachy left all Eden's papers to me. We're not doing anything wrong.'

The unspoken 'yet' hung in the air, and his lips tilted up as he held my eye. I made myself stay still, as if that would quiet the warring going on inside me. I felt a pull towards Linc, but also an instinct to keep back. To stay where it was safe.

'Then why did you pick the lock?' I lightened the heavy moment with a laugh.

'That's just how it opens. It locks automatically, see?' He raised the lid and pointed to the lock. 'The contents of this box, and everything inside the safe, are mine.'

'Amber's dad gave them to you?'

'He left them to me in his will.'

'Can we open the safe?'

'I want nothing more.' For a moment, Linc's eyes were hard. 'The safe is locked and the keys have, since Malachy's death, mysteriously disappeared. I had a vault technician look at it, but drilling in is too risky.'

'Why risky?' A picture was forming now: the arguments I'd witnessed between Linc and Amber, the missing Eden Hale story that Linc had told me about. There was a simmering conflict between Linc, Amber and Ceanna, and the contents of this safe were at the heart of it.

'Well, firstly Ceanna would butcher me with a blunt axe if I even tried.' He smiled, clearly not terribly concerned about this possibility. 'But this safe is an antique, from a time when it wasn't uncommon to booby trap vaults with poisonous gases – before they had alarms and sensors and things. This one has one of those traps, most likely armed with ink, and drilling would destroy the contents. Given how paranoid he was in those last days, there's a good chance that Malachy set it.'

'What's inside?'

'Eden's personal papers. Her letters, notebooks and

diaries. Rough drafts of poems. The only known copy of her story version of "The Heart in the Wood", the unpublished fairy tale retelling I told you about.'

'You want those papers, don't you? You want them badly.' I looked up at him. The mossy green of the ivy on the wall outside fired the green in his eyes.

'I do.' I could sense his need, urgent, pressing, to read these words that were locked away. Linc dropped the letters and pulled out some photographs from the box. 'But unless the keys are found, Eden Hale's journals and lost story will stay locked away for ever. I suspect that's how Ceanna wants it.'

'You don't trust Ceanna,' I said slowly.

'I am almost certain that she took the keys and hid them from me.'

'Why would she do that?' I frowned. 'If Malachy left Eden's papers to you?'

'Precisely because he did that. They were really tight, those two – they were a world to themselves. The only time I saw them argue was when Ceanna learned that Malachy had willed Eden's papers to me.' Linc exhaled with frustration. 'If I'd been able to unlock that safe last November, I would have made Chair. Not that dull professor with her allergy to dogs. The job should have been mine.'

The anger in his voice made me glance up at him, and he added quickly: 'But that's not why I want them. It's not about a promotion or publications, or anything like that.'

'What is it, then?'

'I deserve them.' Three simple words. The entitlement. 'No one knows Eden Hale as well as I do. No one has read her poems as many times, scrutinized and dissected them as I have. No one has spent days, weeks, years, reading every last cryptic word on these walls and floors, or studied these photographs as much as I have.'

Linc handed me three photographs. Eden sitting on a park bench. Eden in a garden. Eden standing in this room, the ink-covered wall behind her. 'No one loves her more.' Again, that zeal in his eyes, in his voice. This obscure poet was religion to Linc.

I thought maybe I understood why Ceanna wanted to keep the papers locked inside the safe. The impulse was protective; making Eden's most intimate records available to Linc meant her private thoughts would be parcelled into lesson plans or dry academic papers. Or maybe it was simply that Ceanna hated Linc so much that she enjoyed denying him the thing he wanted most: to fully own this woman who defied ownership.

'See.' Linc held out a photograph of Eden in the kitchen, wearing a sundress. It looked like she'd been caught unawares in this picture. She'd dropped the ethereal stare, and her eyes were dark and knowing. Hard.

'Do you see it now?' Linc pressed. 'How like her you are?'

I saw what he meant. Apart from a vague physical resemblance, Eden looked like she was hiding something. She looked like a woman who lied.

Handing the photographs back to Linc, I caught the way his eyes lingered over the picture of her in a sundress.

As though he'd fallen in love with a ghost.

Chapter Fifteen

Tuesday

On Tuesday morning, Liadh answered the door with a lacklustre, 'Oh, it's you.'

I stepped inside, wiping my wet shoes on the mat.

'Is Isabelle home?' I hung my raincoat on the hook, the smell of wet jacket deadening the light lavender scent that usually lingered in the hall.

'She's visiting my gran.' Liadh started up the stairs, not bothering to look at me. 'My friends are coming over to study. We'll be in my room.'

After changing into dry leggings, I retrieved the cleaning materials from the utility room. Isabelle had left a list of jobs: change the beds, clean the light fittings, call the birds with my song . . .

Upstairs, Liadh was at her desk, books in front of her and the door wide open. I sensed her eyes on me. She was clearly mistrustful of me, and even as I resented it, I grudgingly applauded her for her good instinct.

I'd finished in the upstairs bathrooms and Isabelle's bedroom – where, again, I fruitlessly searched for the scarf – when the doorbell rang. Liadh bounded down the stairs and a light, happy cacophony of girls' voices carried up.

'It's lashing out there.'

'Omigod, did you see what Caitlyn wore last night?'

They tripped back upstairs, laughing and disappeared into Liadh's room, slamming the door behind them.

Quiet as a thief, I stole into the upstairs sitting room. The sculptures stared at me from their shelf. I appraised the room; it was clean enough. I could leave it today, just wipe down the light fitting as Isabelle had instructed. That would give me time to do what I'd come for.

I fetched the stepladder from downstairs and placed it beneath the light, then arranged the cloths. Deception was largely about the props. It was easier to believe if the stage was set.

Using the duplicate key I'd made, I unlocked the desk drawer, feeling an irresistible pull to the blue notebook. If Nico mattered to Isabelle, if he loved her, I felt certain he would be here, in these pages. I opened the notebook and continued reading Isabelle's unsettling reimagining of her picture-perfect life.

The Danger was protective of her, alert to her every need. He never read books or watched TV, preferring instead to watch her. Always, always watching her. The woman tried to please him, because the Danger liked to be pleased. She learned that the Danger would have her as his, one way or another. If not by his love, then by her fear. It was easier by love.

The sound of the doorbell ringing interrupted my progress yet again, and I let out an irritated growl. From Liadh's room came the sound of music playing, the murmur of voices.

I packed the notebook away and hurried downstairs, my mind racing with what I'd read. Was Isabelle writing some kind of dark romance? Was this a way of escaping the limits of her dull suburban life? I had a sudden terror that if I read on, I would find detailed erotic fantasies between the woman and the Danger.

But I also felt the truth of her story. Isabelle's description of a slow, quiet anguish was the opposite of my own trauma, the violence and distress from which I'd fled. And still her words kindled the never-quenched hurt inside me until it was a roaring fire.

Was it real? I thought of the scar on Isabelle's palm. Who did Isabelle, the stiff, well-dressed doctor's wife, find dangerous?

Was it – I swallowed hard – Nico?

Nico had a strong instinct to protect. He had little appetite for fiction. Again, I felt that gnawing in my stomach.

Through the frosted glass panel, I could see the outline of someone tall. Another of Liadh's friends, no doubt. I opened the door wide, already stepping back to let them in so I could return to Isabelle's words. To make sure that Nico wasn't her Danger.

Instead, a man pushed inside, and I moved back with alarm. He towered over me, menace in his eyes. Then he removed his hat and held it in front of his stomach. Rain dripped from his clothes on to the marble floor. He was staring at me, taking in every detail of my face.

'Do you live here?' he asked.

'Can I help you?' I asked stiffly. Something was off. I knew this with certainty. There was something wrong about this man with his watery blue eyes, holding his hat to his stomach, like the devil hovering awkwardly at the entrance of a church.

'Can I help you?' I repeated, louder, adrenaline coursing through me.

He peered down the hall and up the stairs. A burst of laughter came from Liadh's room, and his head snapped to her door. Then he smiled, a small bitter smile, before turning back to me.

An icy hand gripped my heart. Was *this* Isabelle's Danger? Was I, then, in danger now?

Despite my trepidation, I forced myself to stare at him. To make a note of every detail – the coarse hair of his beard, the hint of grey at his temples. Deep creases on his forehead. He wore a black shirt with jeans and white trainers. His eyes were a remarkable ice blue, a shade I'd never seen before. I touched my leg, feeling for my phone in the slim pocket there.

'I'm looking for Alex.'

He stepped closer to me, and I found myself pressed into the wall where coats hung from the long, thick coat rack. He smelled of rain and must. He felt unstable, as if he was seconds away from drawing out a knife and plunging it into my heart, which beat harder in apparent protest.

'Is that you?' he asked again, his voice harsh. 'You're Alex?'

I thought of Liadh and her friends upstairs. I pulled myself tall, refusing to be intimidated.

'Get out. Now. Or I'll call the police.' I made myself sound loud, unafraid, as I squared my shoulders and pushed away from the wall. I moved into his space, looking right into his eyes. I held up my phone, ready to dial emergency. 'Go.'

He held my gaze, the threat unspoken. Another peal of laughter sounded from upstairs, drawing his attention. He stared in the direction of Liadh's room, before spinning away and striding out of the front door.

Upstairs was noisier now, Liadh and her friends shrieking in merriment, and I felt a pulsing in my ears. I stood in Isabelle's front hall, watching the man walk down the path and out of the gate, and the warning klaxon in my head seemed loud and real.

As I turned to head back upstairs, the boots lined up on the shelf beside the door caught my eye. Three pairs of Paul's thick-soled boots, all neatly arranged side by side. Beside the shoe shelf was an umbrella stand where large umbrellas stood as straight as swords; a hat rack where baseball caps and sunhats were impaled.

I thought about Paul and his nice smile and good manners. Paul, who believed that men should be gentlemen and protectors of women.

That's when I understood. I realized what it was – who it was – that Isabelle found dangerous.

And it wasn't Nico.

Later that afternoon, the sun came out, and Liadh and her friends went outside into the bright warmth. I was becoming accustomed to the changeability of the Irish weather. Liked it, even. It made sense to me that days could be both moody and bright, like I could map my own temperament against the weather.

I peered through the upstairs window, watching the teens lie on the grass and soak up the sun. Then I turned to the drawer and picked up where I'd been interrupted.

4.

The Danger told the woman that she was his world. And he was hers, at his insistence, but one that was too tight, too small.

The first time the woman tried to tell the Danger she was leaving, his dinner plate hit the wall, ossobuco oozing down the matte paint on to the varnished floor. The older daughter, then a toddler in her high chair, had started crying.

Look what you made me do, he murmured. He'd never been violent again. Not physically, anyway, and the woman found herself forgetting. She forgot how afraid she'd been. She forgot what she wanted and needed, lulled into a numb acceptance through the regular rhythms of everyday life.

The Danger never lost himself like that again. He'd learned to hurt more subtly, more brutally. The second time she told him she wanted a divorce, when the younger daughter started secondary school, he neglected to pay the private nursing home where the woman's mother lived. It had broken her heart when she had to explain they'd lost the courtyard room her mother loved.

The Danger warned her again that he would never let her go. He loved her too much to live without her. That if she ran, he would track her down and find her. The only way she was leaving him, he'd said, stroking her hair, was in a body bag.

And that's how the woman realized what she had to do. For the Danger to let her go, he had to believe she was dead. She had to prepare a new life, far away.

In order to live again, the woman had to die.

This is not a story about pain, of all the endless humiliations the woman endured. It is a story of hope. Of a grand escape.

The woman decided she wouldn't leave the Danger in a body bag. Nor would she limp away broke and desperate. She would stay until the younger daughter finished school. She would start her new life with the security and independence she'd never had in this one. And for that, she needed money.

She began squirrelling it away, skimming twenties in cashback when she did the grocery shopping because the Danger rarely checked the Dunnes receipts. She sold some of the expensive dresses and coats he'd bought her over the years.

One evening, she met the Danger at his practice and saw the stack of headed prescription paper in the momentarily unlocked supply cupboard. She slipped it into her bag, her cheeks hot as he came out of his treatment room.

That was the moment that changed everything.

The beginning of her release from her golden cage.

Frowning, I turned the page with a trembling hand.

5.

After years of PTA and sports club meetings, the woman knew which mothers were potential customers. She approached them. Casually, carefully. An easy conversation while washing their hands in the bathrooms at the planning meeting, or while they set up for a fundraising event.

Her business grew through word of mouth, a quiet network of respectable women looking for something to take off the edge. She only sold to women she knew to be discreet, and she only sold sedatives and painkillers.

It wasn't enough though. The woman needed more.

'Liadh,' I heard Isabelle call from downstairs. Quickly, I buried the notebook beneath the folders, acid burning my stomach.

Chapter Sixteen

Tuesday

Isabelle sold illegal prescription drugs.

Nico had been addicted to prescription painkillers and sedatives.

My head throbbed with loud, violent beats.

This was how it started. This was where Nico got his first taste. Isabelle had been Nico's dealer.

Had she taken it a step further and become his lover too? Did she lure him with a trail of pills, like peas in the woods, marking the path to her bed?

I cycled hard, the burn in my lungs a welcome distraction from my thoughts.

My mind turned over everything I'd learned as I sailed along the narrow roads. Fitting and discarding, I tried to match memory to experience. About eleven months ago, when Nico had grown distant, he'd been struggling with his research after suffering a major setback. He was under huge pressure, his supervisor breathing down his neck. He was terrified that his PhD had reached a dead end. That must have been when he'd turned to Isabelle. A little something to help him manage the stress.

Even if Isabelle wasn't the lover who betrayed him, as his drug supplier, she had to take some blame for Nico's unravelling. I felt a tightness in my chest, a burning resentment that they were all just fine, living their lives, while he was in a coma, his dreams in pieces.

By now I'd cycled to a quiet corner of town, right near the lake's edge. Beyond a narrow strip of shingles, boats were moored on the water. A swan glided by.

While I was furious with Isabelle for feeding his addiction, I couldn't ignore that Nico had made the choice to take drugs he wasn't prescribed.

And it wasn't his reliance on drink and pills that had cost him his degree; it was his lover's lies. He'd been clear about that. The drugs were a distraction. I was here to find *her*: the woman who'd lied to the university and got his funding pulled. The woman he'd loved.

And if that person was Isabelle – well, so much the better.

I secured the bike outside the cafe and went inside. This had been one of Nico's haunts, a place he visited often, either to work or meet friends. I'd already come here a few times. The prices were reasonable, and it was popular with students. Students who might have known Nico.

Now, hot after my cycle, I ordered ice cream and went outside to find a seat. My phone buzzed with an incoming text, and I glanced down at today's vitriol.

The messages were coming every day now. A constant reminder that while I was chasing after Nico's lover, she was biding her time. Waiting only for Nico to improve, or die, and then come after me. Each message fed the gnawing anxiety in my gut; a live, growing thing that sent tendrils of unease to every part of me.

The cafe was busy. Merry students drank cider in the sun, and every table was occupied. I searched among the large wooden picnic tables for a place I could share. I was already on my way to a table when I realized I knew the woman there: Linc's research assistant, his right-hand woman.

Fiona, that was her name. The one Amber didn't like. She was in a different faculty to Nico, but perhaps she'd met him at The Woodlands. Linc seemed casual with his PhD students, so it was possible.

'You mind if I sit?' I gestured to the opposite end of the table.

'Go ahead.' She glanced up from the large textbook in front of her and smiled.

'Fiona, yes?' I asked hesitantly, and she looked up at me, expression blank. 'I saw you at Linc's house? I am the cleaner.'

'Oh, right.' Recognition brightened her face. 'You moved here recently. How are you settling in?'

'OK.' I dipped my plastic spoon into the cardboard bowl. 'I like this cafe. Do you come here a lot?'

'Too often.'

'To work?' I gestured to the book in front of her.

'I'm always working,' she said with an exaggerated sigh.

'Linc is a good supervisor?'

'The best,' she said fervently. I suppressed an eye-roll. Fiona was clearly smitten with Linc. But wasn't I a little taken with him, too? I felt suddenly hollow.

'I wondered if you could help me,' I began, then saw pure horror on Fiona's face. It took me a moment to realize she thought that I'd sat at her table to scrounge off her. I felt my cheeks go pink, offended by the assumption.

But it didn't matter what Fiona thought of me, so I pushed on. 'I found something in Ceanna's house. In the room of the man who's gone now. Ceanna,' I shook my head. 'She won't talk about him.'

'Ceanna's old lodger?' Fiona said. I noticed with grim satisfaction that she was blushing too, clearly embarrassed by her mistake. 'Nico? There's a name I haven't thought about in a while. Linc was pretty friendly with him.'

'He was?'

'Yeah – they met for drinks, went on cycling trips, played soccer every week. That kind of thing.'

I knew about the soccer. In the first year, we used to video call as soon as he got in after their game. But the rest of it was news to me.

'What did you find?' Fiona pressed.

'A photo,' I said.

'Of Nico? He was so hot,' she said dreamily.

'Ha, yes. I think the girls would like him,' I laughed, masking my desperation to know more. 'He had many girlfriends?'

Fiona dropped her gaze. She knew something, I realized, my heart racing. And she didn't want to say. I didn't want to lose her, though, so I didn't push.

'You want to get Nico's picture back to him? Hmmm, I don't have his number,' she replied, but then brightened. 'Oh wait, I have his email address. Do you want me to send him a message?'

'I can do it. You look busy already.' I nodded to her books. I couldn't risk Fiona sending an email and mentioning me; I suspected I wasn't the only one monitoring his inbox. And I wanted to know if Nico had a secret email account, one he'd used here. Because there'd been nothing in his old emails from his Woodlands lover. The idea gnawed at me. Did I know him at all?

She hesitated.

'I will send his picture. That is all.' I shrugged. 'But don't worry if you prefer not.'

'It's fine. No problem.' Fiona checked her phone, then scribbled Nico's email address – one I already knew, to my frustration – on a page in her notepad. She tore it out and handed it to me.

'So, who was the lucky girl?' I said coyly. 'Was it you?'

'Me? No,' she giggled. 'Nico was way too . . . worldly for me. He had that bad-boy thing going for him.'

'Bad-boy thing?' I spooned ice cream into my mouth, cold and sweet, to quench the burning in my chest. Nico was no bad boy. I forced myself to match Fiona's giggle with one of my own, and for a second I almost believed it, two young women gossiping and giggling over ice cream on a summer's day. 'He sounds interesting.'

'Only if you like trouble.' She leaned forward, relishing the gossip now. 'He left in disgrace. He must have done something really bad, because he lost his funding and was asked to leave.'

'Oh? You must tell me.' I dipped my spoon into my bowl, my tone admirably light considering the dark churning inside.

Fiona shrugged. 'They kept it hush-hush. I can only guess.'

'And what do you guess?'

'Between you and me? Just a hunch – I have absolutely no basis for this – but I think he was hooking up with Ceanna, she got bored of him and he acted out. He was a bit too fond of the . . .' Fiona mimed drinking. Then she flushed. 'Sorry, I shouldn't have said any of that. Linc wouldn't like me talking about his family.'

'Don't worry. I'm just the cleaner,' I said, taking advantage of how they perceived me – invisible, unthreatening – yet again. 'Linc won't know. Why do you think this Nico was with Ceanna?'

Fiona shook her head. 'I'm only guessing. They spent a lot of time together – and I mean a lot – in that house. He was so gentle with her. And she looked at him like he hung the moon. It's such a shame it turned out the way it did. Perhaps he was a little wild, but honestly, to me he seemed like a really nice guy.'

I felt a lump in my throat, simply from hearing it acknowledged that he was the most ordinary of things: a really nice guy. Because, despite his mistakes, he was. We were all a mix of good and bad. I'd made my own mistakes, things that would forever haunt me. Everyone had.

'He suffered setback after setback with his PhD,' Fiona went on. 'His supervisor was awful. He started drinking more and more, and next thing he was gone. He didn't deserve what happened to him. It was a rough patch, but he would have bounced back because he was smart and hard-working – even with the bad-boy reputation.' Fiona's phone pinged and she reached for it. Our ice-cream intimacy was clearly over. 'Sorry, we're planning my dad's sixtieth party. My sister is a devil for a spreadsheet. I'd better see what she wants. Nice chatting to you . . .' She searched for my name.

'Esmie.' I smiled at her again. My mind was buzzing with information. Ceanna and Nico, sweet with each other. And then the relief: to hear Nico, my Nico, spoken about in a way that I could recognize.

That Nico had suffered a whole series of setbacks with his research was news to me, though. He'd only mentioned the first, and then stopped talking about it.

I wished he'd talked to me.

As I walked away from the table, Fiona's words haunted me: *It was a rough patch, but he would have bounced back.* I forced myself to face that she might be right. Perhaps Nico would have bounced back; maybe never to the same heights as before, but maybe he would have been OK.

Until a few weeks ago.

Chapter Seventeen

Wednesday

Ceanna's room, painted deep green, was the biggest of the three in the rectangular bungalow. A giant brass disc, intricately etched with vines, hung above the neatly made bed. The chalkboard green of the walls, the white duvet covers and chunky knit blanket, along with the leaves, and the grass and bark outside the window, created a quiet, soothing space.

Had Nico liked this room as much as I did? Had he slept in this white nest of a bed, his strong, hairy legs flicking away the covers? He'd never had the patience for duvets or blankets back home, preferring to sleep with a light sheet even in winter.

He and Ceanna had spent a lot of time together here in this house, Fiona had said. I felt itchy, wondering what they did with all that time. Watch TV? Take Moondust? Fucking bake? I ran a hand through my hair, and with a sudden surge of violence, I kicked the leg of the bed. Did she give him a massage? Was that how it all started?

Forcing myself calm, I opened the wardrobe, and checked methodically through the hanging dresses, jackets and skirts packed tightly together, for the green floral scarf. I checked the top shelf, finding no love letters, no hidden photographs, no diary. No scarf. I searched under the bed, inside the drawers, behind the mirror.

No scarf, no scarf, no scarf. I wanted to scream the words. Open the window and yell them to the sky. There was no scarf here, not in Amber's house, nor in Isabelle's.

Where the hell was it?

If Fiona was right and Ceanna was Nico's lover, there was nothing here to confirm it.

Scanning the room, my eye fell on a large silver jewellery box. If Nico had given her jewellery, would I be able to pick out a piece he'd chosen? A year ago, I would have said yes without hesitation. Now, I wasn't so sure.

I lifted the lid, immediately seeing the sparkling green oval stone clustered with diamonds. I picked up the ring and read the inscription inside: *my heart.*

Why was Amber's oh-so-special engagement ring in Ceanna's jewellery box?

I slipped the ring on to my finger, holding it up to the light.

'What are you doing?' The voice came from behind me, and I started. I whirled around to see Caden standing in the doorway. I put my hand down beside my leg, out of sight, hoping he couldn't see how flustered I was.

'Cleaning.' I turned the stone to my palm.

'You're cleaning Ceanna's jewellery box?' He sounded incredulous. 'Were you trying on her ring?'

'No.' I said it too quickly, and Caden smiled. 'What do you want? Looking for Amber?'

I knew as I said it that I'd made a mistake. Better to let Caden think I knew nothing. That I'd seen nothing.

'Why are you here?' I said, louder this time, determined not to let him intimidate me.

'This is my home, Esmie.'

My jaw dropped. 'You're the new lodger?'

'I am.' He nodded at the jewellery box. 'Now, tell me. What are you doing?'

'I told you, cleaning.' I held up my hand, showing a small polishing cloth. Deception really was all about the props. 'Ceanna's silver box is dull.' I gave him a bright smile and injected sugar into my voice. 'I didn't realize you were interested in my cleaning.'

'I'm not interested in your work.' He made no effort to leave. 'I'm interested in you.'

'What do you mean?' My palms felt clammy, my sweat smearing all over Amber's pretty ring.

'I think you're hiding something.' Caden gave me a searching look. 'You're definitely hiding something.'

'I'm not hiding anything.' I turned away abruptly. 'That's crazy. You're wasting my time.' Immediately I realized my mistake: never turn your back to danger. I felt him watching me, but I couldn't see the expression on his face. Couldn't see if he prowled nearer.

I waited a breath, then heard his hand slap the doorjamb and his footsteps retreat down the passage.

When I was sure he'd gone, I pulled Amber's ring from my finger, gave it a shine, and returned it to the box. Then I polished the box until the dull silver was so bright I could see my own lying self reflected back to me.

I went back to the woods that afternoon, once again searching for the tree. The tree at the heart of the wood, where Nico had left his heart.

I walked and I walked, but I could not find it.

Chapter Eighteen

Thursday

The next time I saw Isabelle, I thought about her selling pills to Nico, and a solid ball of hate wedged itself in my throat, making it difficult to speak.

'You're late,' Isabelle snapped. It was three minutes after starting time. 'Liadh and I are going to see my mother. Paul is expecting a delivery – please watch out for it.'

I caught a glimpse of myself in the mirror; my face was mutinous. I was glad they were going out though, so I could ditch the cleaning and get on with what I was actually there to do.

I went directly to the drawer in the upstairs sitting room, impatient to learn if Isabelle had written about Nico. If dealing him drugs had led him to her bed.

The notebook retrieved, I flipped to where I'd left off.

6.
In her secret office, the woman had hidden a box beneath the bottom shelf and covered it with an old canvas. Today she chose a dark red wig and green contacts, and put them inside her sports bag. With her black jeans, a cream shirt and a brown trench coat, she looked ordinary. Forgettable.

The woman drove to the next town where, wearing the wig, she dropped the script with one of her prepared identities, a stolen name and address, at a pharmacy. She feared this five-minute wait most of all. She was convinced that this was when someone would say, 'I'm sorry, we seem to have a problem.'

The woman was organized – she'd practised her copy of the Danger's signature and had carefully studied how to write out prescriptions – but she always felt that sliver of terror.

She loved that terror. Her manically beating heart. It made her feel alive.

The doorbell rang, jolting me from my reading. I packed the book away, thinking that if Isabelle was Nico's lying lover, she was now the easiest to get revenge on. I'd use her own words against her, make her regret ever having put pen to paper with her story.

From the landing window, I looked out to see if it was the courier.

But it was him again, the man with ice eyes, and my gut clenched. The edginess I'd sensed in him had amplified. His face was twisted with fury, and he banged his flat hand against the door, yelling, 'Open up. Open this door.' Each bang, each shout went through me, wearing at my already frayed nerves. He hit the door again, then kicked it.

He stepped away from the door and walked down the white pebble path to the gate. He looked back at the house, right up at me. His eyes cut straight through me.

I shrunk back from the window, my breath coming in gasps, but it was too late. He'd seen me.

Shaking, I pressed my back against the wall. This man had a simmering rage coiled tightly inside him, ready to snap at any moment. But, I reminded myself, I had nothing to hide – not from him, anyway. I had many reasons to be afraid, but he wasn't one of them.

I squared my shoulders, now angry myself. How dare he frighten me when I'd done nothing to him?

Barrelling downstairs, I marched to the front door and flung it open. I walked down to the gate and stepped out into the road.

There was no one there. I looked at the field across, down to the woods. The resting houses. There was no one around. And yet, I felt certain someone was observing me. That an unseen person watched me wrap my arms around myself as though I was cold.

Safe as houses, Isabelle had said. Which suddenly didn't feel very safe at all.

HOME

Nico had gone quiet.

It was more than two years since he'd left. In the be-ginning he'd written letters to Esmerelda, called home frequently. Over time, that had tapered off to a weekly video call and an unsteady back-and-forth through messages.

Esmerelda was worried about him. He'd had a major set-back in his research, he'd told them. Something had gone badly wrong, costing him months of work. Esmerelda knew that he was working through the night to fix things, to recover lost time, so she tried not to mind that he wasn't in touch as often as she'd like.

He was calling and messaging Simone irregularly too, which made Esmerelda feel marginally better. The two women had fallen into an uneasy, necessary peace, living beneath the same roof. Sometimes Esmerelda missed the old Simone, the girl who'd been her friend, with a physical ache. She missed Simone's body wriggling in the bed beside her. She missed Simone's rare explosions of laughter that racked her shoulders.

Then Esmerelda would remember that night everything changed between her and Simone. The night she'd dis-covered the truth about her friend. She would never forget the way Simone had looked down at her father while he slept in the armchair.

Simone had been so calm. So unaffected.

There was something deeply wrong with Simone.

Esmerelda didn't want this cold, rotten woman marrying Nico. The darkness Esmerelda knew was there would destroy him. Simone would snuff out his light.

Esmerelda had to find a way to use his absence to drive a wedge between them. She had to find a way to use Nico's silence to ice out Simone.

She started slowly. In her usual cheerful messages with her latest news, Esmerelda would casually seed in that Simone wasn't helping out around the house. Esmerelda had to be careful, though. She and Simone had always hidden the depths of their ill feeling from Nico, aware that he would have little patience for it. She amplified Simone's sins – rude to Mama Bear, hiding money, indolence, greed. Esmerelda played to what would displease Nico.

He didn't always respond, but Esmerelda knew Nico read the messages. She was careful not to overload the negativity – he would see through that. She played it well, dressing it as part concern, part frustration. Over the weeks, Esmerelda painted an unflattering portrait of Simone. It was devious and wrong, but she had to save her brother. When Esmerelda had seen Simone's true nature, she'd tried to explain to Nico but, caught up in the terror of that night, he'd refused to see it.

Esmerelda knew that Nico's love was bound to his desire to save Simone. He had a romantic notion of her as a damsel in distress. She had to revise his image of Simone, remoulding the distressed damsel into a manipulative villain.

She knew that her poisoned messages were chipping away at the love Nico felt for Simone. His impatience became obvious. If his contact with Simone had slowed to a trickle before, it was almost non-existent now.

Esmerelda tried not to feel bad when she saw Simone's red eyes. It was for the greater good. She couldn't let Nico marry someone who was capable of killing in cold blood. Esmerelda checked Simone's phone – she'd always used the same PIN – and saw that Nico's impatience, then his silence, had made Simone appear even more pathetic: **Why didn't you answer my call? Did I do something to upset you?** The responses from Nico were terse: **I was working** or **Things are busy right now.**

It was a wet night towards the end of September when Esmerelda learned how effective her plan had been. She was adding more garlic to the fried rice when her phone pinged with a message from Nico. He'd sent a photograph.

Esmerelda nearly burned her hand on the pan. She gasped loudly.

'What?' Simone said, pausing with a stack of plates. 'Is it Nico? Is something wrong? What is it, Esmie?'

Mama Bear had come into the kitchen and was looking at Esmerelda curiously.

'He booked me a ticket. I'm going to visit Nico next May.' Her face shone with triumph. She held up her phone, waving the screenshot of the e-ticket. 'We'll take a road trip, go camping. It's going to be amazing. I'll start the paper-work straight away.'

Simone's hands clutched the plates she was holding. Her face was blotchy. When it was still a vague idea rather than a firm plan, Nico had talked about Simone joining him for a visit. But now, he'd booked the ticket and it wasn't for her. He'd chosen Esmerelda.

Simone put down the plates, her hands shaking. Mama

Bear looked at her with concern. Esmerelda was babbling about the things she and Nico would do.

'Esmie, sit down,' Mama Bear said, and Esmerelda obeyed, her lips twitching up into a huge beam.

Simone closed her hands around the seat of the chair. 'It was supposed to be me.' Her voice shook.

Esmerelda looked up, her eyes widening with faux innocence. 'Oh, he didn't tell you? Nico said it's better if I come out and the two of us get to spend some time together. It's been so long.'

'Esmerelda,' Mama Bear said, a note of warning in her voice.

'I'm sure you understand that he wants to spend a little time with me, Simone.' Her eyes were gleaming. 'And with the wedding as soon as he gets back . . .' She trailed off, putting a forkful of rice in her mouth. 'You'll have the rest of your lives together.' Her words were muffled by rice.

'I understand,' Simone rasped.

But Simone didn't understand.

Chapter Nineteen

Friday

I woke too early on Friday morning, my thoughts pressing and nagging until I broke through the thin veil of sleep. It was always like that now, these unrestful nights. The guilt. The relentless unease.

I woke up thinking about how it should have been, my visit here. How these bright summer days should have been spent with Nico. We should have been seeing new places, exploring ancient castles, the wild Irish coastline, stopping at quaint pubs in the countryside. We would have taken the ferry to small faraway islands, feeling like we were leaving the world behind.

Then I thought about the last time I saw Nico. Lying on the rough carpet. How I'd screamed and screamed. Mama Bear's face, stern and resolved, as she swore us to silence. *It was an accident*, she'd said. Lied. *It was an accident, promise me you'll say it was an accident.*

On the other side of our small room, Fabiana dressed by the light of her phone torch with quick, practised movements. I reached for the lamp beside my bed and flicked on the soft light. She flashed me a quick smile as she turned to the small mirror on the wall. We were awkward, Fabiana and I, the enforced intimacy of sharing a bedroom making us excruciatingly polite.

I felt different here. Not myself. When I was done, would there be anything of me left?

When I reached Woodland House, I could tell from the mess that greeted me that Amber and Linc had entertained again. The afternoon room wasn't as bad as last time, but they hadn't bothered to clear the leftover wine glasses, ashtrays and half-empty bowls of dip.

'Esmie, our saviour.' Linc breezed into the living room about ten minutes later. He took a sip from a coffee cup on the mantelpiece and winced – 'Cold, bleurgh.' I examined the walls for cobwebs. 'We're awful, I know.'

'It's my job.' But it wasn't really, I thought, trying not to take out my frustration on the cornices as I brushed out new webs. I was here to clean the house, not retrieve Amber's bra from the coffee table. I had a new respect for Laura, whose life I was temporarily inhabiting, even if she was fleecing me. Laura was a lot older than me, and this was tough manual labour.

Laura had been one of the trickier parts of my plan. The day after I arrived, I visited her with dark chocolate and marzipan. I'd taken the precaution of wearing cheap, heavy-framed glasses and a cap; it was best to leave as few traces of Esmie as possible.

I made her an offer: I would do the work and she would get a third of her usual weekly rate. She'd been suspicious, but I'd told her a sob story about being Isabelle's half-sister and wanting to find the right moment to tell her. It was a delicate matter, I'd said, my hands fidgeting, because nei-ther Isabelle nor her mother knew. Not about me or my poor dead mother – a tear had streaked down my face at this point. My performance was strong; even I'd half believed my stupid story. I felt bad for the lie, though. Laura hadn't done anything wrong and she was a big old softie, just as Nico had said. Addicted to soap operas and secrets and marzipan.

Laura had agreed, though negotiated me up to half her weekly rate. Just enough for her to spend the two months visiting her sister in France. She'd smiled at me with sharp teeth and I wondered if she wasn't such a softie, after all – if she knew my story for the garbage it was – but I didn't care either way.

The front door slammed shut, and I peered out of the living-room window to see Linc walking to his Jeep. He reached inside the back seat, his faded blue T-shirt riding up and exposing the muscle and skin beneath. I had an urge to run my hand just there, and an idea came to me.

Before I could think it through, the sound of raised voices in the afternoon room drew my attention. Amber and Ceanna, getting into it again.

I glanced out of the window, at the Jeep that was parked outside. Linc was nowhere to be seen. He must have gone to Three Oaks.

I hesitated. The voices in the afternoon room were lower now, just the murmur of conversation. I straightened the cushions, then carefully, quietly, I inched down the hall. The door was open a crack.

They were standing in the centre of the room, Amber's arms folded like a truculent teenager as she turned her face to the window. 'How many times must we repeat this conversation? I'm not selling to you, Ceanna. Just leave it already.'

'Why not? Three Oaks means nothing to you. Nothing.' Ceanna moved towards Amber, stepping into her line of vision. 'Is it because you don't want me to have it?' Ceanna sounded hurt.

'Don't be ridiculous.'

'Please, Amber. It's Dad's childhood home. We can't let

some stranger live there.' The women were silent. Then Ceanna said, 'What's your price, Amber? How much?'

'I'm not interested in your money.'

'Then what do you want?'

Amber chewed on her bottom lip. 'Find the keys to the safe. Let Linc have the papers. Then I'll gift you my half of the cottage.'

'I'm afraid that's not possible.' Ceanna sounded colder, more distant.

'That's my only offer.'

'They don't belong to him,' Ceanna spat.

'They do.' Amber let out a laugh. 'Dad left them to him.'

'Dad was sick. He was confused, and Linc was there all the fucking time. Linc manipulated Dad into changing his will. I know it, and so do you.'

'Be very careful what you say, Ceanna.' Amber sounded thin and breathless. 'And how you accuse my husband.'

Ceanna's face was tight with rage as she moved closer to Amber. 'It's our family history. Not Linc's.' Her words echoed in the bright room. 'And it's all I have left.'

'I'm here,' Amber snapped. 'You have me.'

'Do I?' Bitterness seeped out of Ceanna's words.

'God, Ceanna.' Amber sounded like she was gritting her teeth. 'You're not the only woman in the world who lost someone she loved.'

Ceanna drew back with a sharp intake of breath, as though Amber had slapped her.

'I'm sorry,' Amber said quickly. 'I shouldn't have said that.'

Ceanna picked up her phone and keys from the side table.

'You're so desperate. You'd give him everything,' Ceanna said, pulling herself up tall. 'And still not get the one thing you want in return.' She stalked to the garden door, placed her hand on the knob, but didn't turn it. She paused, clearly wrestling with herself.

Amber's face contorted, like she'd been hit by a bullet to the heart. One of the dogs nestled up to her, sensing her distress. Amber put her hand gently in its fur, then she dropped to her knees, burying her face in its neck. When she looked up again, her face was wet with tears.

Ceanna turned around, and I quickly dipped into the downstairs bathroom as she crossed the room to her sister. 'Ah, Amber.'

But I wasn't alone in the bathroom.

Linc was there, his face pale. He'd heard everything. He held a finger to his lips and we listened.

'Come now, we both said more than we should,' Ceanna said gently.

'I know it's what you believe.' Amber sounded dull, and Ceanna's softly murmured response was inaudible.

In the small room Linc and I waited, our breathing falling into rhythm with each other's. The silence stretched, and I looked up at Linc, seeing devastation and fury play across his features. He must have been realizing he was never getting into that safe. He would never read Eden's diaries. He'd never find the lost story.

We listened as the glass door slid open, then shut again. Amber's soft footsteps padded past the bathroom, the dog following close behind.

Linc leaned against the wall and blew out a breath.

'I'm sorry,' I said, but he hardly seemed to notice me.

I was about to slip out when Linc spoke in a low, rasping voice. 'Do you know when I first read an Eden Hale poem?'

I paused at the door, unsure what to do. On the one hand, listening to him would build the trust growing between us. It would make him more likely to tell me about what had happened with Nico. But I didn't know if my exhausted spirit could take yet another lecture about that damned poet.

Before I could make my mind up, he decided for me by continuing. 'It was winter, and I was fourteen. My mother had been recently diagnosed – pancreatic cancer – and home was difficult. There was all this noise, and I couldn't bear it. I began going to the library after school because I wanted silence. But even then, I still felt it. The noise. Under my skin, in my heart. A buzzing in my ears. It was driving me mad.'

I watched him warily. Why was he telling me all this? He took a deep breath. 'The book was on the table, *The Heart in the Wood*. It was pure chance I found it. But when I read it, it felt like those moments of glory you see on TV. The sun on my face. Angels singing hallelujah. And finally, no more noise. I went home, and despite the turmoil there, I could find silence. With Eden's words, I had reprieve. Solace. An inexplicable serenity.'

It doesn't look like they're bringing you serenity now, I thought. He was wrong. Eden wasn't a reprieve. She was an obsession.

Like you avenging Nico? a little voice inside me said.

There was suddenly an unpleasant taste in my mouth.

Chapter Twenty

Friday

I hesitated, then walked down the short passage of Three Oaks, resisting the urge to check my reflection. I'd put on eyeliner, knowing I'd see Linc here. My thin pink T-shirt brought out the colour in my cheeks, with the V-neck accentuating my curves. My black leggings were comfortable, but also fitted snugly and were flattering.

I was nervous about this addition to my plan. When I'd listed my options while sitting in a cramped plane seat less than a month ago, this wasn't something I'd considered. In my twenty-five years, I'd only ever had one relationship, and I wasn't good at flirting.

But when I'd watched Linc's T-shirt ride up earlier that day, I realized that it wouldn't be horrible to get to know him a little better and use his flirtation with me for my own purposes.

Paul and Ceanna had thwarted all my attempts to find out more about the aggressive lodger. Isabelle and I barely spoke. But Linc seemed to like talking to me – or at me – and I could use that.

And perhaps there was a part of me that wanted him for my own sake.

I knocked once, then pushed open the door to Eden's study.

Linc was at the desk. His laptop was closed and he leaned back in the chair, his hands clasped behind his head. He turned to me, and I wasn't sure if it was just the way the sun fell in the room, or if his eyes lit up when he saw me.

'Esmie,' he said, his gaze sweeping over me before he quickly averted it.

'Remember in your study?' I asked. 'When we talked about Eden? And her work?'

'I do, of course.'

I wondered if he'd thought about us alone in the dimly lit room. How he'd leaned towards me.

'You want more, don't you?' He gave me a slow smile, as if he knew that something had hooked into my skin, reeling me in. And it had. He was just wrong about what exactly that something was.

My heart was hammering, but not at the prospect of more dusty letters. I was in uncharted territory, making a detour that could be a shortcut or could get me badly lost. Linc had one great weakness: his obsession with Eden Hale. By some stroke of luck, I reminded him of her. I would be foolish not to accept this as a gift.

Within a minute, Linc had picked open the locked box. He patted the teal velvet bench tucked against the wall, and this time I sat beside him. He placed the pages between us.

'Have you finished *The Heart in the Wood*?'

'No,' I confessed, cursing myself. I should have prepared better. 'I haven't had time.'

'You work hard.'

He was right, I did work hard. In addition to The Woodlands, I had to cover Laura's shifts in town – a young tech professional whose flat I cleaned one evening every fortnight, and on Wednesday mornings I cleaned for a family with three young children. I was tired to my bones, but I didn't want to tell Linc that. It was too honest. Too real.

'You play music, don't you?'

I shook my head. 'Not at the moment.'

He nodded, examined my face while I stared resolutely at the writing on the wall. He held up a sheet. 'Do you want to read, or will I?'

'Is that a poem?' My brow creased with confusion. 'You want to read a poem, here? Now? Like in a class?'

'Not like a class, Esmie.' A smile played at his lips, and he lowered his voice. 'Like we've picked the lock to my wife's dead aunt's special box on this bright Friday afternoon. With the sun streaming in through that small window, and surrounded by books. Like that.'

I laughed softly. 'Fine. You read.'

'You don't do that nearly enough. Laugh, I mean.' His eyes held mine, and his lips quirked up. 'I like it.' His gaze lingered; then Linc started reading and I zoned out a little, only hearing some of the words as I focused on his voice instead. It was enchanting, low and relaxed, and it made me feel softer, looser.

'It's not bad,' I said, my head tilted in what I hoped was an alluring way.

'Now it's your turn.'

'My turn?' I said, forgetting to sound sexy. 'I don't know any poems.'

'Tell me a story, then. Tell me a fairy tale.'

I looked down at my hands. The only stories I knew had terrible endings.

'Once upon a time,' he urged lightly. 'Come on, Esmie, you can do it.'

All at once, I was assailed by the ridiculousness of my plan. 'Maybe I should go.' I made to stand, but he stilled me.

'I want to know more about you.' The way he was looking at me made me catch my breath, and a flurry of agitation started inside me. Good agitation, and bad. I wanted him to look at me this way, and not just because I was trying to get information from him. I'd been invisible for so long. I craved, I realized, to be seen.

Was that what had happened with Nico? Had this woman made him feel seen?

Don't think about all that. Don't think about Nico now, a part of me said. The part that edged closer to Linc. But I had to think about Nico. That was the whole point of being here, reading strange poems. Nico.

'Once upon a time,' he nudged me again, and I took over without pause.

'There were two girls.' The words tumbled out, and I felt breathless.

'Esmie and . . . ?'

'Simone.' I watched him closely as I spoke our names. There was no *Aha, gotcha, you're in with that man, your one, the aggressive fella.* I was safe – for the moment.

'Pretty names.' He shifted and resettled a little closer. The relief that had relaxed my shoulders instantly dissipated. I felt a strain as I watched my thigh only inches away from his, wanting both to reach out and pull back.

What will you give me, Linc? I thought. *If I tell you a truth?*

'Esmie and Simone were close. They lived next door from very little. They went to school together. Played soccer, music, dance – all the things children do, and always together. They liked to say they were sisters. But Esmie already had a brother. His name was . . .'

Here, I faltered.

'Lucas.' I decided on the name I'd given Ceanna. 'He was one of those people, very appealing.' I mimed a magnetic attraction with my hands. 'Everyone loved him. Esmie and Lucas were very close. More than usual for brother and sister.'

Linc shifted again, his leg now touching mine, and a shiver passed through me. I wondered if he felt it too.

'They were poor. Their house was tiny, but they managed. When they were older, Simone started changing. She didn't want to be in Esmie's little room. If Lucas was fixing the car, she was outside. If Lucas was cooking, Simone was there.' My words were now coming out too easily for someone who was here for language lessons, but Linc didn't seem to notice and I was glad. Because, suddenly, I needed to tell this story, and it was hard to hold back.

'She'd fallen for Lucas?' Linc guessed.

'Worse, she preferred Lucas.' An unforgivable sin. 'Esmie had never minded his girlfriends, but Lucas and Simone together – no. It made her sick.' I made myself speak slowly, deliberately, forming the words carefully. 'See, Simone was hers, and Lucas was hers, and she didn't want them with each other. She didn't want to be forgotten.'

I looked at Linc to see if he was judging me, but there was a strange light in his eyes. He seemed to approve.

'Ah, because she was passionate. I often think that grand love is extremely selfish, not selfless, as some like to believe.'

'One night, the two girls went out. They came back at midnight, went to sleep in Esmie's bed. But around two, Esmie woke up, thirsty.'

'Oh dear,' Linc said, immediately seeing where this was headed.

'They were on the couch, naked.'

That night. The dim moonlit room. The rhythmic pumping of Nico's hips.

'Simone had been sneaking into Lucas's bed, or the couch or his car, for months, but they hadn't told her. Esmie was angry and felt left out.'

'Sure.'

'They told Esmie that they'd kept it from her because

they knew she'd react badly. Which she did. She knew she should just be happy for them, but she couldn't. She was jealous.'

'I can see why,' Linc said.

'To make Esmie happy, Lucas broke it off with Simone. Esmie knew that Lucas was only with Simone because he felt sorry for her. He needed to fix people. To save them.'

Linc looked intrigued and murmured, 'I've known a few people with a saviour complex.'

You sure did, Linc. You were friends.

'The girls seemed to make up. But it was never the same.' I shrugged. 'Too much bad feeling. Then, a year later, N—' I caught the near slip with a thud of relief. 'Lucas told Esmie that he couldn't do it. That he'd tried to move on, but he loved Simone. He wanted to be with her. He asked Esmie to be happy for them.'

'What did she do?'

'What choice was there? Esmie couldn't argue – that would be childish. She crossed her fingers and lied, telling them she was fine with it. The bad feelings grew, and she began to hate her friend.'

I had to be careful: talking about this had given me my usual voice – not afraid, not soft and hesitant. Or maybe I was tired of pretending to be a beginner in a language I was fluent in.

'Because of her brother?'

'Yes, but there was more.'

The words were on the tip of my tongue, this story wanted to be told.

'Simone was . . . unpredictable,' I said, a small concession. I shut my eyes briefly, remembering five years ago. The memory was seared into my brain.

'What do you mean?'

I lifted a shoulder, struggling to find the words. 'Simone didn't always know the line between right and wrong.'

'You're saying Simone was a psychopath?' Linc urged, fascinated.

'No.' I pushed back my hair with an irritated hand. Did everything need a label? 'People break the rules all the time. Maybe they use their neighbour's wifi or download pirated movies or speed down narrow country lanes.' I nudged Linc with my knee, and he gave me a rueful smile. 'Wrong but acceptable, they tell themselves. But they draw the line at stealing from a shop. Or punching an old lady in the stomach. Still, stealing is stealing, no matter how you do it. You can hurt people without touching them.' I knew that only too well. 'Simone's life with her dad had been bad. And it affected her. It pushed her lines of acceptably wrong further.'

Linc was peering at me. 'Your English is a lot better than I thought.' He tilted his head, and I shifted uncomfortably. 'You're not really here for language lessons, are you?'

Anxiety spiked in my gut. I opened my mouth, then closed it again, unsure what to say.

'I know why you're here.'

A roaring panic cascaded in my ears. Had I, lulled by a strange intimacy in a beautiful room, revealed too much?

'You came here to escape. You came here because of Simone.'

I wanted to shake my head, to offer a feeble protest, but his words were arrows, hitting true. I sat there mutely, unsure how to steer to safer ground.

'Time and distance will help restore your friendship, if that's what you want. In the meantime, enjoy the adventure,' Linc continued, sweeping out his arms. 'Travel, discover the world for the next few months.'

I held back my sigh. As if I had the money, the freedom of movement, for months of travel. Linc just didn't get it.

'I'm not here to travel.' I made myself sound soft, affable, despite the turmoil inside. I had to patch the damage, and coming across as defensive wasn't going to help. 'My class is intermediate level. When I go home, I want to teach music.'

It was the truth. I was happiest when I was teaching music. In another time, another life, that's how I'd spent my best hours. Placing small fingers on half-sized guitars, helping teenagers coax music from wood and string. Making something beautiful where there had once been nothing.

Suddenly I was desperate to return to my old life. I'd sat down with Linc to get his secrets, and instead I'd nearly told him mine. Talking about home had only made the longing resurface. I had to keep faith that Nico would wake up and it would be safe to go back.

Would it? a little voice nagged at me. Or was I relying on blind faith when I could ill afford it?

No, it would. It had to. Because by coming here, I would fix everything. My revenge was the key. My heart picked up as I realized what I'd not quite articulated to myself before: getting justice for Nico was my ticket home. It would be the peace offering I needed to secure my own safety.

When I looked up again, I saw Linc staring at me thoughtfully. I was trying to figure out how to make the connection to the aggressive lodger, how many conversational steps before I could get him to tell me the story I really wanted to hear – not one about some long-dead, irrelevant poet. I'd spoken honestly to him; now I wanted the same in return.

'Esmie.' Linc had turned to me now, his shoulders squared to mine. 'There's something I need to tell you.'

He placed his hand on my thigh, and for the first time in

months – years – all thoughts of Nico fled. His touch was slow, deliberate. The squeeze was so slight, it was barely there. I sucked in a breath. Heat travelled up from my leg, blossoming in the pit of my belly. He said: 'That was a terrible fairy story.'

Then he clapped the hand again on my leg with a laugh this time, blurring his intent. Had he touched me with meaning? Or was it just a moment of levity after a heavy conversation? I could still feel the warmth of his hand as I stood up, watching him pack away Eden Hale's papers. I touched the nape of my neck, trying to make sense of this sudden confusion.

Then, as if I'd summoned her, my phone buzzed. I was loath to look at it, to break the reprieve I'd felt with Linc. *Don't speak about her, don't even think about her.* But it was too late. A second text landed.

Still fucken hate you.

Can't wait to show you how much.

Linc gathered the papers, then glanced at me, said, 'I have to get back.'

'Me too.'

We left together through the back gate. We were nearing the woods when he asked, 'Is she OK now? Your friend, Simone?'

No. 'She will be.' When I carried Nico's lover's head on a platter. Everything would be set right then. It had to be. 'She'll get her happily ever after.'

Walking between the trees, I thought about what I hadn't told Linc. The memory that had nudged and jabbed at me while we sat together in Eden's study. A memory of violence, that was hinted at in every word I'd spoken to him. A memory that was now the colour and texture of a soured friendship.

A memory that held me like a shackle.

HOME

FIVE YEARS AGO

Esmerelda started, the sound of a dish smashed against brick travelling through the thin walls. On her bed, she'd been trying to finish the song she'd been writing. But now she drew her knees up against her chest, wishing she could mute the fighting next door. Simone's father, AJ, was in one of his rages. Drunk again. He was always drinking away their money. Simone held down two jobs and still struggled to make ends meet. Now, AJ was like a bear with a sore head as he rumbled around their house looking for money and cursing Simone.

Esmerelda sighed, thinking about her friend. On the surface, their friendship hadn't changed too much. They'd still catch a band, or see a movie, or shoot pool together – but where it had once been two, it was now always three.

Esmerelda had been spare, the unnecessary third, ever since that day well over a year ago. The day when Nico had told her that he loved Simone and couldn't be without her. Simone was his life, his heart, he'd said with an odd softness in his eyes. They were sickening, always pawing at each other. Esmerelda knew that she should be happy for them, but how could she when it felt like she'd lost her brother and her best friend in one fell swoop?

Their love had come at too high a cost, Esmerelda thought, and she was the one who had to pay it.

The wall shook again as a door slammed next door. She heard Simone's muffled shout, *leave me alone.* Esmerelda caught the sob in her voice. Simone would have finished her shift at the busy restaurant less than an hour ago, and she was always exhausted afterwards.

Sometimes Esmerelda wondered if AJ hated his daughter. Something else smashed and AJ let out a volley of abuse. Esmerelda put her hand to the wall, feeling her heart pick up pace.

'Take it,' Simone screamed at AJ. 'Take it all. Drink it away. They can throw us out on the streets.' She was crying now. 'Why should I care?'

Esmerelda chewed her lip. Her throat felt thick, as it always did when AJ unleashed his temper on Simone.

Then without warning, it went silent. A drawn out, ominous nothing. Esmerelda got to her feet, and watched the wall. She waited for the slurred insults, Simone's pleas, but there was only a menacing quiet. She took a step towards the wall, then looked out of her bedroom door. Mama Bear had gone to her church meeting and Nico wasn't yet home.

Her body lined with tension, Esmerelda pressed an ear to the wall. Then jumped back when AJ started yelling again. Simone was crying out now, shouting something but the words were too muffled to hear.

Esmerelda pulled on her thin hoodie. She stopped for her shoes, fumbling with the laces as she tried to tie them. By the time she ran outside, it had fallen quiet again.

She looked at the front door, then made for the window at the side of the house. She peered in through the glass. Simone was in the kitchen area. She touched a hand to her head, probing at the roots of her long hair, and winced. Then she crossed the kitchen, slamming the cupboard doors. She bent to retrieve a heavy frying pan from the drawer.

Esmerelda wanted to shush her. Simone knew she had to be quiet, or she'd set him off again.

Esmerelda stepped to the side, searching through the window for AJ. She found him in the armchair in front of the TV. Lights flickered over his face, but he wasn't watching. He'd fallen asleep. All the rampaging, and now there he was, lights out. Like a toddler after a meltdown.

Scanning the living room and tiny open plan kitchen, Esmerelda assessed the damage. A dish had hit the wall and lay in shards on the floor. The side table had been pushed over. She should go in and give Simone a hand; AJ would only get mad again if he woke and saw mess. They might not be as close any more, but Esmerelda knew these episodes took their toll on Simone. She looked again at her once best friend. Simone was motionless now, in the kitchen, just staring at the pan in her hand.

Sighing, Esmerelda went around the back of the house. The kitchen door was further away from where AJ slept, and she had a better chance of not waking him if she entered there. She pushed down the handle, trying not to make a sound. She clicked the door shut behind her, and took in the kitchen. An onion sat unchopped on the cutting board. The TV played quietly, showing a newsreader talking earnestly to the camera.

Simone was slowly crossing the floor from the kitchen area to the armchair. She walked strangely, placing one deliberate foot in front of the other. Esmerelda frowned, wondering why she seemed so strange. And what did Simone have in her hand?

Stepping forward, Esmerelda saw Simone reach her father asleep in the armchair. Simone watched him for a moment. Then she raised the heavy pan and smashed it down on to the side of his head. She hit it a second time, and after the third, Esmerelda lost count. Esmerelda was frozen, her body turned to ice for a few vital seconds.

When she could move again, Esmerelda stepped forward, screaming, 'Stop. You'll kill him.'

Simone turned to Esmerelda, her face spattered with blood. She looked at the pan. She looked back at AJ, at his split-open head. She looked at the pan again, and dropped it as if it had burned her.

Simone stepped towards Esmerelda, pleading, 'Thank God you're here. I was so afraid, Esmie. I thought he was going to kill me.' Her voice racked with sobs. 'He hurt me, see, he pulled the hair right out of my head.' She pointed to the scalp, but Esmerelda couldn't see anything. There wasn't a bruise or mark on Simone.

'He hurt me,' Simone said again, her voice raw with desperation. 'It was self-defence.'

Esmerelda looked down at AJ, at the bleeding mess that was his head. Her heart twisted with disgust at her once friend. 'Stop lying. I saw everything. He was unconscious, and you killed him.'

'Why are you girls shouting?' Mama Bear said, entering through the front door. Her lips were pressed together, she was not happy. She did not tolerate them arguing. They were sisters, Mama Bear told them. Perhaps not by blood, but sisters all the same.

Mama saw the blood on Simone's face and took in a sharp breath. Her gaze tracked down to the armchair, to the once sleeping man there. She shut the door behind her, turning the lock.

'Get those curtains,' she said to Esmerelda, pointing to the side window, as she whipped the heavy fabric across the front window.

'She killed him!' Esmerelda sounded shrill, but still she obeyed her mother. 'He was sleeping and she killed him.'

Mama Bear now folded Simone in her arms. 'My poor child.' She said the words over and over, while Simone's shoulders shook.

'Call Nico. He has to come now,' Mama Bear ordered Esmerelda. She placed her hands on Simone's shoulders. Simone's face was red and blotchy. Nico should see her now, Esmerelda thought.

'He hurt you again?' Mama Bear smoothed her hands over Simone's hair, taking in the slight wince.

'My hair,' Simone whispered. 'He grabbed it and pulled me across—'

Mama Bear made a shushing noise. 'I know, I know, child. I have seen how he's treated you all these years, and God help me, I didn't stop it. His debt with you is huge, he was always going to have to pay for what he's done to you. And today God called it in.'

'Mama Bear,' Esmerelda objected, her voice raised. 'He was asleep. She killed him. That wasn't God.'

'The Lord works in mysterious ways.' Mama Bear went to her daughter and hugged her too. 'You will never, ever utter those words again. We all know what a cruel, abusive man he was. We will tell the police he attacked her first. You saw it all. It was self-defence. And you know it was, Esmie, you know that actions have consequences. Now, say it.'

Esmerelda glared at Simone. 'It was self-defence.'

'Again,' Mama Bear ordered.

She said it again and again. She told the police exactly what they needed to hear, just as Mama Bear insisted. And when Nico came, he said it too, refusing to hear Esmerelda's arguments for telling the truth.

Much later, after the police had left and they'd all four returned to the house next door, Esmerelda took solace in the thought that Nico now knew what Simone was truly like. He couldn't love her now, not when she'd killed her father in cold blood.

But Esmerelda was wrong. When she sank down on the couch, she saw that Nico was even more attentive of Simone. That his hand stayed intertwined in hers, that he couldn't stop looking at her. Esmerelda saw the love and concern in his eyes, and it made her want to scream. Certain that she would explode, she went outside, into the night.

She would go to the police, she decided. She would tell them everything. Nico and Mama Bear might be angry at first but they'd have to forgive her eventually. And Simone would be locked away for a very long time.

Esmerelda jumped when she saw a man standing a few feet away, quietly watching her. He had a hood pulled over his head, hiding the features of his face.

'Nico,' she called nervously. He must have heard the fear in her voice because he was there at once, his hand still laced in Simone's.

The man took a deep drag from his cigarette. 'Which one of you killed him?'

Without hesitation, Esmerelda pointed a finger at Simone. 'She did. Simone.'

He stepped closer, dropping his hood, and in the changing light, Esmerelda saw the neck tattoo that confirmed her suspicion. A small heart made of flames. It was a gang sign, not uncommon in their neighbourhood. They knew to keep their distance from men with that mark. Esmerelda shivered, apprehensive now of what she had set in motion.

The man was inching closer to Simone.

Nico stepped in front of Simone, shielding her. The gangster smiled, and Esmerelda saw that his front teeth were missing, the canines sharp.

'Not going to hurt you,' he said, taking another inhale. 'If you hadn't killed the rat, we would have.' He took something from his pocket and moved closer to Simone.

She stepped out to face him, eye to eye, her jaw tight. He folded a small card with the scribble of a burning heart in her hand. 'If the cops give you a hard time, I can fix it.'

Esmerelda cursed under her breath. With the gang now involved, she knew she couldn't go to the police. These were not men to cross. She clenched her fists, furious that she'd been backed into a corner. Forced to keep this terrible secret.

'Thank you, but they won't give me a hard time.' Simone's voice sounded different, as if she'd lived a thousand years in one evening. She tried to hand the card back to him.

'Keep it.' And then he was gone.

Nico folded Simone into his arms and held her like she was his anchor to the world.

It was as if Esmerelda wasn't even there.

Chapter Twenty-One

Weekend

I dreamed of it again: the heavy pan, the sleeping man in the armchair, the blood flecked on the walls. The shadowy figure with a burning heart tattoo. I dreamed about that dark, hot night. The night we'd buried a brutal violence, hoping it would remain hidden.

But sometimes when burying, we inadvertently plant.

Later, the shoots pushed up – a bloodied statue, a howling scream that tore through the night. The poisoned fruits of our terrible secret.

There were always, always consequences, as Mama Bear had so deeply ingrained in us.

I slept until Saturday afternoon, drifting between agitated dreams and a distant awareness of Fabiana moving silently in the room. Careful fingers smoothing oil through long hair. The sound of a brush on skin, the sharp smell of nail varnish. When I woke towards the evening, Fabiana was glowing. Her hair shining, her teeth polished, she smiled shyly and asked if I minded if her boyfriend stayed the night.

Leaving the room to them, I walked to town, acutely aware of how alone I was. Around me, friends bunched together on a busy, pedestrianized road. The women were dolled up, their hair and make-up and tiny skirts a uniform

I didn't own. People spilled out of pubs, their spirits high. A band of young men with guitars and honeyed voices busked, attracting a dancing crowd. A fire-eater arched back his neck, holding a burning torch to his open mouth. I was right there, in this vibrant new world with its colour and music, and yet I wasn't.

I ate a pizza slice while leaning against a shop window. My phone rang and I answered quickly, my heart bursting out of my chest. Would this be *that* call, the one that confirmed the thing I feared the most?

'Mama B,' I breathed. 'Is it Nico?'

There was only silence on the other end, and I realized my mistake. It wasn't Mama Bear who'd called, of course it wasn't – her name would have shown on the caller ID.

'Hello, Esmie.' The hostility in her voice cut through me. The way she sneered those words.

I clutched my phone tighter, saying nothing.

The silence extended; thirty seconds, a minute. Neither of us spoke.

I could hear the familiar rattling of the wind at the windows, and I remembered how cold the house could get in winter. We'd never find our way back to each other, I realized. Too much had happened.

I ended the call, bumping my head against the wall. She had my new number, I realized, dread curling in my gut. Which meant she knew I was in Ireland. Panic tasted metallic in my mouth.

I'd told Mama Bear that I was teaching music in Dublin. It was a plausible story, the kind of thing I might do if my world hadn't fallen to pieces. But with any scrutiny at all, my cover wouldn't hold. Deep down, they had to know I would come here, unless—

I shook my head. It was pointless speculating. But I had

to move faster. I closed my hand around my phone, staring at the Unknown Number on the screen.

She was drawing closer, I knew that for certain.

I just had to make sure she didn't find me until I had something to offer her.

Stopping in the bar where I'd seen Ceanna dancing in her red dress, I sat alone in a corner. I drank more than was wise, then wandered away from the noise and the people. I went along the river, trying to remember the stories Nico had told us when he'd first arrived, but a kind of cold numbness had settled into me.

The events of the last month demanded a reckoning, but I couldn't face it. Thinking back cast a surreal blur over everything I wished I could forget. Home had become distant, something I both longed for and feared. My thinking felt fuzzy; my body ached from bending and scrubbing. It felt like even if I slept for a hundred days, I would always be tired.

I walked back to the house, getting in after two in the morning. The men drinking in the living room waved at me. The kitchen was empty. In our room, I crept past Fabiana and her boyfriend, who held each other as if her small bed were a boat lost at sea.

I slept until late Sunday afternoon, and woke with the urge to be outside in nature, away from the damp, overcrowded house. I set out on Amber's bike with no destination in mind, but less than half an hour later, I found myself at the outskirts of the woods. It seemed that all roads led back to The Woodlands.

I stepped over moss-covered stones, and again it struck me how different it was from home. Dankness lurked even in the summery woods, where gentle sunlight danced between the trees. The leaves and undergrowth were green and rich, undeniably enticing. And yet, I'd swap it in a heartbeat for brown scrub and sweltering sunshine. The always watching mountains.

I searched again for Nico's tree, trying to identify it from the shape of the branches, the surrounding rocks, but I still couldn't find it. Eventually, I sat on a fallen bough and pulled out Nico's letter to read for the thousandth time.

'You like it here in the woods?'

I wheeled around to see Amber, her thin shoes on the tree roots. Little bird feet on a perch. I stuffed the letter into the pocket of my sundress.

'I'm not sure,' I replied, with more honesty than I'd intended. Amber laughed, and it pleased me, the low chuckle that came from her lips. In the distance, the dogs were nosing, following some elusive trail.

'Is it a guy?' She sat down on a fallen bough and gestured to my bag. 'I saw you reading. A letter from your boyfriend?'

I gave a long slow shrug, a deep breath. She was looking at me with concern, her head tilted and her topaz earrings dangling.

'He's not my boyfriend.' I got to my feet. 'Did you find your ring?'

'No.'

I thought she'd walk away. She was already looking to the distance, ready to move on.

Instead, she peered at me, concern etched on her face. 'You look upset.'

I sucked in a breath. After everything, it was this small kindness from Amber that made me want to cry.

'Esmie, I know it's not my business but you seem so sad sometimes, and I . . . Well, I know a bit about broken hearts.'

I looked up at Amber in surprise. I hadn't thought she'd

noticed me. Feeling reckless, I spoke impulsively, my throat thick. 'Does Linc break your heart? Or do you break his?'

Amber looked at me for a beat, then said, 'I am not easily shamed, Esmie. I eat if I'm hungry. It's so tedious, this coyness about women's desire.' Her kimono slid down her arm and she pulled it up. Then Amber lifted her face to the sun, and it was as if she was declaring something to the woods. 'I have never loved anyone the way I love Linc. He is everything to me.'

She stood up, whistling to the dogs.

'But it is quite something,' she said as she stepped away. 'Unusual. To be loved the way Linc loves me.' She said the words without any malice or triumph. A simple acceptance of how things were. Envy, strong and vicious, filled my heart.

The dogs bounded up to her, all lean energy and long limbs, and together, they walked between the trees.

Chapter Twenty-Two

Monday

Another Monday. Another day clearing the aftermath of Amber and Linc's parties.

Brushing crumbs from the sofa, I peered out of the living-room window. Linc, holding his work satchel, opened the door to his Jeep parked in the driveway. Amber hurried behind him, her long summer dress trailing on the stone path. She called after him, and he paused.

She caught up to him and reached her hands to cup his face. They were so beautiful together, between the tall flower bushes in the gentle morning sun. I couldn't look away. Then Linc shrugged out of her hold, checking his watch, and for a brief second, Amber looked defeated. She watched Linc close the door to the Jeep, then turned to her Mini.

'Esmie.' The voice came from behind, and I whirled around to see Ceanna. I had to remember that she sometimes let herself in through the back lane. That she moved quietly. 'What are you looking at?'

'Nothing.' I shook out the cotton throw from the sofa, and dog hairs floated up. 'It's pretty outside.' In my peripheral vision, the Jeep pulled out into the road. 'I didn't realize you were here.'

Ceanna continued to examine me, a slight furrow on her

brow. As though there was something about me that eluded her. As though she recognized me, but didn't quite understand how. Her scrutiny made me wary. Cautiously, I lined up the edges of the throw. I folded it in half, then in half again, trying to find calm in routine activity.

'Can I help you?' I asked, unable to read her.

'Yes, actually,' Ceanna said, coming in closer, her eye tracking Amber's Mini as it reversed from the drive. 'I wanted to talk to you.'

I nodded, on edge. Ceanna seemed almost hostile. There was no danger of her lighting candles and trying to be friends today. She put her hand in her pocket and took out her phone. She swiped at the screen, pressing something I couldn't see.

'I was hoping you could explain this?' Ceanna came to stand beside me, and I realized there was a video playing on her screen.

'What is it?' I said, stepping back.

I met her eyes, unable to decipher the dark emotion there. I didn't yet have a clear sense of what mattered most to Ceanna. Of what I'd take from her, if it turned out that she was responsible for ripping Nico's future from him.

'You tell me.' She pushed out her phone to me.

For a second, I wasn't quite sure what I was seeing. Removed from its context, Amber and Linc's bedroom wasn't immediately recognizable.

'You put a camera in Linc and Amber's bedroom?' My mask slipped as I gasped at Ceanna. 'Why would you do that?'

Ceanna shrugged. 'Sometimes the end justifies the means.'

I was in no position to argue with that.

'I don't want to see.' I pushed Ceanna's phone away but she held it firmly in front of me.

'I think you do.'

The camera must have been positioned near the door, overlooking the bed and the open wardrobe. A figure stepped out from the wardrobe, sliding the door shut: me.

My mind grasped frantically for an explanation that didn't sound preposterous. Then I remembered, with a heady gush of relief: Amber's ring.

I watched the small black-and-white version of myself move to the bedside drawers where I pulled open the top one, searching it thoroughly.

'I was looking for Amber's engagement ring.' My voice sounded thin and unconvincing. 'She asked me to.'

'Really?' Ceanna fast-forwarded to me rifling through the romance books. Then I was flat on the floor, peering under the bed, then lifting the rug. I'd certainly done a thorough job of searching Amber's room. 'You thought Amber's enormous emerald ring might be under the rug? Inside a book?'

My pulse raced in my ears. She was going to fire me. She'd tell the others, and I would have to leave when I'd only just begun.

Ceanna scoffed. 'Come on, Esmie. It's obvious you were snooping. What were you looking for? Money? Amber is pretty careless with her things.'

Is that why you took her ring? It was on the tip of my tongue, but I didn't want Ceanna to think that I'd been searching through her room as well.

Let her think me a thief, I decided. It was better than her knowing the true reason I was here.

I straightened my back, preparing for my consequences.

'Look, I don't care.' Ceanna exhaled. 'Take her money, it means nothing to me. The only thing I do care about is my cottage. I want Amber to sell her half to me, and she won't.'

I stayed silent. I wasn't sure where Ceanna was going with this, but it couldn't be anywhere good.

'The night of her dinner party, I saw Amber kiss Caden,' Ceanna went on. 'I know they've met since. There is one sure way to make Amber sign over her half to me.'

'Telling Linc about Caden.' Or threatening to.

I knew I had a cold streak, that under certain circumstances I was capable of doing things some would find objectionable. That I didn't always feel things the way others seemed to. It was intriguing to observe a similarity in Ceanna. Not for the first time, I felt a kinship with her. That our losses had reshaped us. That lines had blurred for us, as if smudged by our tears. I studied her, those luminous eyes that showed how deeply Ceanna had loved and lost.

And yet, if it was Ceanna who'd lied to the university about Nico I would destroy her without hesitation. I would burn that cottage to the ground, if that's what it took. And then I would dance on the rubble.

'Amber is still missing her ring, and it's worth a lot.' There was a soft mocking in Ceanna's eyes. 'It would be such a cliché if you were caught stealing from her. I think you're too clever for that.'

The way she was looking at me made my heart stutter. It was a strain, pretending to be halting with my words when I wanted to let them rip at her.

'You're always around,' Ceanna continued in her gentle voice. 'And no one really pays you any attention. It's like you fade into the background.'

'I don't understand.' I turned away and fluffed a cushion, placing it at a neat angle.

'I need evidence, of Amber and Caden. Together. Or I'll tell her you took her ring. That I found it among your things.' Her voice was very soft.

Was that why she'd taken the ring in the first place? To give her leverage over me?

'I don't know what you're saying.' I set the middle pillow down. That one was askew but I couldn't give a damn. I went to leave, but Ceanna blocked my way.

'I took down the hidden camera. They don't meet in her bedroom or at my house.' She held out a hand, extending a small digital camera to me. 'Watch them. Take the picture for me. In return, I won't accuse you of being a thief.'

'You're blackmailing me now?' As soon as I said it, I wanted to clap a hand over my mouth; I doubted 'blackmail' was part of the vocabulary taught in my imaginary language classes.

'You have a choice,' Ceanna said with a shrug, oblivious to my slip-up. I could stand right in front of them, talk to them, and still, they didn't see me.

There was no choice. If Ceanna accused me, I would be in trouble. There were many restrictions to my being here, and being charged with theft could see me sent back home. And right now, with Nico still in a coma, home was the most dangerous place I could be.

Ceanna put the camera in my hand. 'The evidence can't be ambiguous.'

'I cannot understand, sorry.' I felt mulish, resistant.

'The picture has to be clear enough to persuade Amber the cottage is mine, if she wants to hang on to her precious Linc,' Ceanna warned me. 'You're going to have to catch them red-handed.'

I had a sudden, burning need to bring her down, this woman with whom I had felt a kinship not five minutes ago. I wanted to see her mascara smudged with tears beneath those clear green eyes. I wanted to see her broken and begging.

Ceanna turned to leave. She was at the door when I found my voice.

'What if she doesn't? What if she'd rather split with Linc?'

She looked at me over her shoulder. 'She will sell.'

'How can you be so sure?' I pushed.

'Because Amber will do anything – and I mean anything – for Linc.'

The week raced on, and I learned nothing. I expanded my search for the green-and-white scarf, checking kitchens and utility rooms to see if it had been demoted to a rag. I even checked garages and searched inside cars. But the scarf was nowhere to be found.

Ceanna cancelled my shift on Wednesday, saying that she was sick and wanted to be alone. I didn't want to see her either, because it reminded me of the threat she held over me, the task I had to do for her.

And every day, I received a new message.

I dreamed you died last night.

Your head bashed in with a rock.

Better be careful. XOXOXO

Every message heightened my dread, reminding me to work faster. To finish this, before it was too late.

On Friday afternoon, I went to the cottage via the woods. Again, I searched for Nico's tree. I studied the trunks, looking for markings and finding only frustration.

At Three Oaks, Linc was working in the study, and I popped my head around the door.

'Esmie, hey.' Linc smiled at me. 'Come in.'

He stood up and stretched, my eye catching the line of his arms and shoulders. His neck, which I had a sudden urge to touch. I wanted to put my hand right there on the cords of his neck, then run it to his nape. I wanted to tug him—

'Come on, sit down with me.' Linc looked at me, rubbing a hand down his stubbled jaw.

I dropped my eyes to the ground and hurried to plug those thoughts, forcing myself to remember that I was there to get justice for Nico. And a peace offering, to secure my return home.

'Don't you need to work?' I gestured to his laptop, thrown by this unexpected awakening. The inconvenient stirrings of want.

Sometimes it felt like the last few weeks had existed in suspended time, outside my real life. And in this strange in-between place, an absence of desire had settled into everything. I no longer craved the foods I'd once loved; I ate for fuel, to give me energy to work. I hadn't really missed the urgent fumbling I'd witnessed in Amber and Caden, that base sexual desire. I'd been in the waiting place, and it was characterized by a lack of want.

But with Linc, I was beginning to want again.

'I do, but . . .' He beckoned me closer. 'I find it . . . appealing, watching you experience the poems for the first time.' *God, stop with the fucking poems,* I thought, but Linc went on, 'You've such an open face.'

What every liar wants to hear. And still, warmth bloomed in my chest. *Stop it.*

But as I sat with Linc on the velvet bench, daydreaming while he read, it only grew.

Chapter Twenty-Three

Tuesday

Time was a sea, and I was adrift. The days were waves rolling into each other, and I couldn't seem to get to where I wanted – needed – to be.

Cleaning the hall mirror at Isabelle's, I finally admitted to myself that the scarf was a dead end. I'd run through all three houses with a fine-tooth comb, and that scarf was not there. I desperately needed another lead. Maybe I could try talking to Fiona again.

I paused, seeing Liadh's reflection step inside the TV room. Or maybe I should find out what Liadh knew about Nico. Teenagers saw things, heard things.

I shone the mirror vigorously, making sure there wasn't a single streak. Then I stuck my head into the TV room.

'Liadh, can I ask a question?'

'What?' she said, looking at the zombies on the screen. She shook crisps into her mouth, spilling crumbs on to the floor I'd already vacuumed.

'About The Woodlands. I heard it was dangerous here.'

'What are you on about?' Liadh paused her show, a grey zombie frozen mid-feed, frowning at me.

'I heard something bad happened,' I improvised. 'That some man stole money and hurt someone.' I still had no idea how Nico came by that roll of cash I'd found in his suitcase, but it had to have come from here.

Liadh let out a loud laugh. 'Where did you hear this rubbish? I wish something exciting would happen. It's so boring here.'

'They said it was Ceanna's lodger. I think it was . . . Nico?'

Liadh's reaction was nearly imperceptible – but it was there. Her eyes gave her away, a slight widening.

'Nico?' Liadh said. One word, but she couldn't hide that it meant something to her. My heart skipped a beat.

'I heard he was trouble.'

'He wasn't,' Liadh blurted. 'He was kind and funny, and suddenly now they're all saying he was so awful and aggressive. It's not true.'

I froze, staring at Liadh. 'What do you mean?'

She picked up the remote and pointed it at the TV. 'Whatever. It doesn't matter. He's never coming back to this place.' Her face twisted on 'this place'. As though she hated it.

'Liadh,' I said urgently, not bothering to hide how much this mattered, 'what do you mean? Why would they say he was awful if he wasn't?'

But Liadh pressed play, and the frenzied sounds of a zombie feeding filled the room. She stared at the screen, refusing to look at me.

Defeated, I went upstairs. Isabelle was out, and Liadh was busy with her zombies, so the coast was clear. In the sitting room, I took Isabelle's notebook from its hiding place.

Without the scarf, this book was my strongest lead, I realized with a frustrated sigh. It wasn't even a good one. It was clear, though, that Isabelle had sold to Nico, that they were connected by prescription drugs. Maybe I'd find his lover here, along this murky path.

Opening the notebook, I skimmed through the pages until an entry about the Danger made me pause.

9.

On a cloudy Saturday morning, the Danger was in a foul mood, complaining about the cost of groceries again. They stood near the open kitchen door, with the Danger ranting about money.

The woman hated when he went off like this – how he did so much for her, how well he looked after her. How any other woman would kill for a life like hers. She didn't have to work. She wore designer clothes. Lived in a beautiful, large house that was cleaned twice a week. A gym membership, an expensive car. Her sick mother had the very best care. What a life, he said, his arms outstretched.

What a life. She couldn't work; he'd sabotaged her every time she'd tried. She had few friends, none of them close. She didn't even have her own bank account, and it made her feel ashamed. If she stopped for a coffee in town, he knew. If she ate out, she'd have to hear him chuckle indulgently about how his wife was a lady who lunched.

You don't appreciate what I do for you. The Danger had towered over her that morning, his large body making her shrink back until she was small, smaller, smallest. His finger pointing until she turned her face away in fear of it jabbing her eye.

I had to push the book away. It reminded me too much of him, the belligerent little man whose murder we'd covered up. I remembered his small, piggy eyes, how he'd had to put others down to feel good about himself. How horrible he'd been to all of us, even Mama Bear. Despite everything, I felt for Isabelle. I remembered my first impression of her, confident, elegant. I was so sure we couldn't have much in common, that she couldn't know what it was like to feel at the edge of things, without power. Now I realized we shared more than I cared to admit.

A sound from the kitchen door interrupted him. A quiet cough – and while the woman's stomach fell at the humiliation of having a witness, she was glad for the interruption. Because that meant the Danger had to put on his nice smile again, step back from her. But she still felt shrunken, and scurried out of the kitchen with an apologetic smile.

The feeling lingered, and that night the woman still felt small and insubstantial. They were at a party at the house next door. Holding his cocktail, the Danger regaled the guests with some amusing anecdote, while the woman leaned against the wall. She imagined she could push herself right into it, that it would fold around her and she would be swallowed into the building.

She never felt insubstantial when she was Alex, making a delivery to a client.

And then she saw him. The witness. The man who'd glimpsed the truth of her marriage that morning. The man who'd saved her with a quiet cough.

He often met with the Danger, to play sport or take the bikes for a spin. But the woman only knew him casually from strolling together and making small talk when she saw him in the bluebell woods. He was beautiful, strong and vital, now laughing with Linc on the pale stone paving outside.

When he saw the woman watching him through the glass doors, he excused himself, moving swiftly towards

*her. He didn't ask any questions, but it felt like he was
checking up on her. Seeing if she was OK.*

*The woman didn't know him well. But she'd warmed to
him. She felt a connection to him that was hard to
articulate. She felt herself again when she was with him.
She felt safe.*

*That night, beneath the twinkling lights of the chandelier,
the woman had an instinct that he could help her.*

Because this man had seen the Danger in action.

*Because something hard had flashed in the man's eyes
that morning. He knew exactly what he'd interrupted,
and he'd done it deliberately.*

The Lodger had seen that the woman was in danger.

Time stopped. Everything was suddenly silent, the world
around me caught in a freeze frame. The Lodger. Nico. Isabelle was writing about Nico.

Nico had witnessed Paul berate Isabelle. He'd seen the
dark side of their marriage.

Nico's instinct, always, was to save. It would have been
hard for him to watch Paul and Isabelle, and not grab Paul
by the collar and shake him.

Maybe he did eventually, and that's why Paul had called
him aggressive. Projecting his own shortcomings on to the
man who must have confronted him.

The saviour. Always the saviour. Years ago, I used to
admire that about Nico. Now, I hated it.

I looked down at the page again. I couldn't bear it, this
elegant, storied version of Nico. I could recognize the
truth of it, and yet it wasn't my Nico. I didn't want to
think about him making wry comments over cocktails in
Amber's beautiful house. These people were so alien to
me that I could only inhabit this world by hovering at the
edges. It was stupid, but it felt like a betrayal that Nico,

my Nico, was a part of this world. Drinking and flirting. Making Isabelle feel safe.

What else had he made her feel? The question was a stone in my chest.

My hand scrunched the page before I realized what I was doing. I'd acted in rage, balling the paper, tearing it at the edges.

Shit, I panicked. *Shit shit shit.* Isabelle's notebook was open in front of me, the torn page a broken wing.

I had to fix this. My hand frantically smoothed the page. Maybe I could iron it? But no, the creases were too deep to disappear without a trace, even with heat.

As carefully as my trembling hands could manage, I tore out the page. Isabelle might not notice a missing page, not immediately, and I would be gone in a few weeks.

I flipped to the other half of the book, removing the now-loose sheet there. Isabelle had only filled a quarter of the book. There wasn't much left to read. I could finish it today. I checked the time and cursed under my breath: I'd over-stayed my shift by twenty minutes. I chewed my lip, wondering if I dared stay another ten minutes to finish it. I was so close . . .

But before I could turn the page, I heard a loud clang from downstairs, as if something had crashed to the floor.

I put the book away and went to the stairs, calling out, 'Liadh?' The blaring sound of fast, dramatic music and zombie groans met my ears.

Cautiously, I made my way down the stairs, goosebumps forming on my skin. Peeking into the TV room, I saw Liadh riveted by the screen, seemingly unaware of the noise.

I took slow steps to the kitchen. There, on the floor, was a stainless-steel mixing bowl that had fallen from the counter. Strawberries were scattered everywhere. I stared at the mess, feeling my face scrunch in confusion. I bent to scoop them up. Fat and ripe, they smelled sweet, their red juice smearing on the floor. I collected handfuls, dumping them into the bowl.

Suddenly, I sensed movement. Before I could turn, I was grabbed from behind and pulled to my feet. I struggled, pushing back against my assailant. A hand tightened around my throat, and fear flooded my body.

'Be quiet,' a man's voice whispered in my ear. 'Leave the girl out of this.'

'What do you want?' My voice shook.

A second hand reached up to my throat. His thumbs pushed up to my jawline, his sweaty palms around my neck. 'To feel better.'

He squeezed my throat, the unwelcome pressure making it impossible to breathe. I pulled at his hands, but they only gripped tighter. He put more pressure on my windpipe. White spots danced before my eyes.

From the passage I heard Liadh from the TV room, the movie still playing. 'Mam? Is that you?'

He breathed heavily in my ear, his grip relaxing slightly. His jacket smelled of wet dog. 'Tell her you're fine.'

'Just me! All fine,' I called, hoping she didn't hear the shake in my voice.

Taking advantage of his distraction, I pushed out of his hold and reached forward, grabbing the nearest thing on the island: furniture polish that I'd left there earlier.

I turned around and smashed the can against his temple. Scrambling back, I pressed the nozzle and directed the spray at his face, watching a cloud of aerosols form around us. I sprayed again and again, feeling my own lungs burning as I breathed it in. He ducked, moving away from the fumes as I aimed for his face. Near the fridge, he stood ready, poised for a second attack.

It was the man with ice eyes. There were specks of

furniture polish on his beard. He reached for me, but I raised the can to his eyes, said, 'Stay back.'

'What are you doing in there?' Liadh called again. She sounded afraid.

I hesitated. I couldn't let Liadh come in. Not while he was here. His hands around my neck had been no empty threat.

'Everything is OK,' I called to Liadh. 'The bowl of strawberries fell.' Then I said quietly to the man, 'What do you want?' The polish had thickened the air, burning my nostrils.

'You know what I want.'

My stomach flipped. Now, seeing him again, I remembered. Alex. He'd been looking for Alex.

I'd been so preoccupied with discovering Isabelle and Nico's connection that the name hadn't registered. But with this man right in front of me, his stale-smelling coat and the faint scent of something surgical, it was all becoming clear to me. Isabelle *was* Alex. This wired man with his ice eyes must be one of her clients.

In trying to escape her Danger, Isabelle had invited in a host of new threats.

He wanted drugs. Obviously. His eyes were red-rimmed. He looked drained and exhausted. His skin had a waxy cast.

'Leave. Now.' I reached for the second drawer, where Isabelle kept the steel meat mallet. I pulled it out and held it aloft. My throat burned, and I had a sudden urge to smash it down on his head. To make him bleed for hurting me.

He backed away. Giving me a hard look, he disappeared through the rear door. The aerosols still floated in the room, and the scent of Lemon Fresh and strawberries lingered.

Shaken, I returned the furniture polish to the utility, then finished cleaning the red smears on the floor.

He must have been the client in the silver Toyota who'd parked outside the woods on my first day. Isabelle must have messed up, if her clients were coming to her house looking for a fix. I would almost have pitied him – if I couldn't still feel the pressure on my windpipe.

I made a note to keep the garden and back doors locked. Because this man would be back.

HOME

A hand closed around Esmerelda's throat. 'What did you tell him?'

Esmerelda pushed at the hand, but it was too strong. In the dark, she recognized the citrus scent, the smooth, moisturized skin. 'Go away, Simone.'

'I know you told Nico lies about me.' The hand tightened, squeezing hard. Esmerelda felt a beat of fear.

'Let me go,' Esmerelda bit out, and the hand dropped. Released, she rolled away, then sat up. The overhead light came on, harsh and glaring.

'Get out of my room,' Esmerelda spat. But the fury in the other woman's eyes frightened her. There was a strange light in them, as if Simone was possessed by something other.

Simone advanced. 'What did you tell Nico about me?'

Esmerelda leapt out of bed on the other side. 'I told him you didn't help in the house. I told him you were rude to Mama Bear. OK?' There was more, but she didn't want to make Simone angrier.

'Why?' Simone whispered. 'Why would you make things worse when they're already bad enough?'

'Because Nico is too good for you,' Esmerelda hissed.

'You're going to hurt him, I know it. He's my brother, and I'll do anything to protect him.'

'Even if it means getting hurt yourself?' Simone pushed Esmerelda to the bed. She climbed on top of her and pulled something out of her pocket. Esmerelda saw the glint of silver in her hand. 'Don't ever interfere in my relationship with Nico again. Or you'll be sorry.'

She placed the knife to the thin skin at Esmerelda's throat and whispered, 'I'll do it. You know I will.'

Esmerelda could barely breathe as the knife pushed harder into her skin. She'd seen Simone kill her own father. Fear overcoming her, Esmerelda reached out her hand, feeling for something on the bedside table she could use as a weapon. The look in Simone's eyes was soulless and terrifying. Esmerelda's hand grappled, and she knocked over the lamp.

'Girls,' Mama Bear called sleepily. 'Everything OK?'

'Yes,' Simone called, turning in the direction of her bedroom. 'Just knocked into a lamp. Sorry, Mama B.'

When Simone looked back, her eyes were normal again. She lifted the knife from Esmerelda's throat and put it in her pocket, laughing.

'Fuck you, Simone.' Esmerelda got off the bed.

'What?' Simone laughed. 'It was a friendly warning. I wasn't really going to hurt you.'

But Esmerelda had seen the strangeness in her eyes. She knew what Simone was capable of when she hated someone.

And Simone now hated her more than anything.

Chapter Twenty-Four

Thursday

The sun was bright and warm, not a cloud in the azure sky. Bees dipped in and out of flowers. A hare hurried along, disappearing down the drive. I walked down the white pebble path, breathing in the heady scent of rose and lavender. The door to number three was wide open, and strains of piano music carried down the summery path.

But this idyllic scene made me feel cold inside. The gate had been unlocked again, and I scanned the tall shrubs, the trees in the garden, searching the shadows. Looking for him, the bearded man.

I drew nearer to the front door, unable to quash the fear that he might be hiding somewhere inside the house. That he would sneak up behind me while I scrubbed and cleaned. Bash my head against the taps until my blood ran down the gleaming enamel.

I hummed my favourite banjo tune as I went inside to force the violent image from my mind. Checking the time on my phone, I saw a new message. **Watch your back. I'm coming for you.**

My anxiety ratcheted up, and my stomach twisted painfully. I wasn't moving forward quickly enough. I'd reached dead end after dead end, and something had to give.

In the kitchen, I halted when I saw Paul at the island with a mug of coffee, scrolling on his tablet. I ducked my head, trying to make it to the utility unseen.

'Ah, Esmie,' he said in his usual jolly way, and I nearly let out an audible groan. 'Just the person I was looking for.' He patted the stool beside him. 'Come, sit down.'

I didn't want to, but he patted the stool again and his eyes told me this wasn't a request. Paul might sound cheery, but I was learning to recognize the darkness beneath the facade. I climbed on to one of the white leather barstools, my legs dangling like a schoolgirl. His feet easily touched the bar of his stool.

Paul got straight to the point. 'Has everything been fine here?'

'All good.' My eye darted to the fridge, where I'd sprayed furniture polish at a man who'd tried to strangle me only two days ago. 'Nothing to worry about.'

'Any visitors?'

'Liadh had some friends.' My voice was soft and thin again, and I wiped an invisible fleck from the counter. Paul did nothing more than sit on a stool, yet still he managed to intimidate me.

'Not Liadh. Isabelle.'

I shook my head.

'You don't recognize this man?' Paul held out the tablet and I saw an image of the road outside. My stomach jolted. They had a camera on the gate. I cursed myself for my over-sight. That first week, I'd checked each of the front doors and found no camera. Why would they bother putting a camera on the gate when it was unlocked half of the time? Hell, in this tucked away, quiet neighbourhood, even the house doors were unlocked half the time. Everyone seemed lax about security here, and it had lulled me into lowering my guard.

'Only the front gate has a camera.' Paul answered my unasked question. 'But I'm going to upgrade the security. Get more cameras installed, both inside the house and around the garden.'

And Isabelle's cage would shrink even further.

'Isabelle isn't keen, but I want to make sure she's safe.' Paul pinched out the screen to zoom in on the bearded man. 'Did you see this man?'

I looked at the image. He was at the gate, reaching a hand to push it open. There were deep frown lines between his eyes.

'No.'

'Esmie.' Paul chuckled, but he didn't sound amused. 'Are you sure? Look again. Did this man call in for Isabelle?'

'This man did not call in for Isabelle.' I enunciated slowly and too carefully. Paul frowned, as though he wasn't sure if I was mocking him, or if it was my accent.

'Did he come for you?' Paul sat back. He looked properly annoyed now. Self-righteously annoyed. 'Is this your boyfriend? Did your boyfriend visit while you were working?'

'What?' I laughed. 'No. That man isn't my boyfriend.'

Paul let out an irritated grunt. 'I don't think you're being honest with me, Esmie. I know this man went inside the gate.'

I shrugged. 'I wasn't here then.'

Paul tapped at the time-stamp with exaggerated patience. Tuesday afternoon. 'This man went inside the gate at two forty-six, and he didn't come out until three twenty-seven. You left at three thirty-four.'

Forty minutes. That creepy man had been inside for forty minutes before he attacked.

Paul leaned in a little closer, his eyes on mine. 'Why are you lying to me?'

I pulled back, checked the time. 'I am not lying. This man did not visit me or Isabelle. Isabelle wasn't here Tuesday afternoon. He must have been in the garden. Excuse me, I have to work now.'

I got off the stool, but before I could leave, Paul touched my shoulder. Just one hand, but the command was clear. Stay. I stared at his hand on my shoulder. I made myself take a deep breath and smile. 'Is that all?'

He reached into his pocket and pulled out a ten-euro note, stuffing it into my hand and closing my fist. 'Try for a fifty next time.'

'I don't want this.' I reached the money back to him.

'I insist.' Paul could make a simple word sound aggressive without violence or raising his voice. I knew, without doubt, he would take no further argument from me.

He didn't say anything as I walked away, the money in my fist an insult and a reminder.

Upstairs, Isabelle was in the shower. Quietly, I pulled the sitting-room door nearly closed, thinking about the cameras Paul planned to install. How he'd monitor Isabelle from an app on his phone.

I felt a swell of pity for Isabelle. I'd seen only a fraction of his well-mannered tyranny, and it made me feel violent. I got why she needed to run, and yet I couldn't forgive her for selling those drugs to Nico. It bothered me that I understood her, that I felt for her.

Then I realized that with the cameras installed, Paul would be watching me, too.

I was running out of time.

Seething with anger and irritation, I retrieved the notebook, returning to where I'd left off. It was risky, with Paul and Isabelle both here. But I was fraying at the edges. From my mixed feelings towards Isabelle. Because of the ice-eyed man. Because of Paul. A fierce pang of longing – for home, for Nico – shot through me, nearly bringing tears to my eyes.

I opened the notebook and read, preferring to lose myself in someone else's story rather than think about my own mess.

10.

With the Lodger, the woman's world expanded.

The woman no longer relied on tired, overwhelmed mothers. The Lodger was the door to a whole new market: younger, more adventurous university students. There were enough of them looking for something; mood enhancers, maybe to help them focus, stay up all night, party harder.

The woman visited the Danger's work at closing time with a cake for the practice manager's birthday. When they left later that evening, the Danger's arm proudly around her – such a good wife – the woman had had all the additional information she'd needed.

The woman filled the scripts from a rotation of pharmacies in three different counties, preferring busy pharmacies where the staff were stretched, and used several doctor IDs. She always separated scripts for sleepers and painkillers, and only ever for a short-term supply. It was a quick, clean service, and one that couldn't easily be traced back to her.

The Lodger, who was suave, confident and beautiful, helped the woman to see that she could afford to take a little more risk. She began her priority service, an express in-person delivery which added an extra hundred. He helped her to delve deeper for her special clients, sourcing meds that couldn't easily be filled by prescription: anabolic steroids, ketamine, diet pills.

After a month, the woman more than tripled her income.

The Rose was one of the woman's special clients. She was the Lodger's friend.

I paused a moment. The Rose? Who on earth could that be? Nico had never mentioned any particular friend. I exhaled, feeling a little queasy. The idea that he would know how to set up an underground pharmacy in these placid suburban streets was wild. Nico had never felt more distant to me.

The woman first met the Rose in Malloy Park.

The Rose was well-groomed, her hair in a carefully styled ponytail and her make-up precise. She wore a necklace with her name spelled out in gold: Little Rose.

The woman accepted the envelope, quickly counting the notes inside, then took the plain brown paper bag from her tote. But she hesitated. The woman felt oddly reluctant. It wasn't her business, she reminded herself, as she handed over the bag with the banned appetite suppressant.

You don't need this, the woman wanted to say. But she made herself think about the moment when she would drive away for the last time. Music blaring and the windows down. Her hair flying in the wind as she left it all behind.

She couldn't help it. She said, 'Why?' One simple word, that should have remained unspoken.

The Rose glared at her. Then her face crumpled. 'He thinks I eat too much.' She put her hand to her mouth, as if surprised she'd spoken. But more words fell out in a torrent – how the Rose was getting married soon, how she was sure her husband-to-be wanted her slimmer.

The woman touched a hand to her shoulder, a quick gesture of sympathy. But inside she was screaming, Run. This *is the Danger. It will only get harder in time.*

The Rose's eyes were red with unspilled tears. The woman wanted to touch the soft skin of her cheek, tell her how beautiful she was.

She was going off script. But the woman would break her own rules, if it meant she could save someone else from the Danger. She pulled a pen from her pocket and scribbled her burner number on an old blank envelope. If only, she thought, some strange older woman had stopped her when she was tearfully shopping for wedding dresses.

If only someone had told her that running was an option. That she was allowed to waste it all; the planned menus, the expense. That she was allowed to not care about everyone else's expectations if her heart wasn't in it.

Above her number, she wrote, Alex.

The woman turned away. She glanced back once, to see the Rose with red-rimmed eyes and clenched fists. Then she walked on, feeling helpless.

Isabelle's bedroom door opened, and I dropped the notebook, slamming the drawer shut.

I searched my memories of Nico's stories about the people he'd met at the university. But I couldn't match any one to Isabelle's description of the Rose.

I have to track her down, I thought, relieved to have something new to pursue. If Nico knew this woman's secrets, then maybe she knew his. The notebook hadn't been such a bad lead, after all.

My phone buzzed with a message, and I steeled myself for another warning. But this time it was from Ceanna, and brought its own anxiety: **Caden going to Amber's for** dinner tomorrow night at 8.15. Linc away until late. My heart sank and I slunk down the stairs, mulling over the unpleasant task ahead.

Downstairs, I checked the kitchen, relieved to find that Paul had left. As I passed the study, I saw Isabelle staring out of the window. The printer was spitting out a page. I paused, thinking about the sad, damaged woman I'd discovered in her notebook, and my heart reached out to her, despite the reckless things she'd done.

'Is there something you want?' Isabelle sounded cold. She moved to the printer, blocking my view of it.

'Can I clean your room?' I couldn't let my pity for Isabelle distract me. Besides, the way she spoke to me made it easy enough to dislike her.

'Oh, right. Yes, you can go ahead.'

She was printing prescriptions, I realized, anger sweeping through me and wiping out all traces of sympathy.

Was this the secret office she'd written about in the notebook? I doubted it, but nonetheless, I scanned the room for a canvas that might hide a box of disguises. I hadn't stumbled across it in my search. Where did Isabelle keep her supplies? Maybe I'd find the scarf there?

'Is there anything else?' Standing at the window in the muted light, Isabelle looked haggard.

'No.'

This was how it started. Isabelle standing in that room, gazing out into her garden while the stolen prescription printed. While I still blamed Nico's lover and betrayer first and foremost, it hit me in that moment just how different things would have been if Isabelle hadn't stolen that first prescription paper. Maybe she did deserve to pay, after all . . .

'Esmie?' Isabelle called.

'Yes?'

'You haven't been cleaning Liadh's room. It's dirty.'

'She doesn't want me to.'

'She's out today. Go in there now, and give it a thorough clean.'

The page landed; the printer quieted. From the utility room, the washing machine sang that it was finished. Isabelle glanced at her watch.

'You should get started. Liadh will be back soon.'

I left the room, rage curling inside me. I went up the stairs, one stiff step at a time. Discontent was wedged solid in my stomach as I went into Liadh's room.

I folded the heap of clothes on the armchair, then ran the vacuum, sucking up old crisps ground into the carpet. I changed the bedding and collected the scatter cushions from the floor.

There'd been bears on the bed, I half remembered from the first day. Three of them. I looked around the room, finding two face down on the window seat, then bent to search under the bed for the third. I could see the brown furry leg just out of reach, and I flattened myself to the floor to pull it out.

It was an old bear, but the fur was still soft. One eye was missing, and its mouth twisted up into a grimace.

At its neck, wrapped around several times, was a green-and-white floral scarf.

The scarf that had tied Nico to the tree.

Chapter Twenty-Five

Thursday

I dropped the bear as if it had burned my hand. *Don't jump to conclusions,* I told myself. But how could I not?

I picked up the bear and put it on the pillow. I smoothed the cover. Then I dipped into the bathroom and vomited.

The green-and-white flower scarf was Liadh's. That would mean Nico had groomed a teenage girl. My stomach rolled, and I grabbed the toilet. It had to be a mistake. Nico wouldn't. He couldn't. It didn't have to be Liadh's scarf, even if it was on her bear.

But these arguments felt weak. Like I was trying to explain away disaster. Refusing to see what was right in front of me. My stomach lurched again.

Hot and uncomfortable, I touched my face to the cold bathroom tiles. I rinsed my mouth with Liadh's toothpaste, the minty-fresh taste too sharp as I stared at my shocked reflection.

In Liadh's bedroom, I picked up the bear again. She had to be around eighteen now, but she was still a girl. I pulled the scarf from the bear, half strangling it in the process, hoping against hope that I'd made a mistake in identifying the scarf.

There was no mistake. These were the same white flowers,

the same shade of forest green. I held the scarf like a rope, pulled it taut. It felt like my heart was bleeding.

The front door opened, and I heard Liadh calling to Isabelle. I wrapped the scarf around the bear's neck, and left her room.

The afternoon passed in a blur, one question turning over and over in my brain: how could I ask Liadh about the scarf? But when I went downstairs, Isabelle and Liadh were in the kitchen on a FaceTime call. From their banter, it was clear they were talking to Ava – the older daughter who was at university in Dublin – and her girlfriend. Liadh was laughing, and she'd never looked more like a teenager.

I left, mumbling goodbye while Isabelle and Liadh chatted with Ava.

Outside, the sun was too bright. I took a deep breath while I stood on the front step. I felt shaky, unsteady. The Nico I knew inside out wasn't like that. It was inconceivable he'd find an underage girl attractive, let alone act on it. But the Nico of the last year was a wild card.

Liadh was a jeans and T-shirt girl, I tried to convince myself, as I pushed my bike down the path. Liadh had taken the scarf from her mother's wardrobe, and put it on her bear. I couldn't picture her wearing scarves, and this one looked expensive.

But what if, despite all that, it *was* hers?

Still, I was feeling all wrong. My skin was too tight. Breathing had become difficult. I went to the woods, too shaky to cycle home just yet.

Leaving the bike at the entrance to the woods, I walked until my feet ached, my mouth dry with thirst. I forgot the time as I pushed on between the trees, trying to quell the turmoil inside.

Then, something stopped me. A prickle at the back of my

neck. An awareness of someone else in the woods. Some-one watching me.

I thought of the angry man with ice-blue eyes, the feel of his hands around my throat, and fear tore through me. I turned carefully on the uneven ground, searching between the trees. Whoever it was, they were still now, not making a sound.

'Who's there?' I yelled into the trees, suddenly furious. 'I'm not scared of you.'

As soon as I said it, I knew it was a lie. Since I'd felt the hands at my throat, I'd been terrified. Yesterday, walking through town, I kept seeing him, the bearded man, out of the corner of my eye. Yet when I turned to look at him head-on, there was nothing.

I turned abruptly, then started when I heard another tread from behind. I whirled around, sure I'd see him, and terror shot through me. He could finish the job he'd started.

It wasn't the ice-eyed man. Instead, Caden leaned against a tree.

'That envelope you dropped,' he said simply, 'had been opened. You'd been going through Amber's things that day. Snooping through her letters. Why?'

'You do this often?' I felt my lip curl. 'Sneak up on women alone in the woods?'

He pushed away from the tree, slowly creeping towards me. 'Amber says you don't clean for her on Thursdays. So why were you in her house? What are you looking for? Money? No, nothing that banal.'

'What are you saying? I snuck into Amber's house and cleaned it?' I scoffed. 'Find another game, Caden. This is boring.' I sounded unconvincing. Worse, I sounded afraid.

He was right in front of me now. 'But Esmie, I like this one.' He leaned in to me. 'I collect secrets. And I want yours.'

'I don't have any secrets,' I lied. 'I'm just the cleaner.'

'How do you go to language classes when you're here every day?' He dropped his voice. 'When your English is already so good?'

'Evening classes.' My hair had come undone, and I flipped it over my shoulder. 'I'm in the intermediate class, so I can be a teacher.'

Caden's eyes lit up. I could have kicked myself for answering. I'd only fed his interest.

'Maybe, but there's more. I'm sure of it. I'm going to find out, Esmie,' Caden sang quietly. 'And by trying to hide, you're just making it more fun.'

He gave a mock salute, then turned and strolled away.

I collapsed against a tree, winded, as though I'd run a race and lost. I made myself take deep breaths, slowly count to fifty. *Don't mind him. He's all bark and no bite.*

My reassurances felt hollow, though. I suspected Caden had a very nasty bite.

'You look like the ghost of Eden Hale,' a different, lower voice suddenly said. 'A poetry witch, wandering through her woods.'

My chest was heaving from my encounter with Caden, and I was tormented by images of Nico and Liadh, but I still had to stop myself from rolling my eyes. A poetry witch. Seriously? Linc needed to take a break from his ivory tower and make a trip to the real world.

He was ambling towards me, his white shirt standing out against the green of the forest, strong and beautiful as usual. But this time, I felt a burst of irritation. What a luxury it must be, to be Linc. To be obsessed with a dead poet, to have a locked safe as your greatest frustration, when some of us had to share a bedroom and work ourselves to the bone.

He frowned. 'Are you all right?'

I stared at him, trying to find the words. How should I play this? Yes, no? Suddenly, I didn't care any more.

I wasn't sure Nico deserved for me to care.

Hot tears pricked at my eyes. I felt unarranged, as though someone had reached inside, taken me apart.

'No, you're not,' Linc said, kindly. 'Come on, let's go.'

He tugged at my arm and started leading me through the woods towards Three Oaks. After a few steps, he dropped my arm, but hovered close, pointing out exposed roots and loose rocks. His voice was warm and steady. He told me that he'd been in the woods with his graduate students. That he'd taken them to visit Eden's favourite haunt, held an informal class there between the trees, and that Fiona was sure they'd summoned the ghost of Eden Hale. Then, minutes later, he'd seen me. As if they really had called Eden to the woods.

'You're so like her,' he breathed, and I wished he would just shut up about her.

At the wall, we climbed over, crossed the lane and walked to the cottage. I was shivering, though I wasn't cold.

'Amber said you're having trouble. She mentioned a boyfriend?' Linc said as we stepped into the kitchen, and I glanced at him sharply. I did not want Linc and Amber talking about me. 'It's Amber's birthday next week, we're having a *Midsummer Night's Dream*-themed party, and we hoped you could help out. But we won't impose if things are tough right now.'

'No.' I made myself plaster on a smile, tell my usual lies with that shy, sweet voice. Today the veneer was thin and hard, though – as if it could crack at any time. 'I mean, there are problems back home, but . . .' I shrugged. 'I'm here, not there. I can help with the party.'

But I wasn't sure I would be here next week. If the scarf

really was Liadh's, I'd leave. Run and lose myself somewhere far away.

'Nothing like keeping busy to take your mind off your troubles, isn't that right?' Linc handed me a glass of whiskey. He was bypassing the offer of tea today, going straight to the hard stuff.

I nodded vigorously. Then I thought about the green-and-white scarf on Liadh's teddy, and it took everything I had not to let out a sob.

'Hey, you sure you're OK?'

'I'm fine.'

'Esmie.' Linc tutted. 'You can talk to me.' Then he put an arm around me and gave a quick squeeze, and a dark, delicious pleasure streaked through me.

Suddenly, I wanted to break something.

He raised the tumbler to his lips and took a drink, his eyes on mine. 'Is it Simone?'

I nodded. In the end, everything came back to Simone.

'Do you want me to distract you?'

I nodded again.

'Maybe we can try to break into the safe again,' he said playfully. 'It can be our secret.'

Our secret.

He held my gaze a moment longer. Then he tilted his head to the door. 'Let's go in.' He grabbed the bottle of whiskey. I paused a moment, then followed. No lines had been crossed. But I sensed that if I wanted to, I could blur Linc's. That today I could shake things up, change how they fell.

It wasn't even about getting information at this point. It was because I'd been turned inside out by finding that bear. My thoughts, my senses were garbled; I wasn't sure what I wanted any more. Except, maybe, to forget.

I had to find a new way forward. Make a new plan. But today I was lonely, and tired and unsure. My heart felt black and twisted. I sat on the floor again, my back resting against the velvet bench.

Linc picked Eden's locked box again, pulled out her letters. He sank gracefully to the floor to sit beside me.

'Do you want to read?' he asked. 'Let Eden's words distract you?'

'Linc,' I said gently. 'I think you and I are distracted by different things.'

He gave a rueful grin and placed the papers on the bench. Then he lifted a hand to my cheek, and I felt that furious beating in my chest. His voice dropped, husky and low. 'Maybe there's another way to take your mind off things.'

I wasn't stupid. Linc's interest in me was because I was a canvas on which to project his obsession with the dead poet, whom he thought I so resembled. A medium to bring the ghost to life. But I didn't care.

His hand travelled down my jaw, sparking a yearning inside me. His eyes were hooded, as if he were already lost. He leaned closer, questioning, and my head spun. He closed the distance, his lips fierce on mine, and I was lost too.

He kissed me, and I felt like earth so dry it had forgotten water. I clutched my hands to his shoulders, craving the comfort of a human body. I pushed closer to him, unashamed to hide how much I, after weeks of numb detachment, *wanted*. I climbed on to his lap – then I broke away gasping.

'Sorry,' Linc said, but he didn't look sorry.

I thought of the scarf wrapped four times around Liadh's teddy's neck, and I kissed Linc again, his stubble scraping my skin. The letters slid from the seat, fluttering to the floor. Linc ignored them, pressing me closer to him, and just for a moment, I felt beautiful. Desired. As though I meant more than yellowed letters from long ago.

As though I mattered.

The bear with the scarf; the tree I was searching for. Nico's long brown fingers on Liadh's bare shoulders. It was too much. I wanted to be possessed by something else, even if only for a little while. My arms snaked around his neck, and our kisses grew more urgent.

Then Linc was pushing me down on to the hard wood, on to Eden Hale's words that crawled around the floor. I felt the crackle of old paper beneath my arm. I imagined the ink from the letters seeping on to my skin as Linc pushed against me. The words now imprinted on my body, sinking into me. I pulled at his shirt, urging it off his shoulders, then reached for his belt buckle.

'I have a confession to make,' he said thickly.

'What?' I replied, wishing he'd stay quiet.

'I didn't kiss you to distract you.' His voice was little more than a whisper. 'I kissed you because I am haunted by you.'

But it wasn't me who haunted Linc. So I said nothing.

We shed our clothes like skins. My eyes fluttered shut because I didn't want to see the adoration in his gaze, an adoration that was not for me. I felt a hand travel up my thigh, the other tracing the curve of my hip. His mouth moved down my stomach, frantic and urgent, as though he could find *her* through me. I threw back my head, lost to pleasure, but also to the dull, unyielding pain in my heart.

Reality came crashing back too quickly afterwards. I wasn't sure what tasted worse – that I'd been with a married man, or that I'd let him use me as a proxy for the dead woman he wanted so much to possess. I shook my head. It had only happened because I'd been so upset. This was an exception, one that would never happen again.

I got to my knees, watching Linc as he gathered the

poems from the floor. They were mostly undamaged, though a little creased; one was slightly torn. Linc looked at it with a kind of wonder. As if he was pleased we'd left a mark. I had a sudden memory of Amber in the woods, telling me it was unusual to be loved the way Linc loved her.

I realized then what she'd meant: it was unusual because Linc loved her second best. Eden would always be the woman who mattered most. That he wanted to possess her, Eden, entirely, which was why he seemed to be more at home here than at his actual house. Why these papers mattered so much to him. He needed to pin her down, dissect her, understand every small part of her. Amber had meant Linc's love for her was deficient.

I felt sorry for Amber. Then I didn't, because that was probably why she'd married Linc: because he was unattainable, and Amber wanted most what she couldn't have. Linc would always be out of her reach, and that's why she loved him more than anything.

Slipping my T-shirt over my head, I said, 'I have to go.'

I gathered my things, and found a new message on my phone.

I opened it and saw a screenshot of one plane ticket to Dublin in the basket, not yet purchased. I took a sharp breath. My hands were unsteady as I deleted the message.

If the scarf was Liadh's, I was utterly screwed. There would be no revenge, which meant no peace offering.

'You hungry?' Linc interrupted my swirling thoughts.

'No, I have to get back.' I could see his mind was already ticking over what he needed to do the rest of the day. He cast a longing glance at his laptop on Eden's desk. He looked invigorated, filled with ideas for his book.

He said politely, 'I could give you a lift home?'

A ride for a ride? 'I've got the bike. I'll be fine.'

I heard Linc pounding at his keyboard as I left.

Chapter Twenty-Six

Friday

The next morning, I was already awake when Fabiana stirred beneath her covers at four thirty. I'd barely slept the night before, tossing on the lumpy mattress as I thought about Liadh in Nico's arms. Of my body entangled with Linc's. My mind had conjured up relentless images all through the night, both in dreams and in my thoughts.

The morning sun crept in from the sides of the drawn curtains. Watching Fabiana form a neat wing with her eyeliner, I thought through my options.

When I'd arrived here a few weeks ago, I'd been so certain of the clarity of my mission. I was the silent observer, here only for justice. But things had changed, become murky.

Instead of watching unseen, I'd been drawn in.

Fabiana left, and I lay in bed, thinking for a long time.

I was ten minutes early to Amber's house, and so preoccupied with Liadh and Nico that I'd completely forgotten about Linc. I met him on the garden path, rose bushes blooming on either side of us. He was wearing a suit today, looking so fine, and carrying a satchel. And again, there was that disconnect between my physical response – a hunger that zinged through my body and demanded I move nearer to him – and my rational response, which was wariness. I stepped to the side, off the path on to the grass, hoping he wouldn't say anything.

'Esmie,' Linc said. It was a different voice than he'd used with me before. It was a voice that announced an intimacy. A connection. Guilt closed around my throat like a hand. I wanted him to hurry on and go. I wanted him to reach for me and press me against his strong body.

'Hello, Linc,' I replied, and then, my stomach dipping as I looked at the door, I added, 'hello, Amber.'

Amber nodded, then disappeared inside. Linc said, 'I'm in Dublin for the afternoon. I won't see you at Three Oaks later.'

I felt his gaze on me as he lifted his satchel into the Jeep. Then I remembered Ceanna, and how this evening was my chance to do what she'd ordered. I groaned inwardly.

I cleaned listlessly, unable to take my mind off Nico and Liadh. Mopping the kitchen floor, I froze. Suddenly, I couldn't pretend any more. I couldn't ignore the churning in my gut. The anxiety squatting in my throat.

So I stopped. Leaning the mop against the side of a chair, I looked around and thought, *Enough. I've done enough.*

I had an urge to be outside, so I left the kitchen. I walked down the gravel path, past the summer kitchen and through the orchard. I saw a wooden gate in the stone wall, and I pulled it open to find a lane on the other side, fields beyond. I walked a little way down the lane, seeing another gate, one to Isabelle's back garden.

The gate opened easily. The back garden to number three was smaller than Amber's, the house set further back from the road at the front.

Near the gate was an ivy-covered wooden shed tucked into the wall. The grass around it was overgrown, and it looked like no one ever went there.

But maybe Isabelle did. Maybe this was her secret office.

The bolt was oiled and I opened the door easily, finding giant broken pots, weed poison, a few garden tools on shelves.

I crouched down, pulling back the heavy cream canvas, then the box tucked well beneath the wide bottom shelf. The box that I'd read about in Isabelle's notebook.

Inside was a collection of wigs, coloured contact lenses, glasses and sunglasses. I reached inside, feeling around, and at the bottom I found a phone. I powered it on. I tapped on the email icon, seeing three new messages. Ignoring the unread messages, I opened a few at random. They were all orders, mostly for sedatives, painkillers and uppers. One from a few weeks ago caught my eye. It was from Fibear77, confirming a meeting time at Begley's.

It was irrefutable proof that what I'd read in the notebook was true.

I wasn't sure how I felt about that. I didn't want to feel sorry for Isabelle. It was easier to hate her for selling to Nico when I didn't understand why she did it.

Gathering evidence, I took pictures going back two weeks. But there was nothing to show that Isabelle Blake, the good doctor's wife, rather than Alex780421, was involved. She'd covered her tracks well.

Closing the email, I checked the contacts, seeing that only one number had been saved to the phone. Little Rose. I programmed the number into my phone before returning everything exactly as I'd found it.

Since the discovery of Liadh's bear, everything was confused. Uncertain. I had to track down this woman Isabelle referred to as the Rose. If she was Nico's friend, she could help me understand what had happened to him. Why he'd been led so badly astray. This was my last grasp at closure.

I bolted the shed door, then made for the house. There was no point in continuing this charade if Nico had groomed Liadh. But there was one other person I had to talk to before I left.

She was in the kitchen, wearing her school uniform, and she started when she saw me at the door.

'Can I come in?' I asked.

Liadh frowned. 'Yeah. Did you forget something?'

I nodded. The words were stuck in my throat. I took a deep breath. 'I noticed a scarf on your bear yesterday. It's really pretty. Where did you get it? I've been looking for one just like it.'

My explanation sounded lame. I failed in my attempt to pass off the words as casual.

'Scarf?' she said, confused.

'Green, with small white flowers. Silk,' I said, anxiety knotting my stomach as I waited for the confirmation I dreaded. 'The bear is wearing it.'

'Oh, that.' She shrugged, not interested. 'I think it's my mam's? Has to be, because Ava wouldn't wear a scarf if you paid her. It's not mine, anyway.'

Violent relief rushed into my body. Then I realized that, even if it wasn't hers, Liadh had it now. She might have had it when Nico was here. 'Have you had it long?'

'What do you mean?' Liadh was staring at me. She looked at me as if she'd noticed me, really noticed, for the first time. Her head tilted as she studied my face. 'Funny, you seemed really familiar there. Just for a second.'

I frowned at her, wondering what she meant. Was she baiting me? I didn't think so. There was something softer about Liadh today. Kinder. Or maybe she just appeared more vulnerable to me because of Nico.

'I was hoping it's still in the shops,' I improvised. 'Maybe I could get one too.'

'You couldn't afford it,' Liadh said bluntly. 'Look, Mam has loads of scarves. She's totally forgotten about that one. I found it stuffed in the hall closet two months ago when I was making a costume for a party, and then it ended up on the bear.'

Two months. After Nico had left. The relief was hot and liquid, warming me inside.

'You can have it.'

'I can't,' I said, horrified for several reasons.

'I won't use it, and Mam doesn't care.' She stood up. 'Wait here.' Then she disappeared up the stairs.

I shut my eyes, letting it all sink in.

It was Isabelle. She'd been Nico's lover all along. She'd roped Nico into her illegal business, and then into her bed.

Isabelle had lied. She'd hurt Nico, causing him to lose everything.

I would destroy Isabelle. The need to hurt her, to take something valuable from her, burned in my chest.

There was a sound at the front door, and I moved towards it. I could see the outline through the frosted glass, and the height and shape of her looked like Isabelle – the black of her jacket, the white of her blouse. Something thudded on the other side of the door, and I wondered if Isabelle had lost her keys.

I pulled the door open, and Isabelle stumbled inside. My sharp gasp was audible. Her muddied blouse was just about covered by the jacket. The top buttons were missing, revealing a teal lacy bra. There were scratches and bruising on her cheek.

She put a finger to her lips before I could say anything more. Her hands were shaking, huge tremors that made me understand why she hadn't been able to get her key into the lock. She was in shock.

'Where's Liadh?' she whispered.

I inclined my head to the stairs, where Liadh was already bounding down.

'Go in there,' I whispered, gesturing to the downstairs toilet. Then I met Liadh in the kitchen.

She reached out the scarf, saying, 'You're right. It is pretty. It will look really nice on you.'

I frowned at her. Why was she being so nice to me suddenly? I thanked her, slipping the scarf into my shirt pocket. As I left, I glanced back to see Liadh at the kitchen table, her headphones on.

Opening the bathroom door, I saw Isabelle leaning against the wall, wincing as she touched a rib. I studied Nico's lover, this tall, self-contained woman. *I should leave her here, let her daughter find her bruised and hurt.*

But Liadh had been kind to me just now, and I felt a lingering protectiveness towards the teenage girl.

'Let's get you upstairs,' I said, reaching out a hand to help her. It was muscle memory; the times when I'd slipped my arms around Nico, rested his weight against mine. When he was both drunk and high, trying to blot out what he'd lost.

Isabelle. He'd lost Isabelle.

Still, I let her rest her weight on me, and we silently made our way up the stairs. My heart felt strange, as though there was something dark lodged inside. I was holding up the woman who'd destroyed Nico. The woman who'd cost us everything.

I would let Isabelle think that freedom was within her reach – that's when I would take it from her. She might feel she was trapped now, but it was nothing compared to how tight her cage would feel after she'd missed her escape. Her every move would be monitored by Paul's cameras.

I shut the door to Isabelle's room.

She sank to the bed. Her movements were stiff, pained, as she eased herself out of her jacket.

'How were you hurt?' I said, taking the jacket from where it caught at her wrists. Isabelle shook her head. 'I need to understand how bad it is,' I press. 'If you need a doctor.'

'I have a doctor.' Her voice was hoarse, but I could hear the bitterness in her words. Her eyes caught mine, and then she sighed.

'I was mugged.'

'Where?'

She hesitated, and I could see that she was thinking through her story. 'Down on the river walk. Near the old pier.'

She wasn't telling me the whole truth, I was sure of that. I didn't for a second think that this was some random mugging. From her shifty body language, the way she wouldn't look me in the eye, I was sure that this was a drop-off turned bad.

'Did they hurt you?' I said.

'Pushed me to the ground, that's all.' She pressed her lips together, which told me that wasn't all.

She was looking directly ahead, and when I followed her gaze, I saw us in the large mirror with its gilded edges. Me standing over her like an awkward angel in leggings. Large purple bruises were forming on her ribs, as though she'd been kicked there.

'I didn't want Liadh to see me like this.'

'Your face.' I nodded to the mark on her jawline.

'I can hide it.'

Of course she could. I was learning a lot about how very well Isabelle could hide.

'Why are you here?' she said suddenly, her eyes suspicious.

'I forgot these in the utility.' I dug in my shirt pocket, my fingers brushing the soft silk there. I pulled my hand away as if the fabric could burn, grabbing my earphones. I held them up for Isabelle to see. 'But I'd better get back to Woodland House.'

I turned for the door. Isabelle said, 'Esmie,' and when I glanced back she added, 'you really helped me there. Thank you.'

I smiled at her. Let her think she was safe with me. She had no idea what was coming.

The cottage was empty this afternoon, and I was glad for the silence because it gave me room to think. My conversation with Liadh had changed everything.

Not only was my plan for justice back on track, but I now knew who had to be held to account. I'd thought I'd be elated when I worked out who she was, but instead I felt tired and injured, as though I'd run too far, too hard, and the only way forward was to limp on.

While there was no longer any joy in the prospect of revenge on Isabelle, it had to be done. If only because it was my way back home, the peace offering that would allow us to start over.

One thing was certain – Isabelle would not be escaping her life.

After I'd boxed up old curtains, towels and sheets, I went into Eden's study, curled up on the day bed, and thought about the unpleasant task that awaited me that evening. This was the downside to my plan still being intact – I had to do what Ceanna had demanded of me, or risk having her tell Amber and Isabelle that I'd stolen Amber's ring.

It was only a few pictures, I consoled myself. No one other than Ceanna and Amber would see them.

I stayed in the cottage and heated a tin of soup Linc or Malachy must have left in the kitchen. For the first time since the night I ran, I felt oddly comfortable. It was wrong that the cottage was empty; houses needed people to live in them. Sitting in the old armchair, I took out my phone and pulled up the Rose's number. Without thinking what I'd say, I pressed call. The phone rang for too long before I hit end.

From my bag, I took the small digital camera that Ceanna had given me. I'd get a few shots of Amber and Caden kissing. It would be over quickly. Then I'd immediately hand it over to Ceanna and forget this ever happened.

At eight thirty, I made my way through the woods to Woodland House.

Seeing the driveway gate at number three slide open, I pressed myself into the hedgerow. Paul's sleek sedan pulled into the road. Isabelle was beside him, expressionless. In the back seat, Liadh was looking down at something. Most likely her phone.

When the car disappeared around the bend, I went down the side of Amber's house to the back lane and slipped in through the gate there.

At the summer kitchen, I paused. The outside table was set for two, the meal half eaten. The door to the inside dining room was ajar. I inched closer.

The room was simply furnished with an oak table and chairs, a sideboard by the window. In the middle was Amber, naked and blindfolded. Her wrists were wrapped together with red rope and tied to a ceiling beam. The candles in the candelabra were lit.

I breathed in sharply. Caden strolled languidly from the other side of the room, holding a red candle. He stopped behind her, gently brushing her hair away from her neck. Then he dripped a line of wax down her sternum, murmuring, 'Do you like that?'

'Yes.'

'Do you want more?'

'Yes,' she breathed again. Caden paused, then dripped wax between her collarbone and breast. She let out a low murmur. He bent to kiss it, and I lifted the camera and clicked. He moved the candle to the soft skin of her inner thigh. I clicked again.

I took five photographs, none of them ambiguous. Feeling like a dirty voyeur, I edged back. I'd only taken one step, though, when Caden glanced up. His eyes held mine for an endless moment, and the venom in them made my knees weak. He blew out the candle with a loud puff. Then he looked back to Amber, dismissing me.

I knew he'd come for me later, though. I pushed down the urgent, rising dread – that was tomorrow's problem.

I hurried through the orchard, my heart dark and loud. I didn't like Amber, but no one deserved this. I hated that I'd watched. That I'd raised the camera and stolen their intimacy. One of Mama Bear's old sayings came to mind: *Before you embark on a journey of revenge, dig two graves.*

I'd come here to hurt Nico's lover, the woman who'd betrayed him. But what if I ended up hurting myself? What if, at the end of all this, it was me who was irreparably damaged? That's if I wasn't already.

In the back lane, I paused. The Blakes were out this evening. Only the front gate had a camera, and I was nearly finished reading her notebook.

I stepped through the back gate at number three.

Not much longer now, I told myself. The end was in sight. I could take everything to Paul now. I could tell him what Isabelle had been doing. She'd risked his professional reputation, his licence. But what if that made him so angry that he divorced her?

No: Paul was the Danger. I could see in him a violent need to control. Divorce would be too easy; it would be giving Isabelle what she wanted. That wouldn't be an option for a man like Paul. He'd want to punish her, assert his authority.

I went down the side of the house to the back and tried the doors until I found the utility unlocked. As I climbed the stairs to the upstairs sitting room, I thought about how Isabelle had leaned against me as she touched a hand gingerly to her ribs. The bruises on her face. What had happened to her?

Isabelle had clearly been afraid, and Isabelle's fear was my currency.

I retrieved the notebook and this time, I turned to the end.

17.

From the driveway, the woman watched the Cleaner cycling to the house next door. She couldn't pinpoint why the Cleaner bothered her; maybe it was those dark staring eyes or the silent way she moved. The Cleaner seemed familiar somehow, her face brought a nagging awareness that the woman couldn't place.

A bitter laugh escaped as I read those words. I bothered Isabelle? By the time I was done, I was going to haunt her every waking minute.

Lost in thought, the woman didn't notice when the man with pale blue eyes and a short beard entered the driveway. She didn't know he was there until he spoke the words that made her freeze.

'Where is Alex?' He took something from his pocket, pushing a square card towards her. 'I know she lives here. I have a message for her.'

Only after he'd gone did she look at the photograph in her hands.

Driving to the old pier, the woman couldn't get the collarbones out of her head, how pronounced they were. The gaunt, exhausted face.

The woman was out of breath by the time she reached the meeting place, a sheltered spot between the trees. A young man, strong and muscular, waited there. And that was when she realized that in her distraction, she'd forgotten to put on the wig and contacts.

He demanded to see what was inside the bag. With a shaky exhale the woman reached in, bringing out a handful of pills and injectables.

Without warning, he snapped a picture with his phone. The steroids in her hands. The woman, without her disguise.

She lunged forward, but he held the phone out of reach, laughing.

The woman glowered at him. She'd known there would be risks. She thought she'd taken the necessary precautions. But the man looking for Alex had unsettled her. She'd made mistakes.

Frustrated, she ran at him, trying to get his phone. He grabbed her shirt and she heard the thin fabric tear. Fear bloomed through her as murderous rage crossed his face. He shoved hard. She twisted as she landed, scraping her jaw on a stone. Her bag dropped, scattering her purse, a lipstick, into the grass. He towered over her as she tried to get up, demanding that she supply him Rohypnol.

When she refused, a heavy boot landed in her ribs.

He picked up her purse and pulled out her driver's licence. Her heart hollowed out as she watched him pocket the card with her real name and address.

When he left, she slowly got to her feet. Terror gnawed at her stomach.

She would never supply anything that could harm another woman. Then she remembered that picture of the Rose, and it felt like her heart was tearing in two.

She had harmed another woman.

She had to move her plan forward. She didn't have enough money. She wasn't ready to say goodbye to her mother. But she had no choice.

The woman decided. She would hide this notebook in the older daughter's wardrobe to find when she came home. She would leave at Midsummer, during the party. While the Danger was distracted, she would slip away quietly. She would leave her car near a cliff with a two-word note for the Danger: I'm sorry.

The woman would die.

The woman would live.

Then, at the bottom of the page, in a hurried scrawl, Isabelle had written:

My darling, darling girls. Remember how I read fairy tales to you when you were little? Here's one last story for you, the most important one I could ever tell you. I wrote it in the hope that one day you might understand. I have to leave now, but I will find my way back to you girls. I love you and I carry your—

The sound of the front door opening startled me. Isabelle's voice carried upstairs. I froze, petrified, then dropped the book in the drawer. From downstairs came the bustling of jackets and shoes being removed.

Locking the drawer, I heard footsteps climb the stairs. I looked around wildly for a hiding place, then darted behind the door. There was a furious rushing in my ears.

Why the hell had they come home so quickly?

The tread on the stairs was light. It stopped at the upstairs sitting room, way too close to me. Only the oak door lay between us. Steadying my breath, I pressed myself into the wall.

'Mam, are you missing a statue?' a voice I didn't recognize called downstairs.

'Ava, don't shout.' Isabelle sounded fondly exasperated and not far away. 'Yes, I gave one away. Months ago.'

Ava. They'd collected their older daughter from the station.

'You gave away one of your precious statues? To whom?'

There was a pause, then Isabelle sighed. She was on the other side of the door now. 'Someone who'd given me something invaluable.' She sounded wistful.

Given her something invaluable? I burned with incredulity. It took all my strength not to push back the door and leap at her throat.

I shut my eyes, pressing harder into the wall as I tried to will myself calm.

Ava went into her room, and I heard the thunk of a bag hitting the floor. Then both women walked downstairs, Ava talking brightly as if to chase off the shadow she'd sensed.

I needed to get out of here.

I listened. Paul's deep voice playfully chided Liadh. It was coming from one of the reception rooms at the front of the house.

I started carefully down the stairs. Liadh and Ava were laughing while Paul admonished them with faux outrage.

I'd never felt the brokenness of my own home life more acutely than at that moment when I crept down the stairs. What had I become? I, too, had had a family once; one with games and laughter on a Friday night. Now, I was this miserable creature, slinking in the shadows.

Unseen, even when I was right there. Unheard, even when I spoke. Just the cleaner. Then I remembered Isabelle's notebook and how deep the cracks in this family ran. Within days, it would all break apart. And I could go home.

A fierce longing gripped me. I needed to be home. I felt almost feverish with desperation to return to my place in the world. I wanted to be in a valley beneath a high sky painted in the richest blues. In our little house with the giant aloe in the cement and dry grass yard, surrounded by the chain-link fence topped with razor wire. I wanted to step inside and smell onions fried in spices. I wanted to close myself in the arms of the people I'd left behind.

At the bottom of the stairs, I waited. Listened. There was Paul's smugly indulgent voice, the cajoling of his daughters. The girls teasing their mother. They were all in the living room. One big happy family.

Quietly, I eased towards the kitchen. I reached for the door, glancing back as I opened it. Framed in the late golden rays of the sun was Liadh. She watched me, her eyes wide with surprise.

'What the hell?'

I couldn't move. My mind cast around for an excuse, but I couldn't think of anything.

'You OK there, Liadh?' Paul called from inside the living room.

Endless seconds ticked by. Liadh watched me.

'Liadh?' Paul called again.

'All good. Just a message from Kayleigh.' Liadh didn't take her eyes off me.

I mouthed 'thank you' and, still holding her gaze, I opened the door and slipped into the kitchen.

I left through the back gate. I didn't understand why Liadh had let me pass, but she had, and I was grateful. Maybe it was a small rebellion; it couldn't be easy having Paul and Isabelle as parents. They both held on so tightly, in different ways, and I suspected that Liadh might be a little smothered in that house.

Feeling lighter than I had in a long time, I ran through the tall grass in the narrow lane, trailing my fingers through the meadowsweet and cow parsley. I was assailed by colour and scent, a happy banjo picking in my heart. The night sun danced between the trees.

I'd done it.

I'd found the woman who'd betrayed Nico, who'd made him lose his scholarship. The same person who'd enabled his addiction.

I'd discovered what she cared about.

And now I would make sure that she, entirely and irretrievably, lost what she most wanted.

Chapter Twenty-Seven

I made my way to Ceanna's house to deliver the camera. I didn't want to take it back to my small, shared room. Didn't want its accusing eye staring at me all weekend.

It was pushing ten but still bright, as if the day had no intention of giving up. Beyond the bend were more houses, and I wondered what people were doing behind closed doors. Who was cheating on their husband, maybe engaging in wax play? Who was selling prescription drugs to bored housewives and students? Who denied their wife a bank account, who was in love with his wife's dead aunt? Who lifted her red dress as she danced in dingy bars, revelling in being watched?

All of them were one thing on the outside and something selfish and shrivelled on the inside. I was glad this was coming to an end. I had nothing in common with these people. I couldn't wait to leave them behind.

At Ceanna's, I knocked on the door. Arvind, the other lodger, let me in as he was going out, saying that she was in her bedroom.

'Ceanna?' I pushed open the door. She was standing at the window wearing a short silk nightdress. On her tiptoes, peering out into the back garden at the ivy-covered wall and the whitethorn hedging, she was oblivious to my presence in the room.

I crossed the room, pausing halfway. The way she was standing, the readiness of her posture – on tiptoe, hand gripping the curtain – made me stop in my tracks, the hair on the back of my neck rising.

'Ceanna?' I said. 'What are you doing?'

Ceanna turned to me, her face troubled. 'I think they saw me outside the cottage.'

'Who saw you?' I noticed how wild her eyes were, and my alarm ratcheted up. Her gaze roamed the room, unable to fix on anything. This close, I could see the soil stains on her nightdress and on her legs. The dirt ringed around her fingernails. It looked like Ceanna had been out digging.

'The professors.' She squinted at me as if she was struggling to focus. 'They were hiding in the woods. Near Eden's spot.'

'Do you mean Linc?' I was confused.

Ceanna stepped towards me, swaying, and I moved to steady her. She grabbed my wrists with surprising strength. 'They want to come in.' She spoke urgently, squeezing my wrists tighter. 'But I tricked them.'

'Let go.' I tried to pull out of her grip, but it only made her hold on. 'Ceanna, you need to let go.'

'Eden?' Ceanna looked at me with confusion.

'Maybe you should rest.'

Her hair was knotted, the light brown tipped with dirt, as though she'd been lying in soil.

'You're here,' she said, touching my face. I realized how much her hands were shaking. 'You have a halo, so beautiful.'

I helped her on to the bed, arranging the pillows beneath her.

'Tell me a story,' Ceanna said. 'I've always wished you'd tell me a bedtime story.'

'I can tell you a story,' I said, checking her darting eyes. 'What do you want me to read?' I'd watch her, I decided, worry knotting in my stomach. If she worsened, I'd get help. The thought of going back to Amber's made the knots tighten. But I'd have no choice.

'One of your stories, of course,' she said. 'Tell me the one about the sweetheart.'

'Uhm.' I racked my brain but it was late, and the details of the story about the disaster bride and her villainous sweetheart were all jumbled in my head.

'I kept them safe for you, you know.' Ceanna forgot about the story.

'Kept what safe?'

Ceanna paled. 'Going to be sick.' She fumbled with the covers, but I had the wastepaper bin ready. This wasn't my first rodeo. Ceanna was sick into the bin, then lay back, feverish.

'I'll get you some water,' I said.

She clutched my arm. 'Don't let them get it.' Her skin was blotched and pale. She smelled of earth and sweat. Then she groaned, a low pained sound.

'Ceanna?' I said more frantically, as her eyes fluttered and a spasm jerked her body. 'I'll bring that water.' I was afraid now.

'Eden,' she breathed, still holding my arm. 'They're at Three Oaks.'

'It's Esmie.' I placed a hand on her forehead, but she had no fever. 'Who's at Three Oaks?'

'The keys. I buried them under the swing. The professors read my mind and stole the combination to my safe, so I had to hide them.' A sly look came into her eyes. 'So that *he* couldn't have it. He took Amber from us. I won't let him have you too.'

She was delirious, I realized with some relief.

'Going to be sick again.' Ceanna reached for the bin.

I helped her, then smoothed back her hair as she settled restlessly into her pillow. I eyed the armchair grimly. It looked like that's where I was sleeping tonight.

I cleaned the bin and returned it to the bed, then went to the kitchen for water. As I filled the glass, a light rap sounded at the door. A voice called out, 'Hello, anyone home?'

'Linc?' I called, and he appeared in the kitchen moments later. 'What are you doing here?'

'Esmie?' His brow creased with confusion. 'I'm looking for Caden. Have you seen him?'

I had no idea how to answer that.

'I came back earlier than expected, and while driving I had a brilliant idea for a paper and thought I'd see if Cade was up for a drink.'

'He's out,' I said. 'Linc, I'm glad you're here. Ceanna's sick and she's acting really strange.' I knew there was no love lost between him and Ceanna, but he had to hear the agitation in my voice.

'Ceanna's sick?' Linc froze, then stepped towards her room. 'What's wrong with her?'

'She seems delirious. Confused. I think she was out wandering the woods.'

Linc's face creased with alarm, and he strode down the passage towards Ceanna's bedroom. I followed, holding the glass of water. Ceanna was staring up at the ceiling. Linc leaned over her, checking her pulse, her colour.

'I'll stay here with her,' he said, taking the water from me. 'If she gets worse, I'll take her to A&E.'

'You'd do that?' My voice betrayed my surprise.

'I'm not a monster, Esmie,' Linc chided gently. 'We may

have our problems, but Ceanna is family.' He checked the time. 'You should head out if you want to catch the light.'

I hesitated. I badly wanted to get out of The Woodlands. It felt close and claustrophobic tonight. But it seemed wrong leaving Ceanna with the man she despised when she was so weak.

'Linc,' Ceanna groaned. 'I feel so strange. I think I'm dying.'

'I'm here,' he said, his voice unexpectedly gentle. 'You're not dying on my watch.' He glanced at me. 'Don't worry. I'll take good care of her. My dad's a GP – I'll give him a ring.'

Suddenly exhausted, I turned to leave. I was relieved to be going home, relieved that someone else was looking after Ceanna. But I couldn't shake the unease I felt.

I'd left my bike at Three Oaks. The sun was finally beginning to descend, so I hurried down the road towards the woods, eager to get through them before darkness set in. I'd just passed Woodland House when I heard the sound of the gate. Glancing back, I saw Caden leave Linc and Amber's house, whistling as he walked with his hands in his pockets.

I stepped back, hoped he couldn't see me. I couldn't be sure he hadn't.

It was darker between the trees, and I cursed myself for not retrieving the bike earlier. I hesitated, wondering if I should go back and take the road to Three Oaks. But it was more than twice the distance so I went on, picking up my pace.

I checked over my shoulder, making sure that Caden wasn't on my tail. I jogged through the woods, my feet following the now familiar path. The twilit woods felt ominous, the trees seeming to press closer. I thought I heard the sound of footsteps and came to an abrupt halt. Breath heavy, I turned to see if Caden lurked on the darkening path. But when I listened again, it sounded lighter, like the rustling of leaves – or the barely there tread of a dead woman poet. Of a forest villainess. I ran on, faster, and was relieved when I finally climbed over the stone wall.

I went inside the gate at Three Oaks, where my bike waited in the back garden. Pushing the bike back to the gate, I paused at the sight of the wooden swing beneath the large oak tree. Just minutes ago, Ceanna had talked about this swing. She'd said she'd buried the keys beneath it.

The ground beneath the swing was indeed freshly disturbed. With a flutter in my stomach, I put my hands into the soft earth and began to dig.

It didn't take long before I touched metal, and I breathed out a triumphant curse. They hadn't been buried very deeply at all. I reached into the soil and pulled out a ring with three long keys.

Linc was right. Ceanna had hidden them from him. It was both petulant and admirable, her desire to thwart him.

He wore his obsession on his sleeve, making it easy to manipulate him. It was almost a shame that Linc wasn't Nico's lying lover, because he would be the easiest to get revenge on.

I closed my hands over the keys. I'd be leaving in a few days, and this would be my parting gift to Linc. A little something for him to remember me by. As guilt-ridden as it was, I had found some warmth with him.

I dropped the keys into my bag and covered up the hole. I smoothed the ground, trying to make it look as though it had never been touched.

Chapter Twenty-Eight

Weekend

The next morning, I tried calling the Rose again, but her phone rang unanswered. I was eager to speak to someone who'd known Nico away from The Woodlands. I always felt I could breathe better when I left. I wondered what it had been like for Nico when this close, tightly drawn place had been his home. Did he feel it pressing on him as I did? Had he found reprieve outside?

Maybe he had, with the Rose.

Around midday, I cycled into the city centre for a coffee, then walked along the river and tried the Rose again. The fourth time I rang, a man answered, barking an unfriendly, 'Who is this?'

I stayed silent, taken aback by the man's growl.

'I said, who is this?' he insisted.

'I'm looking for . . . I'm sorry, I can't make out the name.' I remembered Isabelle writing that she wore a necklace with her name spelled out. Little Rose. I took a gamble. 'I think it's . . . Rosie?'

'You're looking for Róisín?' he barked. 'What do you want?'

Instinct told me to hedge. This was my only chance to talk openly about Nico. I hoped she could give me an insight into the events leading up to his departure. What exactly had happened to make Isabelle betray him. I knew where the blame lay, but I didn't know yet how everything had unravelled.

'That's right. Róisín. I'm from Universal Courier Services – I need your Eircode for a delivery,' I said quickly. I'd once overheard a courier calling Amber about hers, so I knew it wasn't an unusual request.

'If it's flowers, keep them.'

'It's not flowers.'

The man sighed and rattled off the seven-digit code, and ended the call abruptly. Marvelling at how easy that had been, I called up a map, entered the code, and within a minute had directions. Then, retrieving Amber's bike, I set off to Róisín's house.

When I reached my destination thirty minutes later, I halted at the many cars parked outside. Róisín clearly had a party or barbecue on today, but maybe that would make it easier to talk to her. I could slip inside, lose myself in the crowd, and approach Róisín when her guard was down. No one would notice me.

I chained the bike to a pillar, then edged nearer. To set my mind at ease, I confirmed online that Róisín did indeed translate to 'little rose'. But before I could put my phone away, another message landed.

I'm going to kill you with my bare hands.

I walked up the path, seeing through the window a room filled with people, but I felt strangely detached. Light-headed.

And I'm going to enjoy doing it.

My hands were slick with sweat when I stuffed the phone into my skirt pocket. Through the windows, I saw that the house was packed. A pair of men stood outside smoking in silence.

I went up the path, keeping my head down as I eased between people in the front hall. I was approaching the living room when I noticed the sombre tones of their outfits. The muted colours. I felt a deep trepidation stepping inside the living room. Vases of white roses covered every surface, the scent cloying. I heard muffled sobbing. Then I saw the casket.

My eyes widened at the long wooden box in the middle of an ordinary sitting room. I'd never seen anything like it. My only encounter with death, the murder we'd hushed up, had been neatly contained in the expected ritual of ninety minutes in church. A cremation afterwards that no one attended.

This – the quiet weeping, the stony faces of people sitting on leather couches as mourners approached the coffin – was utterly removed from anything I knew. I was wrong-footed, out of place, and it made me clumsy, stumbling as I took another step forward.

'This way, my dear,' a woman said kindly, gesturing me towards the casket. More roses on either side.

I froze, not yet ready to confront death. I had a sudden overwhelming certainty that if I stepped forward and looked inside the casket, I'd see Nico.

I shut my eyes, thinking of Mama Bear that night weeks ago, frantically pulling out Nico's cheap suitcase, saying, 'She's gone mad. You have to go. She won't rest until she has your blood.'

Maybe I wouldn't see Nico. Maybe I'd see myself.

'Go on,' the kindly woman urged. 'Say goodbye to Róisín. Did you work with her at the boutique?'

Róisín.

I whirled away from the sitting room, stumbled blindly down the passage. All the doors, made of dark wood, were shut. I reached for one, pushing it open. I needed a moment to catch my breath. I hadn't come here expecting death. But it had been waiting for me.

I'd found the Rose – in a casket in her sitting room.

I was in a bedroom. The curtains were drawn, but there was enough light to see a large floor-length mirror with a giant crack as if a fist or stone had hit it. I drifted to the mirror, my face blotted out by the web of faults that ran through the surface. I turned to the wall and saw a wedding photograph beside the bed.

The couple were familiar, but also not. I'd seen them before, but different versions of them, and never together. In her simple white dress, she should have been glowing. But there was a sadness in her beautifully made-up face. Her perfect smoky eye, which I remembered from the night at Begley's.

I'd seen Róisín there that night. She'd been walking down the passage to the toilets, and I'd noticed her rose perfume and how thin she was. Had we spoken? I tried to remember. She'd dropped something, a small brown paper bag. And then, in the toilets, I'd seen Isabelle counting cash. Róisín must have bought from Isabelle minutes before I went down.

I studied the picture again. She wasn't as gaunt and hollowed out as when I'd seen her. She'd changed between her wedding and the night at Begley's.

And the man beside her had changed too. In the picture he was laughing, his eyes filled with light and hope.

'What are you doing here?'

I turned to see the man from the picture standing right behind me. The bearded man with ice-blue eyes.

I stepped back.

'You came here.' His voice was thick with loathing. 'You fucking dared come here.'

I turned, bolting to the window, but he was faster. He grabbed the back of my shirt, shoving me against the wall. My head bumped the edge of the window frame, and sharp pain chased through my body. I regained my balance, but he hauled me towards him by the arm. With both hands on my shoulders, he shook me hard. His eyes were blazing. The anger I'd sensed from him before was out in full sway.

'You came to pay your respects?' he sneered. 'When you put her in that coffin?'

'Stop,' I said, the room spinning around me. 'Please.'

'Do you know what it's like,' he said, his hands moving from my shoulders to my neck, 'to see someone you care about waste away? To watch her slowly die?' Two large hands closed around my throat. He was going to kill me. He would finish the job he'd started in Isabelle's kitchen.

'Yes,' I said, breathless. 'I do.' I clawed at his hands.

He must have seen something in my face, because his hands dropped slightly and confusion clouded his eyes.

'I'm not Alex.' I squeezed out the words. 'I'm just the cleaner. You got it all wrong.'

'If you're not Alex, who is?' he growled, still not releasing me.

Should I tell him it was Isabelle? He would, for sure, make her pay. If he went back to number three, even one more time, he would probably figure it out. But I wasn't going to make it easier for him.

Looking into his violently cold eyes, I knew the anger that pumped through his veins. He wanted to lash out, because he thought that would ease his pain. But he was volatile, and I couldn't trust that he wouldn't run riot through my carefully laid trap. It would be wiser to keep this man at arm's length.

'I'm trying to find out. That's why I'm here. Because Róisín isn't the only one Alex hurt.'

He read it in my eyes, the pain and heartbreak we'd both endured. Then he let me go, devastation folding his body.

'She died a few days ago.' He sank to the bed, hunched over.

'I'm sorry,' I said, feeling a lump in my throat. It felt like my misery was reflected in this hard, cold man. This man who frightened me. There was a kinship between us, whether I liked it or not.

'She'd lost so much weight. I didn't know until it was too late that she'd been taking a dangerous appetite suppressant. Róisín was getting sicker and sicker, but she couldn't stop. If Alex hadn't sold her those pills, Róisín would still be alive.'

His shoulders shuddered, and I realized he was crying.

'I found her stash of pills and made her throw them away. I was terrified she'd buy more, so I tracked her phone. The next morning, she called the same number three times. Then, around ten in the morning, she visited a house in The Woodlands, I don't know which one. It was a Tuesday, at the end of May.

The day I started working at Isabelle's.

'Later, when she got really bad, I knocked at every door until I found you. The way you'd dodged my questions, your shifty demeanour – I was sure it had to be you.' He looked up at me, his eyes wide and urgent. I drew back, away from his intensity.

'Did you see Róisín around The Woodlands? She drove a silver Toyota.'

I'd thought Isabelle had argued with the bearded man in the Toyota. I'd been wrong; she'd been arguing with his wife.

I nodded. 'I saw it parked outside the woods one morning. But I didn't see your wife.'

He reached into the bedside table and retrieved an old blank envelope. On the top was a number and the name Alex scribbled across. 'I found this with the pills I threw out. I called the number, but it went straight to voicemail.'

I exhaled. Isabelle knew. She knew that Róisín had formed an addiction, and she still sold to her. The burning anger I already felt towards Isabelle flared.

'It's not fair.' My words came out in a rush. 'We've lost the people we loved most, and they go on like it means nothing. Planning their travel, having Midsummer parties, shopping. They do whatever they want, not feeling this soul-destroying emptiness inside them.' I bit my lip, immediately regretting my outburst.

He studied me, understanding in his eyes. The silence was intense, too long. This was an unwelcome kinship, for both of us.

Eventually he gave a weak smile, saying, 'Parties, huh?'

'A *Midsummer Night's Dream* costume party. This Friday. No expense spared. I'd invite you, but I'm just the cleaner.'

After a moment, he said, 'I guess I should get back out there.'

'Sorry I gate-crashed your wife's wake.'

The urgency was back in his eyes, and I knew this man was in no way done with his own revenge. 'If you find out who Alex is, then please—'

'I'll do what I can.' It was the truth, but also not. 'Don't go back to number three. There's a camera at the front gate. The man who lives there watches. He saw you. He'll put up more cameras before too long.'

The man nodded. I made for the door, then stopped and turned.

'Did Róisín ever talk about a man called Nico?'

'Nico?' He looked up at me, and I saw again how grief had transformed his face. 'Yeah, I remember Nico. Róisín met him in the library. They'd sat near each other and got chatting.'

They'd met at the library. Yet another detail of Nico's life that I had no idea about. He'd stopped sharing things with me long before he came back, and the pain of that was relentless.

'Did you know him?' I said, but the man shook his head.

'Róisín mentioned him a few times. Said he was having an affair with an older woman. She thought it was a recipe for disaster.'

Chapter Twenty-Nine

Weekend

I left Róisín's house, but I took with me the agitation that had balled up when I entered her sitting room.

I cycled away on autopilot, haunted by that heavy wooden casket in the blue and grey living room. The day had clouded over, matching my mood. I pedalled through town, and back to the house. But outside, I saw Fabiana's boyfriend arrive with a bunch of flowers and I couldn't go in. I couldn't face my room and silently seethe while Fabiana and her boyfriend enacted a cute romantic comedy. Dark clouds in the distance threatened rain, but I didn't care. I turned the bike and continued to cycle.

It was no surprise to find myself back in the bluebell woods. My place of endless returns. Perhaps I came here because this was where I felt closest to Nico. Perhaps because, in the deep green, I could think.

I walked for a little while; then, suddenly spent, I came to rest beneath a tree.

There was no escaping the truth: if Nico hadn't introduced Róisín to Isabelle, she would still be alive. She wouldn't be lying in a box in her sitting room.

I wiped away a tear, then folded my arms around my body. Nico had been a good man. He'd prided himself on his sense of duty, an old-fashioned idea of honour, and he protected the people he loved. He'd had a clear path for his life, and family had been everything to him.

But this evening I had to face the glaring realization that I'd tried to suppress: the Nico I'd known and loved had changed. His intentions in trying to help Isabelle had been good. But the truth was, he had veered off course to the point where a young woman's death was a direct consequence of his actions.

I was beginning to feel like I'd never known him at all.

I took a deep, shaky breath. It was nearly over. Soon, I would demand Isabelle repay her debt. Then, finally, I could begin to heal.

'Esmie?' Linc's voice broke through my reverie, and I peered up at him through the gloom. 'What are you doing here?'

'I'm not sure,' I said with a small laugh. 'Somehow I keep coming back.'

'Eden loved the woods too. She would bring her pens and notebook here, to this very spot. She'd sketch and write poetry. It's no wonder they thought her a witch.'

I wrapped my arms tighter around me. I couldn't listen to Linc going on about his poetry witch. Not now. But he was drawing closer to me so I plastered on a smile, hiding that I'd been crying.

'This spot? Right here?' I said, surreptitiously wiping my cheek. I could see now that the trees formed an enclosure, bunched together as though they were whispering to each other. It was like being embraced by trees.

'Right here. This was her place, here beneath these very trees.'

'How's Ceanna?' I said, trying to distract him. He was watching me so intently.

'Fine. Recovering.'

Linc drew nearer. My heart picked up. He tucked a strand that had fallen from my ponytail behind my ear. He came closer, and I tilted up my face, anticipation dancing with trepidation.

'Malachy had these films.'

I felt my brow furrow. 'Films?'

'Old reels,' he said. 'Short movies of beach trips, parties. He'd had them converted to digital. I can show you, some time.'

'You've watched them?'

'Many times. Frame by frame. I thought if I studied them carefully enough, it could help me discover who Eden was.'

It sounded a little unhinged to me, but what did I know? Maybe this was how things worked at universities. 'And did you?'

'I learned that she was an enigma. She was commanding, and yet hugged the walls and stayed in the shadows. She was a woman who hid.'

I knew that there was nothing Linc wouldn't do to uncover Eden Hale, to strip her down to her barest self. I wondered if he inched closer to me now because this was the nearest he'd ever get to her. Despite him having ana-lysed Eden's every word, inspected her photographs, I, a vague impression of this elusive woman he loved, was the best he had.

'It's not your brown eyes or your skin, or the shape of your face, you know. That's not why you're so like Eden.' He held my face with his hand.

'What is it then?' I was curious.

'Your painstaking control,' he said softly. 'The care you take to hold yourself a certain way; how you watch every-thing around you. As though if you let go even just a fraction, it will all come falling down. The way you're always reading your surroundings, analysing things, making sure you're in charge of a situation. You don't like to be taken unawares, do you?'

My shoulders were stiff with tension. It felt like Linc had pulled at my mask and glimpsed the true me beneath. I ducked my head, but he slipped his hand under my chin, making me look at him.

'You need to control the world around you' – he spoke so gently that it hurt – 'because, like Eden, you feel that everything is precarious. That it might fall to pieces any second.'

I didn't answer, because everything *was* precarious. Everything *might* fall to pieces any second.

'It's the way you're constantly looking around you,' Linc continued. 'Waiting for the axe to fall.' He paused. 'I know a woman with a secret when I see one.'

There was a roaring in my ears. I held myself rigid.

Linc was looking at me as if I mattered, and I soaked it up. I wasn't invisible and unnoticed. His hand trailed into my hair, and there was a determined look on his face. 'I want to know you, Esmie.' But he was lying, I reminded myself. He wanted to find Eden. But did that matter, at this point?

Then his lips were on mine, hungry and searching. This time I kissed him back, not because it was a distraction or I was shaken, but because I wanted to.

He undid each button on my shirt, then dropped it to the roots and stones.

'Someone might come,' I murmured between kisses. The heavy cloud bore down through the treetops. The canopy of leaves pressed in. It felt like we were the last two people in the world.

'It's just us.' Linc tugged at my skirt. 'The last two people in the world.'

He pressed me into the tree. Maybe I *was* like her, his mysterious muse who'd wandered these woods. Maybe I was everything he whispered to me. All I knew was that I was no longer Esmie. I was just a girl beneath a tree in the woods.

The tree was hard against my skin, and the ground was soft and mulched beneath my feet. It was only when he unzipped his jeans that I remembered the photo of Nico naked and ready. Here in these woods. It was as if we'd both been snared in the same trap, neither of us able to resist this dark allure.

Later, when we drew away from the tree, I felt the shame. Thick waves of it. I thought of Amber, and it didn't matter that she too lied and cheated.

What had come over me? Why had I lost myself like that? Suddenly, fiercely, I didn't like myself. Linc was looking at me pensively, as though he could see the regret there. He saw more than he should, and I wasn't sure I liked being visible, now.

'Don't be so hard on yourself,' he said gently.

'You don't understand,' I rasped.

'Help me to understand.'

The truth was right there, a clog in my throat. I wanted to explain everything to him. To unload this burden that had become too much.

The clouds broke then, dumping their rain. It oozed through the leaves and branches. It was a sudden, punishing downpour. *Look what you've done*, it seemed to say. I bent my shoulders, defeated.

How disappointed Mama Bear would be if she knew.

Nico, I suspected – the new Nico – would give me one of those slow unpleasant smiles.

'There's no one else here.' Linc smoothed my hair. 'Just us.'

'I should get back.' I couldn't look at him.

'I'll drive you home. The rain's only going to get worse.'

With a gentle hand, he turned my face to him. 'Let me look after you, Esmie. Please.'

If only he could. But I nodded dutifully, then scratched at my neck as if I could scratch away the guilt and shame settling deeper into me. I hadn't meant for this to happen again.

There was no room for self-pity. There was work to be done. I pushed down the remorse, my rising distress.

I walked away from Eden's copse, tidying my hair and resolving no more. I was loved, I reminded myself. I had a family.

Did I, though? They were so far away. I was so alone, and for a few moments with Linc, I'd felt less alone.

We hurried through the trees to The Woodlands.

'Amber's out,' Linc said, as I looked up at the house. I wondered if she was out with Caden. The thought made the guilt a touch lighter.

I opened the door of the Jeep, and my phone buzzed with a message. It was from Mama Bear.

My heart stuttered.

I opened the message.

Nico's awake.

Chapter Thirty

Monday

At four in the morning, Mama Bear called with an update.

Nico was fragile, more asleep than not, but the doctors were hopeful. He'd asked for me. When I heard this, I wanted to return immediately.

'You can't come back,' Mama Bear said in her gravelly voice. 'You know you can't.'

'But if Nico is fine . . .' I objected, faltering at Mama Bear's stony silence. I tried again: 'If he wants me there then—'

'He isn't fine. Not yet.' She sighed. 'You know there's been too much damage. You can't come home.'

'I'm going to make everything right,' I vowed. I considered telling her about my peace offering, but now, with Nico just awake, wasn't the time. 'You'll see.'

Ending the call, I slumped back to my bed while Fabiana brushed her hair.

I had to rein in my impatience to be home, and keep focused. In a matter of days, my work here would be done. Isabelle would meet her consequences. The scales would be rebalanced.

That afternoon, I left Woodland House via the lane gate and walked through the woods to Three Oaks. It was

Amber's birthday party on Friday, and we'd agreed I'd make up the shift at the cottage this afternoon. Before I left, she'd raised a shopping bag, saying that it was my costume for the party. Everyone would be dressed as a character from *A Midsummer Night's Dream*, she said, then placed it in a cabinet in the utility room.

She'd spent the day planning the party, her cheeks flushed as she arranged decorations and ordered wine. I didn't particularly care to be Amber's dress-up doll, but if all went to plan, I wouldn't even be here then.

Nervous dread stirred inside me, as though I was at the doctor's waiting for bad news.

Walking through the woods, I felt dislodged. Since the weekend, I'd had this strange sensation, as if I'd been knocked out of myself and I couldn't fit in again. I felt overlaid – this new Esmie I'd become fitted over the old me, but didn't quite come together at the edges.

At Three Oaks, Linc was in the living room with a small group of people clutching glasses of wine. I recognized Fiona, with her severe little fringe and dark berry lipstick, curled up in an armchair. Caden shared the couch with another young man. A second woman sat on the floor reading a slim volume, a tower of books perched on the side table beside her. She barely glanced at me.

'Don't mind us,' Linc said cheerfully, as I stepped into the living room. 'This is my Eden Hale reading group. We won't get in your way.'

'You're not in my way,' I said, still glitching between the new Esmie and the old me. I went into the main bedroom. Of course they were in my way. How the hell was I supposed to pack up the porcelain shepherdess and the wall ducks with them right there?

Their words from the living room were a loud babble that hurt my ears.

'Now you're just making things up, Caden,' Fiona laughed.

'The images speak for themselves.' Caden's voice was smug.

'Cade, I don't think this is the most mature interpretation of the poem,' Linc murmured. 'Go on, Fiona, read it out loud.'

Fiona began reading – a melodramatic, morbid verse about a girl being made out of ashes. I tried again to see the appeal, listening carefully. Nope, I still didn't like it.

Linc glanced up and caught my eye as I paused in the doorway. He smiled, a secret smile. The old me bristled. Esmie smiled back.

'Oh, look,' Caden said, openly hostile, having just deigned to notice me. 'It's Esmie. Here for one of your evening classes?'

'Caden,' Linc said sharply.

'What?' Caden said, turning to Linc. There was a challenge in his voice, the hint of a subterranean rivalry.

'Please,' Linc sighed, 'let Esmie get on with her work.'

'Who's hungry?' Fiona smacked her hands to her knees and stood up, breaking the tension that had gripped the room.

I turned back to the bedroom, grabbed one of the flattened boxes leaning against the wall. I opened it with all the aggression I couldn't unleash on Caden. The parcel tape was missing, and I remembered there was some in a kitchen drawer.

I went, quiet as a ghost, through the living room to the kitchen. The door was open the tiniest crack.

Pausing outside, I heard Linc's charming murmur: 'Don't say anything to the others, OK?'

'Of course not,' came the softer sound of a woman's voice.

I put my hand on the door and a sudden sense of foreboding swept over me. As though pushing open this door would unleash something terrible. That story Linc had told me in his study came together with a sudden, unexpected clarity. The one about the bride who went through the rooms in her villainous lover's house in the woods. I was gripped by a sudden certainty that I was the fairy-tale bride. That if I pushed on this door, I would open it into a room with buckets of blood.

And I thought about another door that should have remained closed.

HOME

The two women stood outside the door.

'Do you think he's OK?' Esmerelda asked, pressing her ear to the door.

It was an uncomfortable alliance between the two women. They needed but resented each other.

It had been difficult since Nico had returned. He'd retreated into himself, preferring silence to conversation. Simone didn't know if she was still engaged to him – any intimacy was infrequent, and all talk of a wedding had been dropped. Nico lived inside his head, a now unfriendly terrain. He needed help, but he closed down any attempts to offer it. Only thirty minutes ago, Esmerelda had tentatively brought up an addiction clinic, which had resulted in a fierce argument, ending when Nico angrily withdrew to the bedroom.

Simone opened the door a crack and peered inside.

'I'll go,' Esmerelda insisted, pushing forward. 'Let me talk to him.'

'No.' Simone was firm. 'I'll go.'

Simone stepped into the bedroom, shutting the door behind her, leaving Esmerelda fuming on the other side. The curtains were drawn, and the room smelled stale.

Nico was sitting up in bed, looking at something on his phone. Simone gathered the dirty laundry he'd dropped to the floor, sighing as she uncovered an empty bottle of vodka.

'Esmie's made dinner. You hungry?' she said pleasantly. He'd lost weight these last months.

'Maybe later.' He was still looking down at his phone, and Simone leaned in curiously, seeing an image on the screen. It was a photo from happier times, she knew from a glimpse of Nico's handsome smiling face and shirtless body. But there was someone else in the picture, someone positioned slightly behind him.

Frowning, Simone moved closer, and Nico placed the phone face down on the bed.

'What are you looking at, Nico?' she said, a little too sharply.

Since he'd come home, she'd worried that they were missing something important. Something he'd kept from her.

Simone felt fear thicken her throat. 'Who's in that picture?'

'It's nothing.' He pushed his legs over the side of the bed. Simone hesitated. She didn't want to get into another argument.

It felt like something hidden was coming to the surface. Part of her wanted to pull back. Leave the room. *Don't ask questions if you don't want to know the answer.*

But Simone was tired of evasion and uncertainty. She put her hands on her hips. 'What were you looking at?'

'Leave it, Simone.' He sounded tired. 'Let's go and eat.'

'I want to see that picture.' She sounded shrill.

He looked at her, and for the first time in months it was as if he was actually there. Present in his own life. 'No,' he said eventually. 'I don't think you do.' He turned to his phone again, the conversation over.

Before she realized what she was doing, Simone quickly rounded the bed. She snatched the phone out of Nico's hand, climbing on to the bed to hold it out of reach.

'Give it back,' he growled.

'Who was in the picture, Nico?' Simone was out of breath. Not from exertion, but because she was terrified.

Nico leapt up on the bed with a hint of his former agility, and Simone jumped off. She dodged him, searching through the pictures on his phone for the one she'd briefly seen.

Nico pulled at her dress, and Simone fell back on the bed. She stuffed the phone beneath her dress as Nico loomed over her. She hadn't seen him this animated since he'd returned.

'Who was in the picture?' she said again, as Nico settled himself on her. It was so achingly familiar, them together like this, but it had become strange these last months.

'Just one of the neighbours. From The Woodlands.'

'Neighbour woman or neighbour man?'

Nico hesitated. 'Neighbour woman.'

Simone swallowed. 'Was she . . . Did you . . .' She looked away, certain he could read the question in her eyes.

Then Nico was up, standing at the side of the bed. He was holding his phone, deleting the photograph. Simone was suddenly furious. She got to her feet, launching herself at him.

'What did you do, Nico?' she said, her voice sounding different. That wildness was running through her. A tide of destruction that wanted to damage everything around her. Bitterness flooded her body. 'What did you do?' She was louder now. It was taking over. She reached out her hand to his face. He watched her warily.

'You know what happened.' His words were almost inaudible.

She dug her nails into his cheek and ripped the skin on his face. His hand flew up, shocked, covering the streaks of red. She felt a vicious satisfaction.

'Don't be a coward, Nico. If you cheated, then at least be man enough to admit it.' She spat the words, still wanting to hurt him. To break something. There was an angry roaring inside her, and she couldn't make it stop.

Nico was still holding his cheek. His eyes flashed and he said, 'You want to know? Fine. I loved her. She betrayed me. Because of her lies, I have nothing left. That's why they pulled my funding and kicked me out.'

Simone recoiled, as if Nico had raised his hand to her. Whatever she'd suspected, it hadn't been love.

'The neighbour woman?' She sounded shaky. 'The one in the picture you deleted?'

He hesitated, then nodded.

'How long?'

He shrugged. 'We were friends first. It got physical last May.'

A year ago. Simone hugged her arms to her body. Nothing could have prepared her for the pain of his betrayal. Nothing could be worse than this. She felt a scream starting deep in her gut. She was hurting, and she couldn't hold it in.

'What was she like?' Simone couldn't stop picking at the wound. 'Was she . . .' Better? Nicer? More lovable? 'Pretty? Clever? Who was she?'

'That's not important.'

'You really loved her?'

There was a beating in her ears. Some winged thing inside flapping around furiously. From the bedside table, that ugly statue watched her with its expressionless face. Inside, the beating grew louder.

The door was shut. Esmerelda waited impatiently on the other side, only catching snippets of the conversation. When she heard Simone scream, she hesitated. Then, with dread in her heart, she placed a hand on the wood and pushed.

Chapter Thirty-One

Monday

I eased the kitchen door open a crack and on the other side found Fiona, shaking out a bag of crisps into a bowl. Linc opened another bottle of wine.

My breath came in shallow rasps. My eyes tracked through the kitchen, searching for trouble, but it was only Linc and Fiona. They were standing at the table, talking quietly to each other.

'. . . whatever you need, Linc. And I'll never say anything. You know you can trust me.'

Trust her with what?

'You're a rare one, Fiona.' He hesitated. 'You're not curious? About what I asked you to do last year?'

'I'm sure you had good reason,' Fiona said. She gazed up at him, adoration in her eyes. 'You always do.'

Linc turned around as if he sensed me hovering. It was too late to duck out, so I pasted an unconvincing smile on my face. Fiona's phone pinged, and she sighed.

'Excuse me. My sister again, about my dad's big party. I'll be glad for the peace when it's over.'

She typed a quick reply as she passed me on her way out.

'Esmie, you looking for something?' Linc raised an eyebrow.

Esmie – always looking for something. And I had a

feeling that I had found something I didn't particularly want to find. An understanding hovering just out of my reach.

'Esmie?' Linc frowned, drawing nearer. 'I'm sorry about Caden earlier. He can be obnoxious.'

I didn't need Linc to apologize for Caden. It was sweet that he'd stood up for me. But Linc had no idea why Caden resented me. That I'd twice witnessed Caden and Amber and their inability to keep their hands off each other. Which reminded me: the photographs. I still hadn't handed over the camera. 'How's Ceanna?'

'She's fine. Definitely over the worst.'

'It's lucky you called in to see Caden that night.'

'Hmmm?' Linc was looking at the time. 'Yes, it was, wasn't it?'

'Have you seen her since?'

'I visited Saturday and Sunday.'

'You did?'

'Ceanna asked me to come over.'

'OK.' Something was off, though. Ceanna had never tried to conceal her loathing for her brother-in-law. And now she was asking him over?

Linc moved closer. 'Is something wrong?'

'I'm cold,' I said, inching back, trying to understand my unease. This strange instinct that something was wrong. 'I never seem to get warm enough. Especially here, in this cottage.' The thick walls and small windows where the sun didn't fully penetrate.

There was something that was eluding me. Something I couldn't put my finger on. It was just out of reach, and frustration coursed through me.

'Hey,' Linc said, resting his hands on my shoulders. 'You can talk to me.'

I wasn't sure why, but I felt that when I'd opened the

kitchen door I'd crossed some kind of threshold. Maybe my terrible sense of foreboding hadn't anything to do with Linc, but with me. That this Woodlands Esmie was beginning to unravel faster.

Linc's hand travelled down my back, both calming and disturbing in equal measures. I leaned in to him, enjoying the smell of him. The feel of his shoulders. It made me feel grounded again.

'I should get back in there,' Linc said. 'Come, join us. The others will leave soon, and we can talk then.'

I followed Linc into the living room. He seated himself in the armchair and I hung back, standing behind Fiona on the couch. Fiona stared up at Linc, her face rapt as she listened to him.

Whatever you need, Linc, she'd said in the kitchen. From the first time I'd seen her at Amber's dinner, it was clear she was besotted with Linc. Then, a cold finger on my spine.

That wasn't the first time I'd seen her. I'd seen Fiona before. At Begley's, the night Isabelle had made a drug drop for Róisín. My mind parsed through memories, and I let out an inadvertent gasp.

I pulled out my phone, wanting to test my theory. I checked something, then from my web browser, I accessed Nico's private email account. I sent a quick email: **Hey Fiona, how are you? Thanks for passing on my email address to the cleaner. She sent a copy of a photo I'd lost.**

It seemed innocuous enough. The content of the message didn't matter; that wasn't the confirmation I was seeking.

I looked up at Linc and his reading group. He cradled a glass of wine, explaining something while his students listened attentively. Then Caden interrupted, and from Linc's answer, I realized they were having some kind of pissing contest. Caden was goading Linc, both of them shooting clever words at each other, and I rolled my eyes. Caden might as well announce to the group that he was fucking his supervisor's wife.

I turned to Fiona, who was looking between Linc and Caden with a mix of jealousy and admiration. I looked down at her phone, impatient. It was open to her Notes app, where she was typing RAWNESS.

Then it came. Fiona's phone pinged with a notification. The email icon showed a new message. From Nico.

I was right, I realized with grim satisfaction. Fiona was Fibear77. I'd found her private email address in Isabelle's secret phone, with a message arranging to meet at Begley's. I thought of Fiona with her short fringe, smiling at me in the passage on the way to the toilet at the bar. Isabelle had been in that toilet, having just sold diet pills to a severely underweight Róisín. She'd stayed down there because she was waiting for Fiona. But what would straight-laced Fiona, good-girl Fiona, besotted-with-Linc Fiona, want with illicitly obtained medication?

Fiona read the message and typed out a quick, **This is a surprise! You good?**

I didn't reply. Instead, I left the living room and tidied the kitchen. I cleared away the traces of Linc's reading group party, then started boxing old mismatched storage dishes, thinking about Fiona and the snippets of conversation I'd caught earlier: *whatever you need Linc. I'll never say anything.*

When Linc came into the kitchen after his students left half an hour later, I didn't have a strategy, but I couldn't hold back. I had to speak.

'You did it, didn't you? You laced Ceanna's herbal drink. She wasn't sick that night – she was drugged.'

For one unguarded moment, I saw the truth on Linc's

face. His guilt showed in his eyes, and his jaw locked. Then he checked his features, and smiled uncertainly. 'You think I drugged Ceanna? Why would I do that?'

'That's what I want to know.' Had Linc meant to cause Ceanna real harm, or had he wanted to scare her?

'You serious?' Linc was standing taller, straighter.

'I think you would do anything to get your hands on Eden's papers.' I stepped towards him, refusing to be cowed.

'Like kill Ceanna?' He sounded incredulous. 'You think I'd murder my sister-in-law so I can get into the safe?'

'No. I don't think you tried to kill her.' I sighed, sitting down. I gestured for Linc to sit too. His shoulders were stiff, his body holding the injustice of my accusation.

'I'm not going to tell anyone,' I said, holding his eye. 'As long as Ceanna stays well and undrugged, your secret is safe with me.'

Linc sat down. He placed a hand on the table, near to mine but not touching. He didn't say anything. No admission of guilt, but no more denial either.

'Ceanna told me there was a medicine that affected her badly.' That first day, at her kitchen table. She'd driven thirty kilometres while asleep in the months she'd mourned her family. 'I know you asked Fiona to get that same medicine for you. From a dealer at the university.'

I watched his face for a response, seeing only a light tic in his jaw. 'You put it in that Moondust she takes, didn't you? You knew she would be sick. Confused. And you would manipulate her into giving you the missing keys while she was off her head. Or you'd be the knight in shining armour, and she'd give them to you.'

Linc let out a long slow breath. He dropped his gaze, realizing there was no point in denying it further.

'I never meant to cause her harm.' His placed his hands flat on the table, as if to bolster his insistence. 'I knew she'd

301

take it before bed, and I would be there, making sure she was safe.'

But she'd taken it earlier that night. She'd gone digging at Three Oaks, hiding the keys beneath the swing.

'I only did it to reset our relationship, to make her see that I'm not her enemy. I'm sick of her casting me as the bad guy.' The irony of drugging Ceanna to prove that he wasn't a bad guy seemed lost on Linc. 'I've never been able to do anything right by Ceanna. It was wrong and desperate, but . . .' He stood up, his hands running through his hair in agitation. 'I have to get those papers. I need them like I need air.'

For the first time, I truly saw Linc. I saw a man clawed down to his barest, basest self. For the first time, I saw him without the charm, without the confidence. He was weak, conniving, callous. But who was I to judge? Tired, I stood up too.

'It will never happen again. It was a one-time thing.' He stepped towards me. 'Please, Esmie, I promise you. It was a stupid desperate act. Please don't hate me.'

'I don't,' I answered honestly.

'Thank you.' He shifted closer and I felt again that physical pull, despite what I now knew of him. Distracting me when I could least afford it.

He moved in until we were touching. His lips brushed my neck.

Linc's hands closed around my waist. His lips in the hollow above my collarbone, he murmured, 'I'm sorry. I'm so, so sorry.'

'I'm in no position to cast stones.'

'One day, you will tell me your secrets.' His lips moved to my neck, and despite my better judgement, I felt my body responding. Switched on, even though I was annoyed by his words.

Linc didn't even know where I came from, where I'd lived my whole godforsaken life, and yet he thought I'd give him my secrets.

'You can't hurt Ceanna again,' I reminded him. I was feeling cold, and yet warm. Nausea churned in my gut.

'I won't. I promise.' Pulling my waist, he drew me nearer to him. He needed me, I realized, and it gave me a heady feeling. 'It backfired terribly. I still don't have the keys. Ceanna admitted the next day that while delirious, she took them from her safe and hid them. We can't find where she put them.'

'She doesn't remember anything from that night?'

'She has only fragmented memories, like Eden appearing in a vision on the garden swing outside, here at Three Oaks.' He shook his head. 'Now no one knows where the keys are. They could be anywhere – the woods, her house, the cottage.' He tried to speak lightly, but despair leaked into his voice. 'And worse, Ceanna confirmed that in his last paranoid days, Malachy did arm the hidden trap in the safe after all, so drilling in is definitely not an option.'

'Couldn't you bypass the trap somehow?'

'No. Malachy fitted the trap with ink. Breaking into it will force open the ink canisters, which will destroy the documents inside.'

The three keys were invaluable, then. And I had them.

Chapter Thirty-Two

Tuesday

It was my last day at Isabelle's. When I next darkened the door of number three, it would be to tell Paul every rotten thing his wife had done. How she'd had an affair with Ceanna's lodger, how she'd sold prescription pills using the medical registration numbers belonging to him and doctors associated with his practice. How this had resulted in the death of a young woman. Above all, I would tell him how she planned to run, leaving him and their daughters to think her dead.

It troubled me that I still hadn't learned how everything had unfolded with Nico – the details of *how* Isabelle had betrayed him and convinced the university to kick him out. I ached to know what happened, but without Róisín, I didn't see who would tell me the unvarnished truth.

In the upstairs sitting room, I made a final check through Isabelle's notebook.

I skimmed the few pages I'd skipped over the last time, looking for more information about Nico. Instead, I found another entry on the Rose.

13.
The Danger had given the woman his credit card and told her to get something pretty for a work dinner. At an

overpriced boutique, she found a dress in a bold print that the Danger would like. It sickened her, how he used his money as a weapon to keep her in line.

She'd dropped the garish fabric on the counter when the woman realized it was the Rose working behind the cash desk. The Rose's eyes widened as she studied Isabelle. Despite the lack of an Alex disguise, it was clear the Rose recognized her.

Months had passed since they'd last met. It had been a quick drop-off after her wedding, when the Rose had ordered two more boxes of pills – for her friends, she'd said and the woman had warned her no more.

The Rose had dropped at least two dress sizes since they'd first met. Her waist was small, accentuating the flare of her hips, and her cheekbones were sharper. The woman knew then that the Rose hadn't bought the additional boxes of pills for her friends – they'd always been for the Rose herself.

When the woman took out the Danger's card, the Rose lunged for it and read the name. A satisfied gleam appeared in her eyes. Dr Danger. Doesn't he have that practice near Coach Street?

The woman's stomach knotted.

The Rose let out a light laugh and tapped her painted fingernail on the Danger's credit card. She needed more pills. And she wanted the woman's home address. Or, if you prefer, I'll ask your husband.

The woman couldn't risk the Rose telling the Danger anything, so she stiffly agreed.

The Rose handed over the bag, which was tied with a perfect bow. The woman walked away, carrying the expensive outfit she didn't want. The Rose called after her, cheerfully telling the woman to have a nice day.

I could fill in the blanks. Róisín had been addicted to the pills, getting thinner and thinner. I didn't know what she'd taken, but it was unapproved, sourced online, and likely had dangerous side effects.

Satisfaction settled me, soothed my jangled nerves. I felt armoured, ready for whatever would come next. This here was indisputable proof that Isabelle had provided illegal medication that killed a woman. Isabelle would not escape. She would live out the rest of her miserable days in her gilded cage. She would stay Paul's dutiful wife. She would smile and keep his home. She would never leave her Danger.

Every day she would remember how close she'd come to her freedom, and how I'd taken it away because of what she did to Nico. Her lies made him lose his dream, what he'd most desired. The future he'd planned. And because life demands balance, because actions have consequences, I would do the same to her.

I would direct Paul to the notebook, but I took photos of the most damning pages as a back-up. Then, for the last time, I locked the notebook away.

I went downstairs and in the kitchen, Isabelle was unpacking a large bag, pulling out a long full-skirted dress. She fluffed it out, held it against her and gave a twirl.

She was different, I realized. She had a new energy, no doubt fuelled by her belief that escape was just days away.

'It's gorgeous,' Liadh said, delighted. She turned to me, her eyes shining. 'What do you think, Esmie?'

'Beautiful,' I agreed blandly. 'What's it for?'

'Mam's costume for Amber's party. She's going as Hermia.'

I couldn't have cared less about costumes and parties, so I tuned them out. I began unloading the dishwasher, thinking about how best to approach Paul.

I felt no jubilation, only grim determination. And,

glancing up at Isabelle, a complicated swell of emotion. Having read her notebook, I empathized with her. But Isabelle had made bad choices. And bad choices had to have consequences.

'Has Dad's costume arrived?' Liadh said to Isabelle.

'Not yet.' Isabelle collapsed the billowing dress to her waist, chewing on her lip. 'He won't have time to change it before the party if it doesn't fit. He only gets back Friday.'

'Paul's away?' I said, my stomach plummeting.

They both looked at me, surprised. 'Yes. Why?' Isabelle said.

I shook my head. 'No reason.' But disappointment was lodged in my gut.

Isabelle gave me a sidelong glance, then lifted the dress against her body again and tilted her hip to one side, then the other with an almost girlish glee.

I could try to contact Paul. Send the pictures of Isabelle's notebook entries as proof. But the distance left room for error. It left space for Isabelle to persuade him that I'd made a mistake, that it was just a creative writing exercise that I'd found. Or accuse me of digitally manipulating the images to incriminate her. After everything, I had to see it through until the very end. I could wait until Friday. It was only a few days away.

And on Saturday – no matter what Mama Bear said, I thought fiercely, no matter the danger – I'd be on the plane back home. I had to get to Nico. The connection between us felt taut and urgent; I needed to be with him, whatever the consequences. He'd asked for me, and as always, I would go to him.

The final pieces of my plan, this plan that had started the night Nico bled on the bedroom floor, fell into place.

Isabelle fluffed out her costume, still admiring it. The soft, feminine style was unlike the loud patterns and safe, mom-styles she usually wore. It was a pretty dress, I conceded, to wear when her world came to an end. Amber was going all out with her party, and it seemed a fitting occasion for all my hard work to come to fruition.

I would confront Isabelle and Paul while they laughed with cocktails in their hands. I would tell Isabelle what had happened because of her lies, how broken Nico was when he returned to us. How he was cloaked in misery, and it drew tighter and tighter around him until that terrible night when everything changed.

And then I would leave The Woodlands and never come back.

I was shutting Isabelle's front gate when my phone rang with a call from Ceanna. I hesitated, then answered.

'Esmie.' Ceanna didn't bother with pleasantries. 'Have you taken those pictures?'

'I have,' I said reluctantly.

'Bring them over when you're finished at Isabelle's.'

I told her I'd see her in a few minutes. I walked slowly, pushing the bike, enjoying the mild sunshine on my skin. The air was rich with the intoxicating scent of meadowsweet that had sprung up in the hedgerows, like little bridal bouquets.

At the bungalow, Caden was rooting through the fridge, his laptop open on the kitchen table. He glanced at me when I came in. 'There she is. My little Peeping Tom.' His eyes were hard and hostile. He came towards me, and I felt my pulse quicken. He grabbed my wrist. 'You'd better forget what you saw on Friday night, or you'll be sorry.'

I swallowed, then wrenched my wrist back. 'I'm here to see Ceanna.' *Just until the end of the week*, I reminded myself.

'If you tell Linc,' he warned, raising a finger to my face.

'I won't tell Linc.' I pushed his finger away. 'I don't care what you and Amber do.'

I had to avoid him for only a few more days, then I would be gone for ever. Even thinking about home – the wide-open landscape, the brown scrub and the distant blue mountains – made me feel lighter. Giddy. I was almost there. Almost home.

Ceanna was sitting on her bed. A box of photographs was spilled on the covers, but she was looking out of the window. She glanced at me as I came in, then went back to staring at the view of the ivy-covered stone wall. The silence in the room felt deliberate, and I was loath to break it, so I stood at the foot of her bed and waited.

'Do you ever feel,' Ceanna said quietly, 'like you're in a hall of mirrors and you can't get out? And in every mirror, all you see is your past. There's no way forward, only reflections of what you've lost.'

All the time, Ceanna. 'Sometimes.'

She picked up a photograph and held it out. It was one of herself, younger and with a smile that lit up her eyes.

'I hate her so much,' she breathed, and the venom in her voice made me take a step back. 'She was so stupid. She had everything – her husband, her father, her baby – and she didn't know how lucky she was.' She flung the picture to the bed.

Again, I saw how similar we were. Weeks ago, I'd stepped off that plane with grand ideas about justice and retribution. That I was here as some kind of avenger.

But now it occurred to me that maybe all of this, maybe what I thought was my grand revenge, was just a pitiful attempt to save myself.

'My family has always been everything to me,' Ceanna

said. 'And then it started falling apart. First I lost Amber to Linc, then . . . the accident. When Dad died, it felt like everything was broken. Like a fire had burned through and eaten everything I cared about. In the months after, I became obsessed with salvaging something from the fire. I had to have something of my family that was whole and intact.'

I understood Ceanna a little better after this confession. I understood why she would go to such extreme lengths; putting a camera in Amber's bedroom, making me spy on her sister. Grief had turned something simple and protective into a dark possessive bind.

'You have evidence of Caden and Amber's affair?' Ceanna looked at me pensively.

'I went there on Friday night. I came over after, but you were in a really bad way.'

'You were here? I don't remember that at all.'

'You were confused. I was worried.'

'I've booked a full medical for next week, but it frightened me. Linc was really there for me.' Her mouth turned down. 'I've been too hard on him.'

I felt a wave of guilt, but I stayed quiet. The last thing I needed was to be drawn further into the murk of The Woodlands.

'When I was drifting in and out, I saw her. My aunt. Eden.' Ceanna's face lit up, and it was clear that the apparition, as Ceanna believed it was, had given her a sense of wonder. A brush with magic. I should have told her the truth, but I was reluctant to take this new lightness from her.

'Eden told me to let go,' she said, her eyes shining. 'I've been holding on so tight, and Eden wants me to let go.'

I had told her to let go, but I meant of my wrists.

'They're wise words, Esmie. I have a feeling you need to hear them too.'

Not when the end was so close.

'Do you have the pictures of Amber?' Ceanna said.

I handed her the camera. 'I thought you were letting go.'

'I am.' Ceanna turned on the camera and flicked through the pictures. She was sorrowful as she said, 'Ah, Amber,' then placed the camera beside her.

'Are you going to delete them?'

She shook her head. 'No. No, I don't think I will. But I won't show them to Amber. I won't make her sign over the cottage to me.'

I felt a huge relief wash over my body.

'I'm going to show them to Linc.'

Dread settled in my stomach. 'To Linc?' I started gathering up the photographs spilled on the bed. An instinctive response: when agitated, clean. 'Is that a good idea?' Caden was going to kill me. If I could just hold him off until after the party, then I'd be gone before he could find me.

'There've been too many lies, Esmie. Linc deserves to know the truth. We've agreed to a fresh start, and I can't do that if I'm not honest with him.'

'It's Amber's birthday. Maybe it's better to wait for after?' I stacked the photos together, not daring to look up at Ceanna.

'Maybe,' Ceanna said with a sigh.

And that's when I saw it, there on Ceanna's bed.

A picture of Nico. It was half hidden beneath another, and I tugged it a little towards me. I could see his strong brown arms in a T-shirt, then his chest and face. There were two women in the picture, one on either side of him. My heart in my throat, I looked at one of the women, realizing who it was.

Me.

Something cold swept over me as I looked at this photograph of my past. We were laughing at the camera, big belly laughs that had my eyes scrunched up and my mouth wide open. My hair was long and dyed a caramel brown in the picture. It had been taken near the beach a few days before Nico left to begin his PhD. I didn't even know he'd had it printed.

I envied her, I hated her.

What I wouldn't do to be her again.

Why did Ceanna have this photograph? Did Nico give it to her? Or had he just forgotten it here when he'd packed up in a rush? I looked up to Ceanna, terrified that she'd seen it. That she would make the connection. But Ceanna was wrapped up in her own troubles, her knees drawn up to her chest as she worried about her health, her sister. With the different hair, the open mouth and scrunched-up eyes, it was most likely she wouldn't recognize me.

'Leave those,' Ceanna said gently. 'You're not working today.'

'I don't mind.'

Then she looked up at the door. 'Isabelle, hello. Esmie was just leaving.'

I stared at the edge of the picture, desperate to pocket it. Could I take it now, just reach a hand forward and slip it out? Isabelle was fussing as she came closer; she barely acknowledged me at all, and I felt my hatred swell.

I couldn't risk taking it now. I smoothed the stack, using the movement to hide the picture of us beneath the others. I would come back for it when I could.

I excused myself as the women spoke. Stepping outside Ceanna's room, I walked into Caden, who put out his arms to steady me.

'You really are like a little cockroach, getting in everywhere.'

313

'Sorry,' I mumbled, unable to deal with Caden's taunting today. 'I have to go.'

I scurried down the passage. Glancing back, I saw that Caden had gone inside Ceanna's room.

Just until the end of the week, I reminded myself yet again.

Chapter Thirty-Three

Wednesday

I woke early with the sound of my phone buzzing.

'Say your prayers, my girl,' Mama Bear rasped into my ear. 'Get to a church and light a candle.' Her words were too fast, and she was breathing unevenly.

'What's going on?' Panic chased through my body.

'It's Nico,' she said.

My world bottomed out.

'He had some kind of fit last night. Collapsed. He's back in ICU.'

I pictured Mama Bear standing outside the hospital, pulling on a cigarette. She'd quit a decade ago, but she still reached for them when things were rough. Like the night when Nico lay unconscious on the floor, blood in his hair. My last memory of Mama Bear was of her lighting a cigarette, then taking two puffs as she walked from the door to the car. Then she'd stamped it out, climbed inside. She'd looked down at her son as the car drove away.

'We've been here for hours.' Mama Bear's voice was hoarse with fatigue. 'You know how it goes.'

'I'm coming home.' I was already out of bed, throwing open my drawers, dumping things on my bed.

'Don't.' Mama Bear stopped me with a single word.

'I have to see him,' I begged, gripping the phone tighter. 'I have to be with him.'

'It will only make things worse.'

There was a rustle, the sound of another voice approaching Mama Bear. 'You can't come. You can't be here.'

On the other side was a woman's voice, sharp and demanding: 'Who's that?'

'I've got to go.' Mama Bear sounded panicked. 'Do not come back.' The call ended.

The silence filled my head, like a quiet, almost imperceptible buzz. It was loud, this silence. Oppressive. I covered my ears with my hands and sank to the floor.

'Esmie?' Fabiana's quiet voice broke the silence. 'Are you OK?'

I didn't answer. Couldn't. I felt a light weight around my shoulders, the soft cotton of Fabiana's pink throw. The delicate scent of apple shampoo. Then the door shut, and it was quiet again.

After a while, I noticed that the light in the room had changed; the sun was higher in the sky. From the house came the sounds of talking, languages I didn't know muted on the other side of the door as people called out to each other, went to get their coffee. I didn't know what to do with the day. I didn't know how I was going to get through it, knowing that Nico was worse and I couldn't be with him.

I picked up my phone to cancel work for the day. But before I could text Ceanna, I saw a new message on my phone – I hadn't heard it come in.

I've worked it out. I know exactly where you are. If he dies, I'm coming for you.

After begging off work, I got back into bed and pulled the covers over my head. I shut my eyes, but my mind whirled. *Please don't let him die*, I begged any god who would listen. Assailed by memories of that last night, I curled into a ball.

Was this how Nico had felt? This need to erase myself, a desperate desire for a few hours of being blank and weightless.

If Isabelle had been there to offer me a little something, I would have taken it.

Chapter Thirty-Four

Thursday

This morning I was red-eyed after crying all night, but energized – a manic energy, born from a conviction that only I could save Nico.

I hadn't spoken to Mama Bear since that call, and the silence had been eating me alive. She didn't answer when I rang and sent only one text, reminding me to stay where I was. They didn't want me there, and I felt lost, unanchored.

As I cleaned, I was fired by a certainty that I was saving Nico. That by punishing his lover, I would set everything right. I would do this, even if it meant breaking everything here to tiny shreds. Breaking myself.

I worked like a woman possessed. By the time I was finished, everything sparkled.

When Isabelle arrived home, she looked around, a small smile on her lips. 'You're a good worker, Esmie.'

I nodded, hating her with all my bitter, black heart. A villain in a bold patterned dress.

I was unpacking the caddy in the utility room when the doorbell rang. Isabelle answered it, and hearing Caden's voice, I pressed against the kitchen door to listen.

'About what you saw,' Caden said, 'last night at Amber's . . .'

'I don't want to talk about it,' Isabelle said. 'I shouldn't have gone in through the back lane. I wish I hadn't seen you.'

'Amber doesn't know you were there.'

'What do you want, Caden?' she said tiredly.

'Are you going to tell Linc?'

'It's not my business,' Isabelle exhaled. 'But Linc's my friend.'

'Isabelle,' Caden cajoled.

'You should break it off,' Isabelle said. 'No good can come from this.'

The door clicked shut and I darted back to the utility room. So Isabelle knew about the affair too. Amber really wasn't very good at hiding.

After leaving Isabelle's, I hurried down the road to Ceanna's. The hedgerows were wild with foxglove, bramble, hogweed and mallow. I breathed in the pungent aroma of woundwort and the sweet dog roses. I'd been learning more names, and the landscape was becoming less strange to me.

I checked my phone. Nothing from Mama Bear. *No news is good news.* Ahead was the bend; I noticed that the pothole, the one I'd forced my bike into that night weeks ago, had been filled. New tar layered over the old.

I had to retrieve that photograph of me. I felt the urgency of it run through my body as I opened Ceanna's gate.

There could be nothing left behind. In two days, it would be like I was never here. Only Isabelle would know how I, behind the scenes and invisible, had watched and manipulated. How I'd righted a wrong. The rest of them would continue on, oblivious.

I knocked at the door. I was here for the photograph, but also to check if Ceanna still intended to tell Linc about

Amber and Caden – and that she'd wait until after Amber's birthday. Ceanna was ruthless, but not cruel, and she knew the consequences of her truth bomb.

But my concern was less for Amber and more for myself. I wanted to be long gone when this came out. The pictures of Amber and Caden in the summer kitchen could only be traced back to me, and Caden had warned me that he would strike back if I told. I was so close to the end, and Caden would not get in my way.

Again, that weary web of actions and consequences.

Ceanna opened the door and I said, 'I dropped an earring here the other day. Do you mind if I look for it?'

She stepped back. 'Go ahead.' She was examining my eyes. 'You feeling any better?'

'Mostly,' I lied. 'I'm sorry for missing yesterday.'

'You don't need to apologize for being sick, Esmie.'

I'd grown attached to them, I realized. I'd grown attached to Ceanna, with her broken-hearted beauty. I was even fond of Amber, who was unabashedly selfish and entitled but one of the more honest among us. And Linc – obsessive, ridiculous, sexy Linc. I would miss him and the guilty comfort I'd found in his arms.

I went to Ceanna's bedroom. My gaze fell on her shining silver jewellery box, and I opened it. Amber's emerald and diamond ring winked at me, and I admired it in the light. Both Amber and Linc had broken their promises to each other; whatever this ring had once meant to them had been erased.

But it could be a way back home for me. The ring was worth a lot. Enough to pay for the extended therapy and care that Nico needed. We could heal him, we could remake him. He'd be as he was before. And if I fixed Nico, I would fix every other broken thing.

I slipped the ring into the small pocket of my leggings and opened the bottom drawer of Ceanna's bedside table, where I knew she kept pictures and mementos.

Crouching down, I searched through the box of photographs, quickly but carefully. Ceanna's life flashed in front of my eyes – Ceanna holding a baby, Ceanna kissing a man on the cheek. Malachy, tall and imposing, with his arm around her. She'd been happy before. I hoped she'd find happiness again.

The picture of Nico and me was not there. I emptied the box, going through each individual picture, panic rising. The photo was gone. Had Ceanna removed it? Then, with a terrifying clarity, I realized who had it: Caden.

He'd been there that day. He hated me, was on the prowl to find something to discredit me. He must have seen the picture on Ceanna's bed and recognized me. Ice trickled down my spine.

I went to the kitchen, where I saw Linc at the table with Ceanna. He was smiling, and intense relief washed over me. She couldn't have told him about Amber and Caden – she must be waiting until after the birthday party. My brow furrowed when I realized they were laughing now. Together. I would never have believed it, that those two would be friends.

'Did you find it?' Ceanna glanced at me, and I was momentarily confused. Then I remembered the fabricated earring.

'Yes, thanks.' My hand brushed my leggings pocket, feeling the heavy stone of Amber's emerald ring.

Late that night, I fidgeted in my bed, rehearsing my conversation with Isabelle. I pictured her face, her anguish when she realized how badly she'd hurt her lover. Always, in these imaginings, I stood before her, wearing the same righteous expression as the angels in my childhood books, with their billowing robes and blazing swords.

At midnight, I accepted I wasn't going to fall asleep any time soon, so I got out of bed. I took the keys to the safe from my drawer and went out to my bike. I'd go to Three Oaks, I decided.

It was Friday already – the day of Amber's party. My last day in The Woodlands. These were the shortest nights of the year, and I might as well wait out the rest of this one at the cottage. There was little chance I'd sleep tonight. I was too highly strung.

This close to the solstice, the night sky was the lightest indigo I'd seen yet. I pedalled hard, flying up the hills and reaching the woods in twenty minutes. I pushed the bike over the uneven path between the trees, unafraid of walking the dark woods tonight. If anything, I felt more at peace than I had in my bed. Leaving the bike at the stone wall, I hopped over it and into the lane.

Three Oaks felt different. Maybe because it was the middle of the night, maybe because it was Midsummer. Threshold time.

Unlocking the back door, I remembered the story about the bride walking through the house, gradually embracing her own darkness in each room she passed through. Tonight, the cottage felt cavernous.

I halted at the door to Eden's study. I'd never been superstitious, never believed in ghosts or magic, but entering that room in the heart of the night, at Midsummer, I felt something. As though the walls themselves sighed as I stole across the room. As though the silver bird on the cabinet gently fluttered a wing as I flicked on the lamp. The painted flowers seemed to move as if by an invisible breeze. The writing on the wall shimmered, the ink hearts quivered. The room was a shrine, an altar, and tonight it was awake.

I opened the cabinet where the safe was kept, and kneeled before it. I slipped the smooth key without any grooves into a small circular opening near the bottom. Then I pressed around the brass discs, finding one that twisted up, and inserted the second key. It caught a little – lack of use, I presumed – and then it turned. I searched among the studs until I found the third opening and turned the last key.

I looked inside the safe and all I saw were old papers, old photographs. How had these made Linc desperate enough to drug his sister-in-law? I pulled out the papers, rifling through them until I found the lost story, 'The Heart in the Wood'. I flicked through it, and it seemed like nothing special to me.

I sat on the floor, looking through Linc's treasures, musty papers with little value to me. I thought about desire, and how it could drive any of us to desperation. How each of us wanted something, and at times that hunger was so all-consuming, so utterly obsessive, that we couldn't see past it.

Nico had wanted Isabelle, his mystery lover. Linc wanted to possess Eden, to own her every thought and word. Raise her from the dead, if he could. Amber wanted Linc. Ceanna wanted her family, and to be healed. Paul wanted Isabelle to be his good little wife. Isabelle wanted to escape.

And what did I want?

I looked down at the story on my lap, reading those lines about the bride hiding from her villainous groom as he robbed another woman.

Weeks ago, I'd arrived here hungry for justice. For revenge.

But now, I was exhausted, drained. As though I'd been walking down a long, long road, and I wanted only for it to end.

I made myself think very carefully. Why did I want revenge? Was it for Nico? Or was it for me?

Chapter Thirty-Five

Friday

Nico used to laugh at me when I was little because I was terrified of the world ending. I worried that a meteor would hit Earth, that there'd be a massive series of earthquakes and tsunamis. I feared that moment of reckoning. How I might be playing with a ball down the road, or eating hot corn with melted butter on my fingers, and then, bam, a bright white light and oblivion.

I didn't realize that my world would end while I leaned against a dead man's kitchen worktop, waiting for the kettle to boil. It was morning, and I was still at Three Oaks, preparing to go to Woodland House. I answered my phone, reaching for a teabag.

'Do you have someone with you?' Mama Bear said, and her voice sounded strange, as if she had a cold.

'What do you mean?' I was sluggish after my unrestful night.

'Is your room-mate there?'

'Yes.' I just wanted her to tell me. I had a horrible prickling sensation in my hands, and it began to spread over my body.

'It's Nico,' she exhaled shakily.

'What about Nico?' My breaths were shallow, my head swimming.

'He didn't make it through the night. His body gave up.'
Mama didn't cry, but I recognized the notes of heartbreak
in her voice. I'd heard echoes of it these last months after
Nico returned. But now it was no echo; it was like looking
into the heart of darkness.

Tightness gripped my throat. My heart clenched in a
fist. I raised a trembling hand to my mouth. The kettle
rumbled.

'I'm coming. Now.'

'Please don't.' Mama Bear was weary. 'You'll make everything worse.'

'When, then?' I needed to be there. I needed to see him
one last time. To say goodbye.

The silence grew. In that frightened moment, I couldn't
connect to Mama Bear. She felt so distant to me. Steam
escaped the boiling kettle.

'He's not here any more. He can't help you.'

I didn't say anything.

'I'm warning you, keep away.' Mama Bear sounded so
very remote. 'She wants you to suffer.'

The walls were pressing in.

'Tell her that I already do.'

I ended the call and stared at the now quiet kettle, my
mind strangely blank. I poured the hot water into the mug.
Then, without knowing what I was doing, and with a violence that surprised me, I swiped things off the worktop;
the hot mug, the boxes of pills, the metal tray flew across
the terracotta. I was breathing quickly and still I couldn't
get enough air. The tray clattered as it landed. I let out a
loud animal howl.

I sank to the floor, covering my head with my forearms. I
stayed there for a small eternity.

Near my foot was a small bottle of diazepam. I reached for
the sedative, thinking, *Should I?* But I got up, placed it on the

tray, and picked up the warfarin, an anti-coagulant, then the digoxin, a heart medication that Mama Bear had taken some years back. The corner of the large sticker was curling up, and I smoothed it down.

All the bottles were neatly placed on the tray, and yet they looked wrong, as though I'd replaced them out of sequence. I rearranged the tray of medication until I looked at myself as if from outside: tidying the small boxes and bottles, as though I could impose order on my blown-up world.

Diligent Esmie, even when my heart was in pieces.

I was back in the bedroom, sitting with my back against the wall, when I finally allowed myself to think about him. To remember Nico. How he'd built a fort in the field behind the house, a space for only the three of us. How we'd laughed together, so many times. How he'd made me feel safe and loved, until he didn't. The memories were a deluge: Nico racing us on the beach, giving us a head start and then overtaking us. The power in his arms and legs as he ran. Nico cooking, slapping my hand away as I tried to steal a tomato from the salad. The way he'd look at me, as if I was important. The feel of his hands, large and callused. The solid brown of his eyes.

My eyes were closing, my muscles relaxing. And in my head, Nico.

Nico was dead, and it was too late to save him. But it was not too late to get revenge.

Something dark and wild and broken erupted inside me.

Isabelle deserved every bad thing that was coming to her.

HOME

'You really loved her?' Simone couldn't stop picking at the wound as she stared at Nico after his terrible revelation: another woman. Love.

There was that beating in her ears again. It felt like that winged thing was inside her, flapping furiously. On the bedside table was that awful statue Nico had brought home with him. Simone felt provoked by the statue. Had his lover given it to him?

'But you don't love her any more?' Simone asked, her voice thin and high.

The beating inside grew louder. A scream was building inside her. She hurt too much, and she could not contain it. Simone, knowing that Esmerelda was on the other side of the door, clapped a hand over her mouth to stop herself from crying out.

'Don't do this, Simone.' Nico sounded tired. He closed his hand around her wrist. 'Please, just leave it alone.'

'What happened?' she said, wishing she could just leave it. But the thought of Nico with another woman ate at her. She bit hard on her bottom lip until she tasted blood. Jealousy burned like hot lava inside her. She couldn't stop thinking about the mystery woman. What did she look like? What did they talk about? She imagined Nico's hands touching another woman's skin, and she thought she would be sick.

'Leave it, Simone.' Nico still held her by the wrist. There was a simmering anger inside him. He was often angry these days, with too much time to brood. 'We're not going to talk about this. Like we don't talk about you murdering your dad.'

Simone flinched. It felt like he'd slapped her. Nico had always understood, without having to talk about it, the darkness that had overcome her that day. How it had all been too much.

'I didn't murder him.' Simone tried to pull out of Nico's hold. 'I hurt him and it went too far.'

When she picked up the pan that awful night, she'd only meant to threaten her father. Warn him. Afraid and hurt, she'd thought, *Maybe if I scare him a little, he'll stop.* Maybe if he felt a fraction of the fear and pain he'd caused, maybe then he'd understand.

Then she'd raised the cast-iron pan above him and her teeth clenched together, and something else inside her took over, and she hit once and hit twice and hit again and again, and afterwards she saw what she'd done. The horror: of coming back and seeing what she'd done.

'Esmerelda was right. I don't know if you're able to love anyone but yourself.'

'Nico.' Simone's throat was thick with anguish. 'I love you. I always have. I'd do anything for you, you know that.'

'Would you?' he said, his eyes locking on hers. 'Anything?'

'Anything,' she vowed.

'Then save me,' he whispered. He gripped both her wrists tightly, causing a red welt to form beneath her watch.

'How?' she asked. 'What can I do?'

'I'm trapped.' His face was right in front of hers. He was

pleading with her, and his eyes were wild, but also strangely lucid. 'I'm not there any more, but I'm not here either. It's like I died there, in The Woodlands, and I never made it home.'

Nico let go of her so abruptly that she nearly fell backwards. He sat heavily on the bed, rubbing a hand over his face. He looked at her, begging, 'Find me, Simone.'

Simone sank to the floor, not sure what to make of Nico's garbled talk. On her knees, she took his hands in hers.

'I'll do whatever you want,' she promised. 'Just tell me what you need.'

'I gave her my heart,' Nico said, and Simone felt each word as a stiletto driven into her chest. She pulled her hands away from him, trying to calm the boiling inside her. *He gave her his heart.* She seethed at the thought of Nico loving another woman so much that he felt part of him was thousands of kilometres away.

'Then we'll get it back,' she said, getting to her feet.

'I've never met another woman like her,' Nico continued, and Simone no longer wanted to hear anything about this woman who'd stolen Nico from her.

'Why, Nico?' she said. *Was I not enough for you?* 'Did you forget about me?'

'She was a universe unto herself.' Now that he'd started talking about the woman he loved, he couldn't seem to stop. 'She was difficult, kind, selfish, broken. I've never loved anyone the way I loved her.' He stood up, as if energized from just thinking about her.

Simone took a step away. She couldn't listen to this any more. Nico's confession made Simone feel like she was being torn open. This was worse than anything she could have imagined. She started tidying, picking up beer cans and dirty laundry, trying to block out the terrible words coming from Nico's mouth.

'She was sexy, smart and unexpected. She surprised me every day.'

'Stop it, Nico,' Simone snapped, dropping the pile of dirty T-shirts. It felt like something was breaking inside her. She couldn't breathe. Hot tears were beginning to spill. 'You're being cruel.'

'It was like a magnetic charge that attracted me to her in every—'

'I said stop,' Simone shouted. It was too much. She was on a ledge, about to fall off. Her fingers gripped the horrible bronze statue of the woman Nico had brought back.

She was falling. She gripped the statue tighter.

'I'm not sorry.' The words kept coming, and the statue was digging into her palm, leaving small dents like bite marks in her skin. 'I would choose her again,' he rasped. His eyes met hers. 'You deserve to know the truth.' He touched his hand to his own heart. 'Even though she betrayed me, lied about me, even though she destroyed me. I love her, and I can't live without her.'

Simone's heart was overcome with pure darkness.

She brought down the statue with full force as she screamed, 'Just stop it, Nico, stop it.' The sharp bronze base of the Doctor's Wife hit the side of his head. 'You don't know what you're saying. You love me.'

'I do love you, Simone.' Blood trickled down his temple. 'But I love her more.'

He swayed, and Simone whispered, 'Nico?' Her mouth fell open, unable to believe what she'd done.

She'd only meant for him to stop talking. Simone scrambled to him, falling to her knees.

The door burst open, and Nico slumped to the floor.

Chapter Thirty-Six

Friday

I woke up in Malachy's bedroom, lying on the floor, cold. I sat up, bracing my hands against the rug. I made myself remember: Nico was dead.

Still groggy, I saw on its side the small bottle of diazepam. I had no idea of how much time had passed since Mama Bear called.

Then I realized I wasn't alone.

From the living room came the sound of voices. I knew Linc's at once. I stiffened. I couldn't let him see me – I wasn't supposed to be here. My head was in turmoil. I didn't have it in me to pretend.

'Yes, it is a gorgeous day.' Linc sounded impatient. 'But I don't think you asked to meet to discuss the weather.'

'Amber said she was hiring performers?' Isabelle said. Linc was in the next room, and Isabelle was there with him. I searched the floor for my phone, finding it under the bed. It was just after eleven in the morning. Tonight was Isabelle's big escape. Why was she here talking to Linc?

'You know Amber, no half measures. She's been carried away with the *Midsummer Night's Dream* theme.' He paused. 'Isabelle, why did you want to talk? Is everything OK?'

'What do you mean?'

'Sometimes you seem troubled. If there is anything I can do . . .' He trailed off.

Sometimes you seem troubled. They lived next door, met for drinks and parties and soccer. And yet they knew so little about each other. They'd never ventured deep into each other's houses, to where the buckets of blood were kept. Only ever into the pretty front rooms.

'Isabelle?' Linc sounded gentler now. 'What's wrong?'

Quietly, I got to my feet. I pressed myself against the wall and peered out. Isabelle was perched at the edge of a chair. Her eyes were at war with the smile on her face.

'Nothing. There's nothing wrong. Not with me anyway.'

Linc leaned back in his chair, opening out his hands in a half-shrug, half-surrender. 'Then tell me what's on your mind.'

'Your student Fiona has been buying illegal drugs from a campus dealer.' Isabelle neglected to mention that she was the campus dealer.

'What?' Linc laughed. I had to admire his sincere incredulity. How his body language remained easy. Always the charming professor. 'Fiona? Drugs? I can't think of anything more ridiculous.'

Isabelle waited.

'Where did you hear this? It's impossible.' Discomfort was beginning to show in the woodenness of Linc's smile, the uncertainty in his eyes.

Isabelle remained silent. Waiting. Her marriage with Paul had trained her in the art of turning meekness into aggression. She didn't move, didn't say anything. She just watched Linc.

'Even if she did – which I doubt – it's not my concern.' Linc placed his hands on the arms of his chair, ready to end the conversation.

'You know it is very much your concern.' Isabelle leaned forward slightly, her voice dropping.

Linc was standing now. The straight line of his back was tense. 'What are you trying to say, Isabelle?'

He stepped towards her. But even though he was tall and imposing as he stood over her, it was Isabelle, still perched at the edge of her chair, who was in control.

'We all have our secrets, Linc.' In a quick, elegant move, Isabelle got to her feet. She was tall, nearly eye to eye with Linc. 'I'll let you keep yours. Both of them.'

He watched her warily as she opened her bag and showed him something inside. Linc took a sharp breath. Seconds passed by, and still he didn't say anything. Isabelle held the silence. I peered out, trying to understand what they were saying in between the words. What was I missing?

'What do you want?' he said eventually.

'I need ten thousand in cash by this evening.'

Outside, a strimmer started up in the distance, the low buzz punctuating the tension in the room.

'I'll see what I can do,' Linc said through gritted teeth. I could hear the anger in his sharp, controlled body movements as he picked up his laptop bag, zipping it.

A phone rang and Linc answered, his voice dropping as he spoke to the person on the other side. 'I'm heading to town to pick up a few things.' He listened then said, 'I know, babe. I'll be back in an hour. Esmie will be there soon. There's no need to panic.'

'Find me when the party starts,' Isabelle said. 'You can hand it over then.'

Linc strode to the cottage door and glanced at Isabelle. I was taken aback by the sheer loathing on his face.

Isabelle sank into a chair, dropped her head and exhaled loudly. I was torn between shaking her for the trouble she'd caused and pulling her into my arms for what she'd lived through.

But being a victim wasn't an excuse for how she'd used Nico. I understood she needed money to fund her escape, but I'd run away with far less.

Isabelle was still sitting in the chair, holding her head in her hands. The need to tell her what she'd done was a hot bubbling inside me. I wanted to see her face when she learned her lover was dead. When I told her how her actions had eventually killed him.

'I know you're there,' Isabelle said, not looking at me. 'You may as well come out, Esmie.'

Then she turned her head to where I'd stepped into the doorway. 'Or should I call you Simone?'

HOME

FIVE WEEKS AGO

'What have you done?' Esmerelda was at the open door, hands over her mouth. She rushed forward, to where Simone cradled Nico in her lap. Her hands were covered in blood, and she sobbed his name over and over.

'What have you done to my brother?' Esmerelda got down to the floor, pulling Nico out of Simone's lap.

'He attacked me,' Simone cried, getting to her feet. 'Don't move him so roughly.'

'Attacked you?' Esmerelda growled, facing Simone. 'Do you mean like your dad attacked you?'

'He hurt me.' Simone breathed heavily. 'Look.' She showed Esmerelda the red marks where he'd grabbed her wrist.

'I don't believe you,' Esmerelda shouted, moving closer to Simone. 'You're a liar, Simone.' She shoved Simone hard. Before Simone could recover, Esmerelda hit her across her face. 'If he dies, I will fucking kill you.'

'Enough.' Mama Bear came in, glaring at the younger women. 'This is not the time.' She spoke with her customary calm, but her mouth worked as she examined Nico. 'We need to get to the hospital.'

Nico lay on the rough carpet, his hair matted with blood. Simone's heart sank so deep inside herself she was sure she

337

would never find it again. She was terrified – that Nico would die, that Mama Bear hated her.

Simone was terrified at how she'd lost herself again. She touched a hand to her stinging cheek.

'We should never have lied about AJ's murder,' Esmerelda raged. 'You should have been made to face the consequences of what you did. We buried it, and now look what we've grown.'

'Come.' Mama Bear started for the door. 'We have to go to the hospital.' Her voice was urgent now.

They lifted him to standing, the weight of his body slumped against Simone, with Esmerelda on the other side. Nico moaned as they half walked, half dragged him to his car.

'You're not going to get away with this.' Esmerelda glared at Simone as she helped Nico into the back seat. 'I'll make sure you pay.' Her voice shook with emotion. 'Even if I have to kill you myself.'

'Simone, get the keys,' Mama Bear commanded. 'They're in the kitchen.'

Simone ran back inside, grabbing the car keys from the hook in the kitchen.

She heard Mama Bear in her and Nico's room. There she found the older woman pulling Nico's suitcase from under the bed. 'She's gone mad. You have to get out of here. She won't rest until she has your blood.'

Simone realized the suitcase wasn't for Nico. It was for her.

'Mama B?'

Mama Bear turned to Simone and took her hands, holding them tight as she spoke urgently. 'Esmie will make sure that you are arrested and put in prison. She wants to hurt you.' Her eyes held Simone's. 'He's my son, but you are like

338

my own daughter. I saw what he's done to you. I know he was carrying on with a woman behind your back. He broke his promise to you. I saw it all.' She nodded, as though she was trying to convince herself. 'He pushed you too far. And you snapped. Just like with the old man.' Mama Bear's eyes brimmed with tears. 'He pushed too far and you snapped.' She said it again, firmer this time. 'You didn't mean to hurt him.'

But Simone did. In that moment, she'd wanted him to bleed. She'd wanted him to feel pain.

'You have to be gone by the time we get back,' Mama Bear said, looking ten years older. 'Or I can't help you.'

'I don't want to leave, Mama B,' Simone cried.

'You have to go,' Mama Bear repeated sternly. 'And not just because of Esmie.'

Simone met her eyes and understood. Consequences. She was being sent away for what she'd done. Mama Bear might help her escape prison, but that didn't mean there'd be no consequences.

'I don't have anywhere to go.' Simone was desperate. They weren't her blood family, Mama Bear, Esmerelda and Nico, but they were the only family she had. The only people who mattered.

'Take this.' Mama Bear pushed something into Simone's hands and took the car keys from her.

Simone saw a clear plastic bag with a small booklet and a stack of folded pages. She pulled out the nearest sheet. 'Esmerelda's ticket? To Ireland?' It was scheduled for a few days from now. The dream holiday that was first meant to be Simone's, then Esmerelda's.

Mama Bear said hurriedly. 'All the documents they'll want at Border Control are there. You'll need her passport altered. With your picture. Do you still have his card?'

The man with the black heart in flames tattoo on his neck. Simone nodded. She'd kept it all these years. Her get out of jail card, literally.

'Can I come back?' Simone pleaded. 'After a while? When he's OK again?'

Mama Bear wiped a tear. 'When he's fine, then you can come back.'

Then she went to the door, lighting a cigarette. Esmerelda was waiting outside the car, impatient. Simone followed Mama Bear, unwilling to let them go.

'It was an accident,' Mama Bear said decisively, as the three women stood by the car. 'Promise me you'll say it was an accident.' She stamped out the cigarette and Esmerelda curled her lip, getting into the driver's seat.

Esmerelda shouted from the car window, her face contorted with rage, 'You're dead. You're a fucking dead woman. I will destroy you myself.'

The car peeled away. Simone went back inside and picked up the suitcase. She was about to dump in a stack of clothes when she saw the bulge beneath the lining. She placed her hand inside, finding the single page of a letter. She searched again, marvelling at the roll of cash in her palm.

Underneath her fingernails, Nico's blood was beginning to harden.

From under the lining of her drawer, Simone pulled out the card with the black heart in flames. The card she'd been given the night her father died.

The night she killed him.

She pressed the numbers on her phone with shaking fingers. This was her lifeline – the wily gang leader the neighbourhood feared. The card was a promise to help, if she ever needed it.

Now, Simone needed him. She had to disappear. She needed a safe place for a few nights and Esmerelda's passport altered with her photograph so she could use the plane ticket she held. It had come back full circle: the ticket should have been hers.

'I need help,' Simone said when he answered.

When prompted, she gave him her new name, one that was half stolen, half gifted. The name of her sworn enemy: Esmerelda Lorenzo.

From that night, she would be Esmie.

Chapter Thirty-Seven

Friday

Simone.

I stood in the doorway, paralysed by that one single word. My heart was drumming, memories of that awful night replaying in my mind.

'That is your name, isn't it?' Isabelle was no longer hunched in the chair. She was sitting tall, staring at me with an inscrutable expression.

'It used to be.' I walked out of the bedroom and stopped a metre from Isabelle. 'But it isn't any more.'

Isabelle reached into her bag, then held out a card to me. Not a card, a photograph. I took it from her, seeing the picture of Nico with his arms around his sister and his sweetheart. The picture I'd been searching for. Caden hadn't taken it, Isabelle had.

'He used to talk about you, when we first met. Showed this picture to all of us. I should have recognized you. But I didn't, not until I saw it on Ceanna's bed. You've changed. Lost your softness.'

That's what heartbreak does.

The pain in my chest was sharp and all-consuming. I wanted to double over with it, but I couldn't show any weakness. Not in front of Isabelle.

'I envied you,' Isabelle said simply. 'That a man like Nico

was so utterly enamoured with you. That you were loved so completely. His face lit up, you know, when he spoke about you.'

And Isabelle had decided she wanted that for herself. A rush of fury flooded my body, leaving me shaking with the strength of it.

'Why are you here?' Isabelle said.

'Investigating,' I said simply. 'Nico lost everything when he left here.'

Isabelle's eyes softened. 'It ended badly.' She searched my face, a look of increasing dread settling on hers. 'Is Nico OK?'

'No.' A hard, bitter laugh escaped. 'No, he's not OK, Isabelle. He lost his scholarship. He couldn't afford to finish his degree. When he lost his dream, he stopped caring.'

I had to pause for breath. It had cost me so much, to stand here and have this conversation with Isabelle. I had to stay calm. I couldn't shout; my voice couldn't waver. But hate, pain, anger coursed through my body, demanding to shake Isabelle, roar at her for what she'd done.

She must have seen my struggle, because Isabelle said, 'We should talk over a cup of tea.'

I didn't want tea but I needed a moment, so I nodded, then followed Isabelle into the kitchen. I sat at the table while she filled the kettle.

'I'm sorry that Nico wasn't able to complete his degree. I know how much his work meant to him.' Isabelle kept her back to me as she prepared the cups. 'He was a good friend to me.'

'Do you make all your friends help you sell prescription drugs to university students?'

She exhaled and turned around. 'So it was you who read my notebook. I suspected as much when I realized a page had been torn out.' Leaning against the cabinet, she appealed to me. 'What you read only scrapes the surface of what life is like with Paul. Judge me all you want, but you have no idea of what I've endured these last twenty years.'

'Why didn't you just leave?'

'With Paul, I'm . . . diminished.' She raised a shoulder, bringing out the simple truth of her words. 'I would rather die than run and hide and eke out an existence. I've lived the last twenty-odd years starved of texture and experience.' Her voice sounded guttural; it was the first time I'd heard Isabelle betray raw emotion. 'And now I want to feast. I want to live on my own terms. It's difficult to be truly independent without money.'

She must have caught my raised eyebrows because she gave a short laugh. 'I haven't amassed a great fortune, you know. I worked out how much I would need to pay my costs for six months, for a black market passport, driver's licence and emergency fund. What I would need to travel. I'm leaving earlier than planned and asked Linc to make up the shortfall.' She raised an eyebrow. 'Selling a few pills to bored housewives and university students isn't so terrible.'

'It was for Róisín.'

Isabelle flinched.

'And for Nico.' I made her hold my gaze. 'He was addicted. We couldn't reach him.'

Isabelle took a sharp breath, distress in her eyes. 'I didn't know.'

'Well, you should have.' The anger was bubbling in my chest. 'You hurt him. He was so lost, and it's all your fault.' I was shouting now. I couldn't hold back any more. I felt ablaze, driven by months of heartbreak. 'You cost him everything. And I'm going to make sure you pay for what you did.'

Isabelle reared back. She stared, wide-eyed, as if I'd slapped her. She turned abruptly to the cups behind her.

She held her back to me, and I couldn't see her face. I couldn't see what she was thinking.

I took a deep breath, holding it in my lungs until it burned. I couldn't let my emotions get the better of me. I couldn't lose control.

Not like I had with Nico.

Not like I had with my dad.

'Did you supply Nico with medication?' I said levelly.

Isabelle busied herself with making tea, but I saw her shoulders drop. She stirred the mug in front of her, buying time.

'Did you?' My voice was rougher now. Isabelle took her time with the second mug. She couldn't face me. Eventually she turned, both mugs in hand.

She placed a mug in front of me and said quietly, 'Yes.' Her face sagged. 'I'm sorry.' She added milk and pushed the sugar towards me.

In my many mental rehearsals of this moment, I stood upright and virtuous as I confronted Isabelle with the consequences of what she'd done. Now, I felt depleted, dissatisfied. I straightened my shoulders. I had to pull myself together. I drank my tea, and the heat in my throat was punishing. Welcome.

'I'm sorry that Nico's been struggling,' Isabelle said. 'If it's any consolation, he's the strongest, most determined man I know. I hope that will help him through.'

'Nico's dead,' I said bluntly.

'What?' Isabelle's face was a mask of shock. She clutched the small Formica table. 'What happened?'

'He came here. He fell in love. He developed an addiction. He lost his purpose. And it killed him.' I drank more tea, the scalding in my throat drawing out the words. Words I'd needed to say since Nico returned to us. 'I've taken photos of your notebook and the orders on your phone. I

346

have evidence of you supplying Róisín with the drugs that led to her death.'

Isabelle's face worked, understanding what I was saying. That I had evidence that could cause a lot of trouble for her. 'What do you want?'

'Justice.' An eye for an eye. A life for a life. I took another sip, feeling fortified. I set the mug down neatly, as though it was made of delicate china, and Isabelle and I were enjoying high tea in some elegant drawing room.

'Simone,' Isabelle started cautiously, testing my old name. I remembered how the other Esmie had sneered her name at me over the phone, after she learned I'd stolen it. I didn't feel like Simone any more.

'It's Esmie now.'

Simone lived near the mountains, walked between the midnight vines with her beloved. Simone sat on a beanbag chair listening to him type through the night, spinning his dreams into words. Simone was loved, passionately and completely. Simone had been betrayed. Simone was wild, she hurt those who'd hurt her. I was not Simone any more.

'Esmie, then. I can't imagine what you're feeling.' Isabelle spoke gently. 'I can guess you're heartbroken and angry, and that you want to lash out to alleviate your pain. I understand why you see me as the cause of that pain, the origin of Nico's downward spiral. But talking to Paul about any of this will just make him angry. Furious.'

I relished the desperation that was entering her voice, despite her efforts to hide it. 'I wasn't sure if I should tell Paul.'

'You weren't?'

'I thought it might be more effective to tell Róisín's husband. Everything.' I held her eye. 'He's been looking for you. I suspect he'll take it all to the police.'

Isabelle sat down so heavily that the chair scraped against the hard floor. 'Please don't do that.'

'But I decided that Paul deserves to know.'

'He'll never let me leave.' She clutched her mug, as if to stop her hands shaking. 'He'll punish me.'

I felt a twinge of guilt. *She deserves this*, I reminded myself as I hardened my heart. Her cage was made of gold. There were worse ways to live.

The helplessness in her eyes sliced at my heart. *She deserves it*, I thought again, furious with myself.

She put her mug on the table. 'How did Nico die?'

I thought of Isabelle's statue, covered in blood. Lying on the floor where I'd dropped it. Esmie, the real one, bursting into the room, screaming at me. I felt another sob catch in my throat.

'He started dying the minute you gave him his first bottle of pills,' I said harshly, pushing down that terrible memory. The bitter taste of my own culpability. The weight of it made me feel breathless. 'Did it not occur to you that he was asking for too much? Why did you keep supplying him?'

'He said he was buying for other students,' Isabelle said faintly.

'But you should have noticed that he was behaving differently.' The room seemed to tilt, and I shook my head as if to clear it. Isabelle watched me with her dark eyes.

'You were his lover.' I bit out the words. I was suddenly exhausted. 'He lost his scholarship because of your lies.' My words sounded lazy, half formed. My head was spinning.

Isabelle's face seemed to melt into the wall behind. I blinked to focus. My eyelids were so heavy . . .

'Esmie, I wasn't his lover.'

'Stop lying. I know you were.' I gestured to my bag under the table. 'Your scarf.' I wanted to go over there, but when I tried to move my legs, they were too heavy.

Isabelle rummaged in the bag and pulled out the green floral scarf. 'This isn't my scarf.' Her brow knitted, then she turned to me. 'Oh, Esmie. This was left behind at my house. I meant to give it back, but I forgot about it.'

'Isabelle,' I slurred, suddenly understanding. 'What did you put in my tea?'

'I'm sorry.' She stood. 'I couldn't risk you telling Paul or anyone else what I've done. I've risked his reputation, and I'm trying to leave him. He would make my life miserable for that. Unliveable.'

She stepped towards me, studying my eyes. 'It's nothing serious. It will make you sleep for a while. And when you wake, I'll have escaped.'

I tried to stand, but my legs wouldn't obey. I had to ask about the scarf – if it wasn't hers, then who did it belong to? But my mouth couldn't form the words. My brain was sluggish, my body weighed down by stones.

I needed to know: if she wasn't Nico's lover, then who was? I let out an anguished, formless sound as I forced myself to speak.

But the words never made it out.

The last thing I remembered was Isabelle lifting her mug and swallowing the remains of her tea.

Chapter Thirty-Eight

Midsummer

I awoke in the forest. The sun had shifted, but I had no idea of the time. I lay staring up at the light dancing between the leaves of the tall trees. It was mesmerizing, the wink and sparkle, and I felt as though my bones had melted into the mulch.

Something niggled at me. There was something I had to do. What was it?

Then it all came rushing back to me.

Isabelle.

I sat up quickly, my head pierced with pain at the sudden movement. I must have wandered out here while under the influence of Isabelle's drug.

This isn't my scarf.

Of course she would say that, I reasoned. Of course she would deny it.

I searched my shirt pocket for my phone, but it was gone. I knew Isabelle had taken it. I'd told her that I'd taken pictures of her notebook, of the orders in her phone. She wouldn't have left that behind.

I cursed. Isabelle was likely on her way to the ferry. She'd have abandoned her car with a note for Paul. She would have hidden the notebook for her girls, but not in Ava's wardrobe because she'd know that I'd find it there.

Looking up at the leaves swaying gently, I realized where I was: in Eden's favourite part of the woods. Funny that I'd come here under the influence of Isabelle's drug. It intrigued me that I'd chosen the tree where Linc had pressed against me. Was my attraction to him beginning to push down roots?

After Nico had betrayed me, I'd sworn I'd never love again. I couldn't love anyone the way I'd loved him.

And then I understood what my unconscious mind must have realized. The rock, the tree, the moss-covered roots.

I was at Nico's tree. I'd found it, but I hadn't recognized it until I saw it from this angle.

I stood up, moving towards the huge trunk searching for an etching in the bark.

This isn't my scarf.

Then I saw it. Above my eyeline. Still feeling disconnected, as if I was floating above myself, I rose to my tiptoes, steadying myself on the branch above. A heart shape, tucked beneath the branch.

I'd found it. I'd found the heart in the woods.

And inside the deeply etched heart were two initials: NL. Nico Lorenzo.

And AK.

Amber Kelly.

Amber. Of all the women in the world, Nico had betrayed me with Amber. Small, vain, self-involved Amber.

For fuck's sake, Nico, I thought as I stumbled from the woods. *Her?*

The house was pulsing. Music pumped, and it felt like a steady heartbeat. The regular vibration travelled through the ground, up my thin-soled shoes. The fairy lights at the gate and in the trees strobed in time to the beat. They seemed to beckon.

I emerged from the woods, my head muddled and my heart sore. The world was still slightly tilted, slightly off-centre.

I stumbled on a new pothole as I approached the gate, summoning the spirit to have another confrontation with another woman. Outside Amber's house, the road was packed with cars, some of them parked on the field opposite.

I tried to fight off the spiralling gloom. My careful planning had been all about how to make Isabelle pay. But in my weeks at The Woodlands, I'd inhabited these houses like a silent ghost. I knew what Amber ate for breakfast, when she did yoga, the date of her last period. I knew so much more than I'd realized. I knew, because their houses had told me.

And in Woodland House, I'd learned that Amber was having an affair with Caden. I quickened my pace, my step lighter as I plotted how I could use this against her.

Then I remembered. Of course. Linc.

I remembered that dark, corrosive jealousy I'd felt the night Nico confessed to me. How it had nearly destroyed me to learn that Nico had loved another woman.

Without realizing it, I'd hit bull's eye. Amber worshipped Linc – he was what mattered most to her, just as Nico mattered most to me. If she knew I'd been with Linc, I would hurt her in the same way she'd hurt me. And then I'd tell him about Caden, and make sure she lost Linc for ever. An eye for an eye. I put my hand on their gate, feeling a dark satisfaction.

But that niggling question made me pause. Was I really doing this to get justice for Nico? Or was I doing it because he'd broken my heart?

I shut my eyes briefly, and when I opened them again, he was there, leaning against the wall beside the door. Nico, wearing black jeans and a white T-shirt.

353

The roses were in full bloom. The door was open. The music was louder, the bass now layered to my own heartbeat.

Nico gave me one of his devastating smiles, then jerked his head at the door as if to say, *What are you waiting for? There's a party.* And then he was gone.

'Wait,' I shouted, and ran up the steps. I felt odd: the little parasite me had been dislodged, and was about to be ejected from the host.

Inside, the party was well underway. A couple in soft flowing fabrics and flowers in their hair flirted in the passage, the woman leaning against the wall in the exact spot Caden had fucked Amber. I ducked between them, catching sight of black jeans and a white shirt disappearing into the afternoon room. I passed a man with a donkey head, who brayed at me.

I stumbled inside, and a group of faces turned to look at me for one perfect second. Then they turned back to each other, to their circle of Shakespeare and red wine, their earnest conversation. I went into the kitchen, which was empty of people but filled with crates of wine, caterers' trays heating food.

I grabbed my costume from the utility room, slipping on the silky white blouse. I placed the fairy wings on my back, the flower wreath on my head. I was wearing yesterday's leggings, but I didn't care.

I went through the glass doors, pausing at the spot where I'd watched Amber kiss Caden. Another man, a different one, in a donkey head, was pretending to gallop around. I felt a flash of impatience: is this what rich people parties were like? I looked around the back garden, the garage, the shed, the summer kitchen, and beyond the orchard. Everywhere I turned there were fairies in flowers and flowing

354

fabric, people painted in gold, ladies in beautiful dresses, and more men with donkey heads than I'd ever thought I'd see in one place. The party was well underway, and the guests were loud and merry.

Seeing the flash of a white T-shirt, I set off down one of the paths, winding through the trees. It was so pretty, the smell so fresh. I breathed in deeply, feeling Nico behind me. I turned abruptly.

In the distance, between the trees, Ceanna was talking to Linc. He was dressed as the King of the Fairies, but he looked like a man who had nothing. Even from here, I could tell it was a serious conversation. Linc's shoulders were stooped. Ceanna had the camera in her hand.

She'd told him. And at Amber's lavish, no-expense-spared birthday party. Again, it struck me how cold Ceanna could be.

I had to find Amber. I whirled around, pushing through the apple trees. Down the garden, past the summer kitchen, was an enormous pile of wood, Amber's Midsummer bonfire. Orange flame licked the broken crates and planks, and I watched, momentarily mesmerized by its hunger.

'Esmie, what the fuck?' Amber's harsh voice was unwelcome. 'Why are you weaving between the trees when we're nearly out of fucking glasses?'

And there she was. The woman who Nico had loved so much he carved her initials into a tree. The woman he loved more than me. Amber Kelly. She looked exquisite tonight. She wore a diaphanous ballgown of white and gold. Her cheeks were burnished with gold, her eyes dark with sparkling silver make-up. On her head was a tall gold crown crusted with berries and flowers. She was, without a doubt, the queen.

'Amber,' I said. There was so much I had to say. But the

party was loud, and the noise was stealing my words. I was still struggling with the after-effects of whatever Isabelle had slipped in my tea, which had made me hallucinate my dead fiancé.

Amber's mouth was a tight line as she studied me. 'Are you drunk?'

I shook my head.

'Where were you earlier?' she growled. 'You let me down, Esmie.'

A couple wearing a prince and princess outfit turned to look at us. Another man with a donkey's head gave a braying laugh. Beyond, I saw Isabelle and Paul dressed as a lord and lady. He held her hand, guiding her through the path between the trees.

She was still here. She hadn't left yet.

Isabelle looked as though she wanted to be anywhere but here. I wondered what had delayed her.

'Isabelle,' I said. I had to get my phone. The evidence aside, it was my link with Mama Bear. The only way I'd know if she wanted me home again. I missed her so much.

Isabelle glanced over, seeing me there with Amber. Her face thundered, and I remembered too late that Isabelle knew who I really was.

Paul grabbed her hand, jerking her towards him. She pulled back, saying something to him. She turned from him, moving towards the summer kitchen, and Paul called her name again.

'I'm going to the ladies.' Isabelle sounded exasperated. 'Give me a few minutes.'

'Something strange is going on with those two.' Amber shook her head and turned back to study me, frowning. 'Your eyes are odd. You're high, aren't you? You're supposed to be working.' She didn't wait for me to answer. 'We need to have a serious talk.'

Yes, Amber. We do.

The couple and the donkey-man were still watching us, interested in Amber's obvious displeasure.

'Not here,' she said. 'Come on.' She dipped her head to the summer kitchen.

'Amber,' a voice called, and she cursed under her breath.

'I'll meet you there. Get started on those glasses.'

I set off between the trees, feeling the long grass brush my ankles. Hearing Linc's voice, I hid behind a tree.

'Look, Isabelle, now is really not a good time.' His voice sounded ragged. 'I have five thousand in the study – the rest is tied up.'

'I need it this evening,' Isabelle insisted. She was checking over her shoulder, as if searching for Paul. I pressed closer to the tree.

'I asked my dad to help. He'll be here soon.'

A hand closed over my wrist and whirled me around. I was dragged off the path and between the trees.

'What do you want, Caden?' I said, rubbing my wrist. The fog in my head was beginning to clear.

'Did you tell Ceanna about me and Amber?' He wore an open waistcoat and short trousers, like a bad elf.

'Ceanna knows. She saw you kissing Amber the night of the dinner party.' I craned my neck to see where Linc had gone. I didn't have time for this, and I glared at Caden.

He moved nearer, invading my space. 'If you told her anything, Esmie, I swear you're going to regret it. I know you're hiding something, and if Linc hears a word of this, I will find your secrets and bury you with them.'

I threw my hands up in the air, forcing him back. I'd had it with Caden threatening me. 'Enough,' I spat.

This insignificant man thinking he could lord it over me. Trying to make me afraid with his insinuations. I had faced worse, and I'd survived. Caden was nothing.

I placed both my hands on his chest and shoved, hard. He stumbled back, and I shoved again. 'I think Linc will care more about your secrets than mine.'

A garden shovel stood against a nearby tree. Everything in me ached to pick it up. To shut him up. The flat end would fit perfectly against Caden's big stupid head. I remembered the satisfaction I'd felt when the iron pan had struck all those years ago. When I'd finally shut him up.

I really wanted to shut Caden up.

His eyes followed mine to the shovel, then flicked back to me. He held my eyes, and whatever he saw in them made him swallow visibly.

I stepped back, away from him. 'You don't speak to me again.'

Then I turned away, done with Caden.

Chapter Thirty-Nine

Midsummer

In the empty summer kitchen, I pulled off my wings and washed glasses while I waited for Amber. There was a huge pile of them, and I was grateful for the distraction. Because those glasses stopped me from going back and picking up the shovel.

'You watched me and Caden the other night. He told me.' Amber came into the summer kitchen after a few minutes, every inch a fairy queen. She was beautiful, cruel. Magnificent and otherworldly. Finally, I could see her true appeal to Nico. I could see the woman who'd tied him up in the woods. I could see the woman who excited him, who'd burrowed under his skin.

I could see my rival.

'Why were you here that night?' Amber tilted her head.

I finished the glass in my hand and set it at the side of the sink. I pulled off the rubber gloves.

'That's the wrong question.'

Her eyes narrowed, puzzled and irritated.

'I'm not here to play games.' Her crown made her look haughty and tall. 'I want to make sure you're not going to tell Linc what you saw.'

Too late, I thought. Ceanna already had.

'Please, Esmie.' She softened her voice, trying a different tack. 'Linc is everything to me. You can't tell him.'

'The right question,' I continued, as if she hadn't spoken, 'is: what am I doing here at all? Why have I come to The Woodlands?' I gestured around me, making my voice stronger, harder. Finding my real voice. 'Why do you do it, Amber? Why do you cheat on Linc if he is everything to you?'

She looked at me, furious, as if to say, *How dare you?* But Amber must have seen the fierceness in my face because she answered.

'I want him to care,' she said roughly. 'I want him to be afraid he might lose me. I want him to fight for me. I wanted only to flirt with Caden, kiss him a few times. But Caden is magnetic. He pulled me under his spell. Every time it happened, I swore never again. I didn't mean for things to get out of hand.'

Amber was like the spoilt child who deliberately broke a toy and then cried because it was broken.

She looked at me, curious. 'Why did you come to The Woodlands?'

'You know, I can count on one hand the times you've shown any interest in me as a person,' I said conversationally. 'I am here for the truth. For justice.'

'Justice?' Amber scoffed. 'What justice could you find in my back garden?'

'Justice for Nico,' I said softly, watching fear shadow Amber's eyes.

'Nico,' I repeated. 'Who'd been engaged to marry me. You knew he was engaged, didn't you, Amber? You didn't care about that. Was Nico magnetic, like Caden?' I already knew the answer to that. 'Did things get out of hand? Were you only trying to make Linc jealous?' A distant cheering from the party reached us. 'Did it work?'

360

Amber's mouth opened as if to speak, then she shut it again. 'But you're from Brazil,' she finally said.

'I never said I was. You all just assumed.'

She looked at me, and I couldn't believe it: that we were finally facing each other as the two women Nico had loved.

But Amber wasn't thinking about Nico. 'If you're planning to tell Linc about Caden, don't bother. He won't believe you.'

'He will, when he sees the evidence of you and Caden. A photograph of you, in that room.' I tilted my head to the shut dining-room door. I held back from telling her that he likely already had.

'You took pictures?' she breathed.

'Ceanna insisted.'

'Ceanna?' Amber was bewildered.

'What happened with Nico?' I wanted to bring it back to him. To what mattered.

'What about Nico?' Amber sounded irritable. 'We had a fling. I'm sorry you got hurt. But it was only ever casual. I mean, yes, we shared a strong attraction, but that doesn't mean it was anything more.'

'A fling?' It was like she'd plunged a knife into my chest. My world, upended, for a fling?

'It wasn't serious,' Amber said, and I understood why there wasn't a Nico keepsake in her special drawer – she simply hadn't cared enough about him. 'I can't believe you took pictures. What kind of person does that?'

'You betrayed Nico. You lied.' I tried to keep my voice from shaking. 'And it cost him his scholarship. Was it because Linc found out you were cheating on him? Did Linc catch you in bed together?'

'You don't know anything about what happened that day,' she hissed.

'Then tell me,' I said, my voice rising. 'How did you get Nico kicked out? What did you tell the university?'

She gave an exaggerated sigh. 'Linc found us together, here in this dining room.' She gestured to the shut door. I glanced at it, and for a second, I could almost hear the low murmur of impassioned voices.

Amber continued: 'Nico had bound me to a beam and gagged me.' She shrugged. 'That's how we liked it. He liked it best when I begged. When things got really rough. When we hurt each other.' Her eyes widened mockingly. 'Do you really want to hear details about your fiancé's cheating?'

'I want to know why he lost his scholarship.'

But I was thinking about the photograph of him bound to the tree, and the words from the poem that Nico had scribbled on the back. I finally understood why he'd written them – that this was the nature of their affair: aggressive, wicked, painful.

'We'd been split up for two weeks. Nico dropped by to see Linc, said he needed to discuss something urgent and they'd arranged to meet.'

'Why had he arranged to meet Linc?' I interrupted. Finally, I was getting answers.

Amber shrugged. 'They were friends.' She didn't even look a little ashamed. 'Nico had just arrived when Linc called to say he had a last-minute work meeting and would be back much later. Nico and I – we didn't expect that Linc's meeting would be cancelled.' She took a breath. 'Linc came home, found us together. He was livid. He launched himself at Nico, throwing punches.'

'He fought for you,' I said. 'Just as you wanted.'

'I never meant literally fight, but yes, I liked that he was jealous. I've spent my whole marriage in the shadow of Eden fucking Hale, and to see Linc act like that, like I mattered, it was what I'd been chasing for so long. I'd pushed

Linc's boundaries many, many times to get a reaction, and there it was. Finally.'

I felt my lip curl. 'You used Nico to make Linc jealous.'

'It was more than jealousy. Linc was enraged. If you didn't know me, then I can imagine that it might look bad – the ropes, the gag, how rough and abrasive Nico was. As soon as he saw us, Linc started talking to me like I'd been hurt. He was roaring at Nico for assaulting me.' She looked uncomfortable. 'It all happened so quickly – Linc treating me like I was his delicate flower, the men yelling at and shoving each other. Eventually, Nico said that he'd had enough of this bullshit and left.'

'Did you tell Linc the truth? After Nico left?'

'I tried,' Amber said. 'But Linc was fussing over my bruises and was so incensed, there was no talking to him. I told Linc to have a drink while I showered. I planned to go downstairs afterwards and force him to listen to what had really happened. I planned to tell him that everything we did was consensual.' She lifted her chin, the spark returning to her eyes. 'And I won't be shamed for it.'

'But you didn't tell him, did you? You never cleared it up.'

'I didn't even have time to shower. Ceanna called to say my dad had taken a really bad turn and had gone to the hospital. In the chaos that followed, I didn't talk to Linc until several hours later.'

There was real sorrow on her face now. 'I didn't dream for a second that things would snowball out of control.' She took a deep breath. 'It was raining that day. Nico had run out without even stopping to put a shirt on. I'd never seen Linc like that, gripped with cold purpose. He left while I went upstairs. I thought he was going to clear his head, but within the hour, Linc was in the university president's office showing him pictures of my bound wrists and other bruises. He offered not to go to the guards as

363

long as Nico was immediately expelled. By the time I knew what was happening, the awful chain of events was already in motion.'

'You could have stopped it at any time,' I said coldly, ignoring the tear that ran down her cheek.

'I wanted to,' she whispered. 'I was so afraid. For Nico. And because my dad was dying.'

What she'd really feared, I realized, was losing Linc completely if she told him the truth. Her plan to make Linc jealous, to fight for her, had worked. She wouldn't have risked it for a man she never really loved.

'You saw Nico again, didn't you? One last time.'

Another tear fell down her cheek as she nodded. 'We met in the woods later that night. He wanted to meet because he had something urgent to tell me.'

'What did he tell you?'

She shook her head. 'It was such a mess. He was trying to kiss me, cajole me, tell me he loved me. That I could leave with him, that we'd start over somewhere new, together. He told me that Linc was a bad man – stupid, desperate lies about Linc hurting Dad. He didn't seem to get that it was over. That I will always love Linc more.'

I thought I'd grown numb to the pain, but these words found a new spot to wound.

Her voice when she spoke was husky. 'I told him it was better this way. That he should take this as a new start. That Linc and I . . .' She blushed, because in the end, it had all gone her way. She'd got exactly what she'd wanted. 'That I was going to try to make things work with Linc.'

'You hung Nico out to dry.'

'No! I gave him money. For his new start.'

The cold calculation it took to bring a roll of notes to your last meeting with your lover. It made me hate her with new vigour. One thousand euros to assuage her conscience.

Amber was rich; she thought she could just buy her way out of the mess she'd made.

'I was a coward,' she continued. 'I thought Nico would go home and continue his degree there. Go back to his fiancée – to you – and move on. I didn't know what would happen.'

'You knew how much he loved you.'

'Is that why you're here?' She sounded cold now. 'Because I stole Nico? You came all this way, spent weeks cleaning my house, because I hooked up with your boyfriend? Isn't that a little . . . pathetic?'

I hushed the little voice inside that kept on with that same question. I was there to avenge Nico, not to punish my rival. I was doing this all for him. It wasn't to feed that dark hunger inside me.

Amber clearly had no idea of the wasps' nest she was poking. I felt that wildness again. The one that wanted me to smash things, to break things. To lash out and hurt. When it took over, I didn't care about the consequences. I was pure, unfettered rage and pain.

While I wrestled with myself, Amber continued talking '. . . so I'll never fully understand why he'd go to the president crying assault when he knows from experience what I'm like.'

There was a sudden thumping sound from inside the dining room. It was followed by a crashing noise, like a falling object smashing.

'Is someone in there?' Amber asked me, her eyes wide, then relieved to see the heavy door shut. 'If you tell anyone any of this, I'll deny it.' Amber went to the door, turned the handle. It jammed slightly, but she pushed, then used her shoulder and it opened.

'Nico's dead.'

'What?' Amber's voice cracked. 'How?'

Another sound, a low groan, from the dining room drew Amber's attention, and I saw her face drain of blood. She rushed inside.

I followed her in. The window was wide open. A candelabra had been knocked down. There was something on the other side of the table. Something on the floor.

'A man went through the window,' Amber said, panicked, as we rounded the table.

'Did you see who it was?'

Amber let out a cry. Lying on the floor, in the corner of the room, was Isabelle. Her fairy dress was soaked red at the chest. She was alive, but barely.

We rushed towards her. I glanced outside as I passed the window. In the distance, between the apple trees, was a figure. He wore a black cotton shirt and gloves as he bent for something resting at the base of a tree. Drawn by my gaze, he turned to look at me. It was the bearded man. Róisín's husband. How quiet he'd been. How silently he'd made her bleed.

We were made of similar clay, I thought. Betrayed and broken and lashing out. We were both trapped within our hurt, and now that was all we knew.

He placed a donkey head over his face, and then he disappeared between the apple trees.

Amber was kneeling over Isabelle, giving her CPR. I knelt on the other side, trying to find a pulse, taking over the CPR when Amber flagged.

But it was too late. Isabelle had been stabbed in the chest multiple times. On the floor beside her was a carving knife, one I'd seen in the sideboard while snooping; it looked like the bearded man had done some snooping too. Isabelle must have come into the dining room to hide from Paul while waiting for the money, not realizing another danger followed her in.

I looked down at my shirt, seeing the blood soak into the fabric.

And all at once, I knew the form my justice would take. An eye for an eye. A life for a life.

Amber was on her knees, dazed. I had to make sure they would believe me, and not her. There had to be evidence of an argument. I watched Amber, willing her to move away.

'We should call for help,' I said, hoping she'd go.

But Amber dropped her face into her hands and let out a ragged sob. It would have to do. Carefully, I took Amber's emerald ring from the small pocket in my leggings, yesterday's leggings, and wiped away any trace of me. I closed it in Isabelle's hand.

I stood up, backing away. I pulled the window shut and locked it, replaced the candelabra on the side table.

Then I screamed. I roared, letting out the wildness that had been trapped inside all day.

'Amber, what have you done?' I cried, my hand flying up to my mouth. 'What have you done to Isabelle?'

From outside, I heard the sound of footsteps and I screamed again. 'You killed her. Oh my God, you killed her.'

Linc burst into the room, followed by Caden. They rushed around the table and stared at Isabelle, the blood pooling on the stone floor. Amber kneeling, blood on her white-and-gold dress. There was a streak on her face as she stared, open-mouthed, at me. Caden made straight for Isabelle, and checked her pulse. When he looked up, he shook his head.

'Linc!' I rushed to him, sobbing. 'Amber did it. She killed Isabelle. I heard them arguing, Isabelle said she'd found Amber's ring, that Amber didn't deserve to wear it. She was going to tell you that Amber had been cheating with Caden. I tried, but I couldn't . . .' My voice hitched.

Linc pushed me back to arm's length, his eyes roaming over my face, taking in the bloody shirt. I couldn't read his expression, couldn't tell what he was thinking. Would he believe me over his wife?

'Are you hurt?' he said after a moment, and I shook my head.

'I tried so hard to stop it.' A sob caught in my throat. Another death. When would it end? 'I was too late.' He smoothed the hair from my face, his thumb briefly brushing away a single tear.

'Linc,' Amber said, alarm making her voice shrill. 'Linc, please, she's lying. I would never hurt Isabelle.'

'But you did cheat.' Linc turned to her. He folded his arms to his chest. 'With Caden.'

Caden was staring at Amber, horror on his face. 'I'd better find Paul.' He edged back as Amber lurched forward.

Slipping in Isabelle's blood, she got to her feet. She made for Linc, getting caught in her diaphanous, now-bloody dress, her crown askew. I moved away as she threw herself into Linc's arms, begging him. She told him I was lying. She told him that I couldn't be trusted. That I was a liar and I wanted to punish her. That I wasn't who I said I was. Her words were garbled and incoherent, babbling about Nico and Caden.

Linc's face was stone. He prised her arms from his neck and stepped away. Closer to me.

'Please, Linc, I love you. I love only you,' Amber cried, as he connected to the emergency operator. 'There was a man,' she said desperately. 'Dressed in black. He – he went through the window, see it's open. He knocked over the candelabra.' She gestured wildly, then frowned. Linc took in the locked window, the candelabra neatly in front of it. Pity and disgust wrestled on his face.

I watched Amber beg, and it fed that darkness inside me.

Then Paul lumbered in, his face stricken with grief. He tripped over an uneven flagstone, barely catching himself as he collapsed to his knees beside Isabelle, lifting her still, bloody body to his arms and howled his pain. I felt a horrible knot in my stomach at the sight. *Isabelle would hate this*, I thought. She'd been so desperate to escape him, and there she was, bound by his arms.

Liadh came in, and she was making these small mewling noises, and Paul pulled her into his arms, and I couldn't bear it.

I left the room, stopping to wash the blood from my hands in the kitchen sink. I pulled off the shirt, trying to scrub the blood away before hurling it across the kitchen, where it hit the wall with a wet sound.

I walked out into the orchard, still mildly surprised by the night sun. Most of the guests had left – just the odd hanger-on lingered – but they were up nearer the house, no doubt making cups of tea as they waited for the police.

I followed the path until I reached the bonfire. I stared up at the flames, thinking about that fire the other Esmie and I started all those years ago. The fire that made me first love Nico. The day he first suffered because of me.

'I'm sorry, Nico,' I whispered. 'I'm so sorry for hurting you.'

Then came the distant sound of sirens drawing towards The Woodlands. There was something bothering me, something that still didn't fit. I searched through the events of the day, but it remained elusive.

My mind was haunted by images of Isabelle on the floor. Róisín's husband between the apple trees. Amber's desperate pleading. Liadh seeing her mother's body.

I kept thinking about the conversation in the summer kitchen with Amber, how she had allowed Linc's misunderstanding to gain legs until it ruined Nico's life, and I couldn't shake the feeling that I was missing something.

369

Nor could I forget that one insistent question, the one I didn't want to think about: had I done all this to get justice for Nico? Or was it to punish the woman he'd chosen over me?

A log shifted and the fire flared, then rested. The sirens had stopped.

It was time for Amber to meet her reckoning.

Chapter Forty

THREE MONTHS LATER

People still stopped outside and stared when they walked by. The cottage where the university lecturer now lived. After he'd moved from the big old property, Woodland House, where his pretty blonde wife had killed the next-door neighbour. The neighbour who'd been selling prescription drugs to university students.

Even Ceanna paused a moment, her hand on the front gate of her father's home, the one she'd finally agreed to sell, but only to Linc. She looked at the house, and I couldn't read her expression.

I watched at the window, and Linc stole behind me. I stiffened slightly before he slipped his hand around my waist. This is the thing about living with a murderer: you have to make sure they never catch you unawares.

It was a few nights after Amber's party when I realized what had niggled at me that day, while I watched the fire. After everyone had left, Linc had asked me to stay the night because he didn't want to be alone. One night turned into three, and on the third, he joined me in the guest room. As he kissed me, I thought how strangely fitting it was that Linc and I should turn to each other after Amber and Nico had cheated on us.

I thought how both my lovers had been Amber's lovers.

371

And then I thought of Amber's preference for ropes and pain, and how they might be what Linc liked too. That's when her words, lost in the events of the day, had come back to me: *I'll never fully understand why he'd go to the president crying assault when he knows from experience what I'm like.*

I fell asleep pondering these questions – why *had* Linc gone immediately to the president? Why not wait a day, talk it through? Why the rush?

When I woke the next day, I understood with the clarity of morning. I recalled Fiona and Linc's cryptic conversation in the kitchen at Three Oaks. Isabelle telling Linc that she would keep his secrets if he handed over ten thousand. *Both of them,* she'd said.

I'd looked up the medication I'd found on Malachy's tray. Digoxin was heart medication, derived from foxglove, and toxic if overdosed. The label on the pack had no dispensing pharmacy, no date nor doctor, and the dosage was high.

Linc had been poisoning Malachy, just as he had drugged Ceanna.

Maybe he only meant to make Malachy endlessly grateful to him, for looking after him the way he did Ceanna. Maybe he was simply a murderer through carelessness.

Malachy must have realized what Linc was doing to him. He'd tried to tell his daughters but they'd thought him confused and paranoid. Weak, and knowing he was dying, Malachy had told Nico his fears. Nico, with his saviour complex, would have wanted to help.

Nico would have confronted Linc. And Linc then knew he had to get rid of Nico.

He'd told Nico to meet him at Woodland House. But he'd called home, saying that he'd been delayed. Alone at Woodland House, Amber and Nico, powerfully attracted to each other, did what they usually did.

Just as Linc expected.

Linc knew what he'd walk in on. I'd seen the toys in their bedroom.

With a false accusation of sexual assault, Linc wasted no time smearing Nico's name. And Amber was too slow and too weak to stop him.

The next day, the old man died. In the woods before she paid him off, Nico tried to tell Amber what Linc had done, but she'd thought him desperate and lying.

Linc, Amber, Isabelle and me. All four of us had Nico's blood on our hands.

'Hey, you hungry?' Linc dropped a quick kiss on my lips. If the neighbours were shocked by the speed with which Linc had moved on after his wife's incarceration – with the cleaner, no less – they didn't say it to me.

'Ceanna's here.' I nodded to where she was now walking down the front path.

'Give her some time,' he said, squeezing my shoulders. 'She'll get used to us.'

I wasn't going to hold my breath.

'Linc?' Ceanna called from the ajar front door. She rarely called in, and when she did, she always seemed uncomfortable. Despite everything, she was loyal to her sister. She did not like that Linc had moved on so quickly, and it was me she blamed.

'I'll make dinner,' I said. 'Ask Ceanna to eat with us.' She always declined.

'She went to visit Amber today.'

Linc hadn't been to see his wife. His future ex-wife. Amber still denied killing Isabelle, but the police had found Amber's ring in Isabelle's hand and taken it as proof of a confrontation about Amber's marriage.

When questioned, I shared what I'd seen of Amber and Caden's passionate affair over the last weeks. What I'd

373

witnessed the night of Isabelle's murder. How Amber and I had been in the summer kitchen when Isabelle had emerged from the indoor dining room. She'd asked to speak to Amber alone.

The conversation grew heated enough that I could hear some of what was said through the stone walls. Isabelle confronted Amber, saying that she'd found the emerald ring on the floor in Ceanna's bedroom a few days ago. That same night she'd seen Amber and Caden together, intimate, at Woodlands House when she tried to return the ring.

I described how Amber had demanded her ring back. Isabelle refused, saying that Linc deserved to know. She would tell him that very night, and nothing would stop her. Amber had lost it then, screaming at Isabelle. With the heavy door and thick walls, I hadn't pieced together what was happening until I heard a thumping sound. I tried to get into the room but the door was jammed. By the time I got it open, Amber was standing over Isabelle, the knife still in her hand, and Isabelle was bleeding out.

Amber denied killing Isabelle, of course. But Linc and Caden were there just moments after, and they'd both seen Amber kneeling beside Isabelle, the knife right there. Ceanna confirmed that the ring had been in her bedroom and could have fallen to the floor for Isabelle to find. Caden confirmed that yes, Isabelle had seen him and Amber at Woodlands House earlier that week. Linc verified that Amber was extremely superstitious about the ring.

It all fitted, every last detail.

There were some loose ends. But no one knew about Isabelle's connection to Róisín. If Liadh and Ava found the notebook, they didn't say; it wouldn't have given them enough to point to the ice-eyed man either way.

'Ceanna mentioned that Amber told her something,' Linc added. 'Something about you.'

I raised an eyebrow, but Linc just shrugged as he left the room. I heard him greet Ceanna, and then they disappeared into Eden's study.

I remembered the argument I'd overheard between Linc and Amber all those months ago, when I'd assumed that Linc was the lover and Amber the beloved. I'd been wrong. Linc was Amber's beloved, just as Eden was his.

Amber had thought that being desirable to other men would make her more valuable to Linc, which was such a stupid, Amber thing to think.

It was a dangerous game, because both times she had become ensnared in the trap she'd set. Nico had fallen in love with her, not realizing that her pretty words were only that.

In the kitchen, I opened the fridge and began cutting veg. I'd received only one last message from the other Esmie, who still hated me more than the devil. Mama Bear told me Nico's death had sent her over the edge, and she'd been admitted to a residential psychotherapy programme.

While there, she had emailed me to say that she no longer planned to kill me. Instead, she reminded me of our long-ago conversation, the one where I'd told her that our small family was everything I ever wanted, that I would die without them.

> It consoles me to know that you've lost everyone you've loved – as much as you can love with that shrivelled black heart of yours. You once said you'd die without us, and it gives me joy to think about you dying a little all the time. I had to choose to spend my savings on my mental health or on a plane ticket to kill you, and I chose to save myself. So fuck you, Simone or Esmie, or whatever you want to call yourself. I'm going to forget you now. Unless you come back here, in which case I *will* kill you.

I thought about those words all the time.

Linc and Ceanna appeared after a few minutes. Linc took out a bottle of wine. Ceanna didn't meet my eye. She was even colder than the last time I'd seen her.

'How's Amber?' I asked, sliding the knife through a carrot. She watched the precise movement of my hand.

Ceanna was mute, then finally looked up at me. 'The same.' She sounded dull.

I nodded and continued slicing carrots.

'She insists that you didn't see her kill Isabelle. That this is all about revenge. That you're Nico Lorenzo's fiancée, and you came here for revenge.'

I put down the knife and walked towards her. I'd anticipated this. From a drawer, I pulled out a large travel purse.

'Amber must have misunderstood. I'm Nico's sister. I told Amber that. But then Isabelle called her to the indoor dining room, said they needed to talk. Maybe Amber was already upset with Isabelle. Maybe that's why she didn't listen to me.'

Ceanna's eyes darted away; she knew well that it was just like Amber to not listen, to mix up sister or fiancée or whatever, because she was self-absorbed and paid no attention to anything that didn't involve her.

'Amber had also been drinking, so maybe that's why she got it mixed up. But I'm definitely Esmerelda. Esmie. Nico's sister.' I took my passport from the travel purse and showed her. There was my picture, my name. It was a good job; the trained eyes at Immigration hadn't found fault with it, nor the lawyer Linc had hired to advise on my residence permit. 'I came to The Woodlands to find out what had happened to Nico, after he fell into a coma. I hoped to get his scholarship back.' My eyes teared up. 'I knew it would help him fight to stay alive.'

I'd keep my little plan for revenge to myself.

'It was true, what I told you that first day in your kitchen. My brother, Nico – not Lucas' – a small rueful pull to my mouth – 'had been in a coma. Nico died, unfortunately, the day before Isabelle. When I learned that Amber was his lover, I wanted to ask her to clear his name. I wanted to give him hope.' Such a bright, sanitized version of the truth. Nico would have told them about his sister Esmerelda, how she was kind and caring. Always writing songs about nature. A qualified early years educator, soft-hearted, an all-round good girl scout.

'I am sorry I came here under false pretences. That I deceived you. But I thought I'd never learn the truth if I told you who I was.'

Ceanna was still looking at me with those flat eyes. Linc moved behind me, just an inch between us. If she'd hoped to catch Linc unawares with this information, she was too late. After Isabelle's murder – after Nico's death – I'd told Mama Bear what had happened, and she'd agreed that Amber had to face consequences. She would back me up if necessary. Despite everything, she did love me.

And as for my consequences, I remained banished from my home, from my family. There would be no going back. And I had to live with the knowledge of what I'd done to the man I loved.

In those strange days after Isabelle's murder, I'd told Linc that I was Nico's sister. We'd talked about it the fourth night I stayed over, the first time I slept in Amber's bed. I'd been prepared for him to be angry, to tell me to leave. But Linc had touched my cheek gently and reminded me of the night he'd confessed to drugging Ceanna.

'You're like Eden. Like me. You belong to the woods. The rules are a little different for those that belong to the woods,' he'd said. Then he quoted some impenetrable Eden Hale poem and went on about 'unbecoming'. And even though his words had irritated me, I was relieved that Linc's moral compass had been so thoroughly skewed by his fascination with the poet's philosophy. If anything, confessing that I'd lied and deceived everyone seemed to make him more fascinated with me.

'You can tell me anything,' he'd said, pulling me to him. 'Anything at all.'

But I wouldn't. I didn't tell him what Amber had said to me: *I'll never fully understand why he'd go to the president crying assault when he knows from experience what I'm like.*

They were words I kept close to my heart.

'Before Isabelle called her, Amber admitted to me that she'd lied,' I said now to Ceanna. 'That Nico didn't assault her. She just let Linc believe that he had.' Another twist to the truth, and this one sat unpleasantly on my tongue. I was so weary of the lies. 'I wish with all my heart that things had worked out differently.' A tangled web, and there was no way out for me. 'I wish Nico was alive. But we can't change the past.'

Ceanna was still looking at me carefully as I returned the passport to the drawer. There was more life in her eyes now, but I couldn't tell if it was anger or sympathy.

'It makes no sense for me to falsely accuse Amber. I had nothing to gain from it.'

Ceanna raised an eyebrow. 'You seem to have gained quite a lot to me.'

'I've lost more,' I said simply, and Ceanna had the grace to flush. 'I could walk away from this,' I said, reaching out my arms and gesturing to the room. The cottage. It was true.

And sometimes I thought I would. Make a run for it. Be free. A butterfly emerging from a chrysalis.

But I couldn't. Because I didn't deserve it.

Isabelle and Amber had faced the consequences of their

bad choices, and the remaining debt was for Linc and me to pay.

I leaned into Linc behind me. 'But Linc and I found something in each other.' A beautiful trap. A pretty cage. Linc, ever yearning. Me, ensnared, unable to go home.

He placed his hands on my arms, firm and strong. He was showing Ceanna where his loyalties were.

'Ceanna,' I pushed on. 'I know you don't want to believe this of your sister. I remember when we learned that Nico had cheated on his fiancée, it was devastating. We couldn't reconcile the man we knew and loved with the man who'd lied to us. Sometimes the people we love are selfish, and they hurt us.'

Ceanna looked at me sharply, as though she heard the pain in my voice.

'Amber is in jail because she killed someone.' I believed that completely. Not immediately, but indirectly. The slow death, the long bleed. She'd drawn out her kill, the poison seeping from Nico to me.

I took a sip of the wine. I was so tired.

'I'll think about what you've said.' That was all the concession Ceanna would make.

'Is there an update on the safe?' I said, as she turned to leave.

Ceanna had insisted on relocating the safe to Woodland House when Linc and I moved into the cottage. She was living there now. Caden had transferred back to the States, and Ceanna had decided she didn't want lodgers any more.

'The expert Linc called,' Ceanna said, 'came out yesterday. He was very clear. Breaking into the safe will destroy the contents.'

I made a mental note to send a thank-you message to

Marko, my former housemate. When I rang him for another favour, this time generously compensated, he'd enjoyed the mischief of me swapping the number Linc had scribbled down with his own. Marko was a trained locksmith, among other things, and he would have been convincing.

'I'm so sorry, Linc. I don't know what happened to the keys,' Ceanna went on. 'As I told you, I did hide them, but lost them that awful night when I was sick and went wandering in the woods. They have to be there, or perhaps here in the cottage.'

'We'll just keep looking,' Linc said, forcing a smile that didn't reach his eyes. I'd heard him late at night, searching the study, the kitchen, the garden. I knew he wandered the woods, looking for keys hidden between the trees.

He was tormented by the absence of the keys.

I kept them in a safely locked box in town.

I'd allowed him to find one, hidden behind a wooden panel in the second bedroom. Just enough to give him hope. Enough to keep him searching.

A few days after Isabelle's murder, I'd retrieved my phone from her things at number three, under the guise of helping out. Liadh had been there, and she'd said to me, 'You're Nico's sister, aren't you?'

I hesitated, then nodded.

'It took a while, but I recognized you from that picture of you three. I liked Nico. He was always nice to me. He often spoke about you, about Esmerelda and Simone.' Nico had always called Esmie by her full name. 'I didn't make the connection between Esmie and Esmerelda until that day you asked me about the scarf.' She shifted. 'I don't know the details of what happened when he left, but I know he was shafted. How is Nico?'

'He died,' I said, and she closed her arms around me.

'I'm sorry,' she whispered into my hair.

'I'm sorry too.' I held her tightly, thinking of Róisín's husband disappearing through the orchard.

Paul had put number three on the market, and it sold in the first week.

'Esmie?' Linc came over to me now, his eyes on mine, searching hungrily. 'Where did you go just now?'

I smiled and gave a small shake of the head.

'Sometimes it seems there's a whole other world you escape to. I can never quite pin you down,' he said quietly as he steered me from the kitchen to the bedroom.

Sometimes it felt like Linc wanted to peel me open. That when he unbuttoned my shirt, he wanted to unbutton my skin, find his way in. He wanted to get inside my head, as if I were a cryptic poem he just had to decode. He knew he could never truly know me, that I would always be elusive to him.

He would never know Simone.

She was locked away, so far, so deep, and she would never be found again.

We fell on to the bed, and I noticed the smudges beneath Linc's eyes.

He never really settled these days; his eyes were always darting, always searching for possible hiding places. The hunger inside that made him always on the prowl. The thing he most wanted, the keys to the safe, remained out of reach.

I'd come home once to find him pulling up floorboards. The frustration had settled into him, had become part of him. It was what woke him up in the morning, what made him struggle to sleep. Sometimes he'd leap up in the middle of the night, saying, 'I have an idea where they might be.'

He no longer spent focused hours working at his laptop. His monograph was untouched these last three months. Whenever he started to work, his attention would be snatched by some new possible hiding place, and then he'd be up and looking.

I had him exactly where I wanted him. Consumed by a slow flame of hope and need, longing for something that would always be just out of reach.

Linc was tortured. And it was no less than what he deserved.

I would lie beside him at night, his jailer, his cellmate. I would toy with the idea of sending one of Eden's locked-up pages to his rival professor, the one who got the promotion he'd hankered after, while his own deepest wish remained unfulfilled.

I would dream of a dark room where the walls were closing in on me, and in my dreams I'd smell buckets of blood. I would wake up screaming, and Linc would hold me, asking, *What is it? What is it?* and I would never tell him how I was always, always so cold here in this house in the woods. How I could never really breathe – that deep lung-filling breath that made you feel alive – with the close dampness, these low skies.

I would let him hold me, and I would think, *I hate you, I love you*, because they'd become the same thing.

I would never tell him that I longed for a small four-roomed house, and a woman who hugged like a bear and loved me as her own. The sound of a chuckling banjo as my fingers played a fast tune. The mountain on the skyline. The hot sun on my skin.

All of that was lost to me now. I would stay here in the house in the woods. Like a bride turned villain and her sweetheart, from some long-forgotten story that was locked away, never to be found again.

Acknowledgements

I started writing this book during the first lockdown in April 2020, a time when houses became whole worlds. It was also the time of my father's cancer diagnosis and subsequent death, over six shocking, quick weeks. I couldn't fly home to be with him, but I could write. It seems fitting then, that this one is for him – our beloved CCV, who saw life in its largeness and tried to show me that too.

I am eternally grateful to Claire Wilson, rockstar agent, for nearly ten years of unfailing wisdom and support. Thank you, Safae El-Ouahabi.

Thank you Thorne Ryan, my wonderful editor, for your clear-eyed vision in helping me shape this story. Huge thanks to everyone at (or with) Transworld: Alison Barrow, for all you do to spread the word, Anna Carvanova, Vivien Thompson, Claire Gatzen, Holly McElroy, Catherine Wood, Lucy Beresford-Knox and others; I know I'm missing names, but I appreciate every person who's worked on getting this book out in the world and to readers. At Crown, thank you Shannon Criss and Austin Parks for your sharp insights and guidance. Thanks Natalie Blachere, Andrea Lau, Dustin Amick, Ann Roberts and the rest of the team. Thank you, Sarah Jackson and the team in Canada.

I was inspired by a Norwegian folktale, a Bluebeard variation called 'The Sweetheart in The Wood' which appears in *Tales from the Fjeld* by Peter Christen Asbjørnsen (translator: George Webbe Dasent) published in 1874. The words 'begged so prettily' and 'he tore off her clothes and jewels' were extracted as part of Eden Hale's found poem. This folk tale can be found on Wikisource, under the following license https://creativecommons.org/ licenses/by-sa/4.0/.

Thank you, my dear friends, for your patience if I disappeared into the mist, especially Catherine, Virtue, Karen, and writer pal, Edel Coffey, whose calm, funny reasonableness should come bottled. I, very strategically, married into a family with several medics, just so I could write this book of course – huge thanks especially to Anna, and also David, for tirelessly answering all my dodgy questions with such careful thought; Yvonne, Deirdre and Bríd, thank you too, and any other unsuspecting doctor I might have pounced upon over the last few years.

About a decade ago, when this story was not even a seed, I had inspiring conversations with young women who'd come to Ireland from abroad. Thanks especially Larissa, Gabi, Alé, Caroline, Marianne; your experiences of being new to Ireland resonated with my own, and made me determined to one day explore this strangeness in a book.

Thank you my tower of sisters, Dessie, Lynn, Joy, Jodine, and nieces Zadie and Shannon, for midnight dancing between the trees (and also Luke – huge respect!). I am so grateful to all Tilly's girls (Tracells too), and Madge, for your enduring love. It's slightly alarming how several of my fictional happenings, after I wrote them, occurred in real life – in this instance, the harrowing experience of a loved one in a coma. Fingers crossed all imagined horrors stay on the page from now on.

Thank you readers, lovely book people on social media,

booksellers, and fellow authors – I am ever so grateful to everyone who shares kind words about this book.

Thank you Cathal for walking this road with me, along with Liam, Lúc and Felix who have me as their mama bear and giver of squashy barrógaí.

Mary Watson is from South Africa and now lives on the west coast of Ireland. She has a PhD from the University of Cape Town, where she taught for many years. She won the Caine Prize for African Writing for her adult publishing in South Africa, and in 2014 was named on the Africa39 list of writers under 40 with the potential to define trends in African literature. Her YA novels have been nominated for the Irish Book Awards and the Carnegie Medal. *The Cleaner* is her worldwide adult debut.